Blood Memory Society

BOOK I

Blood Memory Society

BOOK 1

A Novel by

D. A. Field

Cover and Interior design by Glen Edelstein, Hudson Valley Book Design
Chapter opening illustrations by Michael Gellatly

First Edition, September, 2017
ISBN 978-0-9990514-1-2 Hard Cover format
ISBN 978-0-9990514-0-5- trade paper back
ISBN 978-0-9990514-2-9- E-book
Library of Congress Cataloging-in-Publication Data
D.A. Field Library of Congress Control Number: 2017942697
Fiction; Thriller, action, Sci-Fi, Thriller; mystery
Printed in United States of America.

Published by:

Giro di Mondo

www.girodimondo.com
Amelia Island, Florida

THIS BOOK IS DEDICATED TO:

Carla, Madeline and Tripp. Without your constant support and love, I would not have been able to achieve this milestone.

To Ed and Norma. Thank you for instilling a burning need for knowledge and learning in your son's life.

To all of those along the way who have encouraged and inspired me, here's to many more memories to come.

Our virtues and our failings are inseparable, like force and matter. When they separate, man is no more.

—Nikola Tesla (1856-1943)

Blood Memory Society

BOOK I

I

DEATH AND A DIME BAG. Those were the words the man in the long trench coat kept tossing around in his brain. It was simple. After completing this day of death, he would reach into his "dime bag" stash of homegrown marijuana and smoke away the memories.

On this bitterly cold day in Atlanta, the temperature was falling fast under a rapidly graying sky. Approaching a large almost anonymous-looking cement building, the man's coat was so bulky and out of proportion to his thin frame that he slightly stumbled as he walked. Although early spring, the winter had lingered this year, and at three in the afternoon small slick patches of ice hazardously speckled the concrete sidewalk outside of the National Fertility Clinic.

The clinic, located just a block from the Centers for Disease Control and Prevention, was a four-story dull gray building with a curious lack of windows and just one nondescript dense metal entrance door painted solid black. Out front, there was no signage, no identification of any sort except for its address on Clifton

Road etched into the bulletproof glass transom window above the door. Another odd fact about this building was that the lights and power supply never failed. Even when the rest of Atlanta was in the dark, in the cold clutches of an energy blackout, the lights at the National Fertility Clinic never blinked, never even flickered. Only a select handful of people in the country were aware that this drab, unimpressive building had its own power grid, separate and isolated from the entire city.

The National Fertility Clinic, or NFC to those elite few who actually knew of its existence, was a fully functioning fertility clinic where patients both male and female were seen and evaluated on regular intervals. However, this clinic, with its large physical size and stealthy importance, seemed to be out of proportion for the small number of actual patients. A true state-of the-art facility and fully funded by the United States government, the NFC was staffed by only one physician, two nurses, and one receptionist to serve its total patient count of twenty-seven. The average woman who was interested in starting a family and possibly needing some medical advice could not simply call the clinic to schedule a checkup or an evaluation. The truth was that only a few people in the country were ever granted access to this facility.

On this cold day in March, with foul weather about, it wasn't unusual to see a man in Atlanta dressed in a long warm coat. No one took note that such a man was approaching the NFC. At the front door, he swiped an access keycard, leaned down to allow a laser beam to cross his eyes, replaced his broad dark sunglasses, and then entered the building. With the collar of his coat turned up and a black wool cap pulled tightly over his short-cropped blond hair and chafed ears, hardly any of his pale facial features were discernible; even the large scar on his neck was well covered. Pausing on the threshold to stamp his well-polished leather shoes and wipe away a few flecks of sleet from his crisply pressed slacks, he shuffled through the front door and approached the appointment desk. A biting wind blew in from behind him.

The receptionist, a cute young black woman with a round friendly face and large brown expressive eyes, sat behind a sliding glass window and looked up from her computer monitor.

"Whew, it's cold out there," she said with a playful shudder, her smile brilliantly white. "You must be Mr. Fredrickson? We've been expecting you. I'm Rochelle." She spoke in a soft drawl as she placed her hands on her heart, having been instructed never to shake the hands of NFC patients, for sanitary reasons.

"Yes," the man uttered, standing motionless and not removing his sunglasses.

Most NFC patients wore dark glasses throughout the duration of their visit. Rochelle always thought it odd and had not dared to ask them why, having simply been advised by one of the nurses that most NFC patients had sensitive eyes and preferred to shade them from the bright sun and clinic's intense lights.

Rochelle preferred it that way, having been unnerved at the sight of one patient's eyes three months ago. She had only recently started the job and while checking in a patient one day, his sunglasses fell off and landed on her desk. When she grabbed them and looked up to hand the sunglasses to the man, she let out a low shriek as his eyes were sickly green and seemed to dart erratically in their sockets, as though bouncing almost uncontrollably.

She stared up at Fredrickson's well-hidden face. "Okay. It looks like we've received all of your information and documentation. Everything seems in order. I just need to see some identification."

Fredrickson removed one black leather glove, shoved his slightly soiled hand into his pocket, and retrieved a plastic identification card. The receptionist took a cursory glance at the ID and ignored the dirt under his fingernails.

"Great. If you'll kindly have a seat, the nurse will be out shortly

to collect you," she said, wrinkling her nose at the odor of cigarette smoke emanating from him.

The brightly lit waiting room had a high windowless atrium, a
couch, four chairs, a large flat-screen hi-def television, books and
magazines. The shiny white tiled floors, hygienic cream-colored
walls, and piped-in classical music created a calming yet sterile
environment. Shortly after he was seated, a petite, middle-aged
nurse, with tired but knowledgeable eyes and long auburn hair,
arrived to escort Fredrickson to the examination room.

He followed her through the hallway, past the doors of two
empty examination rooms on the left and a large metal door on
the right with a sign that read "Specimen Room," to the next
examination room on the right.

"This is your room, sir. If you don't mind, please remove your
clothes and slip into this gown. The doctor is slightly delayed but
will be here shortly to give you further instructions," she said,
holding out a blue gauze gown.

Fredrickson grabbed the gown and the nurse left the room,
closing the solid wooden door behind her. He set the gown upon
the crinkled paper of the examination bed and began to unbutton
his trench coat, one slow button at a time. A bead of perspiration
trickled down his cheek as he wriggled free of the heavy coat and
laid it on the bed.

The coat unfurled, exposing a ring of explosives interconnected
with electrical wiring, all masterfully woven into the garment's
fabric. Calmly, he grabbed the ends of several shiny wires and sank
them deep into the bricks of C4 plastic explosives before him. With
his finger, he flipped a small switch that was sewn into the lining. A
white light began to blink. He then carefully picked up the trench
coat bomb and placed it on the floor next to the wall adjacent to
the "Specimen Room." Quietly, he slid a small stainless steel table
in front of the jacket to cover it. With sunglasses and cap still in
place, he silently exited the room.

As he made his way to the front door of the clinic, the young receptionist looked up from her monitor with puzzlement. "Sir?"

He did not answer, and his pace quickened.

Rochelle tried again. "Sir, are you okay? Did you leave your jacket?"

After leaving the building and rounding the street corner, the sound of squealing rubber echoed off the surrounding buildings as a black SUV slid to a stop beside him. He pulled out a cell phone, pressed dial, then got into the SUV, which sped away.

The blast came one minute later, as Rochelle was standing just inside the partially opened front door, scanning the street outside for Fredrickson. The enormous explosion plowed through the hallway towards her, violently jolting her through the door, shattering her eardrums and scorching her flesh. As she lay on the sidewalk, struggling to breathe, she batted her eyes open and saw a wave of flames rush along the crushed ceiling of the hallway. The fireball compressed into a tight inferno, and she felt the intense heat singe her eyelashes as its fiery fingers surged through the front door, searing the building into black char. The National Fertility Clinic was engulfed with a tremendous roar of flames. Everyone and everything inside was destroyed.

The "everything" was the real target.

2

IT WAS A CRITICAL DAY at Pasadena's Jet Propulsion Laboratory, probably the most important day in the storied history of this federally funded research and development facility. The atmosphere on campus, inside the secured gates and high electric fences that surrounded the property, festered with tempered excitement. As always, on the first day of such an event, a sober tension suffused the air.

Located just a few dozen miles from Los Angeles and nestled among the sprawling brown foothills of the San Gabriel Mountains, the Jet Propulsion Laboratory, or JPL, is home to some of the world's most elite scientists, engineers, and physicists. But even among the elite, there exists one exceptionally gifted group of scientists who are so important to national security that their identities are, and have always been, hidden from the public. Team X was the name given to this secret group of eight men and nine women, this collection of individuals with supreme intelligence that on this day was on the technological precipice of changing the world forever.

For decades, Team X had been instrumental in enabling a once far-fetched notion of space exploration, once only fodder for comic books and sci-fi novels, into an obtainable reality. Over seventy-five years, they had devised a number of successful missions using robotic space explorers, hi-tech machines sent to survey and analyze every corner of our solar system, to peer deep into the Milky Way and beyond, and to keep a watchful eye on Earth. Known as the Deep Space Network, this program was responsible for achievements like the Voyager's mission to the outer planets, the Viking's excursion to Mars, and Galileo's quest to the Jupiter system. All of these achievements were made possible by a culture at JPL based upon scientific truth and rational thought. So the idea that the brilliant minds at this institution could succumb to an irrational concept, such as a superstition, was beyond the pale.

But such was the case after a particularly painful time at JPL in the early 1960s.

As the story goes, it happened after the Ranger Program had experienced heart-wrenching failure after failure when trying to land a spacecraft on the moon. Finally in 1963, they succeeded. Previous attempts at lunar landings had failed so abysmally that this success caught the mission control team completely off guard, amazed at what they had done that day. And after such an unprecedented achievement, the scientists incredibly bowed to the primal belief in superstition.

It began with one of the JPL mission control specialists nervously eating peanuts as he watched the lunar landing. In their celebratory haze, the JPL staff turned to each other and jokingly decided that the peanuts must have been a good luck charm and they should adopt the habit. From then on, "Lucky Peanuts" would be eaten just before and during every critical mission event. It became tradition, never questioned, never broken. Peanuts were to be delivered at T-minus one hour and consumed with pride by all staff, administration, and mission specialists. Everyone at JPL would eat Lucky Peanuts, like it or not.

Today's campus excitement revolved around the actions in building 321, known to the 5,000 employees of JPL as the Team X Mission Control Center. Over 150 years in the making, the Genesis Project was so highly classified that only a handful of politicians and military officials, among them the president, were aware of its designs and intentions. All the preliminary tests, mathematical computations, and three dry runs had been performed flawlessly. It was now time to go live. All of JPL knew something big, whatever it might be, was about to happen.

Team X Mission Control Center was a multi-tiered, large oval dome much like a planetarium. With three levels of continuously flickering computer monitors atop long uninterrupted oak countertops, two dozen black leather chairs were positioned in front of the monitors in an auditorium-style arrangement. A six-foot-tall, multicolored electronic banner trimmed the entire room in pixilations of light as live video and data streamed continuously from deep-space machines and satellites. On the ceiling, a plethora of small lights scattered throughout the pitch black darkness like tiny stars, representing the exact make-up of the Milky Way. A halo of royal blue light rimmed the ceiling and cascaded in gentle waves down the walls to the floor, bathing the room in a calming hue. Team X was ready.

ㅌ   ㅌ   ㅌ

AN HOUR BEFORE THE FIRE engulfed the NFC in Atlanta, a food-delivery van approached the security gate at JPL. The guard, a stocky woman with short black hair and Asian features, slid open the darkly tinted glass window of the guardhouse. The driver of the white van, a rugged-looking young man with blond hair, a black mole on his cheek, wore a white ball cap pulled low over his ears. He rolled down his window. "Big exciting day today, huh?" he said, extending a lanyard around his neck with an attached ID card.

The guard narrowed her eyebrows as she examined the man's face and matched it to the ID. She did not recognize the driver, yet it wasn't that unusual to have high employee turnover in the delivery business. Driving a food truck was obviously not a well-paying job and this was the fifth driver for this particular company in just over a year.

"Why would you say that?" the guard asked, staring at the man's daunting black eyes. "Can you lift your hat up, sir? I can't quite see your face."

The man pushed up the bill of his cap. "Because I'm delivering the Lucky Peanuts today," he said with a knowing look.

The security guard looked at the ID again. "Oh, okay. Yeah, it's been kind of tense around here for the last month or so. I hope you got some peanuts for me too 'cause I don't want to be the one to jinx this one today."

The driver smiled and handed her a small wicker basket lined with red, white, and blue craft paper and a frilly American ribbon on the handle. A clear plastic bag of roasted peanuts rested on top of the paper and a white label on the bag of peanuts read Jet Propulsion Laboratory, Building 321.

The guard accepted the basket with a smile and waved the van through. The driver nodded, tucked his credentials back into his shirt, casually waved and drove to building 321.

The deliveryman, wearing a white jumpsuit and white sneakers, entered building 321 pushing a plastic cart stacked tall with the patriotic baskets and proceeded to the security check point just inside double glass doors.

Two security guards, one seated at a large metal desk and the other standing by a standard-size metal detector, greeted him as though Santa Claus had just arrived.

"There he is. We were starting to wonder what happened to you, man. Damn," the heavier of the two guards said. He picked up a handheld radio off of the desk. "Peanuts are here. Be there in five."

"Sorry, I got held up for a few minutes. How late am I?"

The guard looked at his watch. "We got eight minutes. Hurry." He motioned the deliveryman through the metal detector without glancing at his ID.

Officer Jenkins, a plump black man with a receding hairline and an awkward gait, grabbed two baskets of peanuts from the cart and set them down on the desk before leading the deliveryman and his cart down a grandiose hallway with shiny granite floors. White columns stood against dark brown marble walls where photographs of historic space achievements hung. The guard stopped just past a brilliant photograph of the Mars Rover, turned his head towards the deliveryman, and grabbed three baskets from the cart. He hurriedly pushed open a glass door on his right and hobbled inside to deliver the peanuts to three secretaries in the administration office, who thanked him enthusiastically. Exiting the office, he motioned the deliveryman to follow.

"They've called me five times already looking for these damn peanuts. Bunch of superstitious nerds as far as I'm concerned but I'm just glad you made it. We only got five minutes till T-minus one hour, you know. Didn't your boss tell you to be here an hour early?" he said, breathing heavily as they walked rapidly toward the Team X Control Center.

"Yeah. I know. Like I said, I got held up."

"Traffic?"

The deliveryman did not answer but walked faster, his cart squeaking.

When they reached the control room door, Jenkins knocked firmly. The door swung open and another security guard, the largest human being the deliveryman had ever seen, blocked the entrance. Standing close to seven feet tall, barrel-chested with deep ebony skin and arms the size of cannons, he grabbed the cart, pulled it inside, and slammed the door without a word.

It was a little thing. But no one in building 321 noticed that the roasted peanut husks were slightly browner that day, a little darker than usual. However, the taste wasn't altered, the size was consistent and they were just as crunchy as always. The secretaries enjoyed them and discussed the superstition surrounding the nuts. The security guards ate them and complained about how much of a pain in the ass it was to ensure their timely delivery. And most importantly to the deliveryman, Team X nervously nibbled them as the T-minus-one-hour countdown began.

The deliveryman sat in the van parked outside for almost fifteen minutes before re-entering the building along with his accomplice, a tall, ghostly pale man with a bald head, eyes with eerily blue sclera. He had sweat on his brow from stowing away in the back of the hot van for the past hour. The two men slipped on black cotton masks, leaving only cutouts for eyes, and opened the double front doors. The security guards slumped lifelessly over the metal desk. The pale man shook the heavier guard but he did not move, his dead black eyes fixed open and a frothy white foam slathering his mouth.

With a firm tug, the blond deliveryman snatched the set of keys from Officer Jenkins' belt and the two men sprinted to the administration office. Swinging the glass door open, they entered a scene that would have revolted a normal person. Two women lay motionless on their desks, white foam and chunky moist vomit oozing from all facial orifices. A third woman gyrated violently on the floor, convulsing as her eyes bulged from their sockets. The deliveryman pointed a small pistol and put a single bullet into her right temple; bright red blood pooled on the off-white carpet.

The two men sprinted down the hallway to the Team X Control Center. After fumbling through several wrong keys, the deliveryman sank the correct key into the keyhole. With gun drawn and clenched jaws, he twisted the key and the door heaved open with a clatter as the enormous security guard fell through the doorway and crashed to the floor, a white froth exuding from his nostrils. The two killers smiled.

ꙮ   ꙮ   ꙮ

MINUTES LATER, AS THE VAN sped away, the assassins witnessed an enormous explosion in their rearview mirror. A ball of fire rose from building 321, angry black columns of smoke swirling high above JPL in deadly concentric circles.

3

CLOUDS BLEW IN FROM THE east breaking up the morning sun
and casting incongruent shadows over the blue Bahamian waters.
The air was fresh and a thin mist of salt haze hovered over the
warming waters.

"Wow, another successful sortie!" a voice yelled from aboard a
glossy-white boat anchored a few yards off a coral reef, a half-mile
offshore of Hopetown, in the Abacos. The voice belonged to
Ashwin, a thirty-year-old doctor of Indian descent, a friend from
medical school of the man in the water. "You're the man, Will,"
said Ashwin.

Dr. Will Dunbar loved to live the Salt Life. With each breath of
air, he could free-dive fifty feet to the reef below, spear an elusive
fish or a spiny lobster and return to the surface, then do it again
and again with unrelenting energy. He'd done this since he was
a young boy and pretty much had it down to a science. Through
trial and error, Will calculated that each kick of his dive fins took
three seconds off of his "bottom time:" the crucial time he needed
to be engaged in the hunt. Adjusting for body mass index and the

density of his wetsuit, with the six and a half pounds of weight, he now could kick only twice and glide down to the reef, leaving him close to two minutes for spearfishing, his favorite sport.

Every time he broke the surface and held up his catch, he heard a "Thatta boy" or "You're on fire today" from Ashwin. Will referred to these underwater forays as sorties, a word he'd become familiar with while a West Point cadet. Sortie usually referred to an aircraft mission over an enemy territory to launch a missile or drop a bomb on a target. To Will, he was the aircraft, the fish was the enemy, and his speargun, the missile.

After several successful sorties, he swam over to his newly purchased boat, admiring the sleek stepped design of the hull. He un-cocked three large black rubber bands from the shaft of his speargun and handed the weapon to Ashwin, along with a stringer full of fish and a yellow mesh bag filled with succulent lobsters.

"Just another day at the office," Will said, grinning, with his dive mask propped on top of his wavy sandy-blond hair.

And it was just another beautiful day in this tropical nirvana called Elbow Cay, a small sliver of earth that stripes the ocean one hundred fifty miles off Florida's east coast. Hopetown, the capital and only city on this quiet island, is bordered on the west by the azure waters of the Sea of Abaco, on the east by the volatile Atlantic Ocean, and is centrally positioned in the most northern chain of Bahamian islands, the Abacos. With spectacular precipices along jagged limestone cliffs swooping down to generous beaches of pinkish sand, Elbow Cay was one of the few places in North America that actually lives up to the mental image of a picturesque tropical island.

Will had been visiting this slice of heaven since he was a child, growing up in St. Augustine, Florida, some three hundred miles as a crow flies across the Gulf Stream. He and his parents often visited Hopetown, a second home in a way until his parents' death just about a year ago.

His family had not been wealthy nor poor, simply middle class. But they had been fortunate. Fortunate that Will's father's best friend was a wealthy Florida doctor with a plane and a vacation home in Hopetown. Excursions to the Bahamas were out of financial reach for the Dunbars, but this friendship had allowed them the opportunity to visit here, costing them little more than gas for the boat or a few fruity umbrella drinks on the beach. The plane crash that killed his parents and the doctor and his wife changed all of that.

Will lifted himself up onto the transom of the boat and dried off his tan, muscular body with a towel. He was a product of the "Lucky Sperm Club," a phrase that his father, Sam, used to describe beautiful people with good genes. At thirty-two years old, six-foot-three with a strong-featured face and smiling blue-gray eyes, he fit into that category. An exceptional athlete, he'd played wide receiver at West Point.

"Put these on ice, Ashwin. I've got a couple more spots for us to hit before it gets dark," Will said, as Ashwin began emptying the bag of lobsters.

"Man, we're going to eat good tonight," Ashwin said, rubbing his hands together.

Will hoisted the heavy anchor and cranked up the triple 300-horsepower outboard engines. Ashwin coughed and rubbed his eyes from the exhaust smoke and fumes. The thirty-six-foot center console rocketed on plane with grace and ease, dodging coral reefs as they skirted the waters around Hopetown. By noon, the tally was fifteen lobsters and a dozen assorted fish for Will's catch, and one lobster, one conch, and three half-broken sand dollars for Ashwin.

As the boat skipped across the small whitecaps whipped up by a gentle sea breeze, Will took in a deep breath of the moist air and exhaled. He was elated to be in the Abacos again. Ever since beginning his residency in OB/GYN and finishing a fellowship in reproductive medicine, he hadn't had much time to visit the Bahamas. But he hoped all that was about to change with his recent appointment in the new Reproductive Medicine Department at the Mayo Clinic in Jacksonville. With a job much closer to his favorite place on earth, he now could visit more often.

ॐ   ॐ   ॐ

HE PULLED THE THROTTLES BACK near the edge of a large reef and the boat coasted to a gentle glide. Just as he was about to drop anchor, his cell phone lit up and chirped with a text.

"Will. Hi, buddy. It's been a long time. Please call me at your earliest convenience. It is very URGENT. Ross Chapman."

"Wow," Will said.

"Who is it?" Ashwin asked as he hung over the side of the boat, staring through the water to the reef below.

"A buddy of mine from West Point. We played football together but I don't think I've seen him since we graduated. I can't believe he even has my phone number."

Will was off the clock. He had been putting in extra time covering other doctors' midnight calls for weeks in order to get off this particular weekend and bring his new boat to Hopetown. "He's just going to have to wait awhile."

After two more hours, they returned to the dock at the Sea Star Marina and Resort. Will had been coming to the Sea Star forever. These days, his longtime Bahamian friend Tiny was the dock master and had given him a special rate on his boat slip rental for the week. As they tied up, his phone chirped again. It was Ross Chapman, this time calling, not texting. Will pushed "Accept."

"Colonel Ross Chapman," Will said with a smile, "what's going on, soldier?"

"Will, how are you, brotha? Let me guess, you're on a boat somewhere?" Ross asked as Will's triple outboards rattled in the background.

"Yep. You know it. I'm in Hopetown. We killed it today," Will said as he looked at Ashwin and gave him a thumbs-up.

"You always do. Will, I'm going to cut to the chase. I have a strange request of you."

Will arched his eyebrows. "Okay. What is it?"

"I ... um we need you to come here to D.C. ASAP."

Will laughed. "What? You're cracking me up, Ross. What do you really want?"

"I mean this, Will. It's extremely important." Ross paused for a split second. "It's a matter of national security."

Will set his speargun on the deck and sat on the captain's seat. "What the hell do I have to do with national security?"

"I'm not at liberty to say any more about it. You're just going to have to trust me, buddy. I'll fill you in when you get here. We'll send a plane to pick you up. What's the closest airport?"

Will had known Ross a long time and although it had been awhile, he knew Ross wasn't much of a practical joker. He was a jovial but serious military man from a military family. After West Point and after several tours in Iraq, he had continued his distinguished career in the military.

"Marsh Harbour," Will said slowly, bewildered. "I don't know what this is all about and you better not be screwing with me but I really need to get my boat back to St. Augustine. I just bought it and I don't want to leave it over here right now."

"I know it sounds crazy, man, but I'm dead-ass serious."

Will looked at the display of his weather radar in front of him as it scanned the horizon for any inclement weather coming across the Gulf Stream from Florida.

"This is nuts. I was planning on crossing back over to Florida tomorrow but if you're serious, I could start making my way back this afternoon. I wouldn't get home until tonight. I'd rather make the run over during the daylight but I've done it before at night. It's no big deal, it just takes a little more concentration." He shrugged his shoulders at Ashwin, still hoping Ross was kidding.

"Okay. Fair enough. Get a good night's sleep and I'll send a jet to St. Augustine to pick you up at noon tomorrow."

"You're not pulling my leg?"

"I'm as serious as I have ever been in my life."

When Will ended the call, Ashwin asked, "What was that all about?"

"I have no idea but let's clean these fish, fast!"

WILL WAS HUSTLED FROM DULLES Airport in a nondescript black SUV lacking government license plates. His flight from St. Augustine had been uneventful, yet his face had taken on a damp sheen caused by his guttural fear of flying. As the SUV weaved its way through traffic, Will recognized many of the iconic buildings and monuments en route, only having seen them in books or on television, for this was his first ever visit to Washington. When the vehicle stopped, he peered out of his darkly tinted window at a massive concrete structure with a maze of steps that rose fifty feet to a grand portico lined by a row of stone columns — the Library of Congress' Thomas Jefferson Building.

In the distance, a man in a military uniform, carrying a small briefcase, hurriedly descended the labyrinth of steps. As he got closer, Will's smiling eyes lit up as he recognized the six-foot-tall figure, close-cropped black hair, and green eyes of his old friend Ross Chapman.

Exiting the SUV, a cold cutting wind penetrated Will's gray cotton twill slacks and thin wool sweater, reminding him that he was not in Florida anymore.

Chapman was smiling broadly with arms extended. His army service uniform was complete with a crisply pressed white shirt, dark blue necktie, and an impressive array of military ribbons, insignias and badges. A West Point man in his early thirties, he filled out his uniform like an NFL quarterback. "Will, how are you? It's been a long time."

The two friends embraced. "Great to see you, Ross. You're looking good, man."

"Me? Look at you. You look like you could still play," Ross said as he shadow-punched Will's abdomen.

"I wish. Hold on, am I seeing at little touch of gray there in that receding hairline?" Will said, pointing to a slight tipping of gray on Ross' temple.

"Hey, leave this old man alone. I got you by a year, right?"

"Ha, I guess so," Will replied, then studied the enormous building in front of him, a row of goosebumps rising on his neck. "What's going on, Ross? Why am I here?"

"You're about to find out. I know this must seem crazy but there is a good reason *you* are here. Just follow me. They're waiting on us."

The two men scaled the steps up to three arched entrances under the portico. To Will's surprise, Ross did not lead him to the public entrance on the right side with its security guards and metal detectors but instead led him to a doorway on the far left.

Ross pointed at the massive bronze front door, looking back at Will. "Do you know the name of this piece of art?"

Will narrowed his eyes. This was no typical door. It was a ten-foot-tall formidable barrier, a protective guardian sheltering the invaluable historic contents behinds its bulky frame. The size was impressive but the unique feature was the etched bronze sculpture on its front of a grieving Roman woman holding a glad-iator's helmet and sword.

"No. Can't say I do," Will said.

"It's called 'Memory.' It was sculpted in 1869 by Olin Warner," Ross said as he pulled a key from his pocket, inserted it with a twist, and then pushed hard against the heavy door. It swung open and Ross led Will inside, down two flights of polished marble steps, through a maze of arched hallways, and inserted another key into a plain wooden door. Ross pushed this open, exposing a long dimly lit hallway behind. He motioned Will to follow.

As though someone had flipped a switch, his face had changed from jovial Ross to serious Ross. He had not said a word since entering the building.

With warm accents of hardwood floors and intricate oak crown molding, the hallway somewhere in the depths of the Library of Congress smelled comfortable and familiar like an old book. Portraits of the presidents hung on paneled walls and crystal statues of at least a dozen eminent scientists were tastefully illuminated. At the end of a Persian rug, just past the illuminated bust of Albert Einstein, the two men entered a steel elevator. Ross inserted a keycard and the elevator descended further.

"Really, Ross. What's this about? I'm starting to get chills, man."

"Sorry, buddy, can't say. We're almost there."

They exited the elevator and made their way down a brightly lit concrete corridor that reminded Will of a 1950s bomb shelter. With every step, he could sense a heightened feeling of tension and anxiety emanating from his old friend. Will's natural instinct was to crack a joke, but he could tell that whatever was happening today would require his full attention and concentration.

❧ ❧ ❧

WILL IMMEDIATELY RECOGNIZED THE MAN sitting at the head of the meeting room's oblong oak table. General Dwight Coleman was dressed in a crisp dark blue Army Service uniform with four silver stars across his broad shoulders. Will recalled hearing firsthand stories about him on several occasions while at West Point. General Coleman had a reputation as a resourceful, tough-nosed soldier, well skilled in the art of politicking, as would be expected of the Chairman of the Joint Chiefs of Staff. His face was well known in the news media, with its almond skin, large bulbous nose, bold lips, and thinning head of black hair graying at the edges. Flanking him at the table were five men and two women. The large concrete room rattled with the low hum of an overly warm vent shuffling the pages of yellow legal pads positioned in front of those at the table.

With eyes wide and nervous, Will briefly examined their faces while Ross greeted and thanked everyone for being present. Will recognized a senator but the others were unfamiliar. He pulled at the itchy collar of his wool sweater as Ross motioned for him to take a seat. The room was stuffy and hot.

The general motioned to Ross, then handed him several sheets of paper to distribute to the group. As Will watched his friend interact with the powerful players seated at the table, a sense of admiration swelled inside him and a twinge of envy.

Through a combination of grit, a tireless work ethic, and sound decision-making, Ross Chapman had risen quickly through the military ranks. On his three tours of duty in the Middle East, he had proven himself a natural leader.

Ross completed handing out the papers and gave Will a quick, serious glance. The degree of tension in the room was like nothing he had ever experienced and Dr. Will Dunbar had been in some tight situations in his life. He had been in the emergency room numerous times with his healing hands working to save lives. On one occasion during his residency he performed heart massage on a young girl, an auto accident victim, his hands clasped around her freshly ceased heart, frantically attempting to force it back to life. As an OB/GYN, it was commonplace for him to be rushed into a hospital room to perform emergency Cesarean section surgery, sometimes with only seconds to spare, occasionally unsuccessfully. But the sense of distress in this meeting room today was different. The tension was suffocating.

"I would like everyone's attention, please." Ross pressed his lips into a thin smile. "I'd like to introduce Dr. William Dunbar and welcome him here to D.C."

There was a smattering of applause, then General Coleman spoke up, "Thank you, Colonel Chapman. You may be seated."

"Thank you, General." Ross sat at the end of the table, leaving several empty chairs between himself and Will.

The general began, his voice crisp, deep and clear. "Dr. Dunbar, thank you for being here. I'd like to start by introducing the members of this panel. I am General Dwight Coleman, chairman of the joint chiefs of staff; on my left is Jane Porter, national security advisor to the president; Colonel James Murray, director of the IMS Secret Service; and General Frank Peterson, secretary of defense." Gesturing to his right, he said, "This is Senator Brad Hickey, ranking member of the House Intelligence Committee; Robert Ferry, director of the CIA; Dr. Mary Ann Wilcox, director of the Office of Scientific Research and Development; and at the end is Dr. Arnold Bamesberger, director of the National Fertility Clinic and the primary physician to the IMS."

Will wrinkled his forehead, unfamiliar with the term "IMS."

"And of course you know Lieutenant Colonel Chapman, deputy director of the IMS Secret Service."

Will looked at Ross, bewildered, but Ross just looked down at the papers before him.

"The video camera that you see on the ceiling above us is hyperlinked to the Situation Room in the White House." The general's deep voice resounded as it bounced off the plaster ceiling.

Will acknowledged everyone sitting at the table in front of him and gave a quick nod to the camera. He thought to himself that the individuals seated in this room were the same players that would be present if World War III were to commence. His throat got a little drier and he swallowed hard.

Coleman picked up his reading glasses from the table and put them on his charismatic face. "Dr. Dunbar, your reputation, your accomplishments and really your unique skill sets are why you are here today. If I may, I would like to briefly review your resume for the attendees in this room and for the audience at the White House."

Will nodded without a word, not sure if he even could speak if asked.

"Dr. William A. Dunbar, thirty-two years old, born in St. Augustine, Florida, to Samuel and Linda Dunbar," the general read. "I won't read all of your high school accomplishments but it is certainly an impressive list of both academic and athletic awards." He looked back down. "BS degree in Mechanical Engineering, West Point, magna cum laude; medical degree from Harvard — ranked first in your class. OB/GYN residency and fellowship in reproductive endocrinology at Department of Defense Uniformed Services University of Health Sciences, where you also fulfilled your five-year military obligation by serving on staff and conducting clinical research. No less than twenty-three journal articles published to date and co-author of a textbook on surgical anatomy of the female reproductive system." Coleman looked up, removed his glasses and stared up at the camera on the ceiling. "Just top of the line all the way across."

He replaced his glasses and flipped the page in front of him. "In your research paper titled, 'Protein Sequence Coding in Human Embryo Development,' you demonstrated that a protein known as ubiquitin plays a vital role in human fetal development. You concluded that spontaneous abortions, or miscarriages for us lay people, occur at higher rates in women who have low levels of ubiquitin."

Will cleared his throat. "Yes, sir, that's correct."

The general did not look up but merely held up his hand before continuing. "For this research, you earned the prestigious American College of Embryology Clinical Science Award. You began your private practice of reproductive endocrinology six months ago at the Mayo Clinic in Jacksonville, where you have been appointed to head the new Reproductive Medicine Department. Dr. Dunbar," he said, removing his glasses and dangling them between his index finger and thumb, "that's one hell of a resume for any man and especially for a man as young as you are, sir."

Will hesitated for a moment, making sure that he was now allowed to speak. "Thank you, sir. I'm quite proud of it but I've had a lot of help through the years."

"I'm sure that's true, but Colonel Chapman here tells me that he thinks you're the most brilliant man he has ever met," the general said.

"Well, I appreciate that, sir, but Ross ... um, Colonel Chapman and I have known each other since West Point. We were—I mean . . . are good friends so he may be embellishing a bit."

"Perhaps, but I have a great deal of respect for Colonel Chapman's opinions. His rock-solid judgment is a major reason for his success. For the purposes of educating the panel, Dr. Dunbar, your job is to help women who can't get pregnant, become pregnant. Correct?"

Will relaxed a bit, finally a question in his wheelhouse. "Basically, yes. We offer various treatments. Sometimes just simple counseling, sometimes medications, or sometimes in vitro fertilization techniques and surgery."

The general dropped his reading glasses on the table. "I see. Well, that's important work and you should be proud. But the information that I'm about to share with you is also extremely important and so highly classified that only a handful of people in this country and in the world, for that matter, are privileged to know it.

"I understand that we have plucked you away from your private life and practice of medicine. For that I apologize, but I want you to know that we have been in conversations with the administration at the Mayo Clinic. They are well aware that your absence is a matter of national security and we've been assured that your position at the hospital is secure when you return. I think it only fair that you also know that you need not be concerned with financial matters. If you elect to undertake the task that will be asked of you, you will be highly compensated."

Will was doing well financially and had no reason for concern. He thought it was polite of the general to offer but he could definitely manage to be away from the office for a few days if needed.

Coleman leaned in, an intense look in his dark eyes. "Dr. Dunbar, what I am trying to tell you is, if you should elect to proceed with this mission and succeed, frankly, you will never need to work again."

Will said nothing, just scratched his cheek and blankly stared at Ross. Ross did not return his glance.

"However, once you make the decision to proceed and are briefed on today's classified information, there's no going back. This information is too sensitive."

Will felt the hair on his neck rise. He searched for answers on the faces of the public servants seated across from him. Poker faces, masks of worry and concern, a look that Will knew well. It was the same look of desperation, anxiety and emotional distress that greeted him as he was about to reveal the results of a biopsy report or an unborn baby's genetics test.

Will squared his eyes to the general, clenched his jaw and replied, "Sir, it is not lost on me how dire the situation must be, whatever it is. You have brought me a long way and I sense the urgency in this room. I'm a soldier and a patriot at heart. I am at attention and I'm here to serve my nation. You may proceed to brief me on the status of affairs."

All those seated at the table relaxed and most shifted slightly in their chairs. The general looked at each person around the table, nodding as he drew their gaze. He gave a nod of approval to the camera and began.

"Dr. Dunbar, we are at DEFCON 3."

"DEFCON 3?" Will said. "The last time I was aware of that status was right after 9/11."

᪵   ᪵   ᪵

WILL'S EYES REMAINED FIXED ON the general's.

"We'll be putting together a program with the help of the Office of Scientific Research and Development." Coleman motioned to Dr. Wilcox, who nodded politely and smiled. "A program whereby we can hopefully regain what we have lost or at least preserve what we have for future generations."

Will drew his eyebrows together. He had no idea what the general was referring to.

"It will all make sense in a few minutes but I must first give you some background information on what we call the IMS. So to begin the proceedings, I'm going to turn it over to Dr. Bamesberger. Dr. B, as we call him is, as I said earlier, the chairman of the National Fertility Clinic. He has a medical degree from Yale and is the primary physician to the IMS. He is a neurologist by training but also has extensive specialty training in reproductive medicine. He spends most of his time treating the IMS but also maintains a part-time private practice in the Neurosciences Center at Emory School of Medicine in Atlanta. He is a leader in the field of human intelligence and memory. Being that you both are doctors, you will speak the same language."

Dr. B stood up and walked to the end of the room, facing Will. He was a small, wiry man with a face so thin and cheekbones so sharp that his thick eyeglasses continually slid down the bridge of his pointed, hooked nose. Will noticed his intelligent brown eyes and his rather oily black hair, parted on the side. The corners of his mouth slightly drooped so he appeared to be frowning.

The doctor's tone was soft yet confident. "Dr. Dunbar, let me reiterate General Coleman's sentiments. We feel honored that we have a man of your caliber to turn to in this difficult situation."

Will's bewilderment grew, but he managed a smooth retort. "Good morning, Dr. Bamesberger."

"Please call me Dr. B, everyone else does."

He shrugged his shoulders. "Sure, Dr. B. Please call me Will."

"Will," the other man began, "in your studies, you've learned an extraordinary amount about engineering, mathematics, genetics and medicine. But surely you have also read about or possibly even taken courses in early civilizations, possibly anthropology or archaeology?"

"Yes, sir. One of my favorite classes at West Point was in anthropology. I wouldn't say it was totally related to my future studies in medicine but it was also not completely unrelated. I thoroughly enjoyed it."

"Oh, good. So you are somewhat familiar with primitive human societies and social structures?"

"Yes, somewhat. I read a lot of *National Geographic*." Will laughed nervously.

"So, Will, when was the first human civilization created? How long ago did human beings organize themselves into villages, towns, communities?"

Will scratched his chin and looked up at the ceiling, searching his brain for the answer. "If I remember correctly, it would be the Egyptians ... the pyramids and all ... about six or seven thousand years ago ... I think," Will answered, taking a sip of water from a glass in front of him.

"Partially correct." Dr. B hadn't made eye contact with Will, or anyone in the room for that matter, but no one seemed to find that unusual. "You're correct about the Egyptians but the first civilization is a little older than that." He was succinct and direct, with a slight arrogance. Will was used to that, having spent years in the Ivy League. "Most scientists agree that the first Egyptian civilization started about ten thousand years ago."

"Okay. No argument here," Will replied with a nervous chuckle. He scanned the table again hoping to receive a return smile from someone in the room, anyone, but there were no takers, only intense concentration.

"I'm sure you'll agree with me that the degree of accomplishments in technology and medicine over the last two centuries is unprecedented. It's like an intellectual bolt of lightning came out of nowhere and transformed society overnight."

Everyone around the table was watching Will's face for a reaction. He just continued to listen intently.

Dr. B rubbed his hands together and paced the room. "Starting in the 1800s, the sheer volume of human knowledge has expanded like a shockwave, each ripple improving man's life like never before. It's as if during the previous one thousand centuries, ten thousand years, people were stuck in a perpetual state of intellectual stagnation. The world was dark, literally, until brilliant minds, like Edison in 1879 and Tesla in 1888, arrived on the scene. These intellectual giants rose out of the abyss and turned on the light. Are you following, Will?"

"I guess. I never really thought about it."

"So what I'm pointing out is that just in the last two percent of civilized human history, the human condition has been revolutionized like never before. For thousands of years, a nation's fighters entered combat on the backs of beasts of burden like elephants, horses, or camels and now, in only three or four generations, we have gone from our cavalry traveling by horseback to jet fighters that fly around the earth in supersonic machines traveling at two and a half times the speed of sound. In only a few decades we, or some machine that we've built, have visited every planet in our solar system reaching speeds of up to 150,000 miles an hour. We've placed a robot on the surface of a comet and on the planet Mars, 35 million miles away." Dr. B gestured loosely at the ceiling. He wiped a bead of sweat from his forehead and pushed his glasses back up on his nose. "In 1900, human life expectancy globally was only thirty-one years old, and only forty-three years in the mighty United States."

Will nodded in agreement. He had learned these facts in med school.

"In less than one century, human life expectancy has miraculously doubled. Doubled, Will. Currently, the worldwide life expectancy exceeds seventy years and it's around eighty in the United States. Nowadays, we can three-dimensionally print replacement human body parts and other devices for immediate transplant for things like heart valves, ears, and teeth." Dr. B pushed up his glasses again. "Now, I'm sure you're familiar with the following information but let me reiterate it for you again."

Will nodded and folded his arms.

"For centuries, the average woman had six or more babies in her life and at least half of these children did not survive childhood. I'm not talking caveman days. I mean the late 1800s and early 1900s. Furthermore, many mothers did not survive childbirth," Dr. B said, raising his hands like Moses. "Tell me, what drastic change has occurred in the last two percent of human history to account for all of this tremendous human advancement?" His beady eyes made contact with Will's for the first time as he awaited a response from Will. "What glorious phenomenon has occurred on this planet to propel us along like never before in human history?"

Will didn't attempt to answer.

Dr. B was eager to continue talking over the silence. "Do you think it's just a coincidence that many, many, many of the greatest minds in human history lived, walked, worked, and breathed at the same time? I'm talking about geniuses like Einstein, Darwin, Nobel, Pasteur, Thoreau, Edison, Van Gogh, Monet, Tolstoy, and on and on and on ...," he said, his voice trailing off.

Will held all those names in high esteem and had never associated the fact that they all lived at roughly the same time in history and breathed the same air.

Dr. B's perpetual frown was more evident than ever. "Dr. Dunbar, I would now like to explain to you what has happened to allow the world to advance so far, so fast."

WHATEVER IT WAS THAT DR. B was about to tell him, Will could feel the degree of importance building.

General Peterson, secretary of defense, released a sigh and seemed a bit agitated with Dr. B's egocentric tone and melodramatic mannerisms. He was ready to get to the meat of the matter.

"A genetic mutation has occurred," Dr. B said plainly.

"A mutation?" Will was on the edge of his seat.

"A mutation in the human genome, in human DNA. This beautiful, transcendent mutation has resulted in the creation of mind power and human intellect like the world has never seen."

"A superior brain power?"

"Yes, but it has occurred only in a small segment of the world's population. You see, there exists a tiny percentage of individuals in the world who are highly, highly intelligent."

"You mean like MENSA?" Will said, shrugging his shoulders.

Dr. B snickered with contempt. "No. That organization of bright people cannot hold a candle to these individuals, not even a smelly rancid one … no pun intended."

The defense secretary crossed his legs and rocked back in his chair, impatiently gripping the table tightly with his fingers.

"We're talking about an intelligence quotient to a degree like we have never seen on this planet and with each generation ..." Dr. B smiled for the first time. "They become smarter and smarter."

"I just ... I'm not sure what to say," Will said.

"Dr. Dunbar, are you familiar with mitochondrial DNA?"

Will sat up straight. "Of course. We all have mitochondria inside our cells. They're like tiny power stations. Mitochondria generate the energy needed for a cell to perform its function."

"Basic explanation, very nice. What about its genetic inheritance?"

Will thought for a moment. It sounded as if Dr. B wanted a real medical explanation. "All mitochondria possess DNA and it's separate from all other DNA in our body. This primordial genetic material is passed down vertically from generation to generation in each of us. It's different from all of the rest of our DNA because no changes occur in our mitochondrial DNA from parent to offspring and ..."

"Yes. Yes. Continue," Dr. B said eagerly.

"In regular DNA, there is constant splicing and rearranging of genes such that the offspring is a combination of its two parents. But mitochondrial DNA is different. It's pure, so to speak."

"Right. Keep going."

"Because of this purity, mitochondrial DNA is a powerful tool for tracing ancestry. I know it's used to trace family trees and to perform genetic research. It's even been used to trace human origins back to our earliest ancestor. I believe they named her 'Mitochondrial Eve'—a hominid that lived somewhere between one hundred thousand and two hundred thousand years ago in East Africa."

"Very good, Doctor. Now, are you also aware that mitochondrial DNA is only passed to future generations matrilineally, on the maternal side?"

"Yes, of course I'm aware of that. Since most of the father's mitochondrial DNA is located in the sperm midpiece—"

"In the mitochondrial sheath," Dr. B interrupted sagely and smiled at the group.

"Yes," Will replied. "The midpiece or let's just call it the tail."

"Whatever you like," Dr. B said.

"Since the tail of the sperm is where energy production is needed so that the sperm can swim and fertilize an ovum, most of the mitochondria are located in the tail. Since the tail is lost at fertilization, all children of the same mother are hemizygous for maternal mitochondrial DNA and are thus identical to each other and to their mother. Mitochondrial DNA does not undergo meiosis and there is normally no crossing over, hence there is no opportunity for introgression of the father's mitochondrial DNA.

"However, there has been some indication that a very small amount of the father's mitochondrial DNA does sometimes cross over but it's somehow removed from the embryo during development. Thus, it's fairly safe to say that all mitochondrial DNA is inherited maternally. That's why it has been used to infer the pedigree of the aforementioned Mitochondrial Eve," Will said fluently and with pride. He could play the Ivy Leaguer's game all night if need be.

"Yes. That is my understanding also," Dr. B replied.

General Coleman interrupted. "Gentlemen, gentlemen. For the sake of the many lay people in this room and at the White House, would you please explain what you just said?"

Dr. B apologized. "Sorry. We were just describing the mechanism by which only the mother's mitochondrial DNA is transferred to the fetus. We're discussing the fact that none of the father's mitochondrial DNA is present in the offspring, not ever."

"Thank you. I think we all can understand that," the general said as he surveyed the faces seated around the table, looking for agreement.

Dr. B began again, his hands working to describe volumes of ideas. "Dr. Dunbar, a very unusual mutation has occurred that influences the processes that naturally occur at the time of conception and into embryonic development. This mutation, this change in the normal flow of things, has allowed the father's mitochondrial DNA to be passed on to the embryo and incorporated into the DNA of the fetus."

"Interesting," Will said and scratched his chin. "Do we know what the mechanism of action is that allows this to happen?"

"In your research, you have identified the fact that there is a difference in the types of proteins present in women who have miscarriages. Correct?"

"Yes. We were able to determine that there's a significant difference in the protein sequence and the concentration of various critical proteins," Will answered confidently.

"Right, and one of those proteins that is present, in abnormally low levels, is ubiquitin. Correct?"

"That's correct. What does ubiquitin have to do with all of this?" Will asked and tugged at his itchy collar again.

"Just follow my thoughts for a minute. I became aware of your award-winning research and began to consider the possibility that ubiquitin may play a role with our IMS patients."

Will interrupted. "I don't understand. What is IMS?"

"I'll get to that in just a minute. What we found was that ubiquitin is the protein responsible for removing all of the father's mitochondrial DNA that may happen to enter the fetus."

"Really? Ubiquitin? I'll be damned."

"Yes, ubiquitin. Basically, it tags the father's DNA for later destruction by the mother's humoral immunity during embryo development. Thus, ubiquitin is the reason that no male mitochondrial DNA ever exists in the newborn child."

"That's a wonderful discovery, Dr. B. We've always known that no male mitochondrial DNA survives embryonic development but I don't think anyone has ever been able to determine what substances or processes were responsible for blocking it."

"That's right. In our lab at the National Fertility Clinic and with some subsequent studies at Emory, we were able to demonstrate this. It's been exciting."

"Why didn't you publish your work?"

Dr. B shot a quick irritated glance at the director of the Office for Scientific Research and Development. "Because I was not allowed to." He pushed his glasses back up on his nose again. "Anyway, the mutation that we're here today to discuss, prevents the formation and production of ubiquitin. This is not a mutation in the male DNA, however."

"It's not?" Will asked, confused.

"It is a mutation in the female DNA and prevents female production of ubiquitin at the time of conception and during embryo development. As a result of the lack of ubiquitin to tag male mitochondrial DNA, the father's DNA enters and becomes part of the genome of the fetus."

"So you are telling me that for the first time in human evolution, male mitochondrial DNA is being incorporated into the embryo's genome?" Will shook his head.

"Yes," Dr. B replied.

"Wow, that's highly unusual, to say the least. These women have no ubiquitin at all?"

"No. Not at the time of conception and during pregnancy."

"Then there must be a problem with miscarriages and being able to complete a full-term pregnancy."

"Yes. That's one reason you're here."

Will looked up at the ceiling, trying to understand the ramifications of what he'd just learned. He now appreciated why he was in this meeting room in the bowels of the Library of Congress. The location seemed a fitting place to gain knowledge, even if it was classified and covert.

Dr. B suddenly walked over to Will and grabbed his broad muscular shoulder. "It is much more than miscarriages, Dr. Dunbar. The remarkable thing is that the male mitochondrial DNA contains a gene that has the ability to transfer a father's memory to a newborn child. We call it ... Inherited Memory."

Will leaned forward in his chair. "Do you mean genetic memory?"

"I mean Inherited Memory. There is a very big difference. As you may be aware, mainstream researchers have known for years about genetic memory."

"I know, I remember. In med school, we read about genetic memory in mice. How scientists painted a line in a cage, then placed one mouse at a time inside the cage and allowed the mouse to explore the cage with no influence from any other mouse. Once the mouse crossed the painted line, it received an electrical shock."

"Yes, an uncomfortable stimulus. Go on."

"After several generations of shocking these mice and without any influence from their parents, baby mice, upon their first introduction to the cage, knew not to walk over the painted line. That is classic genetic memory."

"That's exactly right. The mice were born with knowledge not to cross the line."

"It's truly fascinating science," Will said.

"What we know now is that memories are stored in the hippocampus but are translated into emotions in the amygdala. So there is a physical location where memory is stored versus where it's processed. These individuals with Inherited Memory are passing on their memories just like they can pass on their hair color, skin color and mannerisms."

"Are you saying that their entire memory is being transferred to the fetus?"

"Yes."

"But we all have a little bit of our father's and possibly

grandfather's mitochondrial DNA inside of us and it manifests sometimes in subtle ways."

Senator Hickey unfolded his arms and leaned in. "My understanding," he said in his thick Southern drawl, "is it's just like you can be good in sports and have fast reflexes and instincts like your daddy."

Will stared at the stocky congressman, studying his athletic face. "Do you have Inherited Memory, Congressman?"

"Hell, I wish. Nobody in this room does."

Dr. Wilcox spoke up. "Will, I have a normal memory just like you but I have an unexplainable fear of heights just like my father and my grandfather. It's so strange." She shrugged.

"I got a green thumb like my grandfather and I never even met the man. They tell me that he was so green he could grow an orchid in the desert," General Peterson scoffed.

"So it's not just a basic reflex or instinct that's being inherited?" Will asked.

"Oh, no. You could definitely argue that in their basic form, instincts are a form of memory but the memories that are being inherited in these individuals via male mitochondrial DNA is vivid, real and powerful," Dr. B said.

"I ... I'm ... I am just speechless," Will said, wiping sweat from his brow with a sleeve.

Dr. B was pacing the floor again. "These individuals can remember everything that their father knew and his father and his father before him and so on. This compilation of memory on top of memory on top of memory has resulted in IQs never seen in human history."

"So you're telling me that all of the great scientists, artists, writers and poets that you mentioned, all owe their abilities to Inherited Memory?"

"The answer is a resounding yes! Even more amazing is that every generation becomes more intelligent."

Will gave Dr. B a skeptical look and scowled.

Dr. B stopped pacing and stood still. "I'm not saying that every brilliant scientist that has ever lived has Inherited Memory. Normal smart people with normal memories do exist. I mean, look at you. You're a brilliant young man, much smarter than most. Normal people still have their own sets of abilities, but these minds, the ones with Inherited Memory are the game changers. We are all just piggybacking off of them."

"So you don't have Inherited Memory either, Dr. B?"

Dr. B pushed up his glasses yet again. "Sadly, I do not. The ones I am referring to, 'they' as we call them, *they* are building satellites and spacecraft, *they* are solving the riddles to quantum mechanics and string theory, *they* are designing artificial intelligence. And as I said, the most remarkable thing is that every generation is getting smarter. These individuals with Inherited Memory today are even smarter than Einstein and his peers because their memories are more extensive."

"How long ago did this all begin?" Will asked, feeling numb.

"We are not one hundred percent sure, but our best guess is somewhere around the early 1600s. It took a generation or two before people started to understand what was going on."

"How many people have this ... this Inherited Memory?"

"Not very many because there's only a handful of females who do not produce ubiquitin upon conception. We think that there are currently less than forty-five females of reproductive age in the world who are ubiquitin-free and so we estimate that there are only about one hundred and fifty people worldwide who have Inherited Memory."

Will took a moment to do the math in his head.

"The truth is that other countries do not give out this information voluntarily so we can't be certain."

"How does it break down between male and female? I've noticed that you have only mentioned men scientists so far. Can females inherit memory also?"

"Yes, of course. Sorry, I should have mentioned Marie Curie and Emily Bronte among others. Females, like males, can inherit only their father's memory, not their mother's. But females cannot pass on their memory because the Inherited Memory gene is contained within the male DNA. But remember, the male, the father, can only pass on his memory if he mates with a female who does not produce ubiquitin during conception. What I have termed ubiquitin-free females."

General Coleman uncrossed his legs and interrupted. It was his show now.

"Dr. Dunbar, in the past during the 1600s to 1800s, before anyone knew anything about ubiquitin, this father's memory that was passed down the bloodline from generation to generation was called Blood Memory. Those women who were able to pass along this gift were called Blood Mothers."

Will said the words aloud. "Blood Memory ... Blood Mothers?"

Coleman continued, "Shortly after the Revolutionary War, the American government compiled a list of all individuals with Blood Memory. The powers that be thought it would be in the best interest of these individuals, and our country, that we provide protection and security to them. An organization was created, a society if you will, to which all individuals with Blood Memory belonged. The name of this organization originally was the Blood Memory Society, but in 1945 the government changed the name and we now call it the Inherited Memory Society ... IMS, to more correctly reflect what it truly is."

"Oh. That's what IMS means." Will shrugged his shoulders. "But it's a secret society?"

"Yes."

"Sounds like a good idea," Will replied, stunned. His mind was still trying to process it all. "How many people in the U.S. have this ... Inherited Memory?"

"Of the approximately one hundred and fifty in the world, twenty-seven—well, now only eleven—reside permanently in the U.S.," General Coleman said, shaking his head.

Will ran his hands through his hair to regain his composure and took a deep breath. "That seems like a small number if the mutation occurred over four hundred years ago."

Dr. B pounced on the opportunity. "Your ubiquitin discovery and how it relates to miscarriages, unknowingly to you, gave us the clue we needed. Without the ability to produce ubiquitin, there have always been an extremely high number of miscarriages in these women that can pass along the Blood Memory. I guess that is the trade-off for Inherited Memory. Most ubiquitin-free women—"

"You mean Blood Mothers?" Will clarified.

"Yes. The Blood Mothers usually only have one child if they are lucky and two children is almost unheard of. And sadly, it's not that rare for them to never give birth."

"Have you tried in vitro fertilization?"

"We have tried but unsuccessfully," said Dr. B. "That's why we have you now. We're hoping you can help us with that. We want you to review our protocols and see if we are missing something. I have isolated the gene. I know where it is but I need you to help me implant it."

Coleman spoke up, his voice strong. "Three days ago, sixteen American IMS members who composed an elite team of scientists at JPL, called Team X, were murdered. Being that there were only twenty-seven IMS members in the U.S., this is very alarming. These killers have almost completely wiped out the American IMS population."

Will put his head in his hands and wiped his forehead. "Has this happened before? Have IMS members been targeted?"

The secretary of defense took a deep breath and Will could see frustration on his face. "Back in the 1700s, the United States was the first country to figure out that certain individuals were being born with this ... Blood Memory ... this Inherited Memory thing."

Dr. B butted in energetically. "We were fortunate, Will. A clustering of births occurred in the Northeast that alerted us to this phenomenon. It was termed the 'Stoddard Stock.' When this occurred—"

Coleman shook his head and interrupted. "The important information for you to know at this particular time is that we are not aware of an attack, an assault, or kidnapping of any person with Inherited Memory since World War Two"

"What happened then?" Will asked.

"That is also a conversation for later," General Coleman replied, frowning at Dr. B for opening a can of worms. "Now, right now, we have to focus and we have to succeed. We are at a critical point. Not only is someone killing our IMS, weakening our national intellectual property per se, but the same vigilantes have also destroyed the National Fertility Clinic and—"

Will interrupted. "National Fertility Clinic? What is that? I'm a reproductive endocrinologist. I help couples with fertility issues every day and I've never heard of such a place!"

Dr. B looked at the general for permission and answered, "The National Fertility Clinic, the NFC, was established solely for the purpose of ensuring that we, the United States, have a way to ensure the continued survival of Americans with Inherited Memory. We collect and manage sperm samples and ova from all known American IMS members, some of whom have memories dating back to the 1600s."

"1600?" Astonished, Will took a minute to refill his glass with water, his hands shaking so badly that he spilled a small puddle on the table.

Dr. B's eyes misted and his voice cracked. "All samples were kept in a single location in Atlanta. I am—or was—the director."

Ferry, the CIA director, spoke up. "The explosion destroyed all samples."

"Damn. So what do you want me to do? Hunt them down or something? I mean, it's been a long time since I put on my fatigues." Will chuckled.

"No, of course not. Colonel Murray and Colonel Chapman are in charge of figuring that one out. We need you to head up Plan B," General Coleman said.

"Plan B? What's that? Isn't Plan B an abortion pill?" Will said with utter frustration.

"Actually, it's just the opposite." Dr. Wilcox spoke up. "Dr. Dunbar, because we are worried that there's a possibility of some radical faction succeeding in killing all American IMS members, we need you to find a way to rebuild our stock." She thumped the table with her wrinkled hand. "If you can find a way to prevent the production of ubiquitin in normal women at the time of conception, we can reestablish the ability to restore our IMS population. The evolution of our society and our national security depends on it."

Will stared at Ross with such intensity that he almost felt faint. Ross gave him a fist pump.

He took another deep breath and looked towards General Coleman. "Sir, all I can say is I will do my best but I'll need a lot of support. I'm going to need access to examine any of these Blood Mothers ... these ubiquitin-free women ... who exist. And I will need a state-of-the-art research facility." He paused and ran both of his hands through his hair, pulling gently with his fingers. He then interlocked his fingers, placed his palms together and looked up, directly into the camera. "Most of all, I will need your prayers."

6

WILL AND ROSS MET THAT evening for dinner at Ross' favorite French restaurant. With bold maroon walls and elegant crystal chandeliers, it was designed to look old and European and provided a scenic view across the National Mall to the well-illuminated Capitol. Ross requested his favorite table, a small booth in a back corner. Will wondered how many top-secret conversations Ross had been a part of here.

He had grinned when he saw how Ross was dressed. In black designer slacks, a black V-neck sweater and sport coat, which matched his lightly gelled and spiked black hair, Ross sported an air of success and accomplishment.

Wearing the same sweater and slacks as earlier, and a borrowed jacket from Ross that was slightly too small, Will felt a bit out-classed. Not allowing his competitive nature to get the better of him, he brushed it off. After all, he was at a disadvantage. He had not known what to expect in D.C. and had no idea of his old friend's new appetite for fancy French cuisine.

"It's great to see you again, Will," Ross said, sipping water. The silver Rolex on his left wrist sparkled as it caught the light from a candle on the table, causing Will to squint from the quick glare.

"You too. It's good to see that you're doing so well. I always knew you would. You always were a gunner," Will said with a facetious grin.

Both men laughed.

Will pointed to Ross' hand. "So I see that ring on your finger. Tell me more about that."

Ross gazed down, rotating his gold wedding ring between his thumb and index finger. "How long has it been since we talked?"

Will gazed toward the ceiling in an attempt to recall. "It's been about nine years. I called you to tell you that I couldn't make your wedding. Sorry about that, man. I was right in the middle of my Gross Anatomy final at Harvard."

Ross shook his head. "No worries. I just can't believe it's been that long. That's bad." He swirled ice in his glass. "I got married right after I got back from Iraq. Leslie and I work together at the Pentagon now. She's part of the team that handles the IMS grant applications."

Will was about to inquire about her duties but did not interrupt.

"We have two beautiful munchkins, a three-year-old boy and just had a little girl six months ago." Ross's eyes were big and happy as he talked about his family, and then he seemed to notice a painful gleam in Will's eyes. "Oh, Will. I meant to say something to you already. I feel like an ass." Ross looked at Will with remorse. "I'm so sorry about your parents. I heard about the plane crash through a couple of our buddies from West Point. I tried to call you once but ..."

Will's eyes were misty. "It's okay, Ross. We've both been really busy since graduating. It's been a really tough year, but I got through it ... or I'm getting through it, I should say."

A waitress with ebony skin and long braided hair approached the table. "Bon jour," she said with a French accent. "May I start you with something to drink?"

Will always had a knack for small talk and immediately flattered the waitress on her hair. They began a conversation about where she was from. Born in the Congo, she had been adopted by a French missionary couple and had grown up in Paris.

"I'd like a glass of red," Ross said, interrupting their elongated discussion.

"Hell, after today, I need a bottle," Will blurted.

The young waitress laughed, then placed her hand over her mouth, covering it with embarrassment.

Will pointed to the wine menu. "This '09 Château L'evangile looks perfect."

"Oui, you know your wine, sir. Excellent choice," she said with a bat of her long eyelashes as she sauntered away.

Ross stared in wonderment at his old friend. "You still got it, dog, but I didn't know you were a connoisseur too."

Will shrugged his shoulders. "I'm not. But I've been dabbling a bit lately, trying to impress the ladies. You know how it is when you're single." He continued with the previous conversation before the charming French waitress could distract him again. "Two kids. That's great. Wow, so your wife knows all about this IMS thing?"

Ross lowered his voice. "Yeah, I'm gone a lot and if she didn't know what was really going on, I don't think we could maintain a marriage." He released a deep breath.

Will lowered his voice to match his friend's. "I bet. This is all really hard to absorb."

"What about you, Will? Are you still spending a lot of time in the Bahamas? What's it called, the Abacoocos? I had so much fun on those two trips over spring break. What was the name of that guy who used to take care of us, your buddy?"

"It's Abacos and his name is Tiny," Will replied with a broad smile.

"Oh, yeah, Tiny. What a great guy."

Will's face lit up. Tiny was like family.

"I don't see a ring on your finger," Ross said carefully. "Are you and Sharon still together?"

Will shook his head. "Sharon and I dated for five years. I really thought that she was the one," Will said, then surveyed the restaurant for the waitress with long braids. "Where is our wine?"

"Sorry about that, man," said Ross.

Will picked up a piece of steaming French bread and pulled it apart. "So Inherited Memory? Crazy."

"Took me months to come to terms with this new reality," said Ross, "but you've got to strap those boots on and pull up your big-boy pants because we need you, man."

The waitress returned with the wine, performed the obligatory presentation, and poured the gentlemen a glass each after giving Will another flirtatious glance.

After she departed, Ross raised his glass in a toast. "Officium, honorem, patriae." Will joined in mid-toast as they recited the West Point motto; duty, honor, country.

"All of those scientists and artists that Dr. B mentioned, they all owe their intelligence to Inherited Memory?" Will asked.

"Yep. They were all living in and changing the world at the same time in history. Hell, the Age of Enlightenment was nothing," Ross said, leaning back in the booth. "You're a smart guy. Let's play a game. I'll say the name of a scientist or a writer or a painter and you tell me what you know about them."

"Okay," Will replied. He had always been good at trivia and Ross had certainly never been able to outdo him.

"Let's start with Einstein," Ross said, then extended his hand as if he were lobbing a softball.

"That's easy. Theory of Relativity. Numerous theories on time and space, energy, gravity. You name it. He basically changed the way researchers thought about the nature of light."

"Einstein was born in 1879."

"Okay." Will shrugged and took a sip of wine, then squinted in appreciation of such a fine Bordeaux. His appreciation of the Rhone Right Bank had been increasing as of late, now that he was no longer a poor medical resident.

"Think about this." Ross pointed out the window towards the National Mall. "Lining the mall we have all of these memorials to great men: Washington, Jefferson, Lincoln, FDR, MLK ... all born and bred in America. And then there's the Albert Einstein Memorial. Einstein spent almost his entire life in Germany and didn't even come to America to become a citizen until he was almost sixty, yet we built a memorial to him. No one seems to even notice that fact."

"I guess I never thought about it."

Ross snickered, then continued. "Darwin?"

Will refocused. "Come on. Give me a hard one. He wrote *On the Origin of Species*. Developed the concept of evolution. His ship was called the Beagle."

"*On the Origin of Species,* published in 1859. Next one ... Nobel?"

"Alfred Nobel. He invented dynamite. The Nobel Prize is named in his honor."

"Dynamite was invented in 1867. There's a lot more I can tell you about him, but later. Let's keep playing. Pasteur?"

Will's face lit up. "He invented vaccines and pasteurization. He's probably responsible for saving more lives than anyone in history, no joke."

"Pasteurization was invented in 1862," Ross replied. "Monet?" The bantering continued.

"The 'Water Lily Pond.' He was an impressionist."

"He began painting his major pieces of artwork in 1865. Degas?"

"A sculptor, and also painted all of those dancing pieces, women in ballet outfits and such."

Ross nodded. "Yes. The 'Little Fourteen-Year-Old Dancer' was sculpted in 1881. His parents were from New Orleans actually. Most of his other major works were in the mid-1860s." Ross gulped his wine. "I have to say, I'm impressed with your knowledge of the arts. How do you know so much?"

"Sharon was an art major, remember? I miss all that cultural stuff."

Ross began again. "Henry David Thoreau?"

"*Civil Disobedience*. Man, I like this game. I'm killing it!" Will pumped his fist.

"1849," Ross replied as he gave Will a leer like an exacting Catholic schoolteacher.

Will stared hard at the small candle on the table, his eyes searching the flame for answers, as he processed the similarities in dates.

Ross continued, sternly now. "Manet, Renoir?"

Will was laughing, but it was a nervous laughter. He could tell where this was going.

"Why hadn't I ever wondered about all of this before?" he asked, as he looked at Ross with astonishment.

Ross did not answer his question and did not wait for a reply. "1865, 1874. Mendel?"

"Father of genetics."

"1865," Ross replied. "Marie Curie?"

"I know she was involved with radiation and X-rays."

"1867. She was the first woman to win a Nobel Prize for her research on radioactivity. She actually won two Nobel Prizes."

The waitress returned for their dinner order but Will hardly acknowledged her presence, just ordered another bottle of the same Bordeaux.

Ross looked energized by knowing something that Will did not. He was clearly enjoying showing his superiority, even if it was for only one night.

"Twain, Dickens, Tolstoy, ... 1884, 1881, 1869!" Ross said, more loudly than he wanted to, and then put his hand over his mouth.

"This is incredible."

"Feel like a dumbass, don't you? It's like we couldn't see the forest for the trees."

"If it was a rattlesnake, it would have bitten me in the ass," Will said.

Ross smiled briefly then pressed on, "George Washington Carver?"

"He was a brilliant scientist. If I remember right, he had something to do with agriculture."

"He was so brilliant that even though he was an African American born into slavery, he was able to overcome it. His research was critical to establishing the concept of crop rotation."

Will stared with wonderment and shook his head.

"Thomas Edison, Alexander Graham Bell?"

Will picked up a white linen napkin off of the table and waved it like a flag. "I get it, I get it, I get it. Uncle," he said, laughing so hard that the couple at the nearest table, ten feet away, turned to look.

"Shhhh." Ross placed his index finger over his mouth, smiling. "What I'm telling you is that they all had Inherited Memory and the Americans were members of the Blood Memory Society. What we now call the Inherited Memory Society."

Will slugged down the last third of his wine like a shot of whiskey. "Okay, okay. How do they verify who's who? Do the IMS members get some type of documentation or something? I mean, how do they know who's legit?"

Ross' face became serious. "There's a list. A protected security document that was started over 250 years ago and maintains the names of all certified offspring who have ever possessed Inherited Memory. Fortunately, all offspring to this point have been willing participants in the IMS and their family trees have been closely monitored. But it's not hard to tell who has Inherited Memory.

When you can ask a five-year-old child to explain quantum mechanics or string theory and she does it, with mathematical precision, you can be certain. I mean Beethoven wrote 'Nine Variations in C Minor for Piano' at age eleven. At age four, Mozart could perfect any piece of music for piano in thirty minutes, and at age five he began composing. By age eight, he had written a complete symphony."

"They both had Inherited Memory too?"

"Yes. Both of their fathers were musicians and composers. Think about it. If you were to have a child and could pass your memory to him or her, at birth, they would already know what you know. For god's sake, your son or daughter could perform in vitro fertilization as soon as their muscle coordination would allow it. They'd know algebra and physics. Man, they could even play football like you and know your favorite fishing spot in the Bahamas. Think about how much of a head start that would give them on the rest of us."

Will rubbed his eyes firmly in disbelief, then poured another round of wine.

Ross cheered his glass with a clink. "But to answer your question, yes, the Americans with Inherited Memory do get documentation. It's like a separate birth certificate but it's not issued until they're ten years old."

"Why ten?"

"At that age, they demonstrate their knowledge, and then prove they possess Inherited Memory by recalling something that happened to their ancestors and not to them."

"It just sounds so strange," Will said with a smirk. "Are they weird people?"

Ross swallowed hard. "Look, it's my job to protect them and I don't like to judge them."

"It's just me, Ross. I'm not saying anything to anybody."

Ross glanced around. "Most of them are really weird. They

have crazy eyes that twitch and dart around everywhere. Imagine the biggest nerd from high school and multiply it by ten."

Will belly-laughed so hard that a bit of French bread flew from his mouth.

Ross added, "I don't blame them. I mean, I have no idea how I would be if I could remember things that happened to someone else 400 years ago. It would probably make me weird and crazy too."

"Is there a single normal one in the bunch?"

"A few. Maybe five or six that seem pretty normal."

"I see. And they get a certificate for having this?"

"Yep. Like I said, the society started way back, once they realized that it was some type of hereditary situation. It's actually a very involved and serious process that includes having the acting president sign the certification. I'll show you one." Ross pulled out his cell phone. "I actually have a picture of one from the Team X investigation."

"What was Team X again?"

Ross looked down, his expression sad. "That's how we lost so many of our IMS members. Basically, all individuals with Inherited Memory who prefer the sciences were on an exclusive team of scientists at the JPL in California called Team X." Ross shook his head. "All of them were poisoned."

"Holy shit."

"Yeah, it was my job to protect them and I fucked up." Ross stared at the floor.

"Look, Ross. I know you. Whatever went down must have been something highly unusual to get past you."

Ross just shook his head in disgust.

Seeing the angst on his face, Will did not press for more specifics.

Ross leaned in close. "Only two members of Team X survived. Here is a pic of them," he said and held up his phone.

The first photograph was a professional headshot of an attractive twenty-something blond female in a blue lab coat. "This is Victoria Van Buren. She is a brilliant physicist. She survived because at the last minute she was transferred to another location, to troubleshoot a problem that arose with the mission that they were working on. We have her safely tucked away." Ross held up the next photo. "This is Timmy Mahoney."

This photo was also a professional headshot but the young man in this photo was not attractive. He was painfully pale, with red hair, and a mask of freckles dotting his slender face.

"He is a computer genius, a boy-wonder. Right after 9/11, the government hired him to design a computer networking system that would link all government agencies' computers together. He named the program after his favorite Society member. He called it EINSTEIN. Timmy was only seventeen at the time."

"Whoa. That is impressive. How did he survive?"

"Not 100 percent sure because we have yet to track him down. We think he is alive because his body was not recovered from JPL. But I know in my heart he is okay because he has a severe peanut allergy. The JPL scientists were poisoned by eating peanuts."

"So strange."

"Yeah. I ate lunch with him last week and when I pulled out some peanut butter crackers he freaked out," Ross said. "So I know he didn't eat any peanuts."

Ross motioned to the next picture on his phone. "Here. Look at this. This is an official IMS certificate." He enlarged the picture on the screen and pointed towards the top. "This is the logo of the IMS. You'll see this on every official IMS document."

Will squinted and saw what looked like the bust of an owl and a textbook at the top of the page.

"It's called the Owl of Minerva," Ross said. "This is a current IMS member's certificate, but even if you ever see an old document from back in the 1800s when it was called the Blood Memory Society, it's always the same."

Will focused harder on the image. With large eyes and a sharp beak, it was definitely an owl. "Minerva was a Roman goddess, wasn't she?"

"Goddess of wisdom and, as legend goes, an owl was her pet."

"Oh, so that's why the owl symbolizes wisdom. The wise old owl," Will said. "I never knew where that came from."

"That's right. The owl sits on top of an open book and there's a broken chain that hangs down on both sides of the book. It's supposed to represent the fact that knowledge cannot be bound, knowledge is freedom, you know."

"Oh, okay, I get it. Like breaking the chains that bind you." Will examined the picture carefully. Underneath the book, in bold black letters was written "INHERITED MEMORY SOCIETY." He squinted again. At the bottom left-hand corner of the certificate was the signature of the President of the United States.

"Wow. That is pretty damn official right there," he said.

"It's a big deal and has been for over two centuries."

Will searched his friend's face. "All those names that you quizzed me with. I get that they all lived in the mid-1800s. But why did it all come together then? Why not sooner or later?"

Ross leaned in. "What we think is that the first mutation to allow Inherited Memory occurred in the 1600s but it wasn't apparent right away what was happening. It took a generation or two before family members began realizing that their children were different, very different."

Will lowered his voice to match his old friend's again. "Why did they need to form a secret society and what's the purpose of all of the secrecy now anyway? Why would anyone with high intellect fear for their lives or be ashamed of being a genius, a prodigy? I don't get it," Will said as he cut into his perfectly broiled steak, careful not to touch the scalding hot plate.

"There was a cluster of births that occurred in the mid-1600s. We think that Inherited Memory started with a family with the last name of Stoddard. We think the matriarch, Esther, had Inherited Memory and that all of her eleven children did too."

"Oh. The cluster that Dr. B mentioned," Will said.

"Yes. The Stoddard Stock allowed the government to become aware that people with Inherited Memory existed and they tried to protect them. Without this clustering of births, the government might not have known about Inherited Memory for another century, who knows."

"Well, somebody knew. Surely the families had a clue that something was going on."

"Oh, yeah, the families knew. But they kept it quiet."

Will was perplexed and finished his steak as Ross filled in the details of the Stoddard Stock genealogy, which included the names of many famous clergymen, statesmen, and inventors.

"But why would they keep Inherited Memory quiet? Why would a mother be embarrassed to have a super-intelligent child? What an awesome gift."

The cute waitress came back with an assortment of French pastries and tarts and flashed her ivory white smile. Will eyed a rich dark chocolate éclair with longing but finally declined dessert, as did Ross, and ordered after-dinner cognac VSOP for both of them.

"Where were we?" Will asked. "Oh, yeah. Why would anyone be ashamed to be smart?"

Ross's face turned grim. "Have you ever heard of the Salem witch hunts?"

"Sure I have."

"Mothers were afraid to go around bragging about their children with these strange memories. I told you already that most of the IMS members aren't so well adjusted, socially. Can you imagine in 1600, if you had these odd memories and strange visions that you couldn't explain?"

"I see where you're going. The Puritans of the time thought they were witches or devils and ..." Will paused and grimaced. "They burnt people with Blood Memory at the stake?"

"Yes, that's what we think happened. If not for that, there may have been more Americans with Blood Memory other than the Stoddard Stock and their descendants."

Will lifted his cognac snifter and frowned as the fiery liquor slid down his throat. "Now, here we are again, four centuries later, doing the same damn thing all over again. Somebody is trying to kill these people. It doesn't make any sense. This is just mind-blowing, Ross," Will said way too loudly. The older couple at nearest table turned to look, again. The woman, wearing diamond earrings, a fur shawl, and permed red hair, shot Will a sneering scowl. Ross put his index finger to his lips.

"Sorry," Will said in a lower voice. "But if you don't have a Blood Mother then there is no Inherited Memory; it can't be passed along. Is that why you only hear about famous male inventors? Because the government is trying to hide the identity of women with Blood Memory?"

"Very intuitive, Will. The answer is yes. They always have and still are. Marie Curie was not an American. American Blood Mothers have always been treated like national treasures but our government has tried to dissuade them from putting their names on things. I guarantee you that at least half of all the amazing technological inventions that we know of were a brainchild of a woman with Inherited Memory."

Will collected his thoughts. "When you said earlier that your wife works in the Grant Department for the IMS, what does that mean?"

Ross swallowed another mouthful of cognac. "Ahh," he said and stared at the amber liquid in the stylish bulbous glass. "The grants. Well, it was in America's best interest to foster the needs of people with this memory. Basically, the U.S. set up a win-win situation. The government encouraged them to continue in whatever discipline they desired, whether it was science or the arts, and offered heavy incentives in the form of grants for them to join this secret society. By becoming a member, they receive generous stipends to develop their ideas, and all income received from their inventions or artwork is tax free."

"What a great idea," Will said. "The government basically said, 'Continue your endeavors, your research, whatever your passion is, but don't reveal your gift and in return we'll provide financing and security for all of your needs and your family's needs.'"

"You got it."

"Do other countries have similar arrangements for their citizens with Inherited Memory?"

"They didn't at first," answered Ross, "which was fortunate for the U.S. since we began trying to recruit as many geniuses from other countries as we could. In the mid-1800s, when all of this was coming to a head, we built a 'safe-house' for all members of the American IMS. We call it the Hexagon."

"Hexagon? What kind of safe-house? Like a dormitory or something?" Will said, trying to clear his head of wine and cognac.

"It was built to protect them and it also offered one of the best research facilities of the day. Wait till you see it. It's still around. It's extraordinary and has really stood the test of time."

Will raised an eyebrow. He could not imagine where this "safe-house" would be or what it would look like.

"Really, the security and research environment that was created by the Hexagon is the main reason we were able to get some of greatest minds in the world to this country," Ross added. "It really spring-boarded us as a world power to dominate in technology ever since."

Will sat back and sank into deep thought for a moment, sorting through the list of famous names in his mind. "What about Tesla? I remember reading and learning a lot about him in engineering school. He worked with electricity and eventually developed alternating current. He had an amazing number of U.S. patents, something like 1,500, I think. And there was that whole controversy about how he claimed to have developed a 'Death Ray.'" Will laughed.

"Oh, yeah. Conspiracy theorists love that one," Ross said.

"But I remember reading that he could do anything, a real renaissance man."

"They are all like that, man. Multitalented in every which way you can imagine. Let me tell you about that Tesla though. He was a loose cannon. He almost let the cat out of the bag for everyone. The thing was, the government provided security for all of these IMS members but Tesla wouldn't accept it. He even spoke to the press, talking about his amazing brainpower and about the white light that he sees in his head. Whoever was in charge screwed up because everyone kind of let their guard down. I guess you really can't blame them because there hadn't been any attacks or kidnappings on any IMS member since the Revolutionary War. They just had this *laissez-faire* attitude going. But then someone tried to kill Tesla."

"I recall he was crippled somehow towards the end of his life."

"An intentional attempt to take him out. Someone didn't like all of that talk about his death ray."

"His super-weapon that would end all wars?"

"Yeah."

"So are you telling me that he really did have a death ray?"

"I don't know the answer to that but after his 'accident,' the IMS got serious again about secrecy. However, again, after a few decades of no incidents, they let down their guard." Ross finished off his cognac. "But then World War II changed it all, big time."

"What happened in World War II?"

The waitress approached. Will noticed she had put on a new layer of pink lipstick. She set the check down on the table and a mad scramble of hands ensued to grab it.

"Boys, boys, it's been taken care of." The waitress pointed

across the dining room. Dr. B raised his hand and waved. Will and Ross returned his wave and mouthed, "Thank you."

"That was nice of him," Will said.

Ross began again, not allowing Will to re-ask his previous question. "This is all a shocker, isn't it?"

"That's an understatement." Will felt lightheaded. "Are these memories constant or do they come and go?"

"First, we need to differentiate between the two memories. They have regular memories just like you and me but they can also access their inherited memories from decades or even centuries ago. It's pretty consistent. They all say the same thing. Just before an Inherited Memory surfaces, they get a flash of light. Sometimes, depending of the intensity of the memory, the light can leave them incapacitated for a few seconds."

"Oh, I was wondering what you were talking about when you said Tesla saw white light," Will said.

"They see this light, and after it's over they can solve problems, or paint or even have skill sets like athletics, things they may not necessarily have developed in their own life. Think of how amazing that would be."

"I could finally hit the golf ball straight?" Will laughed, staring up at the chandelier. "Man, there's stuff in my past I wouldn't want any kids I had to know about," he said with a snort.

"You mean like that time when we were at West Point and went to New Orleans for Mardi Gras?"

Will snickered. "Oh, man. We drank *way* too much that weekend."

Ross rambled on for twenty minutes about the trip; naked men in leather chaps bouncing on pogo sticks, women in nothing but see-through cellophane, utter decadence like he had never seen in his life. Will just nodded his head in agreement and laughed at the drunken tale of their glory days.

"So where do we go from here?" Will finally asked.

"The Dry Tortugas!"

THE NEXT MORNING WAS TYPICAL for March, cold and windy with snow patches and icy puddles littering the roads to Dulles Airport. After arriving, Will climbed the ladder to board the same jet that had delivered him to D.C.

Below, Ross shouted over the whine of the noisy turbines. "Go home and pack your bags. We'll pick you up in St. Augustine at ten in the morning, then it's just a quick jump down to Key West. Get some rest, you're gonna need it."

Will's head was a bit achy from overindulging the previous night but he managed to give Ross an earnest salute. "Ten-four, good buddy."

Taking a comfortable seat in the front row, an extreme tension crawled up the back of his neck. Until his flight on this aircraft yesterday, Will hadn't flown on anything smaller than a 747 since his parents' accident, promising himself he never would. But this wasn't an ordinary small plane. This wasn't even a plane, really. It was one of the fastest civilian jets in the world, a Gulfstream G650, the IMS' official but unofficial aircraft.

The jet lifted off with a thundering flash as the titanium blades of its engines sucked the cool morning air into its red-hot compressors where the molecules of oxygen were compressed tightly, then saturated with a high-octane fuel, followed by the discharge of an electric spark that sent gases exploding from its massive twin engines, creating over 6,000 pounds of thrust. All this technology came together with seamless synchronicity to rocket the craft and its passengers through the atmosphere at speeds close to 700 miles an hour.

About an hour later, the modern marvel touched down in St. Augustine. Will unbuckled his safety belt and leaned forward, captivated. As he peered out of the small oval window, the blades of the engine were decelerating, allowing the turbine's sonic whine to wane.

He shook his head over this incredible example of human achievement. "How did they build an airplane that flies this fast?" he murmured to himself, then laughed. In the last 24 hours, the word "they" had taken on an entirely new meaning.

ॐ ॐ ॐ

WILL'S CONDOMINIUM WAS DOWNTOWN CLOSE to the Bridge of Lions and across the street from the oldest fort in the country, Castillo De San Marcos. His European-style condo complex was a tall brown brick structure with expansive windows, generous balconies, and a burnt-orange Spanish tiled rooftop. The building fit well in the oldest city in America. It had recently been converted from an old ice warehouse into a modern living facility, complete with privacy parking and free wi-fi.

The downtown of St. Augustine was built before the invention of the automobile so its streets are extremely narrow by today's standards: barely wide enough for one-way roads in most sections, too tight for most delivery trucks. But it is lovely, seasonally temperate, and has an Old World charm. Will's dad, originally from Louisiana, had turned down better paying jobs as a medical laboratory technologist at other hospitals around the country and had selected Flagler Hospital for its comfortable atmosphere, more than anything else. He told Will that he just felt at home in this old city. With its multitude of Victorian-style homes and elegant oaks, it reminded him of Louisiana for some reason.

"The best decision of our life," his parents would consistently say.

Suitcase in tow, Will rode the steel and glass elevator to the tenth and top floor, fit his key into the lock, and opened the heavy door. A rush of cool air smelling of new carpet and clean furniture greeted him. With a nautical theme, the condo was bright and cheerful.

In the kitchen, he threw his keys onto the white granite countertop and switched on the track lighting, which cast small glows from the inset ceiling. Will grabbed a plastic bottle of cold water from the stainless steel refrigerator and stepped out through wide French doors onto a balcony. The morning sun rose over the quartz-colored waters of the inlet, and glittered off of the evaporating dew on land. "Blood Memory?" he said and reanalyzed the entire set of events from D.C. in his head for at least an hour.

꿁   꿁   꿁

AFTER A DAY OF RELAXATION in the heated pool on the third floor, several doses of ibuprofen to soothe his aching head, and a long sunset jog along the seawall and through the city's narrow streets, Will repacked his suitcase for the upcoming week in the Dry Tortugas, the southernmost group of atolls in the Florida Keys. He was familiar with the place, having been there with friends on three occasions. They had camped at the foot of the enormous, deteriorating Fort Jefferson, where the remoteness of the Dry Tortugas National Park offered some of the best diving and fishing in the world.

Still, while the Dry Tortugas was a beautiful place, its elements were not to be taken lightly, for the lack of food and water is a real concern. There is no running water, no electricity, no ice, no hot showers, and no store you can "run to" for supplies. The place is a spit of land in the middle of the ocean. There are no roads, no way on or off besides seaplane or boat and the nearest civilization is Key West, seventy miles to the east-northeast. His previous trips there had provided Will with fond but hot and sticky memories.

Anticipating the humid environment, he packed an assortment of thin, breathable clothes, mainly shorts and T-shirts, but threw in a few more formal items of clothing just in case. He tossed in his toiletries and added a laptop. His gaze went toward the bedroom's corner. His eyes might have been iron, with a powerful magnet in the corner pulling them. A heavy canvas bag sat there, filled with his dive gear, all neatly organized and tucked away.

The thought of bringing his dive gear on official business seemed unprofessional at best. But as the zipper of his suitcase was halfway closed and it became obvious that the thin clothes inside had not come close to filling the space, he reassessed.

"There's no way I'm going to the Dry Tortugas and not doing some diving," he said with a wicked grin. Inside the suitcase went a dive mask, snorkel, fins, a yellow mesh bag, dive knife and light.

With the sun having set just over an hour ago, the night was still young but Will switched off the light and crawled into bed. As he lay for what seemed like a tortuous eternity, twisting under cotton sheets, synapses of his brain fired mental images of General Coleman, Dr. B, the owl of Minerva, the idea of being burnt at the stake. He turned over on his side, desperate to rid his mind of thoughts so he could sleep, but his conversation with Ross at the French restaurant kept rewinding in his brain.

Suddenly, he leaped from bed and turned on his computer. He typed "Nikola Tesla." A cascade of biographies and conspiracy theory websites appeared on the screen. Studying them all intently, he selected the one that boasted to be the official page of Nikola Tesla.

Will read about the mind-boggling 1,655 patents for which Tesla was credited and re-read how his invention of alternating current changed the world. He browsed quickly until getting to the page on how Tesla claimed to develop a death ray, the ultimate "super-weapon." Tesla described it as the weapon "that would put an end to war by bringing down a fleet of ten thousand enemy airplanes at a distance of two hundred miles from the defending nation's border and cause armies to drop dead in their tracks." Underneath the description was a live thread from various social media outlets, discussions buzzing with conspiracy theories surrounding Tesla, his death, and the famed death ray.

One passage made him feel as if a fist had closed around his heart. It was the most vital information on the entire website, in black and white, a statement for all the world to see. It was a direct quote from Tesla, four sentences that surely hundreds, if not tens of thousands, of people had seen through the years and glanced over without a second thought. It was Tesla's secret.

It read, "I have suffered throughout my life from a peculiar affliction in which blinding light would appear before my eyes, accompanied by visions. Often, the visions were linked to a word or idea that I came across. At other times they would provide the solution to a particular problem that I had encountered. Just by hearing the name of an item, I am able to envision it in realistic detail."

Will next thought about the words of General Coleman. Sixteen IMS members had been murdered in the last 72 hours and for all Will knew, there could have been more assassinations by now. He was headed into the lion's den.

"I need a gun," said his inner voice.

This revelation of a need for self-defense was shocking. Will had not struck another human in anger since he was fifteen years old. He was not an avid hunter, but like most males who grew up south of the Mason-Dixon Line, he did own a shotgun and a deer rifle. He enjoyed an occasional quail hunt and would go for deer maybe once or twice a year when someone invited him to their lease in Georgia. But for the most part, his passion for the outdoors revolved around fishing and diving beautiful clear waters, wherever they might be.

He picked up a photograph of his deceased parents off his nightstand. His parents stood in front of their Victorian style home that they had lived in for 43 years.

He had inherited the house and it had been on the market for the past year. The mortgage crisis had hit Florida hard.

Yet to say Will was trying hard to sell would be an overstatement. He had listed the house as "by owner," but rarely responded to real estate agents' requests to show the home. He just couldn't motivate himself to get rid of a piece of his world that still provided a connection to his parents.

He gently rubbed the photograph. A description on the back read "New Year's Eve 1985." His father, Samuel, wore a bizarre tuxedo with various colors of paint splattered onto a white ruffled shirt. Tight black pants were held up by thin suspenders with the same splatter-paint design. His mother, Linda, was dressed in a skin-tight polyester jumpsuit with loose colorful leggings. Her blonde hair was teased so high that at five-foot-seven she seemed taller than Sam, who was six-foot-two. His mother had once described this picture to him, in her warm Southern twang. "Will, back then, if I could get my hair to touch the roof of my car when I was drivin', that was a good hair day." Will smiled, then set down the picture.

He knew where to find that gun, a pistol in fact.

Will walked directly to his closet. He pulled a thin white string and with a click, a hanging incandescent bulb flickered to life. Spreading apart the clothes that hung in the back left corner, he scanned the closet for an important family keepsake. It was an old wooden chest that had been hand delivered to Will after his parents' funeral by the lawyer who'd settled their estate. The attorney told Will that his father's last will and testament specifically stated the chest was to be placed directly into Will's hands.

He slid the old chest from beneath the hanging clothes. It was approximately three feet in all dimensions, dark blue with faded red sunburst patterns on top. Although he remembered placing it in his closet after his parents' funeral, he had only inspected the contents briefly; his grief was too much to bear on that day.

He unlatched the sizable steel latches and tugged firmly on the lid. The hinges squeaked noisily as the lid released its timeless grip and opened up. Sitting inside the chest was the one item that he knew was there, a black plastic case the size of an attaché. He reached his hand inside, grasped the case and unlatched the steel fasteners. Inside was his father's pistol collection. He counted four pistols in all and began to examine them.

Sam had two passions in life, his gun collection and the Civil War.

His father was a Civil War fanatic, most would say, but his knowledge of those times, places, and wars was unmatched. It seemed Sam had visited every battle site from Texas to Pennsylvania, at one point becoming such a disruption to his marriage that Will recalled his mother, in a sarcastic tone, asking Sam if he had a mistress named Shiloh.

Sam was also a crack shot. It was his thing and he had a knack for it. Never one for athletics, Sam spent many hours refining his skill and teaching his only son the art of marksmanship. Will enjoyed every minute of it and the memories of hours spent at the shooting range with his father flooded his thoughts now. His dad's modest salary as a medical lab tech left little room for indulgences but his pistol collection was his one exception.

The collection was impressive and Sam had meticulously kept them clean, and loaded. Will reached down and touched the barrels, all still slick from a light coating of oil. His father's voice echoed in his head. "It's an assortment of handguns, son. Each one made culturally iconic through use by the military, lawmen, outlaws both past and present, citizens legally and illegally."

Will examined the guns lying on a cushion of soft foam, his fingertips sensing their every nook and cranny, the cold metal warming from the heat of his hands. Starting at the left, as he held each one up into the light, he could hear his father's rich voice again, as he described each pistol.

Will began to consider the qualities and characteristics of each weapon, running through his father's descriptions. "The Glock shoots underwater and if you pour sand in it, it will still shoot." Winner.

The gun was fully loaded and as clean as the day it was purchased. He held it in his hands and pretended to aim.

"No one is going to get this guy," he said, holding up the barrel and blowing away pretend puffs of smoke from the tip, then placing the gun in his suitcase.

Curious, Will placed the chest on his bed and examined the remaining items inside of it. He picked up some black and white photographs, still shots from what seemed to be the turn of the century or possibly before. All had elegant handwriting on the back describing the people and the location pictured.

The first was of a middle-aged couple standing on a broad wide porch in front of a grand mansion. The man, in slacks, a long-sleeved shirt with thin suspenders and eyeglasses, stood behind the woman who wore a hoop skirt and bonnet, their expressions dignified and distinguished. The back of the photograph was labeled "Dr. Leonard Dunbar, Ella Dunbar, 1878, Peachtree Plantation, Vicksburg, Mississippi." Will's eyes brightened as he recognized the names. These were his great-grandparents. He had not seen this photograph for years.

He began to peruse more of them, all of the Dunbar family from the mid- to late 1800s. From what he could remember from his father, the Dunbars had lived in a plantation home in Vicksburg around the time of the Civil War.

Will studied the stack's last photograph. A small boy leaned against an oak tree: "Julian Dunbar, Age 5, Peachtree Plantation, 1883." Julian was his grandfather, and he had seen this photograph framed on his grandmother's mantel as a child.

He sat on the bed with the picture, took a deep breath and concentrated hard, trying to recall the story of Julian Dunbar, as told by Will's father.

The wealthy Dunbar family had owned and operated a massive cotton plantation since the early 1800s. Sam had held his hands far apart when describing how the plantation stretched for miles and miles along the Mississippi River. By the time it was Julian's turn to inherit the plantation, it stretched some thirty miles from the house. But for an unknown reason, Julian left, running away from all the family and prestige and would never inherit one cent of his family's fortune. In fact, Julian never married until he was 60 years old, his marriage producing one son, Sam.

Will remembered the first time Sam had told him this story. He couldn't have been more than twelve years old. He pressed Sam as to the reasons behind Julian's leaving, but Sam acknowledged that he didn't know much about his father's life. Julian had died when Sam was only a boy. The speculation was that he fled because he was no longer a believer in the use of slave labor. But for Sam, Julian's death resulted in hard times: he and his mother struggled to make ends meet, the only ones left to tend to a small farm in rural Louisiana.

"You're a lucky boy, Will. You have a mother and a father. I didn't have both of my parents growing up. You should always remember how fortunate you are," he would say, more times than Will cared to recount.

Will's eyes misted. He was proud of his father and how he'd made good out of a bad situation. And now, as he stared at the picture of Julian, he was even prouder of his grandfather for standing up for what he believed and taking the moral high ground.

He wiped his face with the back of his hand, then felt around in the bottom of the chest to make sure he hadn't missed any family photos. As he slid his hand around, he felt the corner of a leather-covered book. He gripped it firmly and held it up to the light. The book was faded brown, still intact but semi-crusty with yellow-green splotches of mildew on the front and back covers. He carefully opened the front cover and read the words "Diary of Ella Dunbar."

It was his great-grandmother's diary, and he recalled his father telling him about this book years ago.

Ella's diary had mysteriously appeared on Julian's front porch in rural Louisiana when Julian was in his mid-sixties, on his wedding day. Julian could not figure out how or why his mother's diary found him. He had not spoken to her since leaving home and had no idea if she was still alive or that she knew where he lived.

Will's heart was saddened at the tragic story. He thought of what he would give to be able to speak to his parents, just one more time.

Will slumped a little and began to feel a sense of guilt now. Maybe he should have already read the diary? But he just never took the time to appreciate how much his father enjoyed Civil War nostalgia. Maybe he owed it to the Dunbar family to read it now.

As Will closed the old trunk, he kept the diary in hand. Where he was going, with presumably no outside contact, it would help pass the time.

8

IT WAS 11:15 A.M. WHEN the G6 touched down at Key West International and if the rest of the country was suffering from a cold, brutal winter, no one in the Florida Keys would have ever known it.

"Man, I haven't experienced heat like this in quite a while," Ross said when Will met him at the airport. The intense sunshine seemed to give him a furnace boost of energy. He rubbed and patted his stomach. "Let's grab some lunch on Duval Street. The seaplane won't be here for another hour."

Will smiled and nodded. "Follow me. I know just the spot."

Duval Street was packed with artists, jugglers, palm readers, tattooed bikers with various pet reptiles and spiritual enthusiasts from all over the country, meandering souls coming to Key West to finally find their proper place in the world.

And, of course, tourists. The main contingency this time of year was an uncooperative mix of older, sedentary, pale Northern snowbirds and unruly, perfectly tan, college spring-breakers. Ross had told Will to dress like your average tourist so that they wouldn't stand out in any way, shape, or form. Will knew exactly what he meant. He showed up in a wide-brimmed straw hat, flowery Bermuda shorts, and a loud Jimmy Buffett T-shirt—what he and his buddies had coined the "Tourist Trifecta." With a smooth tan, Will laughed at Ross' pale legs, but his old friend tried to ignore him.

Ross followed him past the crowded saloons and the Mel Fisher Maritime Museum, onto a less traveled road to a hole-in the-wall deli. The Southernmost Deli, a reference to Key West as the southernmost city in the contiguous United States, was a small bleached-wood, open-air eatery, with limbs and vines of towering banyan trees draped over its patio like a natural curtain. Inside, Ross picked up a paper menu, grease spots and specks of encrusted food residue obscuring the description of the sandwiches. A woman with dreadlocks and a diamond nose-piercing stood behind the cash register. Will walked up and ordered without even glancing at a menu.

"I'll have a Lobster Reuben, extra sauerkraut, and a Diet Coke please."

Ross immediately set down the menu on the counter. "Uh, make that two, but no extra kraut. Oh, and a water."

He rubbed his belly again and looked at Will. "Damn, that sounds good."

"This is one of my favorite places to eat in all of the Keys. They're famous for their Lobster Reuben." Will grinned.

After taking a small table on the patio, Ross' lips began smacking as he bit into the tender lobster, wrapped in a melted blanket of Swiss cheese, finished off with homemade Russian dressing. His obvious fervor for the sandwich and the mess he was creating reminded Will of a one-year-old eating his first birthday cake.

Will laughed as Ross gagged. "Slow down, you're gonna choke."

"What?" Ross gurgled and looked up at Will, mouth smeared with orange dressing. "It's damn good!"

"I'll get more napkins," Will said.

As he turned to stand up, his eyes caught those of a strange-looking man wearing the "Tourist Trifecta" seated at the table just behind him. The man's skin was pasty white, the sclera of his eyes blue, and his face was further caked with thick white layers of sunblock, forming wet, clumpy patches around his nose and dry red lips. The albino man repositioned himself, breaking eye contact, and stared up into the canopy above of limbs and vines.

Will returned, setting a six-inch stack of napkins on the table with a thump.

"Ross, I need to ask you something."

"Sure," Ross mumbled as he sloppily wiped his mouth with a napkin.

"General Coleman and you both referenced World War II when talking about the IMS. I even asked you about it at dinner the other night and you ignored the question. What's the significance of that war?"

Ross put down his sandwich and thoroughly wiped his mouth with another napkin. Tilting his head to one side, he lifted an eyebrow. "It's not a pretty story. It's hard for me to talk about, really." Ross swirled his water glass.

Will waited silently.

Ross relented. "Okay. It has to do with Hitler and his persecution of the Jews," his voice crackled slightly. Ross came from a Jewish family and Will could tell that whatever he was about to say would be difficult for him.

Will said softly, "Ross, I need to know what I'm up against."

Ross took a deep breath. "You know how the history books always say Hitler was trying to build a master race?"

"Yes."

"Well, the history books will say that Hitler wanted blond, blue-eyed, tall, and strong Germans. But that was only part of his objective. His goal was to build a master race all right, not just through superior physical ability but also by breeding a race of people with superior mental ability, men and women with extremely high intelligence. The Jewish community became his target."

"Are you saying what I think you're saying?"

"Have you ever thought about how many brilliant Jewish scientists there are?" Ross asked eagerly.

"I just thought it was a cultural thing. I mean, I have many Jewish friends, you among them, and I just always thought it was cool how much emphasis you guys put on education."

"That's somewhat correct. There's definitely a cultural component but it turns out that Jews have a disproportionate number of individuals with Inherited Memory."

Will wrinkled his brow. "I guess I'm not surprised. You're saying that they have more people with it than any other group?"

"Yes. Unfortunately, Hitler found out about Jewish Blood Memory and began rounding them up."

Will was dumbfounded.

"All of those medical tests, those gruesome scientific experiments the Nazi doctors performed, those were all about trying to find people with Inherited Memory so that Hitler could interbreed them."

Will shook his head sadly. His mind flashed back to the horrendous Nazi medical experiments that he had read about in med school. Hearing a cell phone ring behind him, he turned to see the pasty-faced man had moved one chair closer, now definitely within hearing distance.

Ross frowned and lowered his voice. "Hitler felt that if he could harness the ability to produce a race with superior intelligence, he would have no trouble taking over the world."

"Obviously he didn't succeed."

Ross cracked his knuckles like a boxer about to enter the ring. "No. The Allied invasion ended his master plan."

A frown of disgust came across Will's face. "But Dr. B said that the mutation only affects .0000-something ... hell, I don't remember ... but a tiny amount of the population, so how is it that the Jewish community—"

"Nobody seems to understand but it's true."

"So if the incidence of Inherited Memory is just slightly higher in the Jewish population then that means that out of six million Jews that were killed ..." Will paused and his eyes filled with sorrow as he worked out the math in his head. "Hitler only found less than ten people with Inherited Memory."

Ross nodded solemnly, holding up five fingers.

"Oh, man, I feel sick." Will shook his head. "What happened to those five people?"

Ross took a deep breath. "Once the Allies were in control of Auschwitz, they came across a sector housing 'The Five,' as they called them. Obviously they'd been through hell, seeing Hitler discard the others that didn't have Inherited Memory, you know, you've seen the photos."

Will nodded.

"I don't have to tell you how many people died like rats." Ross' eyes glistened from a slight film of moisture.

Will changed the subject to one less upsetting. "When do I get to see this safe-house, this Hexagon?"

"That's where we're headed as soon as the seaplane gets here."

Will tossed a napkin over his half-eaten sandwich. "Okay, I think I have a handle on how this memory thing works." He took another swallow of soda.

"Now you understand, Will, how extremely important it is that this society stay secret. It's in everybody's interest. Once we get all of them tucked away safely, I'll feel much better."

"Tell me more about this ... this safe-house."

"Like I said, in the early 1800s when it became apparent that the U.S. government needed to protect their IMS, they started looking for an ideal place to build a secure fortress. However, they also needed to provide a place for these brilliant minds to continue their research and art, what have you. So they settled on a place not far from here, a tranquil natural setting that would foster ideas."

"Interesting."

"And the geographic location was perfect. At the time that the Hexagon was built, in the mid-1800s, the Dry Tortugas was the most secluded piece of land in the U.S.."

"Oh, because Alaska and Hawaii weren't states yet. Got it."

"Yeah. It was far enough away to give protection yet close enough to the mainland in case of some unforeseen crisis. It's huge, the damn thing is not much smaller than the Pentagon."

Staring into the canopy of limbs above him for a moment, Will's mind was churning with an implausible idea. His inner voice already knew the answer but he slowly squeezed out the question anyway. "What ... is ... the official name ... of this ... Hexagon, Ross?"

Ross smiled impishly. "I think you just figured it out."

"Fort Jefferson," Will stated, careful so the pale man would not hear.

THE SEAPLANE'S 750-HORSEPOWER ENGINE ROARED like a cyclone as it took flight, the landscape of Key West fading quickly in the background. As the IMS seaplane climbed to cruising altitude and headed west, the clear, azure waters of the Keys glimmered like diamonds in the midday sun. Will peered out of the small square window and began to see the first chain of islands, the Marquesas.

"How often do you come out here?" Will yelled over the reverberating roar of the seaplane's prop.

"About twice a year, I come down to do an assessment. To ensure all of the Fort Jefferson security features are properly working. But this trip, I'm just your personal tour guide."

Will laughed. "What security measures?"

Ross smiled owlishly. "You'll see."

As they flew over the sandy atolls, Will recognized a few of the protected bays and lagoons safely tucked on the alee sides of numerous crescent-shaped islets of the Marquesas. Leaning forward, he touched the pilot's shoulder.

In his sixties with thinning hair and a grandfatherly face, the pilot turned towards Will. "What is it, son?" he asked loudly.

"Would you fly us over the Atocha, if you don't mind? I've never seen it from the air."

"Sure, no problem. It's basically on our way."

The *Atocha*, a sunken Spanish galleon, was the flagship of a seventeenth-century fleet bound for Spain. Like many ships over the previous 300 years, the *Atocha* and its crew had spent the last year of its existence collecting gold from South, Central and North America and was on its way to Cuba, to convoy back to Spain with its bounty. This flow of wealth was crucial to Spain and there hadn't been a delivery in over four years, making the *Atocha's* cargo that much more critical. When it sank in a storm, Spain's economy suffered a devastating blow. Without the *Atocha* gold, armies did not get paid, and families did not get fed.

"Thar she blows," the pilot yelled.

Will stood and walked over to Ross' side of the plane, looking down at a dark oblong shadow in the clear blue water.

"Fisher found a half-billion dollars of sparkly gold on that spot right there," the pilot said with a wide smile.

"Damn," said Ross. "Must be nice."

"I dove that area the last time that we came out here on a buddy of mine's boat. I didn't find nothin' but a sand dollar," Will said. "But it was still exciting just to be swimming around where all that gold came from."

The pilot chimed in. "Mel Fisher searched for that gold for over twenty years. Couldn't give it up. Hell, it even cost him the life of one of his sons. I don't know what makes gold so damn alluring, but it will make men lose their minds."

"The lure of shiny objects ..." Will chuckled.

Ross thought for a moment then spoke. "'Truth, like gold, is to be obtained not by its growth, but by washing away from it all that is not gold.' Tolstoy." As the words rolled off his tongue, he gave Will a wink.

"C'mon, that's not fair." Will punched at his shoulder as the seaplane gently rolled back to the west. "Do you see that?" he said, pointing below.

"What -- another sunken Spanish galleon?" Ross scanned the ocean's blue surface.

"No. You know what those darker circles are in the water? The ones with green and brown on the edges? Those are coral heads, huge brain corals. They can grow six feet high in these waters."

"Man, that's big."

"Yeah. Dangerous too. At low tide, the tops of big ones stick out of the water. I almost ripped a hole in the side of my boat one time when we were down here a couple of years ago."

"That would not be a good day," Ross said. "Look at 'em. They're all over the place."

"They're more beautiful underwater. What's interesting is that they have all of these corrugations and folds that make them look just like a massive human brain. They can live up to 900 years."

Ross screwed up his face. "Wow, a 900-year-old brain? Now that would be an old memory right there."

Farther west, the edge of the U.S. national boundary in the near distance, they began to see the main islands of the Dry Tortugas, seven in all. From this soaring perspective, Will could well understand where the islands' name originated. Tortugas was Spanish for turtle and the islands resembled tiny humps in an expansive ocean; dry, because Will had not yet seen the first standing pool of fresh water or even a single seasonal stream.

Up ahead, he noticed a strange brightness emanating from Loggerhead Key, one of the larger islands. Now directly over it, he shaded his eyes with a hand as the entire surface of the island glowed painfully bright from the silvery reflections of hundreds of rectangles in neat rows.

Will squinted. "You can't see all of those from a boat."

"Solar panels, for electricity." Ross yelled back.

"Why so many? Where does all that electricity go?"

Ross stretched back in his seat ostentatiously and put his hands behind his head. "Be patient. You're about to find out."

The pilot pulled back the throttles and the seaplane descended, preparing to land in the surrounding waters of Garden Key and its most famous inhabitant, Fort Jefferson. When the enormous brown hexagonal fort appeared, Will's breath caught.

"You're right, Ross. It does look like someone picked up the Pentagon and set it down in the middle of the ocean. You know, the first time I saw this place, I wondered to myself, 'What builder got that contract?' I mean, somebody must have had a buddy in Congress." Will waved his hands. "There's no reason for such a huge fort out here in the middle of nowhere."

Ross laughed. "It was built in 1846. There are sixteen million hand-laid bricks in that old fort. It's almost three-quarters of a mile long."

Will noticed the fort's six opposing walls, four tiers and robust seawall that protected the northern and western facing flanks.

"See all of those arched embrasures? At one time they housed a thousand cannons, all aimed out to sea. To this day, Fort Jefferson remains the largest brick building in the Western hemisphere."

The seaplane's pontoons brushed the surface of the ocean with a gentle splash as the plane came to a smooth glide and began to maneuver around the shallow jagged reefs lining Garden Key like a rocky minefield.

Will's attention perked as the seaplane approached a manmade channel that was cut deep, but narrowly, into the natural barrier. "This is the tricky part right here. There's a huge brain coral on each side of the channel," he said, remembering that the channel entrance was barely wide enough for one vessel, and unsure how the pontoons would manage around the two massive corals.

With a quick snatch of the rudder, the old pilot perfectly taxied through the narrow channel into a tiny harbor. As they reached the outer finger of a large wooden dock, two men in dark green uniforms secured the craft's lines to metal cleats.

From his window, Will recognized a shady oasis on this otherwise arid sixteen-acre piece of sandy beach. It was a clump of trees on the southwest corner about 300 yards from the fort's arched entrance. Here were eight campsites, all empty today. It was the only location in the entire Dry Tortugas where the general public was allowed to camp. Campers provided all their own water, ice, and food. It was a real rustic experience.

Will stepped onto the dock and studied the deteriorating condition of the old fort as two uniformed men approached. They wore cargo shorts, loose-collared shirts with an official Park Ranger badge sewn onto the pocket, black leather belts with two gun holsters, and white cowboy hats.

"Colonel Chapman," the shortest of the pair said, extending a hand. He had tan Mediterranean features and looked no more than 25 years old. "It's good to see you again, sir."

Ross shook his hand. "You too, Rocky. I'd like you to meet Dr. Will Dunbar."

The young man extended his hand to Will. "Good to meet you, sir. I'm Rocco Caruso but everybody calls me Rocky," he said with a Brooklyn accent then gestured to the other officer. "This is Demetrius Dawson. We call him Double-D."

"Double-D," Will said, saluting. Double-D was a bear of a man. With a stone-etched physique and deep black skin, there was a steely edge to his brown eyes.

"How's everything going?" Ross asked.

Rocky spoke up. "It's all been nice and quiet, just like we like it, sir. We really haven't had problems shutting down the tourism. As instructed, we informed the ferry service, seaplanes, and most of other recreational outfits in Key West that the fort site is closed for a while. We told them it's 'under repair' until further notice."

Ross said, "There may be a couple of more people that come out but if they don't have proper documentation, turn them away. No exceptions."

"What? You closed down the fort?" Will whispered.

"Yeah. We closed down the campsite until we catch the killers," Ross said. "Oh, gentleman, Dr. Dunbar will be here on official business for a while. We're not sure how long yet but watch out for him for me. We go way back."

"You got it, Colonel," Double-D said. "Now, please grab your bags and follow us."

Will and Ross followed the two men across a long inclined wooden ramp crossing a deep saltwater moat. This led up to the arched concrete breezeway of the fort.

"I never have understood why these Park Rangers down here wear those stupid cowboy hats. I've never seen that anywhere else in Florida," Will said quietly to Ross.

Ross whispered back, "They're not park rangers." He motioned to the dock and pointed at two large sleek center-console boats, each with four huge outboard engines. Official-looking seals were painted in black and green on the sides of the gray hulls.

Will asked, "Then who and what are they?"

"They're U.S. Marshals."

As they passed through the entrance and began the long walk across a ten-acre grassy field towards the barracks, careful to stay a few yards behind the two uniformed marshals, Ross explained how they became involved with the IMS. The United States Marshal Service, the nation's oldest federal law enforcement agency, had been created with the Judiciary Act of 1789, when President Washington noticed a security gap between the broad scope of the military and the local restrictions of the rudimentary police service. As the enforcement arm of the executive branch of government, the

Marshal Service primarily deals with fugitive operations, protection of officers of the courts, court buildings, and, not coincidentally, the service operates the Witness Protection Program.

"When I think of marshals, I think of the Wild West and folks like Wyatt Earp," Will said.

"I know. Most people have no idea what they do."

"But the more I think of it," Will said, "it seems a natural fit. If they started the Witness Protection Program, hiding the IMS would seem seamless."

"It's actually the other way around. The Witness Protection Program was started because of the IMS, when it was the Blood Memory Society."

Will shook his head. At this point, nothing Ross could tell him would surprise him.

Halfway across the field, Will stopped and slowly looked around in a wide circle, surveying the impressive flanks of Fort Jefferson. He noticed the crumbling mortar and disintegrating bricks as they baked in the tropical heat.

He cocked his head. "It all makes sense."

"What? Why they built it way out here?"

"No. I mean, yeah, that too. But it makes sense why there are so many damn rules out here. It's like you can't take a piss without a permission slip around this island."

"I know. The U.S. Marshals don't play."

"Look, don't get me wrong. This is a beautiful place and the fishing and diving is second to none, but there are so many regulations as far as where you can and can't go. I've been out here three times in my life and every time we've been boarded by Park Rangers in a Wildlife and Fisheries boat."

Ross smiled grimly. "The marshals won't let you get within three miles of this fort without being checked out. I assure you, they did not give a shit if you caught an illegal fish. They just wanted to see who you were."

Will laughed. "No wonder they never wrote me a citation."

Just before entering the barracks, Ross pointed out fifteen marshals stealthily positioned around the fort in strategic locations. "They have enough of an arsenal out here to start a world war."

The barracks, or sleeping quarters, for the marshals, official guests, and other employees of the Dry Tortugas National Park was a sun-bleached, wooden three-story building positioned inside the walls of the fort and along the northeastern flank. Looking slightly ramshackle, with peeling paint and a slightly warped foundation, it offered a dormitory feel by way of small rooms and community showers and bathrooms.

The marshals led them down a bland concrete hallway to the third door on the right. Ross squeezed the doorknob and pushed it open. The room had been uncomfortably warmed by the sun and smelled slightly stale. Two twin beds with thin mattresses and no headboards occupied a cinderblock-walled room about six feet wide and eight feet long with a single window between the beds, a single wooden chair and a plain oak desk bearing a small lamp. With a firm jerk, Will raised the window.

"Feels like West Point all over again, roomie," Ross said.

"Hope you don't snore as bad as you used to," Will replied.

"Fortunately for you, I'm only here for one night. Now, c'mon. Let's go see the Blue Bunker." Ross threw his suitcase on a bed.

"Bunker?" Will asked, placing his suitcase on the other bed and unzipping it, fumbling beneath the clothes to make sure his pistol was there.

"Yeah, the Blue Bunker is what we call the underground part of the fort. You're gonna be spending a lot of time down there, I'm afraid."

After verifying the Glock was safe and secure, Will grabbed his snorkel gear and set it in the corner.

"You planning on diving?"

"Um ... maybe. If I can get above ground."

As he was about to zip the suitcase, the diary fell out onto the cement floor.

Ross picked it up. "What's this old thing? Looks like it's seen better days."

Will carefully took it from him and laid it on top of the desk. "This is my great-grandmother's diary. She kept it during the Civil War."

Ross affected puzzlement as he added up the math. "Civil War? Don't you mean your great-great-grandmother?"

"No. My grandfather was about sixty years old when my dad was born. It's like we skipped a generation or something."

Ross nodded. "Oh, I gotcha. Now, let's go. I can't wait for you to see this."

❧ ❧ ❧

As they followed Rocky and Double-D again across the field, known as the Parade Grounds, Ross said dramatically, "Everyone who works here is an actor."

Will grinned. "But why do they allow tourists? That seems risky."

"By allowing tourism, this secret state-of-the-art security bunker appears to be nothing more than just an old run-down relic of the 1800s."

"If you say so."

"We've never had an incident. It's been secret for over 150 years. Even you didn't know anything about it."

"And all of this is secure?"

"Not the fort itself. It's just a shell in need of constant maintenance and repair. Underground in the bunker, it's modern, comfortable and heavily fortified. It's basically impenetrable, even by today's standards. It is—it's hard to explain." Ross smiled. "The doctor who runs the genetics lab, Dr. Greenwood, is expecting you. I think you'll be impressed with his digs. It's where Dr. B does some of his IMS genetics testing."

"I thought he was in Atlanta, at the NFC and Emory."

"He goes back and forth. Most of the IMS prefer to meet him here at the Hexagon for their annual."

"Annual? Annual exam?"

"Yeah. As part of the agreement to stay in the IMS, each member has to submit to an annual physical and whatever genetics testing that Dr. B sees fit. It's no big deal, really. Hell, they get free health care."

Will stopped and looked around. "What's the status on the remaining IMS members? How many are still alive?"

"We're trying to get all IMS back here right now. Before the incident with Team X, there were 27 members of the IMS. Team X was composed of seventeen."

"All physicists?"

"No, not purely. Team X was a combination of people who thrived in the sciences. Since losing Team X, we've only got a few IMS members left. Besides Dr. Greenwood and one woman, there are nine others -- more artsy types. You know, left-brainers ... poets, painters, musicians. We call them the Juilliards."

"Why Juilliards? Do you mean like the Juilliard School?"

"Exactly. Augustus Juilliard was born in 1836. He had Inherited Memory."

Will could hardly believe his ears. "So there are only nine Juilliards left and a couple of others. We're almost wiped out. Our IMS is almost extinct."

"Now you see how important you are. This is major."

Will bit a fingernail as he walked to keep pace.

"Besides Dr. Greenwood, who has the memory and who lives here, two IMS men and one woman have gotten to the Hexagon safely. I showed you the pic of the young lady already, remember?"

Will nodded.

"I'm trying to get the other eight here as we speak."

"What's her name again?"

"Victoria Van Buren. You're scheduled to see her tomorrow. She's the only remaining IMS woman with a scientific brain. There are five other females remaining in the Juilliards ... no disrespect, they just aren't strong in math and science. Victoria is a mathematical genius and she's invaluable to us."

Will's eyes widened. "What is she like?"

Ross smiled. "She's twenty-five years old and she is ... how do I say this? She's got it all. Her family, the Van Burens, have the oldest memory of all the IMS."

"So she's brilliant?"

"Yep."

"Weird?"

"Nope, supernormal but also ... uh, superhot."

"Yeah, she looked good in that photo. But I thought you said they were all nerds?"

"I said most are."

Will felt a sense of intimidation come over him. "When you say old memory, how old is old?"

"Victoria has memories back to the 1600s!"

Now approaching the northwest corner of the fort, almost a quarter of a mile from the one and only public entrance, they entered one of the huge arches. With a right turn through another archway, a quick left back through yet another, then two more meandering turns through a maze of arches deep inside the fort, they approached a massive door.

Will's jaw dropped. Standing in his way was a replica of the bronze door that safeguarded the entrance to the Jefferson Building of the Library of Congress. Except for a light white sprinkling of dried salt spray on its surface, it was an exact match.

"The Memory Door," said Will before asking, "There's a Memory Door at Fort Jefferson and at the Jefferson Building?"

"That's right. I pointed it out to you for a reason when we were in D.C." Ross grinned wickedly and touched the sculpture.

"Here ya go, Dr. Dunbar," Double-D said and handed Will a plastic keycard, then motioned toward the electronic card reader on the wall. Will swiped the card. After the red light turned green, several booming thuds reverberated through the bowels of the fort as multiple massive padlocks released their hold. With a thump, the huge door swung open, exposing a dark passageway.

"This way, gentlemen." The marshals walked inside and Will and Ross followed them into a dimly lit corridor lined by smooth white plaster walls. Double-D pointed to a silver keycard reader on the wall. "You have to have your keycard to get back out of here so don't lose it." Will slid the keycard into his pocket.

They bypassed a stainless steel elevator and proceeded slowly down a narrow metal stairwell. The air was surprisingly cool, air conditioned, and tinged with a pleasingly fragrant aroma. With each step downward, Will became more aware of a soft blue hue, oddly opalescent, emanating from beneath him. Now ten feet below ground, they were standing in a long white polished hallway reminiscent of a hospital, yet smelling fresh and vibrant, not at all soapy or sterile. With each stride down the hall, the air became even cooler and crisper, smelling of vanilla incense and flowers, spa-like. Will saw the whites of the other men's eyes sparkle blue from the unusual light glowing from every inch of the ceiling and flowing like a thin mist down the walls.

The sides of the hall were composed of tempered transparent glass, which separated the men from large research laboratories on the other side. The ceilings, floors and supporting rafters were built of heavy-duty, thick, polished stainless steel. All the walls lining the labs were glass, so the strange blue light flowed effortlessly throughout the entire space, penetrating every shiny surface and dark corner.

Will followed the procession around the first turn, then stopped, awestruck. "This is unbelievable," he said, gazing at the mesmerizing light.

Ross nodded. "Calming, isn't it? Now you know why we call it the Blue Bunker."

"Please follow me, gentlemen," Double-D snapped.

They continued down the hall, passing several labs on each side. Each was strikingly identical containing four white benches equipped with sinks, four microscopes, three fume hoods, centrifuges, incubators, metal shelves and cabinets containing cases of clear glass bottles filled with buffer solutions and reagents, two stainless steel refrigerators and a panel of computers connected to wireless printers.

About a dozen people in white lab coats, wearing clear plastic safety glasses and white hairnets, scurried about, diligently swirling various solutions in beakers and peering through microscopes. On the walls, computer screens flashed pages of mathematical spreadsheets as the drone of massive mainframe computers hummed continuously.

Will called ahead to Ross, "I thought Dr. B ran the genetics lab."

"Not here. Dr. B mostly just comes out for the annuals. He collects samples, does a few basic tests but mainly just keeps track of the IMS health. Dr. Greenwood is an IMS member. You know, has Inherited Memory. He's in charge of all the genetics research here."

"All right! So I will finally get to meet someone with 'the Memory'!"

"Yes, but tread lightly around him. He's kind of hard to deal with."

After traversing the long corridor, they came to a small office off the main hallway. The door was closed and the dark blinds were shut tight.

Rocky shuffled his feet to attention, looked at Will and Ross, took a deep breath, clenched his fist and knocked on the wooden door. After the third knock and hearing no response, he called out in a concerned tone, "Dr. Greenwood?"

"Ugh. What is it? Come in, come in," a voice screeched from inside.

Dr. Greenwood must not be the happy-go-lucky type. Rocky clutched the doorknob, pushed the door open, motioning Will and Ross to enter.

The office was littered with computer parts of all sorts, flash drives, and folders with papers scattered about. There were no family photos, no paintings or plaques lining the walls. The walls were plain and bare except for a small green felt dart-board in the rear corner, the surrounding drywall dotted with wayward dart holes.

A tall, gray-haired man sat behind a large metal desk in the center of the room, staring at a computer screen. His long, dark blue lab coat hung on his thin frame and his thick round glasses gleamed in the blue light as it ebbed through the open doorway like morning fog. His face wore a look of intense concentration and his wet lips were drawn as he feverishly punched a keyboard with his index fingers. He did not look up from the monitor until Ross approached within touching distance.

"Dr. Greenwood, excuse me. It's good to see you again, sir," Ross said softly and extended his hand.

The doctor let out a low grumble, pushed aside his computer, and stood up. He never offered his powdery soft hand and did not speak.

Ross seemed unfazed, expecting his reaction. "I would like you to meet Dr. William Dunbar." He motioned toward Will.

Will put on a determined face, walked slowly forward, and extended a hand. Dr. Greenwood didn't even seem to notice the gesture. Will attempted to make eye contact but the man's bleary eyes twitched unnervingly behind his glasses. Will noticed the dark age-spots down his cheeks and neck and whiskers on his moles.

The doctor switched off his computer, then spoke. "I have no idea why you are here but …" He raised his hands and shrugged. "I have been told to allow you in. I guess there are certain times in our lives that we must do as we are told." He made a sour face.

Will spoke up. "Sir, let me first say that I am honored to be here and I am willing to do whatever I can to contribute to the cause. I will not get in your way."

"What exactly did they tell you you would be doing?"

"Dr. B told me that I was to analyze your data regarding in vitro fertilization success in ubiquitin-free females. They also said something about trying to find a way to inhibit ubiquitin production in normal females."

Dr. Greenwood snorted. "Dr. B is an idiot. He thinks he is onto something at Emory but he hasn't a clue. I have been instructed by the U.S. government to allow you access to all of my data. It seems like a waste of my valuable time."

Ross stepped forward. "Dr. Greenwood, Dr. Dunbar here is an accomplished scientist. He may not have Inherited Memory but he is a brilliant man."

Dr. Greenwood let out a sort of growl and walked forward past Will, slightly brushing into him and entered the hallway.

Will turned abruptly to follow. "Dr. Greenwood, I don't know if they told you but I was the one who identified low ubiquitin levels as a major factor affecting spontaneous abortions."

"So I heard." Dr. Greenwood turned towards him and held up his index finger and thumb, squeezing them together so firmly that the tips of his fingers blanched. "I was this close," he said with contempt, then briskly walked through the doorway of the adjacent laboratory, his blue lab coat flapping behind him.

"Follow me. I'm a busy man and I don't have time to waste." His words faded out as he walked away.

Will looked at Ross, who just shrugged his shoulders. "Don't worry about him. He's just a grouchy old man," he said in a voice just louder than a whisper.

"A grouchy old genius," Will said softly. He quickly tried to keep up with Dr. Greenwood.

◦❧ ◦❧ ◦❧

WHEN WILL ENTERED THE LARGE laboratory, he noticed three women and two men in white lab coats performing experiments. One of the women, holding a test tube up into the air, was asking Dr. Greenwood's advice about how long she should incubate the orange fluid inside. Will waited patiently for the discussion to end, then approached Dr. Greenwood. "My hope is that I can be a fresh new set of eyes for you. I've been thinking about different ubiquitin scenarios over the last day or two and I would love to bounce some ideas off of you."

The research director turned to face him, his eyes wild and crazily darting in their sockets. Will tried not to stare. "Look. I'm not trying to be rude but I don't think that there is anything that ... you can teach ... me," he said.

"No, sir, but maybe there is an angle that I can find. Something that's been overlooked."

Dr. Greenwood shook his head and walked away. Will followed him like a puppy to the far corner of the laboratory.

He looked around the perimeter of the lab, envying the quality of machinery and scientific instruments, noting the millions of dollars in medical research equipment and computers surrounding him. He searched for a way to soften the grumpy old man.

"This is an amazing laboratory that you've created here, Dr. Greenwood. I don't think I have ever seen anything quite like it," Will said.

The research director's face softened for the first time. "Thank you, it is probably the most advanced genetics research facility on the planet. We have made a real dent in things from here." He took off his glasses and stared at a computer monitor, studying the projected images from a multi-million-dollar scanning electron microscope in the corner. "The quest for knowledge is the most romantic and remarkable thing that we can do with our lives," he said.

Will pondered the statement while he watched Dr. Greenwood pick up a test tube from a metal rack and swirl it in concentric circles.

Ross walked up behind Will and put his hand on his shoulder. "Many of the breakthroughs in genetic engineering and gene therapy got their birth right here." He held his hand up and extended it around the room. "These white-coats you see walking around are some of the most brilliant minds in genetics that you have never heard of. Many have doctorates from MIT, Princeton, you name it, they're here."

"But they don't have Inherited Memory?"

"No. White-coats are normal grunts like you and me. The IMS wear blue coats when they're around," Ross said, pointing out Dr. Greenwood's lab coat.

Feeling the strain of the last few days, Will arched his back in a long stretch, his eyes to the ceiling. The light was interesting and intoxicating. It began at the ceiling as a light baby blue, like the sky on a sunny morning, then converged in the middle of the room into a deeper royal blue, bathing everything and everyone in its relaxing quality. It reminded him of an ocean wave approaching the beach, dark and mysterious in the center, transparent and illuminating on the fringes.

"What is all this blue light about?" he said softly to Ross.

"Turn around," Dr. Greenwood said sternly.

Startled, Will spun around towards him.

"What was your second grade teacher's name?" Dr. Greenwood's eyes were steady now.

Will thought for several seconds, and stared blankly at the wall. Unable to remember, he placed his right hand on his chin, cocked his face skyward and stared into the blue light.

"Mrs. Baldwin," he exclaimed with a sense of achievement.

"Exactly!"

"Exactly what?" Will wrinkled his brow with confusion.

"When you or anyone is trying to recall a memory, especially an old memory, they look away from the person asking them the question. The brain is attempting not to focus on anything or anyone, in an attempt to recall this memory. As a memory becomes more difficult to recall, you tend to look skyward."

"Okay. So?" Will realized now that by looking up, he'd performed the exact reaction the doctor had expected.

"You look skyward because the blue light, the blue sky, the violet blue spectrum of visible light, facilitates your ability to recall memories."

Will shot a quick glance at Ross. Ross nodded. "Yep."

Dr. Greenwood transferred his awkward gaze back to the computer screen, ending his portion of the conversation.

Will looked at Ross. "So by looking to the sky, I'm helping my brain find a memory?"

"People tend to look up for answers. That's why many of the IMS members come here, to use this blue light, to help them recall memories so that they can problem-solve. It's an essential part of our endeavors here. The Blue Bunker is like a ... like an oasis for ideas."

Will stared up at the ceiling again. "If I sit here long enough, will I start remembering things from my past?"

"It doesn't really work that way. It helps ordinary people like you and me a little bit, but it has an especially strong effect on inherited memories. The blue light lets them recall these powerful images and retain them for much longer than they could without the light. They say it fosters complex thinking, you know, total recall."

"Photographic memory?"

"Yes. That's basically what Inherited Memory is, except images from hundreds of years ago appear. Can you imagine how difficult it would be to retain a memory from 200 or 300 years ago? They've even figured out the exact wavelength of blue light that allows the IMS to hold onto these memories, so that they can use them to expand their concepts."

"I've never seen anything quite like it," said Will. "But what if it's a bad memory?"

"That's an entirely different issue."

Dr. Greenwood tapped Will on the shoulder, then looked at Ross. "Follow me."

The three men exited the laboratory and walked down the main hallway. As they passed Dr. Greenwood's office, Will began to see a deep green glow illuminating a section of the corridor ahead. As he got closer, he saw what appeared to be green from a distance was actually a combination of the pervasive blue light being infused by a rich, sparkling gold light radiating from a room on the hallway's right side.

Within five feet of this gold-tinted room's entrance, Will heard muted yelling coming from within. With each step, the muted sounds turned into unsettling screams and moans. The lab director was now far down the hall but Ross was only a few steps ahead and he motioned for Will to walk quickly past the room's entrance. Will increased his pace but as he walked by the doorway, he saw a man lying on a sofa, his body awkwardly contorting. Will stopped, took two steps backwards, and for a few seconds observed the man shaking violently with seizure-like motions.

Greenwood brushed past him and shut the door with a bang. "Keep moving," he barked, continuing down the hallway.

A few feet past the gold room, Will tugged on Ross' shoulder. "What was that all about? Should we help that man?"

Overhearing the question, Dr. Greenwood stopped suddenly, then backed Will into the wall. "No. You are never to go into the Golden Room. If you see someone in there, mind your own damn business. Just let it play out. Let whatever happens, happen. They will twist and gyrate and gurgle but eventually they'll be fine!"

Will held up his hands. "Yes, sir. I didn't mean to—"

Dr. Greenwood scowled and kept walking.

"You didn't do anything," Ross said, knowing that Will deserved a better explanation. "That was an IMS member in there, dealing with a bad memory. Like I said earlier, they have just as many inherited bad memories as they do good ones. Just as the IMS has learned that blue light helps with memory recall, they've also learned that sparkling gold hues dampen memories. It's like if you were telling me a story and describing an idea to me, then I suddenly placed a large shiny bar of pure thirty-six-carat gold like those from the *Atocha* in front of your face, you would most likely forget what you were saying and would instead focus on the gold glitter. For whatever reason, shiny gold creates a vacuum of cognitive nothingness, momentary amnesia."

"So that light dampens bad memories?"

"Yes. If a terrible memory appears and they don't want to deal with it, they get to the Golden Room as fast as they can. It's not foolproof, as you saw with that gentleman ..."

"Is that poor man one of the IMS that you were able to get here safely?"

"Yes, but he's obviously dealing with something awful, possibly a family tragedy from decades or even centuries ago. That's the tough part about Inherited Memory. With the good, always comes some bad. Their brains are brilliant but their souls are tormented." Ross smiled incongruously. "Now come on," he said. "It's time to have some fun."

"What about Dr. Greenwood, shouldn't I follow him around?"

"We'll catch up with him in a little while. C'mon," Ross said and led Will away from Dr. Greenwood and down a passage off the main hallway. After he slid in a keycard, they entered a small room. Ross quickly closed the door behind them. The dark cinderblock room was outfitted with rows of security monitors mounted on all four walls as stacks of computers hummed a monotonous drone. A short marshal with brown skin and a neatly trimmed black mustache sat in a rotating chair in the room's center. His head seemed to be mounted on a swivel as he scrutinized the numerous images flashing before him on the monitors, live feeds of all corners of the fort and Garden Key.

"Every one of these monitors is connected to a security camera outside or inside the fort," Ross said, his green eyes gleaming with excitement. He had spent the entire day in the doctor's unfamiliar world; now it was time to visit his domain for a while.

He dismissed the marshal for a few minutes. "Take a break, soldier. Go get a drink from the café." Then Ross studied the screens.

Several cameras were positioned inside the bunker; in the corners of labs, the ceiling of the cafeteria and along the main hallway. Will counted over twenty mounted outside the fort, two focused continuously on the Memory Door. Ross reached out and grabbed a black joystick between his index finger and thumb, and began remotely operating a camera mounted on the highest point of the fort. "You can see every inch of this island from here."

As Will's eyes followed the camera around the island and viewed the palm trees, placid ripples of the sea against the shore and the fleeting white crests of rolling waves across the reef just offshore, he thought again of the strange dichotomy between the elements of the natural world above ground and the manmade high-tech universe below.

"Now I see why they need all those solar panels on Loggerhead Key," Will said. "Between the laboratories, the security systems, and everything else, this place needs a ton of energy."

Suddenly, a piercing sound like a boat's sonar filled the room. Baffled, Will scanned the room, then saw Ross reach into his pocket and pull out a cell phone. "This is Colonel Chapman," he answered. "Yes ... Yes ... I'm leaving Fort Jeff at eight a.m. ... that should put me back in D.C. before noon easily. Okay ... Yes. See you then." He hung up.

Will shook his head. "I didn't think there was cell service on this island."

"Down here, there is."

"May I?" asked Will, reaching for the joystick.

"Sure."

Will began manipulating the camera, obtaining a panoramic view of the grounds. Now dark, the moonlight glowed through a cloudless night sky, offering clear topographical views. Beginning on the western side, Will scanned downward towards the water. His gaze lit on the large cement and brick seawall ten feet from the fort's exterior. It was wide enough to drive a golf cart on and extended well above the water's surface. Sturdy and strong, it was still protecting the fort on all seaward sides as it had been for over 150 years.

He pushed a button with his thumb to zoom in on a section of the seawall. "I remember when we camped here two years ago. I snorkeled that wall for about an hour. It's full of corals, sponges and all types of exotics. That old brick wall is as good as any natural reef around here."

"Really? Right there?"

"Oh yeah. It's spectacular, especially at night."

Will continued to scan the grounds going clockwise. Now looking north across the open ocean and into the vast darkness, he could see only the sudden flashes of heat lightning streaking across the sky. The screen grew a soft white as the glow of the moon refracted off of the ocean in silvery sparkles. "That's just beautiful," he said. Ross nodded.

As he continued to move the camera to the southeast corner, the orange flickering glow of wharf lights along the dock lit up the screen intensely.

"Wow, that's bright."

"Oh, you've got to adjust the night vision setting," Ross said as he reached over and pressed another button on the joystick, dimming the screen.

Using the zoom, Will focused on the two U.S. Marshalls' boats moored along the northern edge of the dock; the IMS seaplane was still secured just a few feet away.

"I can't believe I never put two and two together. Their boats have four 350-horsepower engines; that's 1,400 horsepower." Will shook his head in disbelief. "Each boat has two enormous radars, a closed array and an open array. One, two, three ... I count five antennas sticking through the T-top, dual GPS and a sonar system. Damn, those are some kick-ass boats. I bet they can go close to 80 miles an hour on a calm day."

Ross laughed and nodded in agreement. "You would know more about that than I would."

Will continued his remote tour of Garden Key. Over the south flank of the fort, he saw the clump of trees that provided the only shade on the island, where the rustic campsites were.

His head rocked back and he squinted as an unanticipated flutter of light illuminated the screen. Will adjusted the night vision setting and refocused. It was a tall campfire, its flames flinging up long yellow arms that snatched at the starry sky.

"Are there supposed to be tourists here right now? I thought you said tourism was shut down for a while?" Will asked, his brows raised high.

"What?" Ross grabbed the joystick and zoomed in. He counted two men sitting around a campfire but could see no other clues to key him in on who they were.

He reached over and switched on a VHF radio, which crackled

with static. "Rocky, Double-D ... come in. This is Colonel Chapman."

"You got Rocky. Go ahead, Colonel."

"Who is that at the campsite?"

A short pause. "We positioned two marshals out there, sir. We thought it would give us another good vantage point."

Ross hesitated for a moment. "Okay, but tell them to cut that fire. Put it out now. It's interfering with the night vision setting on the cameras."

"10-4, Colonel." The voice spoke to someone else on the channel. "You heard the colonel. Put out that damn fire."

They left when the marshal with the neatly trimmed mustache returned. Ross turned left but Will stopped in the middle of the hall and looked down the opposite way. He noticed the glistening of a glass door some twenty feet away.

"What's down there?"

"The living quarters for the IMS. We're not allowed in there."

Will began slowly strolling towards the glass door, his eyes concentrating on the frosted etching in the center.

"I said we are not allowed to go in there, Will. That's where they sleep. We, and all of the white-coats, stay in the barracks above ground," Ross said sharply. "Will!"

"Cool your jets, I'm just looking," Will said with a relaxed tone.

Inching closer, he could see that the frosty etching was in fact the outline of an owl, a book and a broken chain. It was the IMS logo.

"The Owl of Minerva," he said. Seeing the logo here gave Will chills.

He felt a firm tug on his shoulder. "Come on, man, let's get to bed. I'm exhausted," Ross said, yawning.

THE GLOW OF DAYLIGHT SHONE through the open window as the waning early morning trade winds fluttered the inner white curtains. Will pushed up out of bed, lifted both hands overhead in a deep stretch. The island's silence was peaceful but it hadn't really helped him sleep that well.

Last night when he lay down in bed, noticing that Ross was fast asleep, he'd decided to get back up, power up his laptop and sort through various facts and figures gathered in his previous research on ubiquitin. After catching up with Dr. Greenwood, hearing his scientific approach, and sensing urgency in his voice, Will wanted to get a jump on things. After plowing through data until well after midnight, his brain and body had begun to tire, yet he still seemed not to sleep nearly as well as his snoring roommate.

Will gently slipped out of the small twin bed, placing his bare feet on the smooth concrete floor. The room felt drafty, cold even. He slowly shut the window, then looked at Ross, still sleeping, but contorted and knotted in the covers as if he had been playing an all-night session of Twister.

"You still saw logs all night long," a gruff raspy voice arose from somewhere under the covers on Ross' bunk.

"Me? You should've heard yourself last night," Will countered.

Ross stirred under the covers. "Sorry, man. I hope I didn't keep you up."

"I'm good. What time is your seaplane leaving?" Will asked as he wiped sleep from his eyes.

Ross sat up. "I'm supposed to be at the dock at eight. But first, I want to introduce you to Victoria."

Will stretched again then sat on his narrow bed, wearing only boxer shorts. "Victoria Van Buren ... huh?" he said mid-yawn. "How old is her memory?"

"About four hundred years. She is a descendant from a long bloodline of men and women with Blood Memory," Ross said as he yawned.

"Wow. Four hundred years, four ... hundred ... years," Will said. "And she's the last ubiquitin-free female," he stated matter-of-factly, waggling his neck side to side to loosen it up. "At least, the last scientifically-minded one, right?"

Ross grimaced, then stood up. "Yeah. I need to give her my condolences too. I haven't seen her since her parents were assassinated."

Will sat up alertly and looked up at Ross. "Oh, no. Were they part of Team X? Poisoned?"

"They were part of Team X but they weren't poisoned. In some ways it's even worse, being shot to death on your fortieth wedding anniversary."

Will's face paled. "What happened?"

Ross paced the cold floor with his bare feet. "Victoria's parents were members of Team X but weren't at JPL for ..." Ross hesitated. "Um, the commencement of a project that was about to be unveiled. Instead, they skipped the big day at JPL and went on a Mediterranean cruise to celebrate their anniversary. A helicopter dropped out of the sky outside of the restaurant window of the cruise ship and blew them away. Both brilliant people murdered in cold blood."

Will was speechless.

"Victoria's parents were really nice people too. Just kind of normal, you know. Not odd like most of the IMS." Ross shook his head. "and what a waste. Four hundred years of memories down the drain."

"Oh, I see what you mean," said Will slowly, as if he were solving a crime. "Because Victoria inherited her memory from her father. Let me see if I got it all straight. Victoria's dad possessed a four-hundred-year-old memory, passed down to him through the generations. Victoria also has this memory so that means," he said and paused, "that means that her mother was a Blood Mother, she could pass along the memory."

"You nailed it."

"Does that also mean that Victoria is a potential Blood Mother ... you know, ubiquitin–free?"

"Yes."

Will pondered the scenario for a moment. "It wasn't a coincidence that Victoria's four-hundred-year-old memory has lasted this long. Along the way, there must have been planning involved to preserve it. Does the IMS have a tradition of arranged marriages?"

Ross nodded. "Yes. They marry within the society. By the mid-1800s, there were almost a hundred Blood Mothers from four different bloodlines."

"Wow, one hundred? And now there are only a few women left?"

"Yeah. You see the urgency. With each generation, it's becoming increasingly difficult for Blood Mothers to get pregnant and give birth."

Will felt his stomach sink.

"In the 1800s and 1900s, there were plenty potential mothers. It's not like they had to marry their first cousin. I think I read Victoria's parents are like fifteenth cousins or something."

Will stood up and stared out the window. Along the northern flank of the fort he could see through a sizable hole, a soft spot in the wall where the bricks had crumbled away and was now under repair. Through the hole, about a football field away, the image of a "park ranger" vigilantly patrolling the shore along the white sandy beach caught his eye.

"I see. They were trying to protect their lineage, to make sure that the Inherited Memory would survive so they married within the society. It's just expected."

"I wouldn't say it's expected, it's demanded," Ross said.

Will reached down to his suitcase. As he began to sort out his clothes for the day, he began to think about the incredible concept that a single individual could have actual memories of Spanish galleons from the 1600s, with sails whipping in the wind, or of a battle from the Revolutionary War, of horse and carriage, of the Civil War, steam-powered trains, the first automobile. It was mind-boggling.

Will had another question. "Did the Van Burens have a son? You know, so that the old memory can live on? Because Victoria, being female, cannot pass on her memory, right?"

"Unfortunately, Victoria is an only child. The oldest Inherited Memory that we are aware of will die with Victoria."

The room fell silent for a few moments. Will grabbed a bath towel from the small closet in the corner. "Tell me more about Victoria. Is she healthy? I mean, you said she's hot but is she mentally stable?"

Ross followed Will's lead and grabbed a towel and a bar of soap from the top shelf. "Well, she's very distraught right now as you can imagine. She was incredibly close to her parents. They were actually working together on this new project." Ross lowered his voice. "It is a truly revolutionary invention."

"What is it?"

Ross shook his head. "Sorry, Will. I can't say. It's the most highly classified project I've ever been aware of. Anyway, Victoria's nice but reserved. Straight and narrow, though funny too. Her dad was a jokester so she has a million jokes."

"Funny?" Will smiled at the prospect of hearing a four hundred year old joke. He could almost imagine it now. "So a heifer and two roosters walk into a tavern..." He refocused on Victoria and her family. "So her parents were on a cruise, but how did Victoria survive the JPL poisoning?"

"The day before the planned mission launch, there was a system malfunction at Cape Canaveral so she flew there to solve the problem. At the time of the poisoning, she was in Florida. Luck was on her side."

"No kidding," Will said.

"Because she was already in Florida, we were able to get her to Fort Jefferson quickly. But I'm still deeply worried about her safety. We are not certain whether or not the assassins are aware she's still alive. As Victoria was the most integral part of Team X, if those killers know where she is, they'll most certainly come after her."

"Was Victoria the head of Team X or something?"

"They don't really have a leader. Hell, it's hard enough to get them to play together. A lot of big egos, as you can imagine. But from what I've been told, even as IMS goes, she may be the smartest one of the bunch. Supposedly, she's responsible for all of this innovation in Internet streaming over the last decade. Smartphones, Bluetooth, and all of that. Anyway, over the last couple of years, she and her parents perfected a—uh, I'm sorry, Will, I can't tell you exactly what it is. Let me just say this, it's called the Genesis Project and because of the Van Burens, the entire world was about to be turned on its head."

"Is that a good or bad thing?"

"It depends on your perspective but in the long run it was going to be a great thing," Ross stated with certainty.

"So is Genesis off now? Is there no way to fix it?"

"It's going to be tough, I think. After poisoning everyone in the building at JPL, the assassins destroyed all data we had for the Genesis Project."

"Are you kidding me? No backup somewhere? What the hell?

"A decision was made years ago by the previous administration not to store the data off-site. They thought it too risky, I guess. The only possible resurrection of the project lies within Victoria's brain." Ross sighed. "Anyway, Victoria is expecting you. And has agreed to allow you to try and solve this ubiquitin issue. Given the dire situation, she knows what's at stake. I'm going to introduce you to her before I take off for D.C.."

❧ ❧ ❧

After showering and shaving in the community bathroom down the hall, Will put on a slightly wrinkled pair of khaki pants, loose leather belt with a silver buckle, cotton short-sleeved navy button-down shirt, and a pair of tan Cole Hahn loafers. He could not believe he was in the Dry Tortugas putting on dress clothes.

He and Ross meandered their way through the puzzle of perplexing archways, through the massive Memory Door, and down the stairs to the brilliant blue hallway.

About halfway down the corridor, Ross turned to Will. "I need to step in the restroom real quick. I'll be right out," he said and ducked into a men's locker room just off of the main hallway, not far from the security room.

Will stood in the hallway with his back against the glass wall, waiting. As he tapped a nervous drum roll on the glass, he noticed a familiar greenish glow nearby, indicating the Golden Room was just ahead. Curious, he eased his way slowly to the doorway and noticed that the door was wide open. From the safety of the hall, he peered inside. Hearing no screams of misery and seeing no one inside, he inched closer, placing his long-fingered hand flat against the doorjamb. The golden light was more mesmerizing than he had thought, more so than even the blue light. Like an unruly child, Will looked back down the hall briefly, and then impulsively stepped inside through the threshold to enter the Golden Room.

It was comfortably furnished with three suede couches and two reclining leather chairs arranged in a semicircular pattern around a large white coffee table. The ceiling was concave, rounded like a dome, with light radiating from hidden insets in the ceiling. The room was colder than the rest of the facility and a large oak chest was open, containing a stack of fresh white cashmere blankets, neatly folded. Chills began to form on Will's arms and he rubbed them vigorously. He took two steps farther inside.

The character of the lighting was like nothing Will had ever experienced. Intensely bright yet comfortable, golden rays in alternating patterns glittered from the ceiling and shimmered from the walls like a thousand shiny gold coins. He now understood why this room would distract someone from disturbing thoughts. With its intoxicating strobes, the Golden Room made it hard to concentrate on anything at all.

"Are you already having a bad day this morning, Dr. Dunbar?" a feminine voice arose from the far back corner.

Will's heart was hammering and he snapped his head in the direction of the voice. "Oh ... ma'am, I am so sorry. I didn't mean to disturb you." His voice cracked. "The door was open and I didn't hear ..."

His voice fell silent as an elegant silhouette of a female with long flowing hair approached from the corner. As she got closer, the vagueness of her shadow evolved into the vision of a tall, shapely woman, well proportioned, with wavy blonde hair that sparkled in the light. Will was enthralled by her smooth, olive-skinned face, with its edgy cheekbones and full lips arching upward at the corners. She extended her hand and Will accepted.

"I'm Victoria Van Buren," she said, her voice soft, almost sultry. "I believe I am scheduled to see you this morning, Doctor."

"Very ... very nice to meet you." His hand quivered slightly as their eyes met but he managed a genuine smile.

"Will, what are you doing in here?" Ross yelled as he grasped Will's shoulder, pulling him backwards through the doorway.

"Hello, Colonel Chapman. Good to see you again," Victoria said.

"Victoria?" Ross said, caught off guard. "Oh, how are you?" He regarded Will with disapproval. "I see you have met Dr. Dunbar."

Victoria nodded and flashed a brilliant smile.

Ross stepped towards her. "Victoria, I just wanted to tell you how sorry I am to hear about your parents. I hope you know how much I respected them."

Victoria's deep blue eyes moistened. "Thank you, Colonel. That really means a lot to me. I saw on my phone where you called but I just ... I know they thought a lot of you too." She took a deep breath. "It's been the most difficult week of my life."

Ross nodded with sympathy, then turned to again stare sternly at Will. "You have an appointment with the good doctor here at eight o'clock."

"So I'm told," Victoria replied, and then tilted her head towards Will, as if sizing him up.

"It's almost eight, shall we head that way?" Ross said and they began to walk down the narrow hallway towards the medical office.

"How long will you be here, Ross?" Victoria asked as she walked ahead of the two men. Her gait was long and balanced, shoulders arched back slightly, head high as her hands swung gently behind her. She wore long khaki slacks with a loose white linen blouse. Will had noticed its top two buttons casually open.

"As soon as I get Dr. Dunbar situated, I'm flying back to D.C.," Ross said as he caught up to her, gently grabbed her shoulder, and looked into her eyes. "Victoria, we are going to find out who killed your parents ... and Team X. I promise."

"I hope so, Colonel," she said. The three of them took a few more steps before she turned to Will. "Do you mind if I have a brief private chat with Colonel Chapman?"

"Of course not. Please, go right ahead." Will stopped and motioned for them to continue walking.

Victoria and Ross moved several feet ahead and began a conversation, inaudible to Will. Her hands were expressive, moving in a circular motion as if describing the rotation of a tornado. After a few minutes of deep discussion that ended with a heartfelt hug, Ross returned to Will and patted him firmly on the shoulder.

"This is it, old buddy. I've got to get back. Good luck with your research. Let me know if I can help you in any way and you have my cell number. I'm going to be really busy for the next few days trying to piece together all of this but we will find these sons-of-a-bitches, I promise you that. If you can't reach me live, leave a voicemail or text. Be prepared and stay safe."

Will shook his hand. "Tell Leslie hello for me and give the kids a big kiss. And, Ross, you be careful too, man."

Ross saluted and walked away, fading into the corridor's deep blue.

THE MEDICAL OFFICE WAS A typical doctor's exam room; soapy, disinfected smell, slippery polished floors, an awkwardly uncomfortable brown vinyl examination bed topped with crinkled white paper, and a metal stethoscope draped over a silver blood-pressure gauge mounted firmly on the wall.

"Shall we begin, Ms. Van Buren?" Will asked and motioned for her to take a seat upon the crinkled paper.

"Please call me Victoria, Dr. Dunbar," she said, leveling her gaze at him.

"Only if you promise to call me Will." He tried to make firm eye contact but felt slightly intimidated. She nodded and winked, her long eyelashes curled into a perfect crescent.

There was no strange manic twitch in Victoria Van Buren's eyes; her gaze was firm and clear. In fact, there didn't seem to be one iota of eccentricity or peculiar behavior about her despite Ross' descriptions of the odd IMS people.

Will glanced at her stunning profile as she sat quietly on the examination bed, and then he looked around the room, pretending to acquaint himself with the new medical office. The only abnormal thing about her was that she was too beautiful to be so brilliant.

He found her medical chart on the counter between the glass canister of cotton gauze and the stainless steel bin of alcohol wipes. He sat down on a metal rolling stool with four wheels that squeaked as he moved about the room.

He looked into her still-puffy eyes, his face solemn, his tone gentle. "Victoria, let me first say that I'm truly sorry to hear about your parents." He hadn't yet picked up the first pen or paper or even glanced into her chart. It was never Will's style to right away dive into someone's medical history and solicit cold impersonal data. "I also lost my parents recently so I can understand some of what you're going through."

"Does it get any better?" she said, sniffling as a new tear rolled down her cheek. Will handed her a tissue and she wiped her tender red nose. "I've tried to stay focused on my research, trying not to think about my parents and my colleagues as much as possible. All this tragedy . . . ," she said with head bowed, shoulders slumping.

Will gently nudged her chin up, his voice soft. "I think that's the best thing for you to do: focus on what you're passionate about, and with time the pain will begin to subside. I'm not saying that it will go away real soon but you must know your parents want you to be happy, always." He handed her another tissue. "Is that why you were in the Golden Room this morning?" Will asked.

"Yes. I was trying to find some relief, but ..."

"Victoria, this time last week, I had no idea of the existence of the IMS. I didn't have a clue that Inherited Memory was even possible. You and I have both been thrown for a loop lately, in vastly different ways, but we're in this together. We must succeed. We have to figure this out. And to do that, we need to establish a solid doctor-patient relationship. Please know I'm here for you as a friend first, doctor second."

He leaned in a little closer. "I'm a good listener too. You should try me."

Victoria managed a sort of snorting laugh between sniffles. "I can tell you're a good guy. It's not that. You just wouldn't understand—"

"Try me. Did you get any relief in the Golden Room?"

Victoria raised her head and looked up at him. "The Golden Room only works when I'm trying to suppress inherited memories so, no, Doctor, it did not help." She put her head in her hands. "I told you that you wouldn't understand."

He cocked his head to one side. She was right, he didn't understand. How could he?

The awkwardness between them was palpable and Victoria sensed his uneasiness. "Tell me about your remaining family, Will," she said. "Tell me about your brothers and sisters. I have never had siblings and always enjoy hearing stories about them."

Will sat back on the stool, stared at her expressionlessly and thought to himself, "Damn, the patient is now interviewing the doctor."

But in a way, he felt relieved. He had always tried to build rapport with his patients by getting to know their backgrounds, their personal histories, their phobias. It built trust and understanding. Who cared if the roles were reversed? It would still accomplish his goals.

"I'm an only child as well," he said. "I remember my mother telling me that my father desperately wanted a large family because he too was an only child. I think that's one of the reasons I chose to become a fertility specialist. Somehow in the back of my mind the lack of an extended family and the wanting of a brother, a sister or even aunts and uncles influenced me."

"I know how it feels. My parents were the only family I had." She looked down. "Maybe we should hang out on the holidays, Doc," she said, struggling to laugh.

Will smiled and opened her chart. They began to discuss her relatively normal medical history. She took no medications, had no allergies, no health issues at all. At her age, he didn't expect her to have anything of real medical significance.

"Tell me about this white light that people with Inherited Memory experience. Is it painful?"

"For me, it's kind of like a migraine of great intensity but short duration. It occurs on the back of my skull, on the occipital bone." She pointed her index finger to the back of her head and brought it forward, tracing a path around her skull as she spoke, eventually holding it firmly underneath her right eye. "It then travels anteriorly along the temporalis muscle before terminating at the infra-orbital foramen, you know, where the V2 branch of the trigeminal nerve exits the zygoma."

Will was impressed with her knowledge of anatomy but she was not trying to impress him. It was just plain talking as far she was concerned. Why use layman terms when she possessed a knowledge base as deep and complete as hers?

"The white light momentarily blinds me," she said, "and then I envision a memory deep in my cerebral cortex. It's vivid and real, sometimes even clearer than my own actual memories. Then, I have this moment of clarity." She closed her eyes tightly. "With my interest in mathematics, I literally see numbers float by and hear calculations tick in my head. I feel vectors, angles, and tangents as they leap from my mind into space."

She squinted tighter. "It's like my mind swells with a precise, tangible purpose, heightening my patterns of thought and even my basic senses of taste and smell. I'm in the zone and ready to problem-solve." She opened her eyes. She was trembling.

Will grabbed a blanket out of a cabinet and tucked it around her. "That's amazing," he said. "How long does the Inherited Memory last?"

She pulled the blanket in tight. "It depends on what I'm trying to accomplish. If it's trivial or uncomplicated information, I can usually access it without seeing the light and it lasts for as long as I need it to. But complex memories take much more work to recall and hold on to. The blue light works wonders for helping access those memories."

Will's intrigue grew. "I hate to sound stupid, but do you actually have memories of the sixteen and seventeen hundreds?"

Victoria smiled broadly. "Yes, Will. We could sit here all day and discuss all of my memories but do we want to figure out how to solve this fertility problem or not?" she asked with a smile.

Will began the examination by listening to her heart and lungs with the metal stethoscope, checking her ears with the cold plastic of the otoscope. He removed three glass vacuum vials from the cabinet, withdrew blood samples from her left arm, and then delicately placed a Band-Aid over the venipuncture. He asked her to open her mouth and he gently rubbed the inside of her cheek with a small white cotton swab.

"Salivary DNA," he said with a wink as he secured the sample.

Like two old friends, they continued talking about their life experiences and particular interests. She told him about growing up in California, moving to Boston when she was a teenager, and that she had moved back to California two years ago to work at JPL.

"Do you like the ocean?" Will asked.

"I've never really been in the ocean much. It's really cold up in Boston and I've been surprised how cold the water is in California too."

"Surfing in San Diego one time, I about froze to death." Will shuddered. "That said, the ocean is my true passion. Something about the smell of the surf is in my blood, I guess." Smiling, he momentarily lost his doctor persona. "It's the raw unknown aspects of the sea that really get my blood pumping. You know, the complexity of the ecosystem, the symbiosis of marine life, all of that nerdy stuff. The more we know, the more we don't understand."

Noticing that he had strayed from the extreme importance of why he was even inside Fort Jefferson, Will shook his head and regrouped. "I'm sorry I got side-tracked. I get worked up about it. It's that Pisces in me, I guess."

"It's okay. I love your passion. It's great to have something other than your occupation that keeps you alive. I haven't done a good job of that, for sure. I don't seem to do anything these days but work and sleep," Victoria said as she compressed the beige Band-Aid with her slender fingers. "But I do love to look out over the ocean from my balcony in California. It's beautiful," she said, then her eyes twitched. "Actually, most of the ocean hasn't been explored. There are still about two million species yet to be discovered."

Will laughed. "Of course you knew that. Did you ... did you just access an Inherited Memory?"

"I'm not sure where I pulled that one from," she said with a wry smile.

"Okay, smartie. If you added up all of the world's oceans, how big would it be?" he asked confidently, knowing he had recently read an article in *National Geographic* about the oceans.

Victoria closed her eyes and he could see her eyeballs shifting quickly back and forth behind her lids. "The total mass of the hydrosphere is about one-point-four times ten to the twenty-first power metric tons, which is about 0.023 percent of the Earth's total mass. Less than three percent is freshwater, the rest is saltwater, mostly in the ocean." She opened her eyes to pull off the Band-Aid and noticed that the bleeding had ceased. She closed her eyes again. "The area of the World Ocean, that's all oceans combined, is 361 million square kilometers and its volume is approximately 1.3 billion cubic kilometers. Its average depth is 3,790 meters and its maximum depth is 10,923 meters. The world's oceans cover about sixty-six percent of the Earth's surface and that does not include seas that are not connected to an ocean."

"Okay, okay. You definitely know your facts, but have you ever experienced your facts?"

"How do you mean?"

"Victoria, you intellectually know an extraordinary amount of information, but it's irrelevant if you don't experience it, live it, and breathe it."

She gave him a long look. "I know, you're right. I have tunnel vision right now, focusing on this research project and all," she said, digging her nails into the cheap vinyl seat.

"What is this project about?" Will asked, searching her face.

She waggled her finger with contempt. "Nice try, Dr. Dunbar. Hope you didn't give me some truth serum or something with that needle-stick." She giggled and pointed to a small speck of blood that had crusted over on her forearm.

"I understand." Will nodded. "So let me get this straight. You're living down here, in one of the most beautiful places on earth and you haven't even put your toes in the ocean?"

"No. I haven't even seen a sunset."

"That's a crime. You need to go for a swim. The coral reefs here are amazing. You need to see the other world that's just inches, merely inches, below the water. You would not believe it."

"I would love to, but we're at DEFCON 3. That means I'm not allowed to leave the safe-house. I can't go above ground right now, not even for a sunset."

Will rubbed his chin. "That's a shame because tomorrow night ..." He paused, his tone mysterious.

"Tomorrow night what?"

"Oh, forget it," he said, hoping she would not.

"What? What's tomorrow night?"

"Tomorrow night is the full moon in March and the coral blooms are extraordinary. It's the most beautiful that the reef will look all year and night swimming is the best way to see it, in all its natural brilliance." He kissed his fingers and raised his hands as if he describing the beauties of the Mona Lisa.

"I don't know. I can't," Victoria mumbled.

He leaned closer, placing his hand over hers. "Why don't you join me tomorrow night? Experience it, live it, breathe it."

Victoria pulled her long blonde hair back and looked at him. "You want me to swim a half-mile out to that reef at night? That's crazy."

He pointed toward the wall. "No, I'm talking about the seawall right here, that brick wall that surrounds Fort Jefferson. It's teeming with corals, sea fans, and sponges. They're attached right to the bricks from top to bottom and there are a million tropical fish swimming there. I'll get snorkel gear and all you have to do is swim down a foot or two to see it in all its glory. It's magnificent, I promise." His voice broke with enthusiasm. "Okay. You think about it but I'm definitely going. You're welcome to tag along."

He stood up and casually tapped her medical chart on the Formica counter. "We are done here for the day. I'll be in the genetics lab today and tomorrow analyzing your samples. I'll be scanning your DNA, Ms. Van Buren," he said lightheartedly. "I hope I wasn't too rough on you today."

"No. You were very gentle. I'm impressed, Dr. Dunbar. The needle-stick didn't even hurt."

Will grabbed the vials of blood and the cotton swab and headed for the door.

Victoria sat up straight and the paper crinkled loudly underneath her. "If I said yes to you, how would we get out of here tomorrow night?"

"You leave that to me!"

12

IN HIS BARRACKS THAT EVENING, Will lay on the small bed, now without the rumble of Ross' snoring, his solitude interrupted only by the chirping of crickets and the tapping of wind-blown curtains against the windowsill. He hadn't experienced emotional silence of this magnitude for a long time and his ears quietly rang with a disconnected hum. He pulled out his cell phone and checked for service. As expected: no bars. He laughed aloud at the fact that just a few hundred yards down a flight of stairs existed the most auda-cious display of modern technology that he had ever observed.

As he scanned the room, his grandmother's mildew-speckled diary on the desk caught his eye. He picked it up, glad that Ella Dunbar's relic had made it to the Dry Tortugas in one piece. His eyes lit up with intrigue as he rotated it in his fingers, examining the beige cover. With a sigh of relief, he shifted his body to get comfortable in the bed, bracing his back against the wall.

The book was heavily worn and the binding almost completely disintegrated. He opened it carefully, trying not to cause any further damage, if possible. With every page turn, tiny shards of glue residue and bits of decaying paper fell into his lap like ancient sawdust. He grimaced with each crackle as he could hardly open the volume without further cracking the spine. As he lay there trying to decide where to start reading, the moist humid night air caused beads of perspiration to form on his brow, eventually coalescing into a heavy droplet that fell onto the page.

"Oh, no!" Will dabbed it with a corner of the bed sheet, fearing that he might do more damage to this fragile family keepsake.

He closed his eyes for a moment and began to recall the story that his father told him about his great-grandmother. Ella had married Will's great-grandfather, Dr. Leonard Dunbar, just as the Civil War began. Will's father Sam had loved to gather them in the family room and recount, in explicit detail, stories about his passion for the Civil War. His favorite of all involved a battle that had taken place in Vicksburg. It was a tale that hit close to home.

This woeful epic tragedy that Will's father found so fascinating was the Siege of Vicksburg. Lasting from May 18 to July 4, 1863, it was the final major military campaign in the South and is considered by many historians as the turning point in the American Civil War. Vicksburg was a critically strategic outpost, perched high upon a bluff. If the Union, initially led by Ulysses S. Grant, and later William T. Sherman, could seize and hold the city, they would control the lifeline of the South, the Mississippi River. After two failed major assaults against the Confederates were repulsed with heavy casualties, a decision was made to besiege the city.

The Union effectively created a blockade, preventing all food, medicine or other necessities from coming in or out. Scurvy, malaria, dysentery and other diseases became rampant and the onslaught of artillery proved to be even more deadly. As the Union gunboats along the river lobbed close to twenty-two thousand shells into the city, the desperate residents deserted their homes and businesses and dug caves deep into the side of a ridge that was located between the main town and the Rebel defense line. In all, over 500 caves were dug into the yellow Mississippi clay for protection and lodging, the musky, muddy caves deemed safer than any other alternative. Finally, after 40 days and loss of over 19,000 lives, the Confederate garrison surrendered on July 4.

However, the carnage did not stop with the surrender. Once the Confederates waved the white flag, General Sherman led the Union Army in and implemented the "slash and burn" tactics that he had become famous for. Every valuable structure was torched to the ground, an incredibly horrifying story of Americans killing Americans, the likes of which Will's dad said he hoped he would never see.

Yet it was all documented first-hand in Ella's diary. Written in graceful penmanship, a complete opposite of Will's doctor chicken-scratch, the black pine-resin ink was cracked and faded but still decipherable. The first entry was dated June 12, 1862. His great-grandmother, a newlywed at the time, was about twenty years old.

We had a bountiful peach harvest this year. God was good to us. The orchard is verdant with young crops. That orchard has been the Garden of Eden to our family and friends. We must have dragged dozens of heavy loads of ripe rosy peaches today.

Will pictured a blissful scene. Possibly friends and family playing a game of hide and seek among shady peach trees. It all seemed so innocent.

He thumbed through pages, scanning each one for a date, a key word or phrase that would lead him to the Siege of Vicksburg. Finally, after several snaps and crackles, as the old binding gave up its century-old grip on the desiccating paper, Will found the story for which he had been searching.

MAY 13, 1863
The bright beautiful morning was shining over Vicksburg earlier. The daily labor of the place is going as usual except a few people who, more apprehensive of the approaching foe, are hurrying away with their families and effects. Leonard and his pa, Robert, came home troubled and blue. All our clothes are packed and I noticed that the sky was covered with dark heavy clouds.

Will squinted as he read. This passage was more difficult to decipher than the previous one as the black ink faded into pale green at the edges, immersed into each cellulotic particle of the yellowish paper.

MAY 14, 1863
Just before dawn, a Cavalry officer stopped to eat breakfast with us. We all sat at the table. I hope it will not be my last breakfast in the dear old hall with all the comforts of home around me.

For the first time, Will no longer fixated on the historical context of the diary. Instead, he noted fear in her words and focused on the content. The enemy was approaching her home.

MAY 18, 1863
A courier passing said the enemy had planted a battery about a mile up the road. This I cannot believe. I did not realize that they could call upon us so quickly. I turned with heavy step into the house, went to the parlor, opened my piano, and ran my fingers over the keys for the last time. I gave it one affectionate look, closed, and locked it. I will certainly miss my beautiful piano.

Will tried to recall in his mind the black-and-white photograph of the plantation that he'd found in the old chest in his closet. He tried to recreate the elegant white columns and majestic balconies pictured behind the sophisticated images of his relatives, imagining the inside of the house.

MAY 19, 1863

The cannons were booming down the road. The carriage was before the door in a very short time and Leonard and Robert packed us all. We carried two large glass bowls in our hands. I gathered the letters and certificates that were of utmost importance and stowed them neatly in my trunk for safekeeping.

Will yawned and wiped his eyes. He felt sleep tugging at his eyelids but continued to read the entries. He got up from bed and sat in a chair, reading more.

MAY 20, 1863

I did not know or could not imagine what would come next. I feel vague fears of several descriptions. Our troops are retreating and the town is to be evacuated and we are to be left to the mercy of those horrible Blue Devils.

JUNE 2, 1863

Faults both painful and pleasant pass through my mind but it all ends in a hard struggle to choke back my fears that I might say the Yankees never forced a tear from my eyes. We have been in this cave for many days now. I lie down on a blanket at night and try to sleep but when I wake the next morning I feel miserable. My clothes are always damp and I feel every minute as if I have a chill but the morning sun soon warms me up and I feel somewhat recovered.

JULY 3, 1863

A beautiful starlit night. The sky was calm and gray and the myriad of stars seemed watching like so many Angels' eyes. I almost cried tonight as the horizon was red in some places with burning houses.

JULY 4, 1863

A soldier came tonight to tell us that the Blue Devils have left behind unspeakable carnage but are finally leaving. I felt hysterical though I had expected it. I have not seen Leonard for days as he's been busy treating soldiers and townsfolk at the makeshift hospital. I pray for his safe return to me. I cut my name on the cave wall, the name of our camp, the date. I gaze into the campfire and listen to the Blue Devils going over the bridge, which is about a half mile from us. Rumbling of artillery, rattling of wagons, and even the voices of conceited men could be heard.

Will felt a deep sense of family pride. He pictured his great-grandfather on the battlefield and in an improvised hospital doing all he could to save lives. He had known his entire life that his great-grandfather had attended West Point and was a doctor. In fact, Will had actually seen his West Point graduation picture before, somewhere. That image, the distinguished image of his ancestor in a West Point uniform, had always been a source of inspiration.

JULY 5, 1863

We climbed the bluff up to the city today to leave our muddy cavern forever. As far as my eyes could see, every building and home was on fire or already burnt to the ground. Leonard picked us up in a carriage and the horrors of war were all around us as we rode through the city. We were all crying as we turned down the lane to Peachtree Plantation. But our tears of sorrow quickly turned to tears of joy. Peachtree has not been disturbed. Even the grand old orchard is intact.

JULY 8, 1863

Our home has been spared but we are devastated about the loss of our fellows and friends. There was a note on our mantle, next to Leonard's West Point graduation photograph. It was written by the Union general.

"Dearest Dunbar Family,
Liberty costs so dearly. Why must all the noblest die while the chaff of the country is left behind? War is a terrible calamity. I observed your West Point photograph on the mantle. It is my pleasure as a West Point brother to ensure that your home, your property, and your livestock will be spared."

Duty, Honor, Country
General William T. Sherman

Amazed, Will bent over, rested his head between his knees and thought for a moment, trying to gather his mind around the significance of the passage. Peachtree Plantation had been spared because General Sherman recognized a picture of his great-grandfather on the mantle. Dr. Leonard Dunbar's West Point brethren had saved his home and spared his property from certain ruin. Will pumped his fist in the air. "Officium, honorem, patriae," he said aloud.

Why had he not heard this remarkable story before? After reading all entries regarding the war and Reconstruction, Will stopped and smiled warmly at an entry dated June 6, 1878.

We were blessed by God today with the birth of our only child, a baby boy. We knew not if God would ever bless this home but our prayers were finally answered. We will name him Julian.

When his grandfather was born, Will calculated that Ella would have been about 35 years old. He was not aware of any great-uncles or aunts, thus he assumed that Julian was the only child she ever bore. Thirty-five was rather old for a woman of those times to give birth, and for the first time Will realized that there was a strange similarity between his great-grandparents, his grandparents, and his parents. They all had only one child and that child was born to older parents.

He scanned through many more entries about Julian's life on the plantation. He read that Julian had unknowingly disturbed a hornet's nest, "a lesson that he will surely not forget soon." He read interesting accounts of the daily life of a cotton plantation wife, with joyful years of harvest often followed by trying years of shortfall. He read about elegant dinner parties hosted at Peachtree Plantation in which "friends from Memphis to New Orleans were there in attendance, but it was a struggle sometimes to make the men from West Point mind their manners."

Will laughed aloud. He could visualize him and Ross dressed in their uniforms at an elegant gala, complete with rye whiskey and fine young ladies of the South, and imagined that they too would have trouble "minding their manners."

After over an hour of fondly familiarizing himself with the mind of Ella Dunbar, the next entry changed the entire mood of the diary.

FEBRUARY 12, 1898

Our Julian ran away from the house three days ago with Miss Belle Davidson. He and Leonard had an awful argument. Julian took to the road and vowed never to come home again. As hard as I tried, I could not stop him. My heart is broken.

Here it was in black and white. The story that Sam told him years ago was true. But who was Belle Davidson? That was not Will's grandmother's name; she was Grace.

He plowed through several more years of a grieving mother's private thoughts, none of which shed any light as to why Julian had forsaken them and their land. Will held his lips tight as he read the final entry in Ella Dunbar's diary.

JUNE 30, 1908

Today our hearts still ache. Our dearest Julian has been gone for over ten years. He would be 30 years old today. Leonard keeps it all inside and toils day and night. He has been working his fingers to the bone treating patients, looking for a cure for this terrible Fever. He won't say it but we now know that we were wrong about the family tradition that pushed our Julian away from us.

"The family tradition?" Will thought. Somehow Sam had related "the family tradition" with slavery. Will sat back in the chair and wiped sweat from his brow.

His forehead was now dripping with perspiration and drops destructively landed on the old diary like tiny water balloons. He stood up, intending to open the window further and cool off. Holding the diary in his left hand, he reached across the desk with his right, to the window. As his fingers felt the edge of the windowsill and he pulled, the soft wood broke away with a crack. Startled, he lost grip on the diary and it fell to the concrete floor, fracturing into two sections.

"Damn."

Will reached down and picked up the two pieces of the book, remarkably equal in size, and noticed that the humid night air had caused what remained of the adhesive to give. The binding had finally lost its century-old battle of attachment. Then something unusual caught his eye.

Tucked into what remained of the spine was a folded yellowish piece of paper. Will extended his pinky finger, digging his nail between the spine and the back cover, and teased the paper from its hiding spot.

He switched on the small table lamp and, with the tips of his fingers, slowly began to unfold the paper. The crumpled old paper was intact but dotted with brown and orange age splotches.

Unfurled, the center of the page showed a hand-sketched pencil drawing of a four-story antebellum home, "Peachtree Plantation" written in pencil above it. The drawing was blurred and indistinctive in some places as the worn gray lines of pencil bled from the page, breaking the continuity of the lines. The smudgy rendering of the top two floors was hard to discern but the general outline of the home remained intact. The fine architectural elements of the bottom two stories clearly illustrated that the artist had attempted to recreate the mansion in precise detail, right down to every antebellum brick, shingle and shutter.

Will closed his eyes and thought back to the old photo from the chest. From what he could recall, this drawing was a magnificent interpretation. Below the drawing were two sentences, written with classic penmanship, the ink still surprisingly dark:

"For those seeking the truth to our family's past,
"A secret room exists, marked by an ornate mast."

"A riddle?" he said into the silence.

As he scanned the document with narrowed eyes, his focus intensified but his confusion grew with every word he read, then re-read.

His eyes suddenly returned to the top of the page, just above the words Peachtree Plantation. Centered and inked in the fashion of official letterhead was a professionally reproduced image of an owl sitting on an open book, a broken chain hanging down on each side.

"The Owl of Minerva?" Will heard his words echo off of the bedroom wall.

Underneath the logo, in block-style lettering, three words were embossed: "BLOOD MEMORY SOCIETY."

His throat went dry and he pressed his face firmly into his

sweaty hands, momentarily losing his breath. His heart fluttered at the fact that he was staring at the official logo of the IMS atop a drawing of his family's old home. This document had been stashed away in his great-grandmother's diary, waiting for someone, possibly him, to discover it.

He paced the damp concrete floor like a nervous lion in a cage, running his hands through his golden mane. He sat down again before the window, peering through the hole in the fort.

"What am I missing? Is someone trying to tell me something?" he mumbled to himself and studied the words on the page again.

THE TRADE WINDS HAD BLOWN hard the previous night and a lone group of campers scurried about the campsite, tidying up their wayward shelters and broken clotheslines. While the wind on the mainland tends to subside at night, nighttime trade winds in the Tortugas tend to blow at full tilt, only dissipating as the sun begins to rise. Any neophyte camper who didn't tightly secure everything before bedding down likely encountered a nocturnal wrestling match with flapping canvas and slapping vinyl.

Never one to sit still, Will rose early for a morning jog in an attempt to clear his head of the previous evening's confusion. The sun was bright and the air was warming nicely. It was going to be a lovely day.

As he jogged by the campsites, he began thinking about his first time camping out on this remote sliver of paradise. He was a Tortugas neophyte and on that trip, in the middle of a pitch-black night, the wind had literally pulled the retention spikes from their foundation and blown his tent off the campsite and into the ocean.

"Lesson learned," Will reflected as he continued his energetic stride through the campsite, high-stepping wind-strewn items. He noticed a pack of cigarettes sliding erratically in the wind, rolling end to end along the sandy soil, and picked it up. Likely scattered debris from the only campsite, the box was sleek black and glossy, obviously marketed as a sophisticated cigarette, whatever that was supposed to mean. Sobranie. Will had never seen this brand in his life and it was not likely an American brand.

As he looked toward the campsite some fifty yards away, he noticed four men congregated in various states of early morning disarray. Their hair awry except for the one bald man, shirtless except for the one fat man, and two others relieving themselves under a small coconut palm, they looked as if it had been a rough night.

Only two U.S. marshals were camping two nights ago, Will remembered. They must have increased the numbers last night for some reason.

He sniffed and the smell of charred wood filled his nose. He noticed the smoldering logs of a recent fire, its charcoals still glowing red-hot.

If Ross saw that he would be pissed, Will knew. Ross had told the marshals not to build a fire.

He shook his head and continued his run. Now approaching the old brick seawall, he leaped like a nimble cat onto it, never breaking stride. At three feet across and an average depth of ten feet, the seawall created a formidable barrier to the majority of wind-blown waves. As the winds died, the ocean was becoming tranquil, gently lapping against the seawall like a house cat with a warm bowl of milk.

Halfway around the long seawall, Will stopped and bent down on his knees. Placing his face inches from the crystal clear water, he shaded his eyes from the stingingly bright morning reflection off the ocean, peering through the water at the diverse sea life fastened to the submerged bricks and mortar. More than a century of marine growth, vertebrates, corals, invertebrates, sponges of all types, stretched from top to bottom of the entire wall, creating a reef system rivaling anything in the Caribbean.

His upcoming night dive was going to be fantastic.

As he rounded the north side of the fort, his thoughts unavoidably returned to last night's family revelations. It was all so intriguing, a complete cryptic puzzler.

His mind stirring with possibilities, he concentrated on trying to recall the sketch and find the clue in his head, at one point almost losing his balance and falling off the wall. The drawing was too intricate to recall completely. He would have to study it more tonight.

He completed his reconnaissance run and returned to the barracks. As he started across his room to make his way to the showers at the end of the hall, he noticed the yellowed document lying on the desk. He walked over and leaned against the desk, sweat dripping, and studied the paper.

The drawing's lines were so faded in spots that he eventually became confused about their direction. He would play detective all night if that's what it took. He would eventually find the secret room but for now, the morning was getting late and he needed to get showered and meet Dr. Greenwood in the Blue Bunker.

※ ※ ※

ENTERING THE BUNKER, THE BLUE light stirred a sense of relaxation within him again. The cool air inside was invigorating as a result of dozens of interconnected compressed oxygen canisters that created a constant flow into the facility, allowing his mind to clear easily and his burning calf muscles to recover quickly from the morning jog.

He met up with Dr. Greenwood and spent the better part of the morning preparing to analyze Victoria's blood and saliva samples. But after a long morning of pipetting solutions and reagents for PCR and dealing with Dr. Greenwood's pompous pride, pangs of hunger began to rattle his insides. Will rubbed his stomach and decided to make his way to the cafeteria.

About halfway down the long hallway, the glowing light of a computer monitor from a laboratory on the other side of the glass wall caught his eye. Victoria's back towards him, she was motionless. He could barely see over her shoulder as she focused on a screen full of charts and graphs. She hadn't yet noticed him so he quietly observed her, watching as she rapidly scanned the screen from left to right. The monitor feverishly flickered as with lightning speed she scrolled through page after page of complex data.

"No way. That is not possible," Will said softly to himself, his eyes big as he pressed his nose up against the glass.

Victoria read an entire screen of text in less than ten seconds. She was flying through the data. Even her comprehension of complicated algorithms and intricate chart matrices, complex mathematical analyses that would take the average scientists several minutes or hours to discern, never took her more than about twenty seconds to digest. Frozen with disbelief, Will stood in the hallway and watched her work.

After several minutes, the pangs of hunger returned and he slowly moved on towards the cafeteria. As he passed the door to the men's locker room, he stopped, made a sudden pirouette and entered. Dark-stained, modestly sized wooden lockers rimmed the perimeter of the room, and a large restroom with toilets and tiled showers was positioned on the far end. Two long leather-cushioned benches lined each side of the main room and numerous white lab coats hung on gold hooks on the walls.

Will had been instructed that, although he had not yet received his white lab coat, he was to hang it in this locker room. White coats were not allowed above ground, no matter what. This was one of the foremost rules stressed to all employees and it was referenced on every page of their signed contract with the government. If tourists were to see people in white lab coats walking the grounds above, the façade that was Fort Jefferson would be uncovered and ruined forever.

After using the facilities and seeing no one was in the locker room, Will strolled to the far wall and removed a coat that seemed to be barely suspended by a thread on its gold hanger. A plastic access key dangled on a lanyard around the collar. With only slight difficulty, he removed the keycard from its clear plastic holder, slipped it into his back pocket, rehung the jacket, and briskly exited the locker room.

As he walked down the hallway a wolfish smile suddenly appeared on his face.

The day before, when he used the restroom, he had noticed that the same jacket had been on the same hook, hanging the same awkward way. He was surprised to find that it hadn't fallen to the ground overnight. He assumed that the scientist to whom the jacket belonged was not currently on the island, thus the keycard would not be missed, at least not for twenty-four hours. He planned to return it the next morning anyway.

Upon entering the cafeteria, he was surprised to see that Victoria had entered the room before him and was sitting alone at a small table, reading from a silver laptop. She sat with legs crossed, her head cocked slightly, a strand of blonde hair falling onto her shoulder, the whites of her eyes glowing from the reflection of the computer screen.

"Good morning, Victoria, I hope you slept well last night," Will said.

"Well, hello, Will." She sat up straight and firmly closed the lid to her computer. "I had a restful evening, thank you. How are the conditions above ground?"

"It's a glorious day out there. The water is so beautiful and—"

"I meant, how are the sleeping conditions in that old barracks? It looks rather rustic."

Will collected himself. "Oh. Except for the steam-room-like conditions and the constant rattling of windows all night, it's blissful. I think I sweated off about five pounds in my sleep," he said, grinning. "But the water pressure in the shower is impressive."

Victoria giggled. "I'm sorry you didn't sleep well. I don't know why they can't install an air conditioner up there."

Hearing her voice and her laugh was refreshing. Will sat down in the chair next to her. "It's okay. I couldn't sleep much anyway. My mind is in overdrive right now. I just look at it like I'm camping. In fact, if I can scrounge up a tent I might just sleep outside with the 'park rangers' tonight. It would probably be cooler anyway."

Victoria looked past Will's face. "Uh oh," she said and took a sip of coffee.

At first, he wasn't sure what had caused her alarm but then he felt a slight but sharp tap on his shoulder.

"Victoria ... Dr. Dunbar." Dr. Greenwood stood behind him, carrying a stack of papers. His eyes were twitching uncontrollably.

"Hello, Dr. Greenwood," Victoria and Will said in unison. Will cut a sharp eye at Victoria and her face blushed like a teenager's.

"Will, I would like for you to join me in my office. I have data that I want to review with you. Grab a sandwich and meet me there, pronto." Dr. Greenwood walked off into the blue haze.

Will turned towards Victoria. "Well, I guess I better get going. I prepped your DNA samples for PCR this morning and I'll be focusing on that all day tomorrow."

"Good luck. I hope you find the answers. If I can help in any way, please don't hesitate. If you'd like me to review your findings or if you need more samples, just let me know. I'll be here, doesn't look like I'll be going anywhere anytime soon."

"Why? Are they not any closer to finding the killers?"

"It doesn't sound like it."

He pointed towards the research director's office. "Well, I better get down there before he loses it."

Victoria smiled broadly. "Okay. It was good talking to you again. I'm serious, if you need anything let me know."

He smiled and started to walk away, taking a few steps, and then turned back. "You know, I went for a run on that old seawall this morning. It's absolutely loaded with corals. Tonight is going to be spectacular."

Victoria powered off her sleek silver laptop and looked up. "Now what would your girlfriend say if she knew you were night swimming with some random woman?"

"I don't have a girlfriend at the moment, Ms. Van Buren," he said, eyebrows playfully narrowed.

Victoria tapped her fingers on the table as she considered his proposition. "You promise it's safe, no sharks or anything?"

"I promise that you will have the time of your life and I'll be right there to make sure that nothing prevents that."

She shook her head, smiling. "Okay. I'll do it. But how do I get out of here? They didn't give me one of those keycards to get past the Memory Door."

Without hesitation, Will slipped the borrowed keycard from his back pocket and slid it under her computer. She looked up at him with surprise.

"Let's meet at eight o'clock on the west side of the fort and, remember, when you go up top, dress like a tourist," he said quietly, tapped his fingers on the table in a synchronized drum roll and disappeared down the hall.

🐛 🐛 🐛

WILL SPENT THE REST OF the afternoon with Dr. Greenwood, reviewing data. Despite his petulance and strange mannerisms, Dr.

Greenwood's intellectual prowess was overpoweringly impressive. He possessed a true photographic memory, and could recall the minutest detail effortlessly. Although awkward at times, it had been a very enlightening day.

Around seven-thirty, Will bid the doctor farewell, swiped his keycard to open the Memory Door, and returned to the barracks. With spirit in his step, he slipped on his swimming trunks and grabbed the yellow mesh bag containing his black dive mask with attached snorkel, two sleek black fins, a small underwater flashlight, and a large dive knife with both smooth and serrated sides. He lifted his dive knife up in front of him and admired its razor-sharp edge. As he was about to place it in the mesh bag, he recalled Victoria's anxiety over sharks, a fear he often found irrational. Nevertheless, not wanting to make her any more nervous than she already was, he tossed the knife aside.

Just across from his room was a small storage room that, unfortunately, also served as temporary storage for the barrack's trash. As he entered, he pinched his nose with his fingers as a medley of mildew and spoiled food entered his nostrils. Earlier in the day when he tossed away a soda can, he'd noticed a collection of expensive dive gear in the corner of the room and assumed that the marshals used this equipment for maintaining the seawall integrity and other submerged aspects of the fort. Will stepped over several white plastic bags filled with trash, retrieved a set of snorkel gear about Victoria's size and headed to the front door of the barracks.

Daylight was fading fast over the fort as Will opened the heavy wooden front door and descended to the Parade Grounds. Three marshals sat in front of him on the steps, their backs leaning against the handrail. Dressed in standard green Park Ranger uniforms, they looked tired but relaxed. Will had thought he heard laughter just as he opened the door.

"Hello, Marshals," he said with a friendly smile. "Do you guys ever get a break?"

"Hi, Doc," responded the smallest of the three men.

"Oh, hi, Rocky ... Double-D. How are you?" Will said, recognizing Marshal Caruso and Marshal Dawson as the men who'd escorted him to Dr. Greenwood's office two days prior.

Caruso stood up. "Tired, sir. We just finished an all-nighter."

"You doin' some divin' tonight, Doc?" another of the trio asked as he sternly stared at the dive gear in Will's hand, a deep Southern drawl resonating off the barracks wooden walls. Tex, as he was known, was well over six feet tall with salted and stubby brown hair and a round wistful face. His protuberant black eyes seemed very strange as his pupils seemed to glow an eerie fluorescent green.

"Oh, this," Will said, humbly holding up the gear. "I hope you don't mind. I was going to snorkel along the seawall tonight. I saw your dive gear in there and thought I might try it out. Man, I am jealous. You guys have nice stuff," he said with a nervy tone.

The marshals glanced at each other, then Rocky spoke up.

"No problem. Enjoy yourself, Doc. It should be awesome under this moon tonight. Hell, I'd join you if I wasn't so damn beat," he said. The other two men did not smile.

"I appreciate it. I should be okay alone," Will responded. The last thing he needed was to show up with a U.S. marshal to meet an AWOL Victoria. He walked down the stairs, took a few steps forward, and then turned back towards the three men. "Hey, guys, I'm not trying to be a pain in the ass but I noticed this morning that someone built a fire at campsite number five last night. I thought Ross said he didn't want you guys to light a campfire?"

"He did. And it wasn't a U.S. marshal," Double-D responded.

Will raised his brow. "What? Who was it?"

"Some VIP types from Miami. Wait until you see the boats that they came out here in. They look like those badass cigarette racing boats."

"VIPs?"

"Nothing to worry about, Doc," Rocky said. "They have all the official documentation and permits they need."

Double-D piped up. "They must be pretty well connected is all I can say because we even got a call from D.C. saying that they were on their way out here. Shit, we were told to reserve a campsite for as long as these south Florida bigwigs wanted to stay."

Will bid the marshals farewell and began making his way across the moist grass of the Parade Grounds towards the front entrance, the dew collecting on the ankles of his bare feet. When he arrived at the seawall, the last purple hue of light bowed out over the western horizon, exiting the stage for the star of the night's sky, a brilliant white glow of moonlight. He sat on the seawall a long while, feet dangling and his toes wet on the tips, barely touching the surface of the warm ocean.

He waited close to an hour for Victoria and his excitement was waning, slowly being replaced by fatigue. His eyes drooped as he listened to the hypnotizing slap of smooth waves against the bricks beneath his feet. It was now nearly nine o'clock. He stared blankly at the romantic moonlit sea. Taking this risk was a lot to ask of her; she was a very important woman.

She wasn't coming.

JUST AS HE LEANED OVER to reach for his dive mask, a voice behind him called out.

"Oh, my lord," Victoria said, holding her hands over her mouth and staring up at the sky. "What a beautiful moon tonight."

"You made it." Will reached down and grabbed her hand to help her up on the seawall.

With her hair tied in a bun, she wore a snug-fitting gold bikini secured with sequined straps on each side of her smooth rounded hips and a push-up top that revealed three-quarters of her plump breasts. While she had heeded his advice about trying to look like a "typical tourist" there was nothing typical about her; even her body was flawless.

She caught his stare and smiled. "Let's get into the water. I'm ready to do this!"

Will looked at her with genuine surprise, thrilled by her excitement. He helped her adjust the mask and snorkel, placed her fins on her feet, then outfitted himself with the same. He eased off the seawall into the warm water, then reached up, grabbed her hands and helped her in. The water was too deep to stand and their bodies bobbed in the gentle waves.

He grabbed the seawall for support. "If you get tired, hold on to the wall to rest."

She nodded through her mask and calmly reached over to the seawall. She didn't seem to have an ounce of anxiety.

Will pulled the snorkel from his mouth. "Okay. Let's go slow. I need to teach you how to snorkel so you don't swallow salt-water all night. When you go under, only breathe through your mouth. When you come to the surface, the first thing you do is to blow hard on your snorkel. That'll clear water out of the tube— otherwise you'll swallow it and you'll have a miserable time."

He took a deep breath, eased his body underwater, surfaced, and cleared the snorkel with a strong puff of air. "Okay. Your turn."

She had watched him closely and, without hesitation, descended under the water for a few seconds, surfaced and correctly cleared the seawater from her snorkel.

"You're a natural."

"I got it. This is easy," she said confidently and repeated the sequence.

"Awesome."

He pointed his finger down to the water's surface and motioned for her to follow. Taking deep breaths of air, they swam down together, only about three or four feet. Will flipped a switch on his small handheld underwater light and pointed it towards the old seawall. The surprisingly bright light spread out along the wall, illuminating intricate multicolored corals and sponges, their intense colors and vivid pigmentations radiating out like a three-dimensional pastel mural. Pink, purple, orange and blue coalesced into a circus of colors as broad sea fans danced with the rhythm of the tide, swaying back and forth in a nautical line-dance. Transparent anemones lined the rocky crevices as brilliantly colorful tropical fish circled above them.

Will could see Victoria's eyes through her mask as the edge of the underwater light captured it. Her eyes were full and vibrant, her long lashes blinked eloquently. He couldn't help staring at her as she swam. What he was feeling was not scientific or professional.

After they surfaced, Victoria pulled the snorkel from her mouth and grabbed onto the seawall. "This is the coolest thing I have ever done, by far," Victoria said as she pulled the snorkel from her mouth and grabbed onto the seawall. "This gives an entirely new meaning to the term barrier reef."

Will laughed and grabbed onto the seawall next to her, their bodies momentarily brushing together.

"Let's go deeper this time," she said.

He nodded in agreement and counted. "Ready, one, two, three ..."

As they swam down, he felt Victoria's fingers slip gently down his wrist, into his palm and between his fingers. She gripped his hand gently at first, then firmly. As they swam deeper, the sea life became even more diverse and the colors more intense. Will was impressed that Victoria never wanted to stop, not once, only occasionally holding onto the seawall to rest. Finally, she coughed as she inhaled some undiscarded seawater from her snorkel.

"Let's stop for a bit," he suggested as he reached up onto the top of the seawall. Pulling himself out of the water with ease, he reached down, offered his hand to Victoria and hauled her up beside him. Then carefully and gently, he lifted her mask, trying not to tug her wet hair, and shook out the residual saltwater inside her mask.

Victoria smiled, and he wondered if she was assessing him as he had been her. "You said that you don't have a girlfriend?" she asked.

"No. What about you?"

She snickered. "I don't date. Well, I dated a guy for about six months but it was a huge mistake."

"I know the feeling. At least it didn't take you years to figure it out."

Victoria laughed, and then reached over and put a hand on his thigh. He turned to her, tenderly replaced the strap over the back of her hair and gently pulled the mask forward, stopping short of her eyebrows, in the process noticing that her sparkling eyes were now accepting. He leaned in, and their moist, salty lips met for the first time. He looked into her eyes. She was extraordinary in so many ways.

Victoria blushed. "Thanks for bringing me out here. I feel foolish for not ever doing this before." She shrugged her shoulders.

"You're welcome. I know you have a lot on your mind so I thought this might be a good escape."

"It's been perfect."

Will leaned in for another kiss. She met him halfway, kissing him more forcefully this time, their lips slightly sticking together as they pulled apart.

"Let's go," Will said and playfully pulled her into the water.

They swam for another half-hour, all the way around to the most northern edge of the seawall. Now at the furthest point from Fort Jefferson, Will leaped up on the seawall again and sat down; Victoria followed, relaxing onto the warm cement beneath them. Will looked up at the stars and began to think about the diary again and the secret piece of paper hidden within.

He looked at Victoria as she gently combed her hair out with her hands. "Victoria, I have been reading the most interesting--"

Stopping abruptly, he flinched hard, as a tremendous fireball and explosion boomed from the interior of the north wall of the fort. Seemingly coming from the approximate location of the Memory Door, it was mixed with an intense crackling of gunfire and a barrage of intermittent bone-jarring blasts, echoing throughout Garden Key and over the sea. From his military training, Will knew the sound. It was the smattering of automatic rifle fire accompanied by the distinctive bang of hand grenades.

"The fort is being attacked," he exclaimed, his heart in his throat.

He grabbed Victoria's hand and with a swift pull, tugged her off of the seawall and into the water.

"What's going on?" she cried.

They swam around the outside of the seawall, clinging closely to it. Every few yards, Will pulled his body upward, lifting his head slightly above the seawall in an attempt to determine the best plan of action, to ascertain the path of least resistance for an escape. Tall yellow flames soared over the flanks of the fort as faint black plumes of smoke swirled into the moonlit sky above.

Will turned to Victoria. "Come on, we've got to try to make it to the dock on the other side of the fort. Stay tight to the seawall."

She nodded, teeth chattering as her muscles trembled from the combination of cold, fatigue, and fear.

They clutched the old bricks and clung to them, sidling farther to the end of the wall. As she propelled herself along, an intermittent wince came over Victoria's face as sharp corals scraped her knees. After several long exhausting minutes and countless ear-ringing explosive shock waves, they finally turned south as the seawall ended at a sandy beach. Now on the northeast corner of the fort and able to stand on their feet again, the two at last released their grip on the wall.

Will removed her mask and fins first, and then his. "I'll hold on to the gear. Follow me and stay in the shadows. Stick right behind me. If you hear a loud noise, stay silent. I'm gonna get you out of here. I promise you that."

She nodded, her face wrinkled with confusion. The U.S. marshals were putting up heavy return gunfire, trying to hold their own. The constant barrage and onslaught was deafening, but she clearly understood enough of his instructions to ascertain his objective, following his every footstep as they exited the water.

In the darkness, they crouched down and made their way slowly, the dim lights of the dock on the other side of the island growing brighter with every cautious step. Halfway there, several sharp quick bursts of light from inside the fort drew Will's attention. He crouched lower, squinted his eyes to peer through the same hole in the fort that was just outside his bedroom. Through the hole, he saw flashes of light coming from inside the barracks.

"No ... no ... no!" he muffled his voice with his hands, pain in his face.

Gunmen had breached the barracks interior. Through the windows, the white curtains were illuminating with random bursts of gunfire. Will felt helpless. He punched the sandy ground with his fist. He had worked with those men and women for two days, spoken to those marshals just an hour ago, and now they were fighting for their lives.

Victoria placed her hand on his shoulder. "There is nothing you can do."

Will pushed her hand away, his jaw clenched. "I know," he said, his eyes wet. He stared at the scene for a minute longer and turned to Victoria. "I've got to get you outta here. C'mon, we're almost there. Stay down."

He held her hand and they silently snaked their way to the other side of the island, to the beach just east of the dock. As their toes felt the wet sand of the harbor, they crept on all fours and entered the water chest high. Will scanned the dock, his face stoic. He saw two large men guarding all entrances to the boats. Dressed in all black and carrying what looked like automatic weapons, their demeanor caused Will's pulse to quicken and his face flushed as he recognized the physical appearance of both men, one bald and one fat. These assassins were the men that had been camping at campsite five.

He turned to Victoria and positioned the dive mask over her eyebrows, stopping short of her eyes again. "I make out two guards on the dock," he whispered. "They're on the far end from us. I don't see anyone else. Do you?"

Her eyes turned to the dock, surveying it in entirety. Searching through the orange glow of sodium bulbs housed in numerous wharf lights up and down the dock, she shaded her eyes with her hand and squinted her eyes. "I think you're right. Just those two."

About 300 yards away, the two U.S. marshals' boats were moored on the outside dock in the limestone-encircled harbor, their bows pointed towards the narrow channel leading to open ocean. On the other side of the marshals' boats, two enormous and identical speedboats were moored to the dock where the seaplane had been the night before. One sleek black and the other sparkling silver, both boats were almost twice the size of the marshals' and with even more horsepower. Somehow, Will had not noticed these on his jog this morning but he had seen boats like this before, big-time offshore racing boats costing close to a million dollars, usually professionally sponsored and maintained. Their bows were also pointed towards the open sea.

"The tide is coming in against us so this may take a little effort. Keep your head down and breathe slowly. Do not look up." Will secured her mask and snorkel. He reached down and grabbed her leg, ran his hand down her smooth calves, and put the dive fins around her feet.

As a chorus of gunfire and explosions echoed throughout the fort, they exhaled the air in their lungs. Immersing their bodies in the shadowy, unrippled water, they swam quietly down the beach towards the marshals' boats.

Will sensed that Victoria was becoming more frightened with each half-hearted kick as she followed his lead, swimming away from land and farther into the deeper, murky darkness. Will's heart was thumping hard as he battled the strong current. He tried to slow his pace as he watched Victoria try her damndest to coordinate her breathing with the rhythmic strokes of her legs. She was beginning to tire as she kicked against the incoming tide, unable to hold his pace.

Will raised up out of the water and a pang of panic struck him as he lost sight of her. He turned back and kicked fiercely down current, pumping his legs with nervous anxiety. Finally, in the distance, some five feet ahead, her dark shadow reemerged. She was losing the battle against the tide and being pushed downstream. He grabbed hold, assisting her against the unrelenting current. They made slow, steady progress.

As they reached the boats, he turned back and motioned to her to ascend to the surface. Will placed his forefinger over his lips, signaling her to be silent.

With grace and stealth that any Navy Seal would admire, he slowly reached up to the dock and untied the dock lines to one of the marshals' boats, then quietly unfolded a dive ladder that was mounted to the transom.

He turned to her and placed his wet lips against her ear. "Climb up on the boat and lie down on the deck," he whispered. "No matter what you hear, do not raise up, do not move."

She nodded, removed her mask and fins, placed her hands firmly on the ladder, and climbed into the boat, slithering down onto the deck.

He took a few steps up the ladder, just enough to see the helm. As he looked towards the console, just under the steering wheel, he saw the keys in the ignition.

"Yes!"

He eased his way back into the water, braced his legs against the dock then pressed his arms to the transom of the boat. Mustering every bit of core energy that he could, he simultaneously engaged his thighs and arms, propelling the 39-foot boat forward, away from the dock. Kicking feverishly with his fins, he swam behind the boat, pushing it out into the harbor. With every kick, the merciless power of the incoming tide made his task more arduous. As he approached the center of the harbor, a swift tide began to push the boat towards the island's eastern edge, towards jagged limestone rocks.

Will turned to look behind him. The gunmen's backs were still towards the harbor as they stood at the foot of the dock, looking at the fort. Weapons drawn tightly to their chests, they were actively talking into mobile radios, as they raised their hands above their eyes in an attempt to shield them from the ever-expanding inferno ahead of them.

Fort Jefferson was ablaze. Brilliant spikes of orange flames towered over the top of the fort as billowing smoke coalesced into a massive dense cloud extending high above, spewing charred debris. The smell of burning embers and the putrid tang of ammonium nitrate pervaded the dense air. Will's eyes moistened, as he attempted to comprehend the indescribable carnage. The 175-year-old brick stalwart had survived the absurdities of mindless bloody wars, endured countless killer hurricanes, withstood untold ravages of the sea and humbly persisted through the continually unpredictable whims of changing government allocation, but now it was disintegrating into the sandy, cold ground, one old solitary brick at a time.

15

WILL HAD NO CHOICE. HE had to climb aboard and start the engines before the boat plowed into the serrated rocks. He grasped the ladder with one hand and as he placed his foot upon the first step, a man's shout sent chills over him. As he turned to look, a gunshot echoed across the harbor. He spun his head around to see both guards running down the dock towards him.

He lurched across the transom, leaping forward like a spring deer, over a motionless, prone Victoria, to the helm. With a quick turn of his wrist, the 1,400-horsepower of outboard engines roared to life, sputtering exhaust into the air. The two gunmen were now scrambling to their boat, one man untying the lines as the other cranked the engines.

Only inches from the rocks, with the palm of his right hand, Will flushed the throttles all the way forward creating a whiplash of thrust that thundered the marshals' boat out of the water and onto plane, a fine mist of seawater spewing in its wake.

In the darkness, the faded fluorescent markers that lined the edges of the narrow channel were difficult to see. Squinting at the markers, Will hurtled between them, trying desperately to avoid hitting the rocky shallows that lay just inches beyond each pylon. With one hand on the wheel, he pressed the power button on the GPS navigation unit and anxiously awaited the screen to brighten with a marine chart of the channel, trying to find the slender path that cut through the rocky outcroppings surrounding Garden Key. Navigating the waters around the island was difficult enough in daylight; Will couldn't fathom trying to dodge the jagged corals at night without a GPS chart, regardless of the supplemental illumination from the full moon.

As the chart came to life, his hopes brightened with every flickering pixel of the display. Just as he was finally able to see the narrow channel on the screen, the roar of powerful marine engines approaching made the hair on his neck stiffen. He looked back to the oncoming sound. His body felt limp with fear, knees weak, as he recognized, some 300 yards away, the speedboat barreling through the channel at lightning speed, a rooster-tail of white water towering behind it.

As the killers' boat began to gain, Will noticed yellow sparks emanating from their bow like small firecrackers, followed immediately by tinny pings of metal projectiles striking the anodized steel of his center console. They were shooting at him. The glass screen of the GPS unit shattered, went black, as bullets pelted the boat. Splintered fiberglass shards of his boat's transom and gunnels flew through the air, littering the deck.

Before he could crouch to avoid the onslaught, a sharp stinging sensation radiated through his right tricep. He winced in pain as he grabbed the back of his arm and squeezed it tightly. Momentarily numb, his arm hung limp; a warm trickle of blood dripped from his fingers. Unable to attend to his wound, he firmly gripped the steering wheel with his left hand and began erratically turning the wheel. The boat began swerving and veering violently back and forth in the channel in an attempt to avoid the blitz of bullets.

As she lay prone on the deck, Victoria's hair was covered in crumbles of glass from the GPS screen and pieces of fiberglass. She held firmly onto the supporting struts of the captain's seat as the boat pitched side to side.

"Stay down. I'm going to try to lose them," Will yelled. He kept the wheel steady now, straightening his path, and pushed forward against the throttles in an attempt to gain more speed. The throttles were at full power, the boat straight-lining along the surface of the flat shimmering ocean at close to 60 miles per hour.

Will glanced back. The pursuing boat was still gaining.

Near the end of the channel, as it narrowed to its closest point, his throat dried and he swallowed. Through the moonlight, he frantically began looking for the slightest ripple at the channel's end, an indication of the spot where the two massive brain corals resided. From his previous experience in the Dry Tortugas, he knew that low tide exposed the tops of these two marine hazards, revealing that the channel between them was extraordinarily tight. As he concentrated his focus, he began to see small white cresting ripples on the ocean's surface.

He looked back again. The chasers had gained several boat lengths. A bald gunman raised his weapon and tried to steady his aim as the boat porpoised through the water. Will's eyes widened as he directed the bow of the boat straight for the coral head on his starboard side. He flinched down low as another crackle of gunfire erupted, followed again with a generous smattering of pings against the steel of the console.

"Hold on, hold on!" he yelled, grimacing as the boat careened ahead, now just feet from the large coral head. Victoria gripped tighter and put her face flush against the cold wet deck. The killers, merely yards away, were gaining on the starboard side. Will ducked down as far as he could while still managing a view of the ripples in front of him. With a sudden jerk of the wheel to the left, followed by an unnerving screeching scrape on the side of his boat against the edge of the coral head, he threaded the needle between the two massive corals.

The pursuing boat, now slightly starboard of Will's wake, made a hard sharp left, then a jarring right in an attempt to avoid the now discernible hazard. Unable to maneuver the narrow straits, the boat violently slammed into the huge coral. At the sound of the crash, Victoria jumped to her feet to see the 12,000-pound speedboat somersault off of the coral, launching high into the air, a massive hole ripped into the port side. As it landed, the bow nose-dived violently, twisting the hull and viciously ejecting the men into the hard surface of water. The massive engines ignited, creating fiery twisters of flames as each was torn from the transom of the boat.

Will pulled back the throttles to a comfortable cruising speed and hugged Victoria tightly. "We did it!"

Their eyes met and they embraced again. She rested her head on his bare shoulder and looked astern, observing small circular pools of flaming oil in the distance as their boat moved away from the wreckage.

Now just outside the reef, Will pushed the throttles forward slightly to gain a bit more speed.

"Where are we going?" Victoria asked.

"I'm just headed out to open ocean for now. Let's just get as far away from Fort Jefferson as we can."

She nodded nervously. "Where did those guys come from, Will? How could they just show up all the way out here?" she said, now visibly crying, her cold muscles shaking uncontrollably.

"Hold the wheel," he said and opened the door to the marine head.

Fumbling through a half-dozen orange life jackets, inflatable life raft, EPIRB satellite beacon and an assortment of other nautical safety equipment, he found two sets of bright yellow neoprene slickers and one soft fleece jacket, dark green with the official seal of the Florida Wildlife and Fisheries embroidered onto it. He wrapped the warm fleece around Victoria, and then handed her a set of the foul-weather gear.

"Here, put this on. It'll help keep you warm." He jostled into the other set of slickers and retook control of the helm.

"They were campers. I saw them this morning. I knew there was something not right with those guys. I knew it!" Will punched the steering wheel with an open fist.

"How could this be allowed to happen? No tourists were supposed to be on the island."

"Somebody in the government told the marshals to save a campsite and let those men, those killers, stay as long as they wanted."

Victoria pulled the fleece tighter around her body and wiped her eyes with a sleeve. "Did they say who made the call?"

"No. I didn't get that part."

"Who is doing this?" she asked, her voice cracking, tears streaming down her cheeks.

With the boat continuing to move into the open ocean, Will scanned the dark horizon in front of them and then looked at her. "I think one of those marshals might be in on it," he said, his voice stern.

"Why would you say that?"

"It was the weirdest thing. When I was talking to him, the pupils of his eyes were glowing with this strange fluorescent green color. It was just too weird. The other marshals looked normal."

Victoria teased a few more shards of smooth glass from her hair. "I don't think he was in on it," she said calmly. "Was it getting dark when you were speaking to him?" she asked over the low hum of the engines.

"Yeah. The sun was setting," Will said as his head continuously swung forward and back, surveying the moonlit ocean from bow to stern for the possibility of a second boat on their trail.

"Will, that green tint was an invention that Team X released to the U.S. military last year. He was wearing night vision contact lenses."

"That's cool."

"Not only night vision. They auto-focus and can zoom in on objects at five times normal vision." She cracked a quick smile that quickly faded. Now, the people that invented them were all dead. All of those brilliant minds would never contribute to the broader good again.

"Who is doing this!" she yelled at the top of her lungs. Her face screwed into confusion.

Will gently grabbed her arm and tugged her towards him, wrapping his long arms around her. She buried her face against his broad chest as he caressed her wet hair, removing a few more fragments of glass and fiberglass, trying to prevent further entanglements.

"Somebody wants Team X and maybe all of the IMS dead," said Will, and thrust his hand forward on the throttles as they planed into the darkness.

Victoria sat next to him on the white cushioned captain's bench seat, adjusting her head from his chest to his shoulder as they bounced rhythmically through the waves. She finally looked down at the crusted blood splayed out across Will's hand and forearm, and a fresh, bloody abrasion striped his bicep.

"Oh, my god. Are you shot?" she said, her eyes wide, focusing on his arm.

Now well offshore, Will pulled the throttles back to idle, and the boat coasted off of plane. He reached over and cocked his head towards his right arm, palpating the edges of the wound with his hand.

"I'm fine, I think." He squeezed his tricep muscle firmly, rolling it back and forth between the balls of his doctor fingers. "It didn't penetrate the muscle. I was damn lucky considering how many bullets were flying at us."

"I'm going to get something to clean that up. There's got to be a medical kit on here." Victoria slid off of the bench, walked behind him, and bent down to a set of inset tackle drawers under the captain's bench.

"It's fine—don't worry about it. We have much bigger problems. Some bullets took out our electronics. The entire navigational system is out of commission including the compass."

There was no way of knowing their position, their latitude or longitude on the ocean, and no way of navigating the treacherous rocky shallows close to land. The moon was full but without the use of a detailed marine map, a chart that highlighted the shallows and the coral reefs, without navigational electronics or even a simple compass, they were stuck, adrift at sea. There was no way they could approach land, be it Key West or any other town in the Keys.

As the boat came to a simple drift on the calm ocean, Will looked out at the horizon; every direction looked the same. He continued to press buttons, even removing, cleaning, twisting, and then replacing multiple fuses. Nothing. No power.

"We're sitting ducks out here. I have no idea which way is east or west."

He looked down at the fuel gauge. Fortunately, still powered and intact, the needle was touching full. "We've got plenty of gas but we might just have to wait until daylight." He walked briskly to the bow, scanning the horizon keenly. "I'm just not sure which way to go but I really don't like the idea of waiting until morning either. Whoever is after you is not going to stop and they'll be looking hard early tomorrow for sure," he said, his usually calm voice laced with a sense of fear.

"What I would give for a pair of those night vision contacts right now. Hell, I'd even settle for the old-school night vision binoculars," he said, attempting a laugh.

His feeble attempt at humor elicited no response from Victoria. Realizing that she had not responded to him in several minutes, he peered around to see her motionless body sitting on the rear seat just in front of the engines. Her torso was stiff and her eyes wide and fixed, but twitching, as she peered skyward into the stars. She wasn't moving and Will couldn't even tell if she was breathing.

"Are you okay? Oh, no, are you shot?" he asked frantically as he reached for her hand. She didn't react. He placed two fingers on her wrist and compressed her soft skin. Her pulse was rhythmic and slow, her chest rising ever so slightly with each shallow breath.

"Victoria. Victoria, are you okay?" He touched her shoulder and gently shook her. She remained motionless and silent as he positioned himself in front of her, staring into her eyes. Wide and wet, her eyes no longer twitched but glistened with the reflection of starlight. As he waved his hand over her face, her body suddenly gyrated and slumped forward. She gasped for air. Her eyes blinked wildly as she returned from a trancelike state.

Will placed his hands on each side of her head and turned her face toward him. "Are you okay?"

She reached up and grabbed his hand, squeezing it tightly. "I can get us where we need to go," she said softly as she struggled to catch her breath, her eyes still transfixed on the sparkling sky.

Will could barely hear her over the clatter of the engines. "What?"

She stood up, took a deep breath; small beads of sweat had collected on her brow.

Victoria pressed her lips to his ear. "I've got a memory now. I can read the stars." Her voice was calm, with a firm confidence.

Will followed her gaze with his eyes, slowly turning his head upward. He traced her focus up to the heavens as it landed on the brightest star in the sky.

"I can navigate by the stars," she said. "Do you see that bright star there?" She pointed to the sky. That's Polaris and over there is Jupiter." Victoria began a detailed account of how she would determine their approximate latitude and longitude by using the transit of the moon, the positions of Polaris and Jupiter and other stars, combined with the fact that the earth rotates fifteen degrees every hour.

He could not believe what he was hearing. "So you are now using an Inherited Memory—a Blood Memory?"

"Yes. A really old one too, I can tell. Probably from the 1600s or 1700s. Obviously somebody in my family spent a lot of time on the ocean."

Like a victorious prizefighter, Will pumped both fists in the air twice. "Yes!" he exclaimed. "Let's get out of here."

"But where to?" Victoria's eyes were still focused on the stars.

"Somewhere off the grid," Will said. He looked down at the fuel gauge again and tapped it with his finger.

"We're going to see Tiny. He'll know what to do."

"Who's Tiny?"

"Just get us to the Bahamas. We'll be safe there."

THE FULL MOON WAS FRAMED by a twinkling background of beautiful and navigational stars. Will pushed the throttles forward and the boat roared onto plane. Victoria pointed at strategic stars, giving him instructions. To Will, her direction seemed accurate. With every new bearing, every change of heading, his confidence in her new memory grew. It was working well and he thought it best for them to stay as far away from shore as possible. Safety was in the stealthy darkness, away from the lights emanating from the islands of the Florida Keys.

They were headed east, past Key West, past Marathon, past Islamorada, and past Key Largo. Will calculated that the trip from Fort Jefferson to his next destination was just over 300 miles and fortunately, their boat was full of fuel. The Bahamas, the Abacos to be specific, were in range.

After several long hours of slicing through the Atlantic waves, a white glimmer appeared on the horizon. As the moonlight beamed off the ocean's surface, a froth of small white lines began to fleetingly appear, then disappear. As they got closer, Will narrowed his eyes. He could now see that the bubbly foam a half-mile ahead of them was actually the cresting of waves crashing onto a slender sandy beach. Off to the right and a little further away, sitting high upon a small rocky cliff, stood the dim outline of a badly deteriorating cylindrical structure that had, a hundred years prior, served as a lighthouse to wayward mariners. Will recognized the lighthouse and the tiny island in the middle of nowhere. He had seen it once before, from a distance, on a previous fishing trip in the Keys.

"That's Cay Sal!" he exclaimed with uncontrolled exuberance. "You did it, Victoria! You did it! We made it to the Bahamas!"

Cay Sal is a one-mile, desolate outcropping situated on the southwesternmost point of the Bahamas, closer to Cuba than to the Keys and equally as far away from the next inhabitable Bahamian island. Although its small size and extreme remoteness make human life unsustainable, those same characteristics make it a gem of the sea for fisherman, for its steep vertical banks teem with sea life of all variety.

Will pulled the throttles back and the boat slid gently through the water. He walked back and stood in front of Victoria as she sat on the gunnel of the boat. Obviously exhausted, she looked up at him, managed a brief smile, and reached her arms out. He bent down to her, gave her a firm hug and kissed her cheek.

"You got us here," he said. "You are amazing."

"No, you are, Will. Why are you doing this? You don't have to, you know. This—all of this—has nothing to do with you. Just drop me off and save yourself," she said, searching his tired face for a response.

He sat down beside her. He looked back behind the boat as it slowly pushed forward through the waves. Purple incandescent glows radiated from the ocean as millions of luminescent microorganisms collided with the swirling surface of their wake.

"Do you see that?" he said as he pointed to the purple sparkling glimmer on the water.

She turned and studied the water. "Phosphoilluminescence. Oh, my. I've only read about it, I've never actually seen it." Her eyes were wide like a schoolgirl's.

"We evolved from those tiny one-cell organisms over billions of years. Modern man has been trudging along on this earth for two hundred thousand years, apparently at a snail's pace. And now, I've just learned, that only in the last 200 years, thanks to a genetic mutation in your DNA," he said pointing to her head, "now, we've begun to make real strides. The kind of strides that will continue to propel our species light years ahead. The kind of strides that will most likely double life expectancy again, that will make miscarriages a thing of the past, which will even cure cancer for god's sake."

Victoria looked up at him, listening intently.

"Sure, by practicing medicine, I've contributed a little to helping my fellow man and I was hoping to help a lot more by trying to figure out this ubiquitin question, but . . ." He scooped a handful of water, the purple luminescence sliding through the creases in his fingers. "The most important thing I can do now, for everyone, is to protect you. I've been thinking about it for the past few hours. I know what I have to do. Please don't question it. I'll do whatever it takes to make sure you're safe."

Victoria slid her fingers between his and pulled his hand to her face, pressing it firmly against her cheek, and then cocked her head up and kissed him deeply on the lips. His mind was soothed by the warmth of her kiss and embrace. Their lips released but their noses were still pressed tightly together, breaths connecting.

He smiled. "Besides, I kinda like you. I mean, you did get us to Cay Sal," he said in a playful tone. "Now, let's keep moving. We need to head northeast, just north of Andros Island," Will said.

Victoria raised her head and peered up at the night sky. She wiped her eyes with the fleece again but the wet wool did little to dry her eyes. She focused on the stars, and after a few minutes, she gave Will a confident heading. Her uncanny ability to navigate was flawless.

They continued northeast through the deep canyon waters of the Tongue of the Ocean, turned due east and passed just a few dozen miles north of Nassau before taking dead aim on the North Star and skirting the majestic cliffs at Hole-in-the-Wall.

Will kissed her on the forehead. "I've got it from here. That's the Hole-in-the-Wall Lighthouse." He smiled and pointed at the swirling beams of a fully functioning lighthouse atop a steep limestone cliff. "We're in the Abacos. I know these waters like the back of my hand."

She shrugged her shoulders in relief, and the tension rolled from her neck. "Where are we going exactly?"

A broad smile covered Will's face. "Next stop … Hopetown!"

17

THE FIRST USEFUL RAYS OF sun were just cresting over the swaying palms of Hopetown as Will and Victoria pulled into the Sea Star Marina. They were tired and hungry, their neoprene rain gear was encrusted with a layer of salt, and their exposed skin slightly burning from the elements. Will nosed the 39-foot boat into the closest slip to the marina office, tossing his dock lines to a familiar face, a young thin Bahamian man with a cumbersome limp and a mild speech impediment.

"Eddie," Will's hoarse voice bellowed as if the young man were a close friend.

"Dr. Dunbah, goo … goo … good to see you," the young man managed to say as he tightly cinched the ropes to the dock cleats.

"Is Tiny around?" Will asked as he reached over to the dock and doused his salty face with fresh water from a hose.

"Tiny is in da ma … ma … marina office," Eddie said, pointing towards a pale yellow Victorian building. Trimmed in fluorescent green with a generous porch and four variously colored rocking chairs, the office looked out upon 285 boat slips that comprised the Sea Star Marina.

Eddie extended his hand down and helped Will and Victoria climb up. He seemed confused as he surveyed Will's demeanor.

"You okay, da ... da ... doc?"

"I'm good, Eddie. I really need to talk to Tiny."

Eddie nodded and moved to the side, clearing a path.

Victoria followed Will as he dashed to the marina office; a small bell clanked as he swung the door open. The inside of the building was trimmed in muted white wood paneling and exhibited the customary tourist trappings: thin cotton T-shirts in multiple colors displaying *Sea Star Marina* broadly across the chest; necklaces made of sharks' teeth and available with gold chain or black twine; handcrafted Bahamian wind chimes constructed from strands of sand dollars. A computer monitor, a squawking VHF radio, and several rechargeable walkie-talkies sat atop a worn wooden counter in the corner.

"Well, I'll be damned. Look what the cat done drug in," said a large Bahamian man seated behind the counter. His broad white smile flashed as much as the sparkling gold chain around his thick neck and the shiny gold watch that barely latched around his massive wrist.

"Docta Dunbah. What you doin' here?" Tiny chuckled, pretending to look at his watch as if uncertain of the date. "I thought you were at work in Florida, saving lives? They told me you left here like a bat outta hell da other day." His distinctive Bahamian tone was fluid and smooth.

"Tiny. It's been a long night."

Tiny stood and approached them. At six foot six with deep black skin, bull-bellied, a glistening bald head, and biceps the size of Victoria's waist, he was an intimidating specimen of a man. Yet, for all his imposing size, his baby face and gentle eyes gave him an air of relaxed warmth.

Victoria leaned into Will and mumbled with bewilderment, "That's Tiny?"

Will just nodded to her quickly.

Tiny put a hand on Will's shoulder and looked into his bloodshot eyes. "You look tired, mon, beat up. What in da world, Will?"

Will clutched onto Tiny's stout wrist, his speech somewhat disjointed. "Tiny, there's been an attack. Some guys came out of nowhere. We were just swimming around and then boom, nothing we could do ... explosions, gunfire, they were coming from all directions. I couldn't—"

Tiny interrupted by grabbing the sides of Will's head with his massive hands, to steady his gaze. "What are you talkin' about, mon?" he said, scrutinizing Will's face, and then looking to Victoria for an answer. Victoria remained silent, face pale. Her damp blonde hair was tangled in knots as she stared down to the black-and-white checkerboard tile floor. She rubbed her eyes.

"Tiny, I need your help, man. We drove all night from the Dry Tortugas in that Wildlife and Fisheries boat out there. It took us eight hours to get here."

"What? You done gone and stole a government boat? Are you crazy?"

"It's not like that. I was trying to tell you. We were at Fort Jefferson and all of a sudden, we were under fire." Will's speech accelerated with every word. "These guys, these military types, charged the fort. Victoria and I climbed into that boat and tried to get the hell out of there but they chased us through the channel. They hit the reef and their boat just exploded. It was crazy, man."

"Oh, my." Tiny let go of his grip on Will's head and held his hands out. "Whoa, whoa. Slow down now. You mean that old fort out in the middle of nowhere?" He pointed towards the western wall of the marina office. "You're telling me that somebody wanted to attack that dilapidated old thing and blow it up? Why would anybody want to harm that place? It's already falling to pieces."

"They weren't trying to harm the fort, per se." Will turned toward Victoria as he spoke. His eyes narrowed. "Someone is trying to kill this lady."

Tiny's clear brown eyes went blank with confusion. "Trying to kill her?" He shook his head then focused his gaze on Victoria. "Now why would someone in their right mind try to harm such a beautiful young lady?" he said as he studied her face.

Victoria looked up from the floor at Will, her eyes saying it all. But Will had no intention of disclosing her secret.

He put his hand on Tiny's shoulder. "I just need you to trust me, Tiny. I can't get into the specifics, at least not right now."

"I don't know what the hell is going on," Tiny said, "but give me something, Will. This sounds crazy, mon."

Will shrugged deeply, then began to recount the specifics of the attack but left out any detail of the IMS or the Blue Bunker that existed below ground. His current predicament and Victoria's safety were tenuous, their story strange and nearly unbelievable. Now was not the time to completely boggle his friend's mind, not the place to permanently alter his known reality.

He explained how eight professionally trained men, posing as campers, raided the barracks and the old fort, attacking the building and its occupants with automatic weapons and explosive devices. He said he wasn't sure how successful the assault was but that the Park Rangers, as he called them, had valiantly fought back but were unfortunately caught off guard, in fact, deceived.

"Victoria is a very, very important person. Some bad people are trying to kill her. I don't trust anyone in the government right now because the one thing I'm certain of is that someone in the U.S. government is in on this whole thing."

Will strained his face. "I need you to help me hide her. I have to protect her for a while."

Tiny frowned. He stepped back and grabbed two cold water bottles from inside a small refrigerator next to the desk. He handed a bottle to each of them, and then turned down the volume on the annoyingly loud VHF radio, instantly quieting the room.

He turned to Will, his infectious smile now in place again. "Will, how long have we known each other? Huh? You're like my brotha from anotha motha. You know dat."

Will had heard that line dozens of times through the years but it still brought a smile to his face when Tiny said it with that cool Bahamian accent.

Will guzzled the entire bottle of water in only seconds. "I know, Tiny. That's why I came here. I don't know what else I can do."

Tiny reached out, encompassing Will's tired body with a powerful embrace.

"Let's go. I know exactly what to do," he said, removed two more bottles of water from the refrigerator, several candy bars, two bags of chips, and snatched a walkie-talkie off the desk.

Following Tiny's lead, they walked around behind the marina office and got into a shiny red golf cart, complete with custom leather seats and a hi-fi stereo system with deluxe speakers, delivering a soft rhythm of reggae music. The gasoline-powered golf cart, the main form of transportation on the island, pushed north on the sole blacktop road.

After a twenty-minute meandering drive, in which Will and Victoria tore through the snacks like ravenous animals, Tiny turned onto a winding, seashell-covered driveway. Hidden by a canopy of coconut palms, sea grapes, and thick underbrush, it was barely discernible from the road.

Nearing the end, a compound made up of three coastal conch cottages appeared. Painted in vibrant pastels, periwinkle blue, rosy pink, and canary yellow, and protected on all sides by a six-foot-high stone wall, they sat in a row atop a high cliff overlooking the Atlantic Ocean.

Tiny looked up and down the drive, surveying the scene. "I'm gonna put you two in da blue house in the middle. I'll put one of my men in da house on each side of ya and I'll have several men stationed at da driveway entrance and on da beach."

"This place is beautiful. Is this where you live now?" Will asked.

"No. Just some rental property I own. I only let special guests stay out here," Tiny said, smiling broadly.

"I can't thank you enough," Will said.

"No problem, mon. I got you guys covered. Now, you two go on in and relax. Get some sleep. You look like shit, Will." Tiny's deep voice rumbled with laughter.

Will and Victoria rolled their tired bodies out of the golf cart and turned to face the cottage. A wooden placard hung above the front door: "Oasis of the Ocean."

As Tiny began to drive away he stopped and yelled back. "There are towels under da sink in da bathroom. I'll be back shortly with some clothes and more food for da both of ya."

Will waved appreciatively, and then looked back up at the placard.

He admired the design of the cottage again. He thought he knew the names of almost every house on this island and was surprised that he was not aware of the Oasis of the Ocean. Positioned deep into the thickest foliage in Hopetown, Tiny's oasis was well hidden. He turned the door handle and with a slight jarring thrust of his shoulder, the door released its tight seal with a pop, swinging open. There was a slight musty smell in the air as if the door had been shut for weeks.

Flicking the light switch in the small foyer, he led Victoria by the hand into the cottage. Warmly decorated with teak wood floors, Venetian granite countertops, and white wainscot paneled walls, the den held a comfortable brown leather couch flanked on each end by leather recliners. A flat-screen television occupied an oak entertainment center and a slightly dusty but nicely balanced black Steinway upright piano sat in front of two large bay windows with views of the waves below.

Will walked across the room to the recliner. His body unwound on the cool leather as he collapsed into the seat, still wearing his well-weathered rain suit. Crusty pebbles of salt broke free of the neoprene and tumbled into the creases of the chair like tiny snowballs rolling downhill.

"Oh, this feels good," he said with eyes closed, smiling from ear to ear.

"I've got to get out of this," Victoria said as she jerked on the zipper of her damp fleece, removing it and the rain pants, tossing both in the corner of the room. In her scanty gold bikini, she walked over to the couch and lay down, her sweaty, salty skin sticking fast to the leather.

"I need a shower," Will said as a faint scent of rank body odor rose from his armpits.

"Me too." Victoria giggled. "Your friend Tiny seems really nice."

"They don't come any better."

"But, Will, you can*not* tell him about Inherited Memory or the IMS. You have to keep that secret."

"I know, but I'm going to have to tell him something. He's really sticking his neck out for us. Look at this place. This is the perfect hideaway."

"But are we safe here?" As she sat up, her back released from the bare leather with a sticky, crackling sound, and he laughed. "Stop laughing, I'm serious."

"Sorry, it just sounded like you were stuck to the couch like a fly to flypaper."

She laughed with him for a few moments then collected her composure. "But really, how can Tiny protect us against professional killers? Let's call someone and get them to fly us out of here tomorrow."

"First off, who can we trust?" Will said. "Someone in the government is in on this. The marshals were lied to and set up for slaughter. Second, there's probably no safer place than right here with Tiny's Army."

"Tiny's Army? What's that?"

"Let's just say that Tiny's official title is general manager and dock master of Sea Star Marina but he's unofficially the chief of police, the mayor—he basically runs this island. Hell, he's like ... like a Bahamian Godfather."

"Godfather?" Victoria said uneasily.

"Um, ambassador. Ambassador is more like it. Tiny is as honest as the day is long. He loves the people of Hopetown and will do anything for them. That's just the way he is. If you're a friend of his, he will do anything for you. A few years ago he put his life on the line to save Hopetown from going bankrupt."

"Bankrupt? Okay, you're confusing me." Victoria leaned over the arm of the couch, and stared directly into his eyes. "Can you trust him?"

Will lowered the foot prop of the recliner and sat up, deciding to start from the beginning of the story.

"We go way back. I've known Tiny since I was a little kid."

He told Victoria how they had met when Tiny was nine and Will was eight, and they'd first encountered one another on a white sand beach just inside of Tilloo Cut. During almost every trip that Will had subsequently made to Hopetown, the two of them fished, dived, and caught lobsters together. Will's parents adored Tiny and when he was fifteen years old, the Dunbars paid for him to travel to St. Augustine where he spent the entire month of July living with the family and enjoying everything that the States had to offer. Tiny loved baseball but he had never seen a professional game, so on the Fourth of July, they drove him to Atlanta to watch the Braves play. To this day, he still talked about how much fun he had swilling sodas and devouring bags of cotton candy, eating so much that he eventually got sick to his stomach.

They tried to convince him to stay in the States, even offering to pay for him to complete high school in Florida but Tiny's impoverished family was too dependent on him for financial support. It had taken an extraordinary amount of coaxing for Tiny's father just to allow him to leave for a month. In fact, unknown to Tiny, it had actually taken a slight bribe from Sam, a small compensation for any loss that might result from Tiny's absence.

Tiny's father, a stern man, was a commercial fisherman and the older and more arthritic he became, the more heavily he relied on his son's physical strength to haul in the heavy gill nets. The family managed to live day to day but Tiny's education paid a heavy price in return. However, after a month away from the islands, he became homesick.

"My bones belong in the Bahamas," he had said.

And as the coming years would reveal, it turned out to be a good decision. Through the combination of a magnetic personality and imposing size, Tiny had thrived on his small island paradise. At the age of eighteen, after his father's death, and emotionally and physically worn from the tremendous toll that commercial fishing required, he obtained a low-level job working the docks at Sea Star Marina. After only a few short months, Tiny was appointed dock master. With his sound judgment and ability to relate to people, he had risen quickly as a star at the Sea Star Marina and Resort, the largest and most lucrative business in Hopetown.

Consisting of a full-service marina accommodating yachts up to 150 feet, two restaurants, and 36 high-end villas for rent, the resort employed dozens of local workers, in turn feeding hundreds of hungry mouths. The success of the island's largest economic engine directly affected the livelihood of the local people. As the Sea Star went, so went Hopetown. Something had to be special about an eighteen-year-old kid to have such an important job as dock master.

Tiny was special, as Will told Victoria. In another life and given a better education and chance to succeed, he had often said Tiny would have been a billionaire. His charismatic charm and innate grounded approach to resolving human conflict made even the most pompous tourist surrender and crumble in his large and humble hands.

At 21, he was appointed general manager for the entire marina and resort. What had started as a simple job on the docks had turned into a life-changing career. So naturally, a couple of years ago, when a crisis almost brought Hopetown to its fiscal knees, the political leaders of the area approached Tiny for help. There had been a rash of boat thefts out of the Sea Star and other smaller marinas on Elbow Cay. Dozens of boats were commandeered from the marinas at night, unmoored from their bindings and stealthily floated away. Stolen, never to be seen again.

It didn't take long before word began to spread among the boating community in Florida and up and down the entire east coast that Hopetown was to be avoided "on your next island hopping vacation." The revenues of the marinas, rental properties, and restaurants on the island began to feel a financial pinch.

Finally, as federal Bahamian tax revenues dropped in Nassau, the Bahamian government decided to take action. Determining that the local police force was ineffective, if not corrupt, the government approached Tiny. They offered him whatever resources he needed to put together a band of brothers, an island militia with the sole purpose of stopping the thefts, to restore order to his peaceful island. They gave him carte blanche authority to find, capture and even punish the perpetrators as he saw fit.

Tiny dipped deep into the government's pocket and installed a state-of-the-art technological surveillance system. Every phone call, text message and email that entered or left cellular towers and Internet servers of Hopetown was monitored and traced. Through monetary enticement, he gained the cooperation of airport officials in Marsh Harbor, only a few miles across the Sea of Abaco, and on Spanish Cay, some forty miles away, to report to him any suspicious persons or activity.

After merely three months of work, Tiny and his men knew everyone who came and went on the island, and within six months, his army had captured the crooks and sentenced them. Rumor abounded on what punishment was brandished on the thieves, but the overwhelming sentiment was that Tiny sent a strong message that Hopetown was not a place for criminal activity.

"Tiny don't play! That was the phrase that everyone used during those days," Will said, yawning widely and stretching out his hands. He looked over at Victoria, whose face held a clear oily sheen. She seemed exhausted but had listened intently to Tiny's tale, searching Will's words for some sense of security.

"There hasn't been a boat theft or any other serious crime on the island since Tiny took over. There's no better place you could be right now. I promise," he said as he leaned forward and touched her hand.

Victoria gripped his hand firmly. "I feel so lucky that you came into my life when you did," she said, voice unsteady.

"You're safe now. You're among friends."

She sank back onto the couch and gave a delicate shudder, closing her eyes.

18

A RAPPING SOUND JARRED WILL from an intense sleep in the leather recliner. What felt like a momentary lapse of consciousness had actually been several hours. The sound resumed and he realized someone was softly knocking on the villa's front door. Rising from the recliner, he noticed that Victoria was no longer asleep on the couch. As he walked toward the front door, he heard the sound of the shower down the narrow hallway to his left.

"Will, you up?" a deep Bahamian voice inquired from outside the front door.

Half awake, Will opened the door to see Tiny standing on the front porch holding a blue canvas duffle bag in one hand and a large brown paper bag chock full of groceries in the other.

"Sorry it took me so long. I know you guys must be starving," Tiny said as he entered the villa and set the bag down on the kitchen counter, resting the dufflebag on the white tile floor.

Will flashed a playful wink. "I'm no stranger to island time. I know that 'be back shortly' is Bahamian for 'be back in four or five hours.'"

"Well, I had the damnedest time trying to find some clothes to fit your skinny friend. I had to go by my aunt's house and borrow a few tings," Tiny said, slightly out of breath.

Will began handing him the items from inside the grocery bag and Tiny began filling the fridge and cabinets with fresh groceries from the local market. A half-pound each of thinly sliced honey-baked ham and white breast turkey, two generous Ziploc bags of cheddar cheese, three vine-ripe tomatoes, two loaves of homemade white bread, and an assortment of fruit including whole pineapples, mangos, and bananas. Will reached deeper inside the paper bag, wrapped his hands around the necks of two bottles and removed them.

"Cabernet?" he said, smiling.

"I know you like your red wine, Dr. Dunbah. You guys enjoy that tonight and I'll get you some more for tomorrow."

"I don't know—we're pretty damn tired after that crazy night we just had. I think I'm going to hit the hay in a little while." Will wiped his eyes, trying to get his second wind.

"Tiny, I don't know how to repay you for all of this. This property is amazing. How many rentals do you own now anyway?" Will asked as he began laying out slices of bread on the small kitchen table. He walked to the fridge and removed a couple of nearly expired condiments, a small plastic bottle of yellow mustard with crackly dried crusty remnants covering the cap and a large glass jar of real mayonnaise. The kitchen was small yet quaint and generously illuminated by three large windows that captured the last of the day's rationing of sun.

"No sandwich for me, I'm good. But yeah, mon, I'm doing all right. I bought this here property about a year ago, which gives me now ... uh ... eight places. But this one is my pride and joy. I got some business acquaintances now in Nassau and we fly some of da high-rollers from da casino out here and put them up here. You know, when dey want to see da real Bahamas, not some big congested city in da middle of da ocean, dey come here to Hopetown. Big money types that like their seclusion."

Will grabbed a butter knife from the drawer and as he began to spread the mayonnaise, he reflected on Tiny's statement. After he'd solved the problem of the boat thefts, he must have undoubtedly made some good connections, including powerful people in influential positions in the Bahamian government. Tiny was a humble man and for him to say that he was doing "all right" most likely meant he was killing it.

"How're Anna and the boys doing?" Will asked, referring to Tiny's wife and his three young sons.

"Oh, e'rybody doing just great. The kids are getting a good education at that school in Marsh Harbour, I'm telling ya. I'm not goin' to let them be like their dad, with no college education."

"Well, you've done pretty damn well for yourself, my friend," Will said as he topped each piece of bread with a pile of cheddar cheese, his mouth watering more with each scrumptious slice.

"You know what made me smile the other day?" Tiny said, grinning.

Will shrugged his shoulders, keenly focused on his task.

"My oldest son, Thomas, said—"

"You mean Junior?" Will interrupted.

"Yeah, Junior. We call him Thomas around the house."

The name "Junior" was an oxymoron just like "Tiny." At nine years old, Junior was already five foot nine and 160 pounds.

"Junior said he wanted to be a docta one day just like Uncle Will."

Will's hands stopped their busy work and he looked up at Tiny. "You tell him that I have no doubt in my mind that he can do it and Uncle Will is going to help him any way he can."

Tiny chuckled with pride. "Okay, I'll tell him. Now, how are you doing? I haven't seen or talked to you in over two months. Did you sell your parents' house yet?"

"No. I just can't seem to pull the trigger on that one."

"Look, Will, it's been long enough. You got to get on with your life. That's what Mr. and Mrs. Dunbah would want."

Will was not offended by Tiny's comments. Tiny was the closest thing he'd ever had to a brother and Tiny was just giving him brotherly advice.

"I know. I'll do it as soon as all of this is over."

Tiny peered around the corner of the kitchen, eyes wide as he scanned the living room for Victoria. "Now dat brings me to this situation. How did you get involved in all of dis? Who is dis girl and why are you playing Indiana Jones?"

Will had anticipated that this point of the conversation was coming. He had never lied to Tiny and wasn't about to start now.

Will looked over his shoulder, trying to ascertain if Victoria had gotten out of the shower. He took a deep breath. "It's a very, very long story but the bottom line is that Victoria is part of a very small subset of individuals that have an incredibly powerful memory."

Tiny grimaced, then burst out into rolling deep laughter, rattling the wooden paneled walls.

Will placed his finger over his lips. "Shhh."

"You mean to tell me that somebody has gone to all the trouble of blowing up that old fort, chasing you in boats in the middle of the night, shooting at you with machine guns, trying to kill her, all because she got a photogenic memory? Come on, Will, do I look that stupid?"

"You mean photographic memory?" Will grinned.

"Yeah, that."

"No." Will quickly turned toward the living room. He looked down the hallway, then back at Tiny's puzzled face. "It's much more than a photographic memory. She ... she inherited her father's memory."

Tiny searched Will's face, estimating the situation. "No shit. Are you pulling my leg?"

"No, she also has her grandfather's memory and his father's memory and his father's memory, all the way back to around 1600."

Bewildered, Tiny looked as if someone had punched him in his full round belly. He sat down in the small kitchen chair, which creaked loudly and swayed from his enormous mass.

"What the—? I didn't know that was possible," he said, his forehead wrinkled like a washboard.

"I didn't either, not until four days ago."

That's crazy."

"What's crazy?" Victoria asked, entering the kitchen, loosely wrapped in a large bright beach towel and drying her damp hair with a smaller white hand towel.

Will looked at Tiny and held up a turkey sandwich. "He was saying it was crazy how we made it all the way here from the Dry Tortugas last night. Here, I made you a sandwich. Hope you like turkey?"

"Oh, wow. Thanks, chef."

Tiny picked up the duffle bag. "Here, Victoria, I got you and Will some clothes. It ain't much but it should do for now," he said, his voice cracking as he handed the bag to her, eyes wide and fixed on her face.

Will snickered to himself as he noticed Tiny's massive hands slightly trembling.

"Oh, you're the best, Tiny," Victoria said and kissed his round cheek.

The small walkie-talkie on his belt squawked with activity. Tiny picked it up. "Ya ... go ahead ... you got Tiny."

The walkie-talkie crackled back with another Bahamian voice. For several minutes, Tiny communicated with his man on the other end. Even for as long as Will had been coming to the islands, he still had difficulty deciphering the conversation when two Bahamians began jawing. With rapid speech and jangled diction, their expressive colloquialisms were unrecognizable to outsiders.

Sitting down at the kitchen table and devouring her turkey sandwich, Victoria watched Tiny thoughtfully as he moved around the room. He ended the conversation with "sounds good" and signed off.

"Everything okay?" Victoria asked.

"Yeah. Everybody's set. We got this place surrounded." Tiny bent down on one knee in front of Victoria, noticing her anxiety. "I don't want you to worry. This is what I do, I'm good at it."

She nodded and tried to swallow.

Tiny stayed around for a while longer, past sunset, and Victoria asked him a million questions about the history and culture of Hopetown. He began a long and descriptive story about the largest festival in the Bahamas, the Junkanoo Festival. But as he finished off his story, the sound of a slight rattle, a snore, made Will look around. Amused, he noticed that Victoria was asleep on the couch underneath a comfortable cashmere blanket.

ख़   ख़   ख़

THE MORNING SUN ARRIVED OVER the sand dunes, creating splatters of gold on the rear-facing porch of the villa, with nearby tall thin sea oats gently bending in the cool breeze. It was starting out to be a picture-perfect Bahamian day but it had been a sleepless night for Will. Although secure about Victoria's safety, waves of emotional torment had continually rolled through his restless body since three a.m., as he experienced a raucous nightmare about his parents' death and the mysterious diary; his thoughts consumed with the possible existence of a secret room. At sunbreak, confounded by the bizarre possibility of his family's involvement with the Blood Memory Society, he had given up on sleep and descended the long flight of wooden steps to the beach below.

After a few minutes of swimming, he heard a voice. "Will!"

He lifted his face from the ocean and swung his hair wildly, looking back at the beach. He bobbed with the waves momentarily until he spotted Victoria waving energetically, gave a wave back, and then swam towards her. As he stood up and walked out of the water, Victoria blushed slightly as his borrowed loose swimsuit hung down in the front, slightly exposing him.

"Sorry," he said, embarrassed and breathing heavily as he tugged up on the swimsuit. "It doesn't fit me well."

"How did you sleep? I slept like a rock," Victoria said as she dipped her toes in the warm water.

"I ... I didn't sleep too well really, but I'm fine. Let's go swimming." He began to pull her playfully into the water with him.

"Let me get my swimsuit on," she said, laughing.

"You don't need one." Will picked her up and walked out into the incoming surf. She squealed with laughter as he held her tightly and they fell into the ocean, floating down to the soft sandy bottom. Surfacing, she wiped strands of wet hair from her face and stared into Will's eyes. Suddenly she pressed her lips to his, passionately kissing him.

Undaunted by the intermittent salty white spray of the crashing surf, they kissed again and again, as Will held her against him, their bodies enveloped in rolling waves of water and their minds consumed with yearning swells of desire. He slid his hand over her entire body, and felt her tongue swirl warmly against his own as he gently squeezed her bottom.

"I think I'm falling for you, Doctor," she said.

WILL AND VICTORIA SPENT A carefree day playing in the ocean and strolling the beach. They searched for seashells and sharks teeth, and at noon, spread beach towels over the sand, ate more turkey sandwiches, and kissed some more.

"A perfect romantic picnic," Victoria said. "The sand is so soft. It really cushions your feet as you walk. It's not like any other sand I've ever felt." She bent down and squeezed a sample of pinkish sand in her hand, rolling the grains between the balls of her fingers.

"I know. It's not sticky like the sand in Florida. It's crushed coral from all of those reefs out there," Will said, pointing out to a small patch of reef just offshore. "I'm going to catch us some dinner. I'll be right back."

He scurried up the steps to the house and came back clutching a long, thin yellow shaft. As tall as Will with three sharp pointed spikes on one end and a large dense black rubber band on the other, the slender weapon was formidable and impressive.

"What is that?"

"It's a pole spear. I noticed it earlier in the bedroom closet."

Victoria smiled. "I can honestly say that for some reason I have never seen one of those."

"Stick with me. I'll show you some fancy handiwork," he said playfully and ran out into the surf, weapon in hand.

The sun's intensity was beginning to wane as he swam out to the reef, the yellow shaft glimmering in the water. A few hundred yards out, he dove down to the coral reef below, kicking hard with his bare feet. Without a mask to protect his eyes from the stinging saltwater and no dive fins, his task was much more difficult than he was used to. His eyes burned as he fought the current for close to a half-hour, his vision blurry as he surveyed the reef for table fare.

Victoria sat patiently on the beach and dug her feet deep into the soft sand, wiggling her toes.

"Woo hoo," Will's faint voice called out over the low rumble of the surf. He held a large fish high above his head, his body bouncing up and down with the waves.

"Way to go," she called out.

Will left the water, set the pole spear on the sand, and kneeled down before her, holding out his catch. "We're not going to have to eat cold-cut sandwiches tonight. Do you know what this is?" he asked, holding out an orange-colored fish with an elongated snout.

"It's a hogfish. It's a species of wrasse," she said. "Their meat is sweet because they use that snout to eat crustaceans that are buried in the sand. They're one of the best tasting fish in the sea."

"Of course you know that," Will said under his breath.

"Great job. I'm starving. Let's make dinner."

❧   ❧   ❧

"Wow," Will said as he entered the kitchen, surveying the spread as he dabbed his wet head with a bath towel. "That looks impressive." He was wearing a simple white V-neck T-shirt, blue shorts, and leather flip-flops. His nose and forehead glowed red from sunburn.

Freshly showered, Victoria was standing at the kitchen table dressed in thin, white cotton pants and a loose beige rayon shirt, slightly unbuttoned, exposing a portion of her sunkissed breasts. The aroma of a charcoal-fired grill filled the air. On the granite countertop, resting on tin foil, were two beautifully grilled pieces of fish, succulently white with perfect hatched grill marks on the side that Will had cooked before showering. Next to the fish were two large bowls, Victoria's contributions to the meal. One was filled with mashed potatoes and the other macaroni and cheese.

"I rummaged through the cabinets and found a bag of potatoes and box of mac and cheese," she said. "What do you think?"

"Looks perfect."

Victoria bent down underneath the sink and found two candles, half-melted with charred wicks. Lighting them, she placed them in the middle of the table. The sun was setting and she turned off the lights to observe the room's glow in candlelight.

Will felt truly content as he stood back and admired their combined resourcefulness—it was a very appetizing ad hoc meal.

He untwisted the loose cork from a bottle of cabernet that he had opened a few minutes earlier, filled two small clear plastic cups, and handed one to Victoria as she sat at the table.

Victoria took a bite of the fish and pursed her lips. "Pretty spicy."

Will laughed. "Sorry. I found cayenne pepper in the cabinet. That's my Cajun roots coming out, I guess. Hope I didn't overdo it?"

She took another bite. "No. It's actually really good."

Smiling, he scooped two large helpings of potatoes and pasta onto his plate.

"I am so hungry," Will said happily.

After a few bites, he settled down to conversation. "Where do you live in California? JPL is in Pasadena, right?"

"Yes, but I live in Malibu. It can be quite a commute."

"With that famously bad L.A. traffic, how do you do it?"

"Well, they have a nice dorm for us at JPL so I often spend the night there and avoid the commute. I'm up to all hours of the night working anyway. But the weekend, now, the weekend, I spend the entire time in Malibu at the beach: volleyball, hiking. All the good stuff. My favorite hiking trail is just up north in Big Sur."

"Malibu. Sounds nice. That's a good quality of life you have there, Ms. Van Buren." Noticing her cup was getting empty, he leaned over and refilled it.

The next question had been eating at him ever since they arrived in Hopetown. He had been trying to sort out why the attack happened and who was the target. He waited for her to finish a glass of wine, hoping the alcohol would help nurture an honest answer.

"So what is this project that you guys have been working on at JPL?" he asked with a casual shrug.

Victoria's eyes narrowed to slits. "How do you know we were working on something?"

"Ross said you and your parents were working on something important. Can you tell me about the Genesis Project?"

"I can't, you know that."

Will clenched his jaw. Victoria settled into her chair and drew her shoulders back.

"I'm risking my life for you, and I think that these murderers are after you because of this project you're working on."

Victoria swallowed hard and looked toward the window. The moonlight was soft tonight as thick passing clouds dampened its intensity. The reflection of the candles glimmered in the glass.

"I can't tell you what it is, Will. I ..." Victoria reached out and gripped his hand. "I care for you so much. Please just don't ask me to talk about this. I'll tell you anything else you ever want to know about me. Ask me anything."

"I just don't want you to get hurt. The more I know, the better job I can do protecting you."

"You knowing about the project may actually put you at risk. Just let this go." Victoria steadied her gaze into his eyes. "All I can say is that we are so close to something extremely important to all of us, me and you, everyone. It has the potential to transform the world. Ross shouldn't have even told you the name. Me either. Please."

He took a deep breath then held his hands up. "You're right. I'm sorry. I'll drop it."

Both extremely hungry, it didn't take long to devour every flaky morsel of hogfish and demolish several heaping mounds of carbohydrates. The wine went down smoothly. Will stood, grabbed another bottle and removed the cork with a smooth pop. At the same moment, from behind him, rich melodious tones arose from the piano, reverberating through the villa.

Complex and intricate, the notes of a familiar classical composition flowed from the piano. Holding the bottle in his hand, mouth agape, Will strode into the living room and watched as Victoria moved her slender fingers, in perfect coordination. On top of the piano sat one of the candles from the kitchen, and her blonde hair glistened in the flickering light.

Dazzled, he slowly slid his body next to her on the bench seat. Victoria completed the sonata.

"Did you like it?" she asked softly.

"That was incredible," Will said, then reached forward and filled her empty cup. "I've heard that piece before. What is it?"

"'Hammerklavier' by Beethoven."

"I loved it. You're like a professional pianist. How old were you when you took lessons?"

She dabbled her finger in a small warm pool of melted wax that was collecting on the piano, delaying her response. "It's part of my Inherited Memory," she said, her voice almost sad. Victoria talked over the awkward silence that followed. "I told you about me earlier. I want to hear all about you. You said you're Cajun? Are you from Louisiana?"

"My family is. I live in St. Augustine now. My dad and mom moved to Florida before I was born but they both grew up in Louisiana," he said, staring into the mesmerizing light of the candle, still half pondering her exceptional inherited gift.

"Come on. Let's sit over here." Victoria picked up the candles and placed them on a coffee table in front of the couch.

As Will's back conformed into the cool leather of the couch, she nestled up against him, laying her head on his shoulder.

"So tell me about your family. I mean, unless it's too hard to talk about." She squeezed her lower lip between her front teeth, probably hoping she hadn't breached a boundary.

Will kissed her on the forehead. "No. It's fine. It's kind of a screwed-up family tree though. I just don't really know a lot about my extended family." He ran his hands through his hair. "What's strange is that there has always been a mystery of sorts surrounding my grandfather's side of the family."

"What do you mean?"

"Just a missing branch in the family tree, I guess. My grandfather was so old by the time my father was born that we lost touch with that entire side of the family. My dad was into this whole genealogy thing and spent years trying to put together the pieces of our convoluted family puzzle." Will laughed and took a slurp of wine.

"What was your dad's name?"

"Samuel. Called Sam. My mom's name was Linda," his voice cracked slightly, eyes misty. "My grandfather was Julian."

Victoria took his hand gently.

"But just before I came to Fort Jefferson, I found the coolest thing in my closet, my great-grandmother's diary from the Civil War."

"So have you read the diary?" she asked. "There must be some answers to your questions about your family in there."

As Will's eyes focused on the candlelight again, his face flushed as he thought about the drawing of Peachtree Plantation, the strange riddle, and the IMS logo. "I was just thinking about this really good story in the diary about the Siege of Vicksburg," he said.

"The Battle of Vicksburg, Mississippi? I've heard of that."

For almost a half hour, Will went on to tell Victoria about the siege, when over 19,000 lives were lost to gunshot wounds, starvation, and disease. He finished the account of the horrific battle by telling her how, by the grace of his great-grandfather's West Point photograph on the mantle, the family home and livestock had been spared from ruin. As best he could recall, Will recited the note from General Sherman.

Victoria wiped her eyes. "That's an amazing story. Your great-grandfather must have been an amazing man."

"Yeah. I guess he was. I'm not clear where he went to med school but I know he was a doctor."

"Just like you. You went to West Point and you're a doctor. It's all come full circle."

Will looked at her with surprise. "How did you know I went to West Point?"

"I researched you, Dr. Dunbar. Do you think I'm going to let just any ol' doctor examine me?" Victoria clapped her hands together. "Where is this diary? I want to read it."

His lips tightened. "It's at Fort Jefferson. It probably got burnt up in the fire. I'm sure it's gone."

Victoria's eyes widened with horror. "Oh, no. I'm so sorry," she said, and then began to softly caress the wound on his arm. "Your family story is amazing. It's not screwed up at all." She bowed her head. "I'm just so fortunate, Will. I've been so blessed in my life. I've never wanted for much. My Inherited Memory can be difficult at times but, trust me, I know I'm supremely fortunate for it."

"I can't imagine how it feels and I never will but I am here for you if you want me to be, as a friend. I know I don't have the kind of brain power that you do but in general terms, I'm pretty bright."

Victoria curled her big beautiful eyes up to his gaze. "You're one of a kind, Will Dunbar. You come from good stock. I figured that out already. I'm not letting you go anywhere."

He leaned down and closed the gap between them. He caressed her cheek and kissed her cabernet-flavored lips.

She pushed back. "*Coup de foudre,*" she said in perfect French.

"What does that mean?"

"I've been waiting my entire life to say that," she said, running her hand along his carved jaw, his whiskers tickling the tips of her fingers. "It means when two lovers look into each other's eyes and, suddenly for the first time, realize that they are in love."

"Do you mean like love at first sight?"

"I felt it the first time I laid eyes on you in the Golden Room. I didn't want to acknowledge it but it was there."

"*Coup de foudre,*" Will whispered.

She grabbed the back of his head and pulled him down towards her. He kissed her lips, her cheek, her nose, her neck as they twisted their bodies together, their breathing more intense with each second. Victoria never uttered a word and never resisted his touch. With the slightest pull, like a row of stacked dominos, the small clear buttons of her shirt slipped effortlessly through their loose holes, one by one, exposing her breasts.

Will suckled her stiff, hard nipples and she writhed, moaning softly and viscerally as he caressed her with his long fingers. She tugged his shirt, pulling it over his head, and then slid her head down and gnawed passionately on his bare chest as he kicked aside his shorts. With one long swoop of his fingers, he interlaced both her thin cotton pants and sheer panties and gave a gentle downward tug. With a steep arch of her back and a slight upward thrust of her hairless pelvis, she consented.

Will searched her face as he entered her, her tongue becoming motionless, paralyzed, as a wave of pleasure rolled through her body. Her eyes rolled back, then refocused, looking directly into his. Her steady gaze captivated him as he made love to her. Her scent filled his senses and he felt consumed with an all-encompassing tender warmth, almost as if he had transcended his body becoming one with hers. The taste of her skin and touch of her breasts, pressed firmly into his bare chest, stroked him into an erotic trance. Her eyes widened and she shuddered, thrashing beneath him. She closed her eyes and let out a loud wail, wrapping her long legs around his back. Unable to withstand the intensity, he climaxed and their bodies simultaneously became limp.

"I'm speechless," she said.

Will lay beside her on the couch, wiping away her damp hair from her face and admiring her long firm body.

She turned on her side and propped her head on one hand, smiling as she stared into his eyes. "What do we do now?" she asked.

"Let's take it to the bedroom."

They made love twice that night as a constant drizzle of rain fell on the tin roof, filling their ears with a peaceful sound like a long, slow music box. With only a thin cotton sheet covering their bodies, arms and legs intertwined, their shared warmth provided a comfortable lovers' cocoon.

WHEN THE PHONE CALL CAME, Ross was staring through his office window, peering out in amazement at how brutally cold this winter had been and that in March, large snowdrifts still blanketed the grounds outside his D.C. office. He looked hard at the phone's display. It was a number he didn't recognize but he answered anyway.

"Hello?"

"Is this Colonel Ross Chapman?" a high-pitched male voice asked. "Is this a secure line?"

"Yes, it is. Who am I speaking with?"

"This is Timmy. I'll call you back in thirty seconds."

"Timmy? Timmy Mahoney?" Ross asked, but the phone had already gone dead.

The name brought to mind the image of a painfully thin man in his late twenties with fiery red hair and freckles, of Irish descent. Ross bit his nails as the long seconds elapsed. Finally, his phone buzzed again, this time from a different phone number.

"Hi. It's Timmy Mahoney."

"Timmy. Are you okay? Are you injured?"

"No. I'm fine, well, at least I'm not dead," he said, his tone scratchy and nasal.

"I knew it. I knew you were alive. You didn't eat the peanuts, did you?"

"No. I guess for once in my life I was fortunate to have this damn allergy." A faint alarm sound rang in the background of Timmy's phone.

"I'll call you back in 30 seconds."

Before Ross could respond, the phone went dead. He released a huge sigh of relief and awaited Timmy's next call. For an instant, he considered making a phone call to his squad but decided against it, not wanting to tie up his phone. Thirty seconds elapsed and his phone rang again. The number was different than either of the first two.

"Timmy?" Ross asked.

"Yeah. I'm here."

"This line is secure. I promise. You don't have to keep calling from different numbers. This phone line has the same secured connection as the president."

"I know way too much about all of that to feel comfortable right now."

"Whatever you say. Let me come get you. I'll send G6 to pick you up immediately."

Timmy paused, the sound of a clicking keyboard audible in the background of his phone. "No. I don't think so, Ross. I'm better off on my own."

"Timmy, you don't know what you're up against. You can't stay alive. They'll find you. I'll personally take responsibility for your safety. Let me come pick you up."

"Who is 'they'?"

Ross paused, his blood pressure rising. "I don't know yet. I'm working on it."

More clicking in the background, and then the familiar alarm sound rang again. "I'll call you back." Timmy hung up.

"No—"

Thirty more seconds passed until the next ring, from yet a different phone number.

"I think I can figure out who's behind all of this." Timmy coughed, sneezed, and then Ross heard him blow his nose several times. "I saw their faces and heard them speak."

Ross' eyes widened. "Really? How did you get away?"

"It was horrible, Ross. I panicked—" The faint alarm sounded again. Timmy hung up and called back 30 seconds later. Each time, the numbers, including area codes, were different.

"He's using different cell towers all over the country every time so no one can locate the origin of his calls," Ross thought. After the last call, Ross had also punched start on the stopwatch function of his cell phone. Timmy was speaking in no more than 58-second intervals.

"I was in the mission control room. As usual, the peanuts were being passed around and like always, I faked it. Before I knew it, people were falling to the floor. Their mouths were foaming. It happened so fast, Ross. I don't know what kind of poison was in those peanuts but it was really fast-acting." The alarm sounded again.

Ross had eaten away half of his fingernails at this point. His pinky was bleeding.

"It was a form of cyanide," Ross said when he answered the phone the next time, not waiting for Timmy to identify himself.

"Cyanide? Hell, I thought it was some new type of poison. They were gone like that."

Ross paused, thinking. He had to get Timmy back in the fold.

"Is everyone dead?" Timmy asked. "All of Team X?"

"Yes, except for you and ... and hopefully Victoria. We had her tucked away at Fort Jefferson but it was attacked yesterday."

"Is Victoria okay? Is she hurt? What do you know?"

"As far as we know, she got away and she's on the run somewhere."

"How can she be on the run? That place is surrounded by ocean for a hundred miles in all directions."

"It's ... it's a long story, Timmy. I'll fill you in, if you will just come meet me."

The alarm sounded and Timmy hung up immediately. Ross paced his office for close to ten grueling minutes this time before he called back.

"What else happened?" Timmy asked when Ross picked up. He seemed to be sniffling now, possibly more from tears than a runny nose.

"They also bombed the NFC."

"The NFC? What the hell? Did Dr. B survive?"

"Yes. He's fine but they managed to destroy all of the samples."

A long pause developed on the phone.

"Tell me what you saw at JPL." Ross said

"I saw two masked men opening the front door so I grabbed keys from the belt of the dead officer and hid in the remote server room." The alarm sounded.

When Ross answered 30 seconds later, he was still speechless.

"Are you there, Ross?"

"Yeah. Sorry. What happened next?"

"I hid behind the main frame, squeezed myself real tight, my back against the wall. Through the cabinet, I saw two men walk in. The first thing they did was shoot out the security camera. I even let out a squeal, I can't believe they didn't hear me. Ross, I can't believe he didn't see me when he bent down to place the bomb under the computer."

Ross switched his phone to the other ear, incredulous. "How did you see his face?"

"He got frustrated trying to activate the bomb. The ski mask was interfering with his vision, I guess. His friend was yelling at him to hurry up so he pulled off his mask and I got a good look at him. He was just a couple of feet from me. I was shaking *sooo* bad."

"What did he look like? Timmy. Let me come get you—" Ross pleaded loudly.

"Ross, I'm going to work on this and I'll be back in touch with you soon." Timmy disconnected.

2I

AFTER HIS SECOND NIGHTMARE IN one night, Will slipped into his shorts and walked outside to the back porch. He fell backwards, limply, into the porch swing, nervously rocking back and forth. It was a warm morning but he felt cold, as layers of sweat evaporated quickly from his shirtless body, his teeth chattering. Listening to the breaking surf, he had never felt so confused, so unsure of his life as he did right now.

His nightmares had seemed more real than any other dream he had ever experienced. He effortlessly drifted into a deeply dark room. From beyond the shadows, the ghostly emanation of a young woman appeared. With dark hair pinned in a bun, she had sickly white skin that seemed loose and dysplastic. Black circles rimmed her dull eyes.

"Find it, Will," the weak raspy voice called out as if in pain. "Julian wants you to find it. There is no one left," the vision uttered with dried cracked lips.

Will shook himself out of his nightmare induced stupor and gazed across the ocean at a sailboat dodging whitecaps, the sail and its mast pitching softly from side to side in the quartering wind.

He recited the riddle in his head again. A mast? Where would a mast be in an antebellum home?

"You are not a good bed partner," Victoria said, smiling as she stepped onto the porch. She held a cup of black coffee in her hand, the words "Don't Worry, Be Happy, You're in the Bahamas, Mon" printed in bright yellow lettering on the white porcelain cup. She sat beside Will and curled into his arms.

As she stared out at the ocean, he studied her face in the low morning light, taking note of her plain and unfettered features, free of pretentious makeup, the natural flow from her brow to her pointed cheekbones, to her strong chin. He caressed her smooth lips with his fingers. She blushed. He inhaled her intoxicating scent.

"Tell me what's bothering you," she said.

"There's something I keep trying to figure out," he mumbled.

"You mean like who attacked us?"

"That's part of it but there's something else that's got me confused."

"What is it? Tell me."

"I found out something recently about my family, and I don't exactly know what it means."

"Maybe I can help."

Will shifted his body. "I just need to figure it out my own. I'm not sure what to do about it."

She stroked his cheek. "Do whatever it is you need to. I feel safe here. Tiny will take good care of me, you know that."

"I know, I just—"

Victoria sternly looked him in the eye. "Will, I want you here with me, you know that, but if there's something bugging you so bad that you can't sleep, then you need to figure it out and come back to me." She put her arms around him and gave a strong, fulfilling hug, tenderly kissed him, and then pushed back. "Besides, you're no good to me anyway in this condition," she said, nuzzling his lower lip.

ª   ª   ª

AROUND NOON, THEY HEARD THE sputtering sound of Tiny's golf cart barreling down the long driveway and walked outside into the humid midday air. They waved vigorously as Tiny skidded to a spirited stop, small white seashell fragments careening from the rear tires' wake.

"How's everybody doin' on this beautiful morning in paradise?" he asked, his smile broad as ever.

"We're doing great, Tiny," Victoria said. "I can't thank you enough for all you're doing."

"No problem. Will is my boy. If he says you're a good person then I know ya are, without a doubt."

Will excused himself from Victoria and grabbed Tiny by the arm, pulling him towards the ocean. "How does everything look so far?"

"You're golden, mon, relax. No one's been asking about two beautiful Americans who arrived in da Wildlife and Fisheries boat," Tiny said, his gregarious laugh booming from his barrel chest.

Looking Will in the eyes, Tiny's face lost its shine. "What's wrong?" he asked.

Anxiously, Will looked back at Victoria briefly then faced Tiny again. "I might need to leave for a day or two. There's something I have to do."

Tiny lifted an eyebrow. "Leave? Where in da world would you go?"

"I'll explain it all when I get back, I promise. It won't take long. I should be back in no more than two days, tops. Will she be safe here while I'm gone?"

Tiny placed his hand on Will's hunched shoulder. "They gonna have to go through ol' Tiny to get to her and dat ain't so easy." He chuckled, and then paused for a moment to consider the situation. "Besides, it might actually do some good if you two split up for a couple of days. I mean, if you both weren't so damn pretty, you wouldn't draw so much damn attention," he said and gave Will a sudden bear hug.

Will groaned with laughter as Tiny's massive arms wrapped him tightly, constricting like anacondas around his lower back, his feet dangling in the air. As Tiny released his powerful grip, Will caught his breath with a visceral cough. As long as they'd known each other, Tiny's raw strength had always amazed him. He couldn't leave Victoria in any better hands, he was sure.

"Okay. Can you get somebody to fly me out of Marsh Harbour tomorrow?"

"No problem, mon. I'll have my best pilot, Gregory, fly ya wherever ya need to go." Tiny grabbed Will's arm and led him farther toward the ocean, away from Victoria. "But, friend, if they're looking for her, they will surely be looking for you too now. They'll use you as bait to find her."

"Okay. I'll be careful. Whoever 'they' are should be hundreds of miles away from where I'm going," Will said with a wry smile. "But, Tiny, wherever Victoria goes on this island, I want you to go with her, no matter what. Okay?"

"You have my word ... my brotha."

❧   ❧   ❧

THE COCONUT PALMS WERE SWAYING vigorously in the brisk northwest wind as large thunderheads shaped like pink elephants danced across the morning sky. The wet smell of rain filled Will's nostrils as an intense storm built on the western horizon. Tiny skillfully drove the skiff and the ten-minute boat ride from

Hopetown across the Sea of Abaco to Marsh Harbour had left Will's borrowed clothes a little damp. A small black man standing on a sunbaked wooden dock grabbed their dock lines and secured the small boat to the dock.

"Will, meet Gregory Albury, da best pilot in all of da Abacos," Tiny said.

Will shook Gregory's outreached hand, swung a backpack around his shoulders, and stepped onto the dock beside him.

Gregory Albury was a native Bahamian. With a thin, limber frame and a worn but friendly face, his wide smile was highlighted by two shiny gold front teeth. "Nice to finally meet you, Docta Dunbah. I've been hearing about you from Tiny for years," he said, his accent richer than most. "Let's put your bag in my car. It's just a short ride to da airport."

"Here, I want ya to have dis." Tiny held up a small black nylon bag. "Just a little sumting."

Will unzipped the bag and pulled out a neatly rolled bundle of crisp hundred-dollar bills, bound by a red rubber band. He fingered the money, counting it in his head. "This is ten grand," he said, baffled. "I can't take this. I'm only going to be gone for a day or two."

"You never know."

Flustered, Will shuffled through the bag some more, this time pulling out a small soft-plastic blue book, a passport. He opened it to the front page and saw a picture of his own face. Underneath his professional-looking photo was the name Cyrus Burke, the country of birth, Bahamas. "How in the world? How did you get a picture of me?"

"I pulled it off of the Mayo Clinic website. If anyone asks, you are Mr. Cyrus Burke."

Will could feel from the weight of the bag that one more item remained. He reached in and clasped his hand around the cold metal of a .38-caliber pistol. As though he had done it a million times before, he examined the shiny silver revolver then calmly unlatched and slid out the fully loaded cylinder, and spun it clockwise. "I'm not going to need this," he said.

"Take it anyway, to make me feel better," Tiny said. "Stay in the shadows."

"Okay, but I'm bringing this money back, all of it," Will said, holding the ball of cash up and shaking it.

He gave Tiny a heartfelt wave, and then followed Gregory toward the car. As he reached the end of the dock, Will looked at the passport again and chuckled at Tiny's resourcefulness. He turned back toward the boat to thank Tiny one last time but he had already unmoored and was headed back towards Hopetown.

With over 5,000 feet of well-maintained runway, Marsh Harbour airport is the main thoroughfare in the Abacos for incoming and outgoing air traffic. Gregory's 1985 Buick Regal passed the main building and drove another half-mile to the private terminal.

"What should I do with this gun?" Will asked.

Gregory just shook his head. "Just put the black bag underneath your clothes inside your backpack. Don't worry: they never check anyting here."

The terminal was a small ramshackle wooden building with a notorious reputation for delays. In addition, its security measures, thanks mainly to apathetic personnel, hadn't quite caught up to the post-9/11 standards to which most of the world's airports subscribed. Slightly nervous, Will presented his fake identification to a rotund woman with well-gelled red and black hair. She looked at it as she ate a bag of potato chips and picked her teeth with a fingernail. Never inspecting any luggage at all, she waved them through with an aggravated expression.

As they crossed the wet steamy tarmac to Gregory's 1969 Cessna 180, Will felt weak in his knees, the sight of the small plane striking pent-up anxiety within.

Extremely nervous but also exceedingly grateful for the ride, Will settled into the plane's gray leather passenger seat just as a smattering of rain began to pelt the windshield. Peering out, down the long wet runway, his mind became clouded, a cold sweat filling his palms. The lack of sleep could have been responsible for his dizziness but, more likely, it was the fact that he was doing it again, flying in a small plane when he promised himself not to, not after his parents' accident.

The emotions he was experiencing were much more intense than when he flew in the G6 a few days prior. It wasn't just that the Cessna was a single-prop, aged aircraft. There was an even darker reason for his uneasiness today.

Gregory turned the key. The vintage engine grunted, groaned, then sputtered to life, the plane's entire body bouncing and creaking like an old worn box spring. "We need to get turned, Docta Dunbah, so that we can take off directly into da wind," Gregory yelled over the engine's roar.

As the plane approached the southeastern end of the airstrip, Will opened his eyes. His stomach knotted, twisting in on itself, and he felt nauseated as he looked through the window to the exact location where his parents' lives ended.

Still visible after all this time, a large, circular, ashened divot on the edge of the runway stood out like an ugly scar; loose chunks of black asphalt still dirtied the bordering grass. The airplane that was piloted by his dad's doctor friend, the plane that his parents boarded, had crashed upon takeoff, creating that scar, killing everyone inside.

Will's eyes watered and he clenched his jaw. He glanced over at Gregory, who was intently engaged with the control tower, waiting for the all-clear. Will sat up straight in the seat and shouted with anxiety over the roar of the engine. "Are you sure we are taking off into the wind? No tailwind?"

"Yes, mon. I never take off with a tailwind! E'rybody know dat," Gregory said with a relaxed smile, his gold teeth sparkling.

Will wished that was true. He wished that Dr. Lazarus had known.

The Cessna bounced and rolled its way down the asphalt like a wobbly boulder. Gregory pulled back the controls and the plane clawed and crawled skyward, straining to push through the ominous envelope of blackness, violently rocking as dense downdrafts strafed the light aluminum frame. Finally leveling out at 15,000 feet, their flight pattern stabilized along with Will's breathing.

"You and Tiny go way back, huh?" Gregory asked, turning to Will.

"Yep. He's like a brother to me," Will said.

"Tiny is a good, good mon. Ever since he caught those crooks and proved himself to be a leader, he's made a lot of friends in Nassau. People talkin' bout him running for office soon. President Tiny," Gregory said, laughing loudly and slapping the steering wheel with the palm of his calloused old hand.

Will smiled at the possibility. His stress was beginning to dissipate and he took a deep breath of the thin air.

"E'ryting gonna be all right."

22

THE FLIGHT FROM MARSH HARBOUR was, without a doubt, the roughest flight of Will's life. Despite Gregory's skill as a pilot, the Cessna struggled in Mother Nature's wrath. A cold front had pushed down from the north creating a treacherous maze of towering cumulonimbus clouds. Gregory veered the small plane around as many of the thunderheads as he could, skirting the edges of the mushroom-shaped monsters. But the plane intermittently caught the center of nature's fury. The terrifying rollercoaster ride of steep nosedives, gut-wrenching drops, and dizzying bankrolls made Will chew his fingers to the bone, until the airplane finally pushed through, reaching calm cool air on the other side.

As the sun set over the horizon and the miasma of pink and blues faded to darkness, Gregory pointed down to two rows of flickering yellow lights that were emerging in the distance. "That's Vicksburg Municipal." With relaxed calm, he guided the plane down with precision, coming to rest on the damp runway, and the smell of wet asphalt and rubber filled the cockpit. Gregory reached over and patted Will on the shoulder. "Told you, mon, you are in good hands with ol' Gregory. I will wait right here for you, Doc. I'll just sleep right here in da plane until you get back from whatever it is you're doing."

Will looked over at the tough old man with admiration. Gregory had never displayed an ounce of fear on the ride over and had spent a tremendous amount of energy simply attempting to reassure Will's spent nerves. Now grounded safely, he felt slightly embarrassed for his fear of flying, his ineptitude. Getting to know Gregory had been the only positive about the entire ordeal.

"No. That's not necessary. It might take a day or two for me to do what I need to do," he said.

"Tiny told me to wait. I can't leave you here."

"You tell Tiny that I'll be fine. I'll be back in a couple of days."

"But Will?"

"Thank you for getting me here. I appreciate everything you've done for me. You rest here tonight and be safe on your way home tomorrow." Will grabbed his backpack, shook Gregory's hand, and walked toward the small brown airport building. He didn't actually know how long it would take but he was certain of one thing, there wasn't a chance in hell that he was going to fly on that small plane back to the Abacos. His intentions were to find out if there was any ounce of truth to the secret document, then take a very large, commercial airliner back to Victoria.

ॷ   ॷ   ॷ

WITH BACKPACK FIXED FIRMLY TO his shoulders and wearing red high-top sneakers that Tiny had supplied for him—at least a size too large with a worn hole in the toe, Will walked briskly across the tarmac, self-evaluating his duds as he walked. He was a bit embarrassed to be wearing red basketball shoes but he didn't feel that much better, stylistically, about the tight green camo fatigues and the white T-shirt. Red, green, white and out of place, he felt like a cheap Christmas sweater. He waved his hand at the only yellow cab that was parked out front of the Vicksburg airport and the old cab driver motioned for him to get in the backseat.

"Good evening, son. Where we headed?" the cab driver said with a shaky Southern drawl, putting the car in drive. His face was pitted, his silver hair was covered by a faded green and yellow John Deere cap, and he wore a torn blue denim jacket. He puffed on a Marlboro Red as he awaited Will's answer.

Will was in Vicksburg, Mississippi.

Located on a west-facing bluff overlooking the Mississippi River, Vicksburg is a city of roughly 25,000 residents, and similar to most towns in the state, it has seen its better days in the decades, if not a century or two, before. These days, with an economy based mainly on dockside gaming, tourism, and timber, it's a mere shell of a city that it once was.

During the 1800s, it had been a thriving, vibrant city owing its prosperity to the fertile soil of the surrounding Mississippi Delta, where the majority of the world's cotton was grown. In many respects, cotton's financial and political influence in the nineteenth century could be compared to that of the oil industry in the twenty-first century. And Vicksburg was geographically positioned perfectly to reap the rewards.

In its heyday, or more accurately in its cotton-day, massive plantation homes dotted the rolling hills and looked down over the wide, flat fields. Many blue-bloods from the North moved to the Delta planning to make their fortune in the promise of this enormous emerging agricultural market. For the Southern elite class, times had never been so good nor would ever be better.

Before Will could answer him, the old man asked another question. "Where'd ya fly in from, young man?"

"From Florida," said Will." Name's Cyrus. Cyrus Burke."

"I'm Billy, but people call me Buster. Florida? What brings you to Vicksburg?"

"Um...I'm researching Civil War history and I just want to see Peachtree Plantation for myself," he said as he looked out the car window. He wondered how this was going to go over.

The car jerked suddenly and Buster stomped on the brakes.

"You want to go where?" he asked and released a tower of smoke.

Will coughed. "Peachtree Plantation."

"Son, do you know anything about that place?"

Will was caught off-guard. He'd assumed that Peachtree Plantation still existed and had remained a private home. But between fleeing for his life and trying to protect Victoria, he hadn't had the time or capability to go online and research the estate's history or current status. "No. Not really. Why? Is there a problem?"

Buster let out a loud chuckle then spat a piece of phlegm into a napkin. "That house is haunted. I mean big time. Everybody around here knows that."

Will searched for a response. "Could you tell me about it? I'm trying to write a book on unsolved Civil War mysteries."

"Well, it was the only house standing in Vicksburg after the Civil War. Every other house was burnt to the ground. The rumor goes that the Yankees got so spooked when they went in that house that they ran out screaming for their lives. Nobody till this day will go in there. You just don't do it."

"Wow. What's it look like now? Is it still standing?"

"Still there all right. I haven't been up there for years but for being abandoned for a hundred years, it seemed in decent shape, at least from the outside." The old man began to drive again. "Now back in the day, it was a dandy one. Supposed to have been the most beautiful house in the South. Old man Dunbar did a good job when he built that one. He was one hell of a builder. It will stand the test of time, that's for damn sure."

Will looked puzzled. "I thought the Dunbars were just the owners. Did they physically build the house?"

"Oh, yeah. From what I've heard, the Dunbars were jacks of all trades."

"So did Dr. Leonard Dunbar, the one that graduated from West Point, build the house?"

"Now I don't know for sure because you're talkin' about times long ago, even before me, and hell, I'm almost 75 years old. But from what I know about it, it was his daddy. I think his name was Robert, who built the house. Hell, all those Dunbars went to West Point. They were all real, real smart. Kinda a legend around these parts. They even named the library after Dr. Dunbar and his wife, cuz they were real big on education and all that."

Will leaned forward from the backseat. "How were they real big on education? I don't really know much about them yet."

"Oh, hell. The Dunbar Scholarship Fund. They paid for college for anybody that lived in seven counties around here and still do to this day. If your son or daughter had the mind to go to Ole Miss or Mississippi State or that other one down south ... uh ... USM, then they paid for it, books, dorms and all. A helluva deal." Buster took a long draw off of his very short cigarette and concentrated on the dark road ahead.

Will grimaced from the smoke and stared out the window blankly, taken aback by this news. He had no idea that his family had offered some type of scholarship.

"I shoulda gone to school but I just needed to work. My people work off the land. Always have," Buster said. "Now I'm too old and I just drive this cab at night. Trying to make ends meet."

"Why didn't the Dunbars pass the house to their children or relatives? Why did it just sit there?"

"They didn't have no heirs. They had one kid, a boy I think, and he done run off or got sick and died or somethin'. Way before even I was born." Buster laughed, then spat another chunk of lung into the napkin. "But my grandmaw used to live close to there and she said that once the Dunbars died, the government swooped in and held onto Peachtree for a long time, like they were protecting it or something. Damn Commies. Think they can take anything they want. They never let nobody buy it. It just sits there. Hell, I don't know who in their right mind would want to buy a haunted house anyway."

THE OLD YELLOW CAB DROVE west of Highway 61 and north of Interstate 20 to a recessed road that cut through the heavily wooded hills of Warren County, Mississippi, carrying Will miles and years away from the twenty-first century. After a twenty-minute drive, they emerged onto a narrow road that coursed next to the muddy Mississippi, the chill off the river dropping the air temperature several degrees. In the distance along the riverfront, he noticed one particularly large, modern building less than a mile away, keenly out of place against the historical backdrop of the city.

Looking like an incongruous combination of a large Southern Baptist church and a glitzy hotel on the Vegas Strip, the bright pastel building was trimmed in a sleek stream of neon lights along its steep pitched rooftop. A neon sign in front flashed "Lucky Lady Casino" and grew brighter and brighter as each second of daylight waned.

"A casino?"

"Oh yeah. You didn't know we had gamblin' here in Mississippi?"

Will shook his head and as he scanned the shoreline, the sound of "Dixie" guided his eyes to a quaint white riverboat approaching the dock; black block lettering on her side read "Magnolia Queen." White puffs appeared over the top deck of the three-storied riverboat as steam from the golden cylindrical whistles of the calliope played the melodic notes of the most distinctive song of the South. The tones pierced the air, bouncing off of the solid earth bluff, clearly audible from several miles up and down the riverbank.

The *Magnolia Queen*, like those that sailed the river a century before, sported a red paddlewheel on the stern and a small yellow pilothouse between two towering black smokestacks, which rose 30 feet above the top deck. On top of the pilothouse, Will counted five multicolored pennants flapping vigorously in the twilight breeze. The three decks were trimmed in small white lights, the rising fog on the river refracting the lights so they appeared to twinkle. The boat was positioning to dock on the extreme southern end of the landing.

"What is the *Magnolia Queen* all about?"

"Oh, that's a gambling boat," he said. " It's run by the same company that owns that big casino right there, the Lucky Lady. Be careful, they will take *all* your money in a New York second."

"The same company, huh? Does it travel out on the river, then come back to dock or something?"

"Oh, no. Several big casinos on the river got together a few years ago and built four of those riverboats. They travel from casino to casino up and down the river. There's a different boat here every day. If that's the *Magnolia Queen* ...?" He leaned over and narrowed his eyes, looking out the window. "Yep, that's the *Magnolia Queen*. My eyes are getting' bad but I can tell 'cause it's got the biggest smokestacks of 'em all," he said and lit another cigarette.

"That boat will be leavin' here about midnight and then, in the morning, either the *River Queen, Mystic Queen*, or the *Lucky Queen* will be parked right where she is."

"Oh, I see. How far down river does it go?"

"That boat will take you north to Tunica, and then south all the way to New Orleans and back. But you got to stop several times between here and there, ya know, 'cause they want you to gamble some at their big casinos along the way."

"Do people spend the night on the boat?"

"I mean, you can. They got cabins that you can rent on the second and third floors, but if you're just going to the next stop, then I'd say just hop on. It's only ten dollars to the next stop and then you catch a ride on the next boat back. But I'm tellin' ya, they say there's a new boat at each stop every six hours or so, but I spent all day one time waitin' for the *Lucky Queen* to pick me up at Tunica and bring me home."

Will wiped the condensation from the window. "It looks pretty fancy. The rooms must be expensive."

"Oh, no. You can get to New Orleans real cheap, if you don't gamble. Only fifty dollars a night and the food is included, well, as long as you go into the casinos along the way."

"Do you need a reservation?"

"Oh, no. They're never completely full. I mean, I would be surprised if they were. I never heard of no one having any trouble gettin' on. Now, if you're gonna stay two weeks or somethin', then that might be a problem." He laughed and put both hands on the wheel again. "There's a different boat here every day. You just buy a ticket and tell 'em how long you'll be on the boat. The rooms are real nice."

"Where do you buy a ticket?"

"You know how they are. You got to walk all the way through the Lucky Lady and out the back door. There's a ticket booth before the ramp that goes out to the boat."

Just after passing the docking *Magnolia Queen*, the cab made a sweeping swerve to the left and began to climb a very steep road. The Bluff Road, appropriately named, rose from the river to the top of the bluff at close to a forty-five-degree angle, the steepness of the road reminiscent of a double black diamond run in Colorado. Finally at the top of the bluff, Buster turned left for another half-mile, then stopped at the entrance to a gravel driveway. A crucifix hung from his rearview mirror and Buster reached up to remove it, grasping it firmly in his calloused hands.

"This is as far as I go, young man," Buster said, his voice unsteady. "Cyrus, I don't think you need to be here. I'm telling you. I'm not the superstitious type, but there are stories that have been passed down the generations about this old house. I..."

Will saw the whites of Buster's eyes in the rearview. Buster truly believed every word that he spoke.

Will felt his pulse quicken. Narrowing his eyes, he studied the dark driveway ahead, the limbs of large oak trees soaring up and meeting in a dense canopy above, filtering out all but a few rays of the full and bright moonlight. He had come a long way, through a heart-stopping storm in a small airplane, but even more taxing on his mind was the fact that he'd left the comfort of Victoria's arms, leaving behind the most remarkable woman he had ever known. He ran his hands through his thick hair. It had come down to this, after coming all this way, he was damn sure going to give it his best effort, intending not to leave a single stone unturned, at least not tonight.

Will gripped the door handle and pulled. "Don't worry, Buster, I'll walk the rest of the way. This is something I have to do."

But before Will could place a red high-top on the gravel drive, Buster said, "Oh, hell. I'll drive you all the way. But I'm not staying a second longer than I have to."

Will smiled and closed the door.

Buster eased the cab down the winding driveway, cut into a leafy, dirt embankment, forming five-foot walls on each side. The roots of centuries-old live oaks met Will's eye level. Between gaps in the huge trunks, Will could see grassy land sprawling over undulating hills, all contained within a sun-dried, cross-hatched wooden fence. At the center of the field, three rows of flowering peach trees swayed in the gentle breeze—the orchard, he recalled from his great-grandmother's diary. His heart pounded heavily as the road twisted and turned, finally terminating at a formidable black wrought-iron gate.

Will began to see the remarkable mansion, encircled by a dozen flowering magnolias and two majestic live oaks entrenched on the sides of the house. Planted more than a century ago, by the same family that had endured war, occupation, and heartache in their quest to hang on to this serene plot of land, these trees towered over the four-story home like giant strong-limbed guardians.

"You really need to think about what you're doing. This house is possessed or something, I'm tellin' ya. Why would nobody have bought it and lived here? Yes it's got a beautiful view of the river but there's got to be a really bad reason, son."

Will got out of the car. "Look. Here's 500 dollars for bringing me out here. Pick me up in two hours and I'll give you another 500," Will said, his breath showing in the cooling night air as he handed the money to Buster.

"A thousand dollars?" Buster said and put his hand to his forehead. He exhaled. "Okay. I'll do it. But I don't want to be here any longer than I have to, so take my card and call my cell phone when you are about ready," he said, reaching into his glove box.

"No, I—I don't have a cell phone with me."

"What? No phone. Did you lose it or somethin'?"

Will paused. His phone was somewhere among the ashes in Fort Jefferson. But in fact, he had intentionally decided not to bring a phone to Vicksburg or any other device that could be tracked remotely by someone somewhere, and Tiny had not even offered to give him one. Will suspected for the same reasons.

"Yes," Will said. He had probably already said enough.

"You got a flashlight in your bag?"

Will shook his head.

"Here." Buster reached back into the glove box and handed will a flashlight. "Give it back when I come back in two hours. When you hear me coming up the driveway, you better hurry because I'm not hanging out at this old-ass spooky house waiting on you."

"Thanks," Will said.

As Buster pulled away, Will turned and made his way closer to the "old-ass spooky" house that, at one point in time, his family called home.

❧   ❧   ❧

THE WIND WAS PICKING UP off of the river and sweeping high up the face of the bluff. Will folded his arms tightly as he felt a slight chill and slowly approached the dark lifeless structure. The wind was whirling in his ears and the only other sounds were the intermittent clattering of broken window panes and rotten shutters.

He felt strange. His eyes saw an old dilapidated house that looked like a haunted mansion from any horror movie but his nose smelled sweet air infused with the aroma of azaleas and the perfume of peach pollen. His mind told him to be terrified but his racing heart somehow seemed soothed.

Slowly, he walked toward the front, with its colossal Corinthian columns. The roof extended over the front gallery and was pierced by one central round room, an observatory, he assumed, which was crowned by a maroon onion-shaped dome giving it a slight Byzantine accent. But what shocked Will was when he realized the house was fashioned in the form of a hexagon, its sturdy red brick walls placed at 120-degree angles from each other, fortressing the home on six sides.

His mind could hardly believe it. "It looks just like Fort Jefferson, the Hexagon." He had studied the secret drawing for hours and it was detailed and remarkable but only in a two-dimensional scale. He hadn't thought about it before this moment, but the sketch only illustrated the front elevation of the house. Now, seeing the massive structure in 3D, he was speechless.

The first question that crossed his mind was one of pure intrigue. Was it possible that the Dunbars had constructed Fort Jefferson? After all, Buster had told him that they were master builders, jacks of all trades. Was that the IMS connection, that somehow the Dunbars had been retained by the federal government to build the safe-house? It was far-fetched, but not illogical.

Will stood still, trying to absorb every minute detail, every structural intricacy, hoping a clue might guide him to the location of a secret room. Suddenly, a dizzying sensation overcame him. He stared blankly into space as a powerful sense of *déjà vu* swelled in his mind. The feeling gripped him so intensely that he stumbled on the porch's bottom step. Will placed his head into his hands and closed his eyes, massaging his forehead.

He must have been here before. But that wasn't possible. He'd never even been to Mississippi in his life. He must have studied the sketch for too long, concentrating on its details too intensely. Then, just as fast as it had come, the *déjà vu* left, returning him to his usual senses. He shook it off and reached his hand out to the decaying wooden porch rail for support but it snapped in half.

The moon was slightly canted out of the east as passing clouds cast shadows across the plantation, with an occasional sprinkling of starlight. Will strolled around the eastern flank of the house, close enough to the red bricks to look for even the smallest flaw. As he walked, he ran his fingers along the coarse concrete mortar, tugging an occasional brick. He stepped backward a few dozen yards and intently scanned the walls. He recited his great-grandmother's riddle in his mind again, ending with the words "an ornate mast."

The clue had to be in the word mast. A mast ... a support beam for a sail. There had to be something around the house that looked like a sail.

With no sense of what to do next, he walked to the west side of Peachtree Plantation, the breeze off the river 200 feet below brought a freshness to the air. An enormous live oak rose from the ground beside the house, its limbs almost enveloping the western wall. As Will looked high up into the tree, studying its intricacies, a flash of moonlight briefly escaped its gray confinement. The beam of light struck his eyes with unanticipated intensity, momentarily blinding him. He squeezed his eyes shut and rubbed them.

A peculiar feeling overcame him again. Dizzy, his knees wobbling, he braced himself against the rough bark of the tree trunk and his stomach tightened as a slight nausea began to roil. As Will opened his eyes, that same sense of *déjà vu* returned, but with greater intensity. He felt he had seen this view of the tree and house together, from this exact vantage point before.

Finally feeling normal again but somewhat sweaty and slightly dirty from the day's travails, he rose to his feet and walked away from the house and toward the wooden cross-hatched fence that separated the lawn from the bluff. He leaned against the fence and noticed how the earth fell away dramatically just a few feet on the other side. As he looked down from the high bluff, he could clearly see the *Magnolia Queen* and the Lucky Lady Casino.

The twilight view was spectacular. Moonlight created a mirrored silvery slick, like a layer of mercury, on the river's surface. The residue of day's end bounced off the western sky with hues of pink and orange that striped the sandy sloping banks along the river's edge. Sandbars just offshore created swirling eddies that coalesced into pink foamy froths, then faded into the dark. This dazzling view rivaled all of Will's favorite tropical destinations.

Will turned to face the house and his focus returned to the old live oak, its enormous branches brushing against the side wall.

Cradling the back of his head with his hands, he looked up into the ancient tree and deeply sighed.

As his tired eyes stared blankly up into the canopy of thick limbs, a shimmer of light glistened above, somewhere past the fluttering green leaves. Intrigued, he sidled slowly to the right, clearing from beneath the large limbs. Head cocked, he back-pedaled until he had an unobstructed view of the top of the house and the maroon dome on the very top of the observatory. The glimmering moonlight caught a three-foot staff-like rod that extended heavenward.

Will stepped back farther from the house for a better vantage point. The metal rod was unusual and intricate, more like a king's scepter. With not much daylight remaining, he scanned the scepter so intensely that it almost crossed his eyes. Then a tingling sensation of disbelief made his heart jump in his chest. On the top of the ornate iron rod, sculpted from the metal itself, was a bird of prey, a silver owl. Its feet were perched on a solid square block. The distance and lack of daylight prevented Will from deciphering the detail but he was sure that the block-like structure represented a book.

He raised both hands over his head, shaking them like a marathon runner breaking the tape. He had found what he had come here for.

"The Owl of Minerva, the crest of the IMS. This is the clue," he said, his blood pounding. "It's a mast, *the ornate mast!*"

All his years and time spent boating and fishing on the waters of Florida and the Bahamas had conditioned Will's mind to think only of a sailboat mast. "A mast! Not a sailboat mast. A mast does not have to be supportive. It's simply a vertical pole, dummy."

He focused his attention again on the dome, the long iron mast piercing it like a needle impaling a pincushion. The onion-shaped dome looked more like something that might top the Kremlin rather than any Greek Revival home in America. He tried to recall the photograph from the chest in his closet. He didn't remember seeing this odd dome on top of the house in the photograph that was dated in the late 1800s, when Julian was a child.

"It looks like a big purple Hershey's Kiss sitting up there. How did I miss that?" he laughed, shaking his head.

The truth was obvious. The dome had to be the secret room.

STANDING AT THE FRONT DOOR of Peachtree Plantation, Will clicked on the flashlight. He scanned the heavy mahogany door with the light and his eyes lit on the tarnished brass doorknocker. As he wiped away a layer of soot, his mouth went dry, and he felt as if he could not swallow. Stunned, he wiped away more dirt and held his flashlight close. The brass ring of the doorknocker was attached to a brass doorplate. Carved into the brass was an intricate design and, after seeing the motif in his dreams for days, it was now familiar. The ornament was in the sculpted shape of the IMS trinity: an owl, a book, and a metal chain.

Will exhaled nervously then pushed open the front door; it squeaked loudly and seemed to barely hang on its hinge. Slowly and cautiously he put one foot in front of the other, head on a swivel. Pushing forward through the dark, he studied the deteriorating walls of crumbling plaster and rotting wood. The air smelled damp and stale. He had taken only five steps when the first cobweb wrapped his face, sending his pulse soaring. He frantically wiped away the uncomfortable tingling remains of spider web and brandished his flashlight around the room in a panic. But his light lit nothing more of interest than crumbling walls and the intriguing interaction between a flashlight and spider web, as small rays of light pierced the darkness.

Dodging spider webs, rotten boards, and hoping not to encounter anything not of this world, he cautiously proceeded from the foyer to a spiral staircase, anxious to get to the fourth floor observatory. Hearing his own pulse in his ears, he carefully began to ascend the stairs. As he finally reached the last step before the doorway to the observatory, he paused before entering the room, listening for any sound. The house was silent. No voices from the living or dead were heard, only a smattering of rain on the shingles, some muted traffic down below the bluff, and the faint chug of a tugboat churning upriver.

The observatory was rimmed with a panorama of arched windows, encircling the room with glass. One hundred fifty years ago, this room would be a beautiful space offering stunning views of the Mississippi River. But tonight it was covered in layer of dirt and at least half of the windows were broken or cracked. The room was furnished in the manner of the Victorian era with one full size couch and one meridienne facing each other; two marble end tables were positioned in between.

Will tilted his head upward, looking for an attic door or another entrance to the dome above. Positioned exactly in the middle of the ceiling was a large circular ceramic ceiling medallion with the same inscription as on the doorknocker: the IMS trinity.

The six-foot-diameter medallion was completely oversized for this room. With his index finger, Will caressed the smooth deep grooves of the crest.

Staring up at the IMS crest on the ceiling, his mind was pushing a thousand directions. He stepped up onto the marble end table and firmly pressed his palm against the medallion. As if unscrewing a bottle cap, he tried to move it. He twisted hard several times but it would not budge. He knocked against it with an extended knuckle but it was solid, no echo to indicate space behind it. With a sense of urgency, he grabbed it with both hands and pulled.

With a crash, the entire medallion and a yard of plaster came crashing down, the dust billowing into the room and out of the broken windows.

Will lay on his back on the cold rotten floor, the medallion beside him. As he wiped the dust from his eyes, he saw the hole above him.

Will fumbled for his flashlight, pointing it toward the ceiling. The plaster and medallion had stood the test of time but was no match for a determined man on a mission. He stood up on the end table again. Will froze, startled by what he saw. As he slowly peeled away the final thin shards of plaster, a dark, circular outline appeared, a foot deep into the ceiling. Hands shaking, he shined the flashlight deeper into the hole then tapped against it, producing a clanking sound. His already tachycardic heart skipped two beats. As the light bathed the round metal disc above him, the same sculpted image that he had seen at the Library of Congress and at Fort Jefferson stared back at him. It was the etched likeness of a woman holding a Roman helmet, an exact replica of the Memory Door.

Holding the flashlight in one hand, he placed the other hand against the corrugated metal surface and half-pushed upward, but it would not move. He scanned the obstacle with his flashlight but there was no handle or keyhole—it was just some plain, heavy barrier. Holding the small flashlight tightly between his teeth now, he placed both hands, palms up, firmly against the metal and pushed hard, straining his aching muscles. Thirty persistent seconds of strain finally resulted in the smallest, ever so slight movement to whatever this was that was preventing him from entering the dome. He repositioned the old end table, placed his hands determinedly again, bracing them against the metal. Counting to three and with all of his strength, Will pushed upward, the rickety table swaying beneath him, crackling with strain. Sustaining an intensity that few could muster, he drove his arms upwards, his hands burning with pain. He heard a creaking sound, like the opening of an old treasure chest, as the heavy metal disc began to move.

Finally, the heavy obstruction lifted up and skidded to the side, the sound echoing eerily into the pitch darkness above. Without hesitation, he placed both numb hands on each side of the opening and lifted himself and backpack upwards into the blackness. Feet dangling through a three-foot-diameter hole, he paused to catch his breath.

He reached over to assess the metal obstruction, baffled by its stubbornness. It was a large cast-iron plate, resembling a six-inch-thick, three-foot-diameter manhole cover. Its sheer weight and mass had created such an airtight seal that Will could barely break it.

A manhole cover? How ingenious. A sense of lost family pride stirred inside him.

Rotating the flashlight around the stifling hot room, he narrowed his eyes as he investigated his surroundings. There was no covering on the floor, no seams or corners in the wall, no rafters or trestles, not even a ceiling, just a matte gray rounded enclosure that merged into a point ten feet above.

With the butt of his flashlight, he gently tapped the wall of the dome and a steely ping bounced from side to side, the echo seemingly lasting forever. As he looked around, there were no broken picture frames, no suitcases against the wall, no holiday decorations in storage bins, nor any other item one might expect to find in an attic. This was no ordinary storage space. In fact, nothing about it seemed old except for the stale and flat air.

Cautiously, Will stepped towards the center, until his light illuminated the only shapes in the room, a rectangular wooden table and a single wooden chair. As he swung his light across the table, it seemed to shine, glossy. He swiped a finger across the surface; it squeaked. He lifted his finger and shined the light directly at the tip. It was clean—the room remarkably void of any dust or lint.

With a sense of wonder, Will turned in a complete circle, studying the room's construction. With thick metal walls and airtight seal, the room was reminiscent of some type of bizarre time capsule. He inhaled forcefully again, trying to fill his lungs with oxygen. There was no substantive smell and it was difficult to breathe. A drop of sweat splattered on the tabletop as he leaned over it again.

An assortment of items lay on the table. Will fell back into the chair and began to analyze them. From left to right, a thick stack of white papers sat next to a small white envelope, all squared to the edges of the table and neatly arranged.

In the center stood a white pillar candle, a small cardboard pack of stick matches at its base. The entire scene looked like it had been staged in anticipation of someone's arrival. Will took a match from the pack and struck it against the flint strip of the matchbox. To his amazement, the match lit on the second strike. It did not break in half as he expected a 100-year-old match to do. He lit the candlewick. It sputtered and crackled at first until a yellow flame took hold and illuminated the table.

25

WILL STARED IN AMAZEMENT; A tall stack of papers and a small white envelope, the candle flame casting an orange glow across the table. His hands trembled and his breathing was erratic as he surveyed them. The preservation of everything seemed so remarkable. The papers were crisp and white, as if someone had placed them there only days before.

Starting in a systematic and orderly pattern, as was his nature, Will began on the far left and picked up the first paper off of the stack. He could barely hold it steady, the combination of nerves and fatigue taking their toll.

It was unbelievable. In mere moments his questions about his family tree might be answered. Pulling the candle closer, he tried to read the heading on the top page. As the soft glow lit the words, his jaw went slack as he scanned the page and read the first passage.

Stunned, he placed his elbows on the table, braced his forehead with both hands and closed his eyes tightly. "I don't understand. I—I don't know ... how?" Will opened his eyes and focused on the document again, trying to see if his eyes had played tricks on him.

The same crest that topped the old yellow document in the diary and the one that was engraved deeply into the doorknocker and ceiling medallion, the unmistakable logo of the Blood Memory Society, was embossed on the top of the page.

The document was dated September 17, 1831. It read:

The BLOOD MEMORY SOCIETY, in good faith and with honor, recognizes Robert Dunbar, born September 17, 1821, to Joseph Dunbar and Frances Smith Dunbar, as an official member. All privileges and rights offered by the United States government bestowed upon you. May the Lord help to guide your thoughts and ideas.

The signature at the bottom was President Andrew Jackson.

Will touched the signature with the tip of his finger. His hands tingled and he felt a bit faint. He was staring at Robert Dunbar's official IMS certification letter. It was signed by the president of the day, Jackson, exactly ten years after Robert's birth, certifying his great-great-grandfather as an individual with Inherited Memory. Pristinely preserved. The wording was identical to what Ross had showed him on his phone a few days ago.

Will nervously flipped to the next page in the order, dated January 23, 1832:

The BLOOD MEMORY SOCIETY, in good faith and with honor, recognizes Elizabeth Ogden, born January 23, 1822, to James Ogden and Elsa Stoddard Ogden, as an official member. All privileges and rights offered by the United States government bestowed upon you. May the Lord help to guide your thoughts and ideas.

President Andrew Jackson

The name Elizabeth Ogden was unfamiliar to him. He turned to the next page. April 14, 1851.

The BLOOD MEMORY SOCIETY, in good faith and with honor, recognizes Leonard Dunbar, born April 14, 1841, to Robert Dunbar and Elizabeth Ogden Dunbar, as an official member. All privileges and rights offered by the United States government bestowed upon you. May the Lord help to guide your thoughts and ideas.

President Millard Fillmore

Will almost choked on his dry tongue. His great-grandfather, Leonard, also had Inherited Memory? He reread the previous document. For the first time in his life, he now knew the name of his great-great-grandmother. "Elizabeth Ogden," he said aloud.

He stared into blackness above, contemplating the bizarre fact that his blood relatives, his direct ancestors, possessed Inherited Memory. He scratched his chin, the name Stoddard resonating in his mind, oddly familiar.

With a resurgence of energy, he flipped to the next page. June 3, 1852

The BLOOD MEMORY SOCIETY, in good faith and with honor, recognizes Ella Solloman, born June 3, 1842, to Gerald Solloman and Francine Kirkland Solloman, as an official member. All privileges and rights offered by the United States government bestowed upon you. May the Lord help to guide your thoughts and ideas.

President Millard Fillmore

The last name Solloman was unfamiliar but his great-grand-mother's name was Ella, so Solloman must have been her maiden name. Will shook his head in confusion and turned the page until his eyes lit on the name that paled his face completely. June 6, 1888.

The BLOOD MEMORY SOCIETY, in good faith and with honor, recognizes Julian Dunbar, born June 6, 1878, to Leonard Dunbar and Ella Solloman Dunbar, as an official member. All privileges and rights offered by the United States government bestowed upon you. May the Lord help to guide your thoughts and ideas.

President Grover Cleveland

Every single one of his paternal grandparents, both grandfathers and grandmothers, possessed Inherited Memory. The only certificate he had not seen yet was his grandmother's. Except for a constant stream of perspiration that trickled down every inch of his body, nothing on his lanky frame moved. It all felt like a fluffy and feathery dream.

In the pure silence, he snapped out of his self-induced stupor and stood. It was time to leave Peachtree Plantation. Yet, fighting an intensely inquisitive urge with every bit of strength he had remaining, he could not help himself. He reached out and flipped over one more page to see whose certificate followed Julian's, fully expecting it at this point to be his grandmother's.

It was a half sheet of paper, a handwritten note. He squinted hard as he tried to read the words. He recognized the sentences. This was the actual letter from General Sherman that his great grandmother had referenced in the diary, except the first line he had never seen. He read it twice:

Dearest Dunbar Family,
As you are members of the Blood Memory Society, we have been ordered by President Abraham Lincoln to protect

your home, property, and livestock at all cost. Liberty costs so dearly. Why must all the noblest die while the chaff of the country is left behind? War is a terrible calamity. I observed your West Point photograph on the mantle. It is my pleasure as a West Point brother to ensure that your home, your property, and your livestock will be spared.

Duty, Honor, Country
General William T. Sherman

Will shook his head in disbelief. In her diary, Ella had intentionally omitted the first line containing any reference to the Blood Memory Society.

He sat down, and again, pulled the candle closer, trying to read the next paper in the stack, trying to see the much smaller typed print on the document now before him. It was different from the others, not a Blood Memory Society certificate but some other type of document. He held the paper closer to his eyes.

The top of the first page was embossed with the seal of the United States of America and displayed a semi-glossy gold seal with a faded red ribbon. In the center was a diagram showing a schematic of some type of machine. The lettering of the body of the document was much smaller and he could not quite discern the exact wording. The bottom of the page exhibited a faint signature with a title underneath: U.S. Patent and Trademark Office, Director.

He flipped through the stack, flicking through page after page with the edge of his fingers like skimming a deck of cards. One after the other after the other, the entire stack was filled with United States patents. Laid one on top of the other, the stack measured close to a foot tall. There had to be over a hundred, Will thought. He had never actually seen an official or original patent in his life but the incredible number of patents on this table made him think about Tesla and his remarkable number of 1,600 or so patents.

Will began to chuckle like a child at the idea that his family's accomplishments could possibly rival the great inventors of all time. He couldn't wait to read them in detail, to see what magnificent inventions were detailed within. His mind was so enthralled now that he lost all sense of urgency to leave the secret room. He reached over and picked up the small envelope next to the papers, twirling it clockwise between his fingers.

It was still crisp to the touch. He opened it gently and removed a tri-folded letter from inside. He unfurled the creases and squinted to read it. The blue ink was still bright and unfaded. Will paused and examined the paper again, comparing the unspoiled condition of this letter, in its vacuum-sealed environment, to that of the yellowed and deteriorated paper in the diary. He began reading. It was dated December 16, 1928.

My Dearest Julian,
If you are reading this letter then you found the hidden note in the diary. I have built this room so that you or possibly your children would know the truth about our family. I am an old woman now and I find these things become increasingly more important. My strength is almost gone and I even find it difficult to steady this pen but I need to tell you how much I love you, for the last time.

My heart is so tattered and broken. A mother's love begins before her child is born and to lose a child is more than a mother can bear, especially when she is at fault. You were our life, our reason to live. When you left in anger on that fateful summer day in '98, with Belle at your side, we had no idea that we would never see you again. When we received word that your Belle had succumbed a few months later from the "Nervous Fever," we were devastated. You should know that Leonard searched New Orleans day and night for you for over a month.

Julian, I am writing this letter so that you will know that we realize the error of our ways. We were wrong about trying to force you to marry within the Society. We should have allowed you to marry Belle, the love of your life. We too would have loved her like a daughter. Your father was never the same after you left. He hardly slept but worked his fingers to the bone, day and night. Leonard passed away last year, his heart broken till the end.

My eyes have grown tired and I know that I have few days left before the good Lord takes me also. However, to live in the hearts of those that we love is to never die. I pray that I will see you again, my precious boy. If not here in the flesh, then in heaven where we can all be a family once again.

With all of the love in my being,
Your mother,
Ella Solloman Dunbar

Will's eyes watered as he set down the letter and rubbed his forehead.

Just as his hands touched the next page, what appeared to be a one-page genealogy with the diagram of his family tree, he heard the distinctive sound of rubber tires on gravel.

Buster.

He walked over to the edge of the manhole. The 50–something-degree night air was pleasing and refreshing as it rushed up through the hole into the stifling chamber. He lowered his body down and peered through a broken window. The flash of Buster's headlights was clearly visible on the gravel driveway.

"He came back," Will said, breathing an intense sigh of relief.

Not wanting to miss his ride and knowing Buster would not wait long, he rushed over to the table. He hurriedly attempted to place the letter and tall stack of papers into the backpack.

Only able to fit half of the patents inside, Will grimaced with frustration. His flight emotion was overtaking his patience at this moment but he could not leave the evidence on the table, the undeniable proof of the existence of the IMS open for all to see. After centuries of protecting the IMS' anonymity, involving hundreds of dedicated men and women, he was not going to be the fool who let the cat out of the bag.

Desperately, he removed all of his clothes from the backpack, firmly tapped the papers to pack them tightly together, then squeezed all the items inside and zipped the bulging backpack as much as he could. With it secured to his shoulders, he eased down through the manhole, onto the end table. But just as he was about to place one foot on the floor, he saw a flash of headlights. It was another car pulling up behind Buster's cab.

He heard the sound of men arguing and their voices escalated. Will swiftly walked across to the window. As he placed one hand on the damaged pane, he flinched at the sound of a gunshot. His stomach seemed to fall to the floor as he saw Buster's knees buckle then his body limply collapsed to the ground.

Panicked, Will scrambled down the stairs, bursting through the front door in a full sprint and out onto the lawn, his shoes becoming soiled from the splatter of numerous muddy puddles. It was raining hard now.

As he passed the enormous oak tree and reached back to examine the condition of the backpack and its contents, he felt a powerful squeeze against his chest. Someone grabbed him from behind and they were strong, really strong.

Will contorted his shoulders and hips, struggling to free himself. Fortunately, the bulging backpack prevented the assailant from being able to wrap his arms entirely around Will's body, unable to interlock his fingers. In one fluid motion, Will slung the attacker to the left and, in a simultaneous move, swung his clenched fist with a right hook, his punch landing directly into the square jaw of his attacker, knocking him out cold.

Will's first thought was that the men might have been waiting for him. But how would they know that he was here, in Vicksburg?

He didn't have time to ponder the question before another shot rang out. This time a smack hit the live oak right next to Will's shoulder. Having not the foggiest clue as to where the shot originated from, he peered at the tree, trying to catch a glance of what had barely missed his shoulder. Sticking into the trunk was a white plastic capsule with a thin needle-nosed point: a dart.

In pouring rain, he sprinted towards the crosshatched wooden fence at the edge of the bluff. Another shot, another whizzing sound over his head. Without a second of indecision, Will leaped the fence, his feet touching nothing but air until he began tumbling down the bluff, over and over, at times landing on his feet only to be violently somersaulted forward into a downward freefall. He tried to slow his descent by bracing his thighs and squatting down tight, but gravity and wet, sticky gumbo-mud were winning. Through bone-snapping branches, lacerating limbs and small scraping rocks, his limp body finally came to rest at the bottom of the bluff.

Lying in the mud, dazed and semi-conscious, Will felt his eyes getting heavy, sleepy. A shriek above the bluff awakened his groggy brain back to reality. He sat up and wiped dirt from his eyes. He was scraped and scratched, shoulder bruised, felt as if he had been beat up, but he could walk and was pretty sure that he had somehow avoided a significant injury. As he got to his feet, he heard the shriek again, closer. The squeal of car tires on pavement was coming from up on top of the Bluff Road.

Moments later, through the heavy downpour, the flash of head-lights appeared about a mile away, speeding down the steep road towards him. With his backpack still secured to his shoulders, he hobbled stiffly. Then as the car was gaining fast, Will used all the energy he could summon and sprinted towards the neon lights of the Lucky Lady, a few hundred yards away. Striding hard across the road, he looked back over his shoulder. The car was less than a football field away now.

Just as he opened the massive glass double doors to the casino, three men jumped out of a black Mercedes, and for a split second, Will's eyes met the stony, malevolent stare of the tallest of the three.

Will entered the main floor of the casino in full stride, dodging slot machines, card tables, and patrons. The incessant clanking of slots ringing in his ears, he made it through the room and out the back door into an alleyway. The narrow concrete walkway split into two directions. He turned left, towards the river, following the path between two buildings, then around the back of the casino, across a rainy field and down a flight of brick steps, passing several gamblers as he ran.

The walkway terminated in front of a small wooden green booth with a sign that read "Riverboat Gambling Cruise. Daily Departures. Stops in Tunica, Vicksburg, Natchez, Baton Rouge, and New Orleans."

Dashing underneath the protective eave of the booth, he approached the smiling, middle-aged man behind the counter just as he handed a ticket to a customer and wished him good luck. The hands on the clock behind the man read eleven-forty-six.

"I need a ticket please and a cabin," Will said, out of breath and wiping away the water from his face.

"Slow down, slow down," the ticket salesman said. "You still got about fifteen minutes till they push off and we got plenty of cabins left."

Will nodded and looked over his shoulder down the concrete path. Seeing no one, he stared back at the man again, eyes darting nervously.

"Do you even know where this boat is going, son?" the man asked.

Will hesitated, took a breath, and then offered a guess. "I was assuming it was headed south to New Orleans?"

The man raised his hands with compassion. "It is, it is. I was just making sure. People stumble out of the *Lucky Lady* all the time and get on these boats not knowing where the hell they're goin'. Most of 'em drunk but some are just plain stupid," he said with a smile, his face illuminated by the screen of a small computer in front of him. "Okay, let's see here. Yep, I got ya a nice room right here on the corner of the third floor," he said, staring at the monitor. Will's nervous energy was causing the man to proceed a little faster than he was used to.

"That will be a two-night stay, which will be a hundred dollars one way or two hundred for a round trip."

Will slapped down a one hundred dollar bill. "One way please."

He grabbed the ticket and sprinted through a white picket gate and onto the long metal gangplank that led to the *Magnolia Queen*. Reaching the end, he saw a male security guard standing under a large rain tarp waving a small black wand over the clothes of the woman in front of him as another guard, a female, searched through the tourist's small duffle bag on a table to the side.

A shot of fear breached Will's insides as he remembered that he had a pistol inside his backpack. He looked back behind him, considering walking the other way, until he began to see the shadowy silhouette of one of the men from the black Mercedes approaching through the heavy rain. He had a noticeable limp and his head was shifting from side to side, scanning the drenched field as he slowly approached the brick steps.

Will tensed, his muscles freezing in paralysis, as a loud foghorn pierced his eardrums and echoed into the night air, a ten-minute until departure warning from the *Magnolia Queen*. He had no choice. He approached the security checkpoint.

"Place your backpack on the table and hold your arms above your head, please," an enormous black security guard who could have been Tiny's brother said. Will placed the bag on the table and held his arms up as if surrendering. The female guard unzipped the wet backpack completely, and the loose dry papers wavered in the freshening breeze.

"Be careful, please, those are extremely important," Will barked.

He closed his eyes and shook his head as the wand passed over his body, certain to hear a female voice yell "Gun!" at any second.

"Okay, he's good," the officer said.

Will opened his eyes, slowly clutched the backpack that she extended to him, and nonchalantly walked onto the first deck, perplexed.

Unable to take the time to contemplate the guard's failure to find his gun, he ducked behind a supporting I-beam, keeping his gaze on the assailant, who was now slowly descending the brick steps. His body partially hidden, Will could tell the man was extremely agitated. His head was jerking hard and he was cursing, but not in English. The rant was so barely audible that Will could not place the dialect. It was raining too hard and the man was too far away. He stopped at the base of the steps, placed his hands on his hips, spat on the ground, turned, and limped back towards the casino.

Will released an anxious breath and entered the steamboat.

In the main gambling room, he counted one roulette table, two blackjack tables, no craps, and only about three dozen slots, yet it was just as annoyingly loud as the larger Lucky Lady casino, thanks to the piped-in sounds of constantly clanking jackpots. As he set the backpack down and braced his body against the wall, he reached into his pocket and pulled out the ticket.

"I guess I'm headed to New Orleans."

AS THE *MAGNOLIA QUEEN* PULLED away, the lights of Vicksburg faded into a rainy river mist. Exhausted from a combination of mental anguish and physical fatigue, Will started up a spiral metal staircase to make his way to his designated room, 3E, for the next two evenings. As he gripped the rail, he looked down at his hands and saw an assortment of scratches and abrasions covering them, the bloody striations just beginning to form a soft layer of hemostasis.

He paused on the second-floor landing under the glow of a large lantern and further evaluated his appearance. His T-shirt was soaked with sweat and had a torn collar. His cargo pants had two rips on each leg and were now more black than green. His high-tops were coated with a thick layer of gumbo-mud and small twigs, looking as if he had just walked through the middle of a Mississippi swamp.

But as he gave himself a onceover, he felt a tremendous sense of guilt and responsibility for Buster's death. There was nothing he could do about it now, but he resolved himself to the fact that he would gain justice for Buster.

"Looks like you had a hard night, my man," a thick gravelly voice said. Will looked up to see a short black man wearing a red-and-white vest and a red captain's hat with a yellow tassel on the side, briskly pulling two large roller suitcases behind him. Will tried to focus on the bellhop's name tag, but he had walked by so fast that Will couldn't read it.

"Yeah, it's been one for the ages that's for sure," Will countered, feeling his words could not have been more appropriate.

"Well, the bar is open all night if you need a drink," the man said as he placed the two suitcases at the sides of the door for room 2A. "You don't got no luggage?" he asked.

"No, sir, I'm traveling light this time."

The bellman smiled and nodded. "Name's Ramsey, if you need anything on your stay."

Will reached out and shook his hand. "Okay, Ramsey, will do." He took one step onto the staircase then turned back. "Ramsey, how long until we get to New Orleans?"

"Everything's on a six-hour schedule, sir. It's gonna take us six hours to get to Natchez. So we get there about six a.m., stay there for six hours until noon, then we're off to Baton Rouge. Takes six hours to get there, stay there six hours, then all the way to New Orleans. So we should get there about six o'clock Wednesday morning."

"Oh, I see. Well, that's easy enough to remember." Will pulled out a five-dollar bill and handed it to him. "I appreciate the help."

Continuing up the staircase towards his room, Will was ready for a bath and a new set of clothes. He was eager to get cleaned up but he also knew he needed to be as inconspicuous as possible. As he made it to the third floor, he entered a narrow, musty hallway and examined his ticket again to verify the room number. Walking forward with head down, his foot caught the edge of a lone suitcase and he fell to the ground. Embarrassed, he looked around but no one had seen him fall. Down the brown carpeted hallway, he counted at least a dozen suitcases positioned in front of ten cabin doors, five on each side of the boat. He had been on a cruise only once in his life but remembered the routine. Shortly after departure, the luggage that had been checked at the landing was delivered and left in the hallway outside the cabins, awaiting their owners.

He stood up and began to examine the androgynous suitcases, all about the same size and with no particular gender indicators like pink frilly ribbons or floral patterns. He couldn't tell which of them contained useful men's clothes and which ones might contain useless women's attire. He slowly walked the dimly lit hallway until a particular candidate drew his attention. The hard-sided suitcase was purple for the most part but several patches of black and yellow on the exterior caught his eye. As he got closer, his suspicion was confirmed as the suitcase was covered with Pittsburgh Steelers stickers and decals. Obviously a man's suitcase.

He clutched it with a snatch of the wrist and whisked it away to his cabin, only two doors down.

The cabin was a respectable size with a sliding glass door that connected to the outer third floor deck and provided a much more expensive view than the price it garnered. As his lungs filled with the first breath of cabin air, however, he smelled a twinge of mildew permeating from the linoleum floor in the small and heavily stained bathroom. The plastic lamp on the brown particle-board nightstand had a floral-themed shade but the switch was loose and almost fell off when he turned on the light. He lifted the suitcase onto a beige polyester bedcover, its ends frayed and ragged.

Anxiously fumbling through the garments with shaky hands, he opted against the Pittsburgh Steelers T-shirt autographed by Terry Bradshaw, figuring that the owner would certainly recognize it from across the deck of the boat. Instead, he chose a pair of nondescript blue jeans, a plain white crewneck T-shirt and a generic gray cable-knit sweater. The clothes were slightly small for Will's frame but he would adjust by leaving the top button of the jeans unfastened. The cable-knit sweater was a real prize though. It would certainly come in handy on chilly foggy nights along the banks of the Mississippi River. He re-latched the suitcase and hurriedly pushed it back to the rightful owner's door.

As he fell back onto the thin mattress, trying to convince his tired bones to take him into the much needed shower, the question of how the assassins knew he was in Vicksburg, at Peachtree Plantation, was burning a hole in his brain. He began retracing his steps until the image of gunfire, the flashing bursts from inside the barracks at Fort Jefferson, came to his mind.

He sat up, mouth agape. "Oh, my god. They found the diary and the sketch of Peachtree. It was lying on the desk in my room." He punched the pillow with his fist. His lips were pursed with anger, his knuckles blanching with fury. He felt like he had just been mugged.

Frustrated beyond belief, he lay back down and closed his eyes again, trying to calm his mind, to think clearly. Finally, as he rubbed his eyes and fell asleep, he dreamed only of one thing, one person, one entity, only Victoria.

The following morning, Will awoke with an ache that encompassed his entire body. His face was swollen, his back and head hurt from a number of scratches and his stomach growled from lack of breakfast. In his core, he felt baffled about everything.

How had they not found the gun in the backpack?

He reached down, picked up the backpack and removed all of the contents: certificates, patents, a crinkled letter, wad of money and a passport. But no gun. He felt around into the empty space inside, pulled the flaps apart wider and peered inside. The gun was missing. He closed his eyes, trying to recapture the frantic moments in the secret room when he removed the clothes from the backpack. He couldn't be sure, but he must have taken the gun out when he was trying to make space for the documents. It was so dark and the moments so tense, he must have left it on the table.

"Whew, that was a close one," he said with a sigh.

In the bathroom, he stared at himself in the mirror. Hair messy, face sweaty and oily, three days' growth of beard, and scabby abrasions down his arms.

"I look like a real catch."

He washed up and brushed his teeth with his finger. As he was putting on the jeans and T-shirt, he heard the sound of the calliope playing "Dixie" again. He finished dressing, slid open the glass door, and walked out on the deck, taking in a deep breath of fresh air as he leaned against the rail. The *Magnolia Queen* was securely docked now and Will watched as numerous passengers shuffled their way off the boat and over to a larger riverboat, a casino that was permanently moored next door.

The sun was bright without a cloud in the sky and Will shaded his eyes with a hand. He narrowed his gaze and surveyed a small group of shops and restaurants on the other side of a steep road that snaked down from the high bluff. He drew his brows together momentarily; the road looked exactly like the Bluff Road in Vicksburg. Out of the corner of his eye, he saw Ramsey walking the other way along the outer deck.

"Ramsey. Excuse me, Ramsey?"

Ramsey turned. "Yes, sir?"

"Where are we? That road looks just like the Bluff Road in Vicksburg."

"We're in Natchez, that road is called Silver Street and that there is what they call Natchez-Under-the-Hill." He pointed a finger toward the row of brick buildings across Silver Street. "Natchez is my home town."

"Wow, those buildings look really old."

"Oh yeah. Natchez is the oldest city on the Mississippi. They say that back in the day, it was the epicenter for cotton exporting, more so than even Vicksburg."

"Really?" Will said, somewhat surprised that the bellhop used words like epicenter and exporting. "Okay, great. Thanks, Ramsey."

The small tourist district sat at the foot of Silver Street and looked as if it was built directly into the side of a tall brown bluff. It was a charming row of old red brick buildings, some with broad wooden-planked false fronts. A rickety wooden walkway with a long hitching rail ran the entire quarter-mile length. To Will, it resembled something out of an old Western, like *Gunsmoke* or *Bonanza*, more than anything else that came to mind.

Will stood silently on the balcony, absorbing the scene while trying to sort out the treasure trove of information that was in his aching head. It seemed that every answer Will was discovering only offered up more questions. Who was Belle and what was "Nervous Fever?" When Ella wrote "succumbed to Nervous Fever," did that mean Belle had died or gone insane?

He stared down at the swirling eddies of brown water, his mind whirling just as rapidly with a thousand questions. Did the Dunbar family tree fall off of the IMS' map when Julian ran away? The bottom line was that, in the end, Julian had married and sired children with Will's grandmother, Grace, not Belle. Grace was an ordinary woman, not a Blood Mother, thus could not genetically pass along Julian's memory.

Will looked sadly at the foaming eddies with an unexpected sense of ineptness tinted with a little guilt. Guilt from the fact that he did not possess Inherited Memory thus generations, possibly centuries, of Dunbar Blood Memory had disappeared, erased with his grandfather's death.

Pieces of the puzzle were finally beginning to fit, yet there was a lot more to learn, Will felt it in his bones. He could not wait to investigate the stack of documents in his backpack. He had a true sense of purpose. He could hardly wait to tell Victoria all about it.

He stretched his aching back, raising his hands high overhead just as his stomach gave grumbles of hunger. With nothing to eat onboard except for a battery of vending machines on the first floor, he disembarked and meandered over to Natchez-Under-the-Hill. He looked up and down Silver Street. To the south, he saw a smattering of familiar tourists from the *Magnolia Queen* making their way up the long gangplank to the large casino boat, the *Shooting Star*. A flashing marquee sign in front read, "Free Buffet All Day, All You Can Eat. Our Portions Are As Generous As Our Slots." Will laughed at the lunacy of it all.

He turned his head back to the north, seeing a flapping yellow banner secured to the hitching rail in front of the last building on the right. It read, "Stiff Drinks. Hot Breakfast and Lunch. Live Blues at Night. Come Experience Classic Natchez Like It Used to Be." A wooden sign attached by two metal chains on the front porch swayed in the breeze, announcing "Under-the-Hill Saloon. Est. 1818."

Will decided to experience Classic Natchez and hopefully a decent breakfast. As he strolled along the dusty road across from the saloon, he tilted his head skyward to study the exterior of the building, fascinated by the date 1818. The 200-year-old building was composed of hand-laid red bricks and mortar, held loosely together with the tincture of time. An obligatory swinging double door formed the entrance to the saloon and Will anticipated seeing a cowboy in a pair of leather chaps and ten-gallon hat walk through the doors at any moment.

Staring up at the sign again, he again felt a tingle behind his eyes. It quickly turned into an itch but before he could rub it, the itch morphed into an oblong circle of light. The white circle radiated out into his eyes like flashing strobes, growing stronger and more intense with each pulse of his blood until Will was blinded by a dazzling white light.

Clasping his head with his hands, he fell to his knees, gravelly rocks digging deep into the thin skin of his kneecaps. His brain felt as if it was being squeezed like a sponge from the inside, collapsing in on itself, and then, it stopped.

Will removed his hands from his face and stood up, his balance unsteady. As he regained his focus on the saloon again, the surreal *déjà vu* overcame him. He dry heaved. As he wiped the thick ropy saliva from his mouth, a strange vision entered his mind. Like a dream, but clear and richly detailed, it was an image of an attractive woman. He did not recognize her face or her look, and her clothes were of another time, some bygone era. Slimly built with confident jade green eyes and ruby red lips, her reddish blonde curly hair was wrapped in a blue bandana, pin curls hanging stylishly on each side. She wore a white low-cut Henley with ivory buttons exposing a small tattoo of a red rose on her left shoulder.

"Rose?" A name was beginning to assimilate from somewhere in the depths of his memory. "Rosie ... Rowdy Rosie." Will swallowed hard and shook his head. "Rowdy Rosie Waters?" he uttered loudly with surprise.

He said it again. "Rowdy Rosie Waters? Who's that?"

He could see the vision clearly now and it seemed brilliant and alive but slightly odd, like a digitally-enhanced old movie. Will sniffed, inhaling splendid scents of rich cigars and pipe tobacco as he watched the movie in his mind. The woman's arm moved vigorously as she mixed a tall cocktail with a long, thin brass stirrer.

Another word started to form in his brain. "Reviver. Rosie's Reviver ... Rosie's Reviver? What the hell?" He shook the vision from his mind.

With all his senses returned to normal but confused and not sure if he should go to a local hospital for professional treatment or continue across the road to the saloon for a dose of self-medication, he elected the latter. He crossed the street, picked up a newspaper off the bench outside, and entered through the swinging doors.

The inside smelled of stale beer and hot biscuits. Larger than it looked from the outside, it contained a dozen four-top tables around a concrete floor, a small carpeted stage in the southeast corner and a vintage wooden bar running the entire length of one wall. A collection of Civil War memorabilia sat on a high shelf behind the bar and above a long mirror that ran from one end to the other. Will examined the antique collection; an old musket and Confederate soldier's hat, a model replica of the *Mississippi Queen*, several vintage bottles of Coca-Cola, empty jugs of corn mash and an assortment of faded black-and-white photographs gave the bar an old-fashioned feel.

Through a doorway leading to a small kitchen, he could see an undersized man with long, thinning gray hair removing a silver pan of fluffy biscuits from a gas oven.

"Be with ya in just a second," the man shouted in a hoarse voice as he basted the tops of the biscuits with melted butter.

Waiting patiently, Will was tickled at the sight of a large ship's wheel mounted on the wall behind the bar. On the edges of the wheel were the names of about twenty different types of liquor drinks, a flexible plastic arrow was mounted on a spring at the top, and a sign above the teak helm read "Shot Wheel."

He unfurled the newspaper and scanned the front page. His eyes narrowed as he read the lead story: "President Denies Terrorist Attacks after Explosions in California, Atlanta, and a National Park in Florida."

"Can I help ya?"

Slightly startled, Will looked up to see the bloodshot eyes of the bartender/cook now a foot above his own, a gold earring dangling from his left ear. Will repositioned his stance, slightly taken back. The bartender was not an inch over four feet with hands the size of a small child's, stubby arms and legs. He had an interesting square

254 / D. A. Field

face with pirate-like good looks and stood with a slanted smile atop a tall leather stool, hands braced against the top of the bar, his face a little too close in Will's opinion.

"Name's J.R." the bartender said, extending a hand across the bar.

Will shook his hand. "I'm Cyrus. Good to meet you."

"You hungry, Cyrus? Want a biscuit or a drink or both? Hell, it's almost ten o'clock. I make one hell of a Bloody Mary."

"I'll have a biscuit and a coffee. My head is still a little foggy," Will said, rubbing his eyes.

"Nothin' better than a good Bloody Mary to get you right again. You want sausage or ham?"

"No Bloody Mary but a sausage biscuit would be great."

The bartender placed a large steaming buttermilk biscuit with a sausage patty the size of a hamburger on the bar, a cup of piping hot coffee in a small foam cup right next to it. Will's mouth watered.

"May I ask you a question, J.R.?" Will asked after he pursed his lips and took a sip of coffee.

"Sure, you go right ahead, son."

"Do you make a drink called ... Rosie's Reviver?"

J.R. smiled, reached back and spun the Shot Wheel with a clicking sound. The wheel spun loudly for three or four rotations.

"Aw, almost got it," he said as he reached over and turned the wheel a few more clicks until the plastic arrow was directly over the name "Rosie's Reviver." "There, that's it," he said and turned back to face Will. "That's our specialty, the drink that put us on the map."

Will coughed, and then took another long swallow of coffee. "Who is Rosie?"

J.R. pointed to a large metal plaque on the wall. "It's all right there."

Will slowly walked over to the wall, his eyes focused laser-like in front of him. Right beside a small placard proclaiming that "The

Under-The-Hill Saloon Has Been Placed on the National Register of Historic Places as Certified by the United States Department of the Interior" was a much larger bronze plaque. His eyes lit on an eight-by-eleven-inch black-and-white photograph of an exceptionally attractive woman. Framed and well-preserved, the photo depicted the woman, hands folded and face stern, as she stood on top of the very bar that was now in front of J.R. Below the photograph, etched into the bronze, was a description.

"Rowdy Rosie Waters, possibly the most famous bartender on the Mississippi River, tended bar here at the Under-The-Hill Saloon from 1860-1897. In those days, Natchez-Under-the-Hill was the most notorious town on the River. Gunfights were commonplace, but everyone seemed to get along when Rosie was around. She kept a Colt .45 tucked tightly under the bar and legend has it that she used it on more than one occasion. This is the place where she perfected the drink that put this saloon on the map. People came here from all around to imbibe her famous concoction, Rosie's Reviver."

Will studied Rosie's face. In his vision earlier, he had seen her face in full color but in the picture her green eyes were black, her blue bandana just a dull gray.

He grabbed the newspaper and biscuit off the bar and sat at the table closest to the stage. He wiped away a small standing pool of last night's beer from the table and set the newspaper in front of him. His long legs were uncomfortably tucked under the table, so he turned his body in the chair and stretched his legs out towards the wall. As his foot brushed against the corner of the floor, he heard a plastic skidding sound across the cement floor. He looked down at the floor. Adjacent to his foot was what appeared to be a black cellular phone. He picked it up and held it in his hands for what seemed like an eternity in his mind, pondering a thought. It was a smartphone, most likely lost on the dance floor by one of the previous night's revelers. With a slight sense of foreboding and deep breath, he pressed the power button.

27

SITTING IN THE SALOON IN Natchez, Mississippi, the smartphone in Will's hand sounded with three chirps as he pressed power, and then a small green LED screen gradually lit up. His eyes brightened with the display until he looked at the upper left corner of the screen and saw that the battery life indicator was blinking red, only five percent. The phone was almost dead.

Will shook the phone in his hand nervously, debating whether he should attempt a call to Ross. With a quick press of a button, he launched the Internet browser, clicked on the Department of Defense website, scrolled down until he found Colonel Ross Chapman, National Security Advisor to the President, and clicked dial when Ross's office phone number appeared. Will's hand was shaking but his mind was twitching even faster with nerves.

One ring, two rings, three rings, four rings, voicemail. "This is Colonel Ross Chapman. Please leave me a message and I will return your call as soon as possible. If this is an emergency, please press 0 and you will be transferred to my assistant. God bless America."

Will began, his voice crackling with anxiety. "Ross, this is Will. I am in, um, let's just say that I will be in New Orleans this time tomorrow. I need to get back to Victoria ASAP. Call me at this number." He looked at the home screen on the phone. "601-555-5774." The borrowed cell phone went dead.

He scarfed down his breakfast and approached J.R. at the bar, now tending to the only other customer. "Do you have a cell phone charger?" Will asked.

"Never had a cell phone, never gonna have one," the buccaneer bartender said with a snide smile.

Will grimaced, then took two steps toward the swinging double doors.

"They might have one at the beauty shop three doors down though. Those dames are always gabbin' on their phone," J.R. said, winking at his customer.

Will entered the hair salon or, as the sign out front read, "Hair Saloon." The stylists were all dressed strangely similarly to Rosie but not a one was half as pretty. There were four large silver mirrors fronting four blue rotating chairs but only three customers seated for hairstyling. The stylist in the middle gave Will a quick smile of acknowledgment then stepped on a small hydraulic pedal to raise her client to a more ergonomic position. "We'll be right with you," she said.

Will recognized the client in the stylist's chair. Portly, with slanted bangs, she was a passenger from the *Magnolia Queen*. He looked to his left at the only other male in the shop, seated in a metal chair in a row of similar chairs along the wall, a *Southern Living* magazine lying in his lap. Will took a double-take. The man waiting on his wife wore a Pittsburgh Steelers shirt, signed on the front by Terry Bradshaw. Will's jaw muscles clenched as he acknowledged the man but the man just nodded and did not recognize Will's stolen clothes, simply returning his gaze to the magazine.

A young woman appeared from behind a curtain that separated the styling room from the break room. She was young and thin with dramatically projecting breasts that did not match her narrow frame.

"You need a haircut?" she asked. "It's okay, we take walk-ins." Her Southern accent was thick.

"Um ... do you have a cell phone charger?" Will asked.

She looked at him blankly. "What kinda phone you got?"

He held it up.

"Let me look in the drawer," she replied and began to rummage through a small drawer underneath her mirror. "Yeah, I think so. Yes. I got one right here. Now do you need a haircut?"

"Yes," Will replied with a wide smile. This would buy him time to charge his phone.

He plugged in his phone to the charger, took a seat in the blue chair, and she placed a stiff vinyl drape around his torso, securing it so tightly around his neck that he looked as if he had a double chin.

"My name's Mary. So where you from?"

"I'm Cyrus. Cyrus Burke from Florida," he answered, trying to avoid as much conversation as possible.

Mary began snipping away at his long curls. "My, oh my, you got some hair. Now, what brings you all the way to Mississippi?" Her sweet voice struck a chord.

"I came to Vicksburg to see the Peachtree Plantation and now I'm headed to New Orleans."

"Oh. Peachtree Plantation? Are you a ghost hunter or somethin'? It's haunted, right?"

"You're familiar with the plantation?" Will asked, surprised.

She giggled. "Not really but I've heard rumors. I know some things about the family that owned it though, the Dunbars. I go to college on a Dunbar Scholarship."

Will wrinkled his brow. "I heard about that. The Dunbar Scholarship pays tuition for anyone who wants to go to college around here. What's it all about?"

"Well, I go to Ole Miss. Go Rebs!" she roared, lifting the scissors dangerously close to Will's ear. "I'm just cuttin' hair during spring break to make a little extra money but I'm headed back Sunday." Mary wiped freshly cut hair off his brow. "I actually know a lot about the scholarship 'cause I'm just like that. I feel like I should know about the people who paid for my education, you know, outta respect. But, I gotta admit, I never wanted to visit Peachtree Plantation."

Will loved her accent. "So where does the money come from to fund the scholarship?"

"I'm not super-sure about this but I think that the Dunbars' son died of typhoid or something and they didn't have anybody to leave the money to, so they set up a scholarship fund."

Will's eyes grew bright but he said nothing. Julian had not died of typhoid, of that he was certain.

Mary continued to clip away and talk. "It's a sad story. Dr. Dunbar traveled all over, treating patients, and trying to develop a cure to the disease that killed his son. They say that after about three years of trying, he finally invented a cure, a vaccine. He even got a patton, is that how you say it?"

"Patent," Will responded.

"Patent—yeah, patent. Anyway, he made a lot of money off of that vaccine and all of the income from it they used to set up a scholarship fund. He must have been a wonderful man."

Will was speechless and slouched his shoulders. He was more confused now than before he walked into the Hair Saloon. Who died of typhoid? Did Julian have a brother that died of typhoid?

"You know what's funny? Some of my friends, the ones that didn't go to college, they call me Typhoid Mary because I used the Dunbar Scholarship for my education!" She laughed.

Will wiped the clippings of blonde hair from his neck and looked at her with sincerity. "First of all, you need new friends, Mary."

She batted her long fake eyelashes.

"Secondly, do you dye hair?"

ॐ ॐ ॐ

As the *Magnolia Queen* pulled away from the mud-covered bank and began to sail southward, the skyline of Natchez became fully visible from the first-floor deck of the chugging steamboat. Unlike anything along the river that Will had yet seen, an impressive array of antebellum homes lined the bluff, monumental relics of days gone by. Still confused from the information he learned from Mary the hairstylist, Will edged past several intoxicated gamblers and made his way back to the aft section of the boat. He covered his ears from the thunderous sound of the steam engine and stared at the massive red paddlewheel as it churned through the water, tossing up a thick cool layer of mist overhead. As rays of sunshine penetrated the spray at an angle, Will's face relaxed, and he smiled at the sight of a small rainbow hovering over the river.

As he watched the paddlewheel, he reflected on the remarkable amount of technology that had ensued since. He grabbed the newly charged cell phone from his pocket and checked it again. His home screen was blank, as Ross had still not returned his call. Now, somewhere halfway between Natchez and Baton Rouge, in the middle of nowhere USA, his mobile service was fading in and out. Will had noticed that as the steamboat approached small townships along the river, the phone would display a momentary spike in signal strength but would gradually fade away as they continued down river. He wrinkled his brow, wondering if he had already missed Ross' phone call during a low signal point in the trip.

As he studied the face of the phone, he noted that it now had three out of five bars displayed along the top of the screen.

Not wanting to miss this brief opportunity, he pressed redial on Ross' office number. One ring, two rings, three rings, four rings ... voicemail. Will quickly hung up. A slither of nausea swam through his stomach again but it was not from another intense episode of déjà vu this time. He was worried about his friend.

Will ran his hands through his new hair-do. Now, after Mary's handiwork, it was short and stubby with no long waves and dyed midnight black. He scratched at his slightly stinging scalp and pondered the idea of calling someone else. Concentrating intensely, he walked to the bow of the boat, up the staircase, and sat down upon a bench seat on the third deck. The mirrored surface of the river against the late afternoon sky was hypnotic and Will considered his options.

He struggled to rationalize a call to the Sea Star Marina. He thought about disguising his voice and asking for Tiny.

Too risky, he decided. If the assassins were able to figure out that he was in Vicksburg, able to poison Team X, and attack Fort Jefferson, then they were a sophisticated outfit with unlimited capabilities. They certainly could possess the technology needed to tap the phone lines and cell towers that serviced Sea Star. If anyone had been tipped off about a stolen Wildlife and Fisheries boat that was moored in the marina, although it was only there for a few hours, then it was a real possibility that the marina could be under surveillance. It was a risk he was unwilling to take.

He was becoming more and more unsettled, his mind desperate to know of Victoria's status. He scratched his scalp again then typed in "Emory School of Medicine." The website appeared. Will clicked on Department of Neurology, then on the phone number listed under Dr. Arnold Bamesberger. With each ring, he was feeling better about his decision to call Dr. B.

The fourth ring. "Hello?" a woman's voice answered.

"Yes. Hello. Is Dr. B—ahem, is Dr. Arnold Bamesberger available?"

"I'm sorry, sir, but you're breaking up. Could you repeat that?"

Will looked at his phone. One bar now. "Could I speak to Dr. Bamesberger?" he said loudly and slowly.

"One moment."

Will's legs were shaking. As he placed a hand on his knee to stop the uncontrollable tremor, he noticed a small green pamphlet on the ground under his red shoes. "Things to Do in New Orleans." He picked it up.

"Hello?"

"Dr. B?"

"Yes."

"Dr. B, this is Will Dunbar."

"Will, are you okay? Where are you?" Dr. B's voice was so loud that Will pushed the phone away from his ear.

"I'm fine. Have you heard anything about Victoria? Is she okay?"

"Will, we don't know where she is. The last thing that we heard was she was with you, that the two of you left together in a boat from Fort Jefferson. Are you not together now?"

"I was with her but we separated and now I'm desperately trying to get back to her."

"Where are you? I'll send the plane immediately to pick you up."

"I can't tell you where I am. I don't trust anyone right now and I don't know who might be listening. I was almost killed last night by some thugs and I don't think they were American."

"Will ... Will, are you there? The phone is breaking up. Can you repeat that?" Dr. B asked.

Will paused and clenched his teeth. "I said, I don't trust anybody right now."

"Will, listen to me. I will personally come on the plane and be there when you board. I'll guarantee your safety. We have to get Victoria somewhere where she can be protected. It is of the utmost importance. Do you understand?"

Will's shoulders slumped and he let out a troubled sigh. He knew Victoria was going to need the best protection that she could possibly have. He loved Tiny like a brother and trusted him to the nth degree, but Tiny had no way of knowing what he was up against. These assassins were sophisticated, not some third-world-country drug smugglers.

"I know," Will said. "Pick me up and we'll go get her but I'm not going to tell you where she is over the phone. I am on my way to ... to New Orleans."

"New Orleans? But I thought—"

"It's a long story, Dr. B. All I care about right now is Victoria's safety." He flipped open the brochure and stared at the inside cover. His eyes lit on a five-dollar discount coupon to the Audubon Park Zoo. The hours read nine a.m. to six p.m. daily.

"I'll meet you at the Audubon Park Zoo in New Orleans at nine tomorrow morning," he said.

"You got it. Audubon Park, nine a.m. I will be there. And, Will—"

"Yeah?"

"Don't call anyone else. Stay low and out of sight. Be safe!"

The phone was crackling loud, losing signal. "I will. And, Dr. B..." A broad boyish smile split Will's face. "I've learned some amazing things in the last twenty-four hours. I can't wait to tell you all about it."

ª   ª   ª

THAT EVENING, THE SCENE ALONG the riverfront in Baton Rouge was much different than those upriver at Vicksburg and Natchez. Baton Rouge had more of a big-city feel. Will sat on the bed in his cabin and pulled the white gauze curtain away from the glass door, peering out to see a gray concrete dock that led to a gray concrete riverwalk, which in turn led to another larger riverboat casino, all framed by a dull concrete downtown skyline and a cobalt sky. He wasn't much impressed.

Now somewhat relaxed and no longer pressed for time, he reread his great-grandmother's letter to Julian. One by one, he reexamined the Blood Memory Society certificates of his ancestors, including that of his grandfather Julian. He ran the tips of his fingers over the presidential signatures again, the slightest indentions of the pen still perceptive to his touch after all these years. He grabbed a beer from an iced-down bucket of beers next to his bed that he purchased from the bar. He took a long pull from the bottle as he studied the words and intricacies of the documents for close to a half-hour.

Will pulled out the one-page genealogy diagram from inside the backpack and brought it close to his face. In elegant cursive writing on the top of the page was "Dunbar Genealogy," and below, "All Names Listed Herein Are Beneficiaries of The Family Blood Memory."

Then a six-inch space. "Updated this 25th day of May 1915 by Dr. Leonard Dunbar."

He traced the line from Julian's name up the family tree to the name of Leonard then higher to Robert. He thought about what Buster had said about all of the Dunbars having attended West Point and grinned with approval, as he had no idea that West Point held such a strong family connection.

Will focused on the matriarchal name at the top of the family tree, Esther Stoddard. It was written in extremely heavy, bold capitalized letters and encased, like a modern text box, with a thick outline of ink. It was obvious that the author of the genealogy wanted this particular name to stand out. He stared at the page, the name Stoddard suddenly registering in his memory.

This was the Stoddard Stock genealogy, the genetic cluster of women, the Blood Mothers, the ubiquitin-free females with Inherited Memory who started it all. A wide smile came across his face.

"Esther Stoddard may have been the first ubiquitin-free female in history, the first American Blood Mother," Ross had said. Will sucked on the bottle of beer and shook his head. He did not think it possible that he could be amazed any more, but now, on this page, it was written, he was directly descended from the Stoddard Stock.

Esther Stoddard was his ancestor!

With his mind becoming numb from the baffling information, he placed his finger on the diagram and continued to follow it down further from the matriarch, to successive generations. He saw a litany of distinguished names littering his genealogy like a Colonial Who's Who. But the name that intrigued him the most was that of Eli Whitney.

"Get out of here. Eli Whitney?" he said loudly. "He had Blood Memory?"

He reached in the backpack and took out the stack of patents. Barely able to hold the large stack at one time, he held them up into the light and recalled a statement made by Tesla, when a reporter asked him about his remarkable number of patents. "The patent is what made the United States unique. The idea that you could invent something and own it and keep it for your own transformed the world."

He thumbed through them briskly, and again, just like the IMS certificates, all of the patents were organized in chronological order. He scanned the first one, dated August 22, 1792, with the patent number 11-X, and registered to Pierpont Edwards. Will glanced back at the genealogy diagram in the book and found Pierpont's name, a distant uncle. The patent was for a flour-milling machine. He scrolled to the bottom of the page and gasped loudly. There were three signatures, President George Washington, Attorney General Edmund Randolph, and Secretary of State Thomas Jefferson, all verifying this document as an original and no less historical patent. Will's hands were shaking as he felt the signatures with his fingers. Anxious as to what was next, he flipped the page.

His jaw dropped to the mildewed floor. The second patent was dated March 14, 1794, the patent number was 72-X, registered to Eli Whitney for a "Cotton Engine." Will held the old document up to the lamp and studied the design. He was not sure if he was more amazed by the mechanical illustration or the fact that he was holding, in his hand, the original patent for the famous "Cotton Gin."

Will was ecstatic. What else could there be? He laid the patent carefully atop the others on the bed beside him and studied the next several. Five were related to the "Cotton Engine" and were labeled, with an official United States government seal, as improvements upon the original design. Will squinted to examine each of them closer. Astoundingly, three of the "Improved Cotton Gin" patents were registered under the name Joseph Dunbar and two under Robert Dunbar.

Will felt an overwhelming sense of awe. Even more intently, he scanned each patent listed under the names Joseph and Robert Dunbar. They were dated 1815, 1817, 1819, 1829, and 1832. Will examined the mechanical design of the one from August 6, 1819. He laughed with reverence as the illustration on Robert Dunbar's patent depicted the incorporation of a steam engine into the cotton gin. The Dunbars' invention, his family's design, had transformed cotton as a crop and the American South into the world's first agricultural powerhouse.

He set down the patents and stared up at the ceiling. Slowly and methodically, like playing a game of Clue, he began to connect the links in his family's chain together in his head. He reread the title page: "All Names Listed Herein Are Beneficiaries of the Family Blood Memory."

He stared at the names. Joseph Dunbar had married Eli Whitney's daughter and because they were both brilliant, both possessing

Blood Memory, they were able to advance the functionality and efficiency of her father's cotton gin. It was only natural that the family would move from the North and settle somewhere in the South. Now with their brilliant agricultural tool, they would work the soil, make their fortune in cotton. And there was no better location than the most fertile soil in the country, the Mississippi Delta.

Will felt connected now, in the loop, the links were reconnecting. His great-grandmother's secret room had fulfilled its centuries-old obligation. His face flushed and, in a strange way, he had not felt such a connection to family since before his parents died a year ago.

Will cracked open another beer, lay back against the flimsy headboard, and began flipping through the stack of patents. He grabbed all of them with both hands and held them up, waving the impressive stack high above his head like a championship trophy. But he lost his loose grip on the patents and they tumbled to the floor. He shook his head and leaned over to pick them up, counting as he reassembled the stack together again. About halfway through the stack and on number 134, he caught a glimpse of a familiar name in the upper right corner. He held the patent up to the lamp.

Wanting more light, he reached over to turn the switch clockwise, hoping it was a three-way bulb and that the next click might be brighter. As he fumbled around under the shade, the loose plastic switch fell to the ground and the room went completely black.

"Shit," he exclaimed. He felt his way around the nightstand and grabbed the cell phone. He pressed the power button and used the light of the cell phone to illuminate the patent, the one that was somehow still secured in his wobbly hand.

The light from the phone showed the name Dr. Leonard Dunbar. Will batted his eyes and tried to focus harder. It was dated July 18, 1896, and the number was 174139-M. The next line stopped his breath.

"Purpose of Patent: Typhoid Fever Vaccine."

Mary's voice at the "Hair Saloon" echoed in his head. "Dr. Dunbar's son died of typhoid so Dr. Dunbar invented a vaccine."

Will shook his head; that sentence made no sense. Dr. Dunbar's son was Julian, his grandfather. Julian had died in his seventies. Will was familiar with typhoid fever. He learned about the awful disease in his second year of medical school. He recalled that the progression of typhoid fever was divided into four stages, with each stage lasting about one week.

He launched an Internet search again from his phone in an effort to refresh his memory. After all, he was a fertility doctor, not an infectious disease specialist. With a hunch, he typed in "Nervous Fever."

A menu of listings appeared on the web page. He clicked on "Typhoid Fever, known years ago as Nervous Fever."

He scanned the online document, the words familiar. "Delirium gives typhoid the nickname Nervous Fever."

Will dropped the patent to the ground and using the dim light of the phone, he shuffled through the maze of papers, finally placing his hand on his great-grandmother's letter. He read the sentences again, slowly.

"When we received word that your Belle had succumbed a few months later from the Nervous Fever, we were devastated. You should know that Leonard searched New Orleans day and night for you for over a month."

Will pictured the images he had seen in his Infectious Diseases textbook, recalling gruesome photographs of suffering patients in the 1800s wasting away in pain, emaciated. It was a terrible, grotesque way to die. In previous centuries, this disease was often fatal. In his textbook, he had learned that typhoid was responsible for wiping out the entire original Jamestown settlement in Virginia, killing 6,000 souls.

He put his hand on his chin. Will winced at the idea of Belle dying painfully, and only months after she ran away with the man she loved. But why did they run away? He knew. Subconsciously he had already figured it out. Yet suddenly, as if hearing a whisper in his ear, his eyes widened as Ross' voice confirmed his theory.

"It was tradition for the IMS to marry within the Society, it was just expected."

Will guzzled the last bit of beer in his bottle and reasoned that Belle was not a Blood Mother, thus not a member of the society. Another link, and possibly the most intriguing in the long chain, had just been coupled. Julian had run away because he was not allowed to marry the woman he loved. He had run off with Belle.

Will's medical mind began spinning. How would Belle have contracted such an awful disease? Leonard looked for them in New Orleans, thus he must have gained some knowledge they were living there. Having rejected the family fortune, they probably had no money. Perhaps they ended up living in squalor, in the ramshackle, poorest parts of New Orleans.

"Belle died as a result of poor sanitary conditions ... and as a result of having no money ... and as a result of the Dunbars not allowing Julian to marry her." Will sat up straight in bed, his pulse thumping, eyes wild. "Julian never returned to Peachtree because he resented his parents. He blamed them for Belle's death."

It made sense. Julian had turned his back on the family fortune, not out of principle, but out of spite. And this spite had torn out the hearts of his parents. The hairstylist had been misinformed. Neither Julian nor any other child of the Dunbars had died of typhoid. Will suspected that the entire story had been warped by a century of time until it now appeared that Julian had been the one to die. But it wasn't him. It was Belle who had died.

The pain of losing his son and his potential daughter-in-law clearly tormented Leonard's soul. After Belle's death, the doctor must set out to make it right. He made it his life's ambition to discover a vaccine for Belle's killer.

28

WILL LAY AWAKE IN THE riverboat cabin for nearly an hour before falling off to sleep, wondering about Julian and Belle, drawing a mental picture of what they must have looked like, their facial features, old-fashioned clothes. When he finally closed his eyes, he was awakened seemingly just moments later by the sound of the calliope as the *Magnolia Queen* announced her arrival.

"New Orleans," he muttered, opening reddened eyes, squinting at the sunlight pushing through the glass door.

He felt an uncomfortable weight on his chest and an awkward prickly sensation over all of his nearly naked body. He lifted his head and observed the mayhem. The genealogy book was splayed across his bare chest and hundreds of invaluable historical documents were strewn across the bed, at least a dozen of which he had used as some sort of makeshift paper blanket during the night. His head pounding from the bad combination of too many cold beers on an empty stomach, Will cleaned up the mess and stowed everything away properly in his backpack.

Strapping on his backpack, he stepped out on the walkway, the air more humid than upriver. As he peered down at the skinny dockhand securing the last of the large ropes to the dock, mooring the *Magnolia Queen* to the New Orleans Landing, he began rubbing his aching head.

As he approached, Ramsey asked with a wide smile, "How you doin' this morning, Cyrus?"

"Ugh, I drank a little too much last night, and I didn't really eat either. I'm a little hung over."

Ramsey cackled loudly and pulled out a small plastic bottle with an orange label from his shirt pocket. "You need a couple of Motrins? I always carry some around with me on this boat. People always drinkin' too much."

"Oh, thanks a lot, man," Will said, as he promptly popped four doses of ibuprofen down his throat, swallowing hard to get them down without water.

"You just hold onto that bottle, you gonna need some more out there," Ramsey said, as he pointed at downtown New Orleans.

For a city of 500,000, its impressive skyline resembled that of cities twice its size. Protecting his sensitive eyes from the bright sun, Will observed a multitude of elegant old hotels and a smattering of glass skyscrapers rising from the low-lying land, enclosing the city in a steamy womb of Old World charm and modern sophistication.

He looked across the Landing at wide, busy downtown streets. Standard yellow cabs, sleek tinted-glass sightseeing buses, and several touristic horse-drawn carriages all jockeyed for position. The relative seclusion that Will had experienced over the past week in the Dry Tortugas, the Bahamas, and along the rural banks of the Mississippi River was now replaced with bustling, big-city clamor. The delicate swish of dolphins breaking the ocean surface for a breath of air or the gentle trickle of ripples along the riverbank gave way to crass and often unnerving sounds of automobile horns and ambulance sirens.

From high on the third deck, he could already see numerous *Magnolia Queen* tourists scurrying across the gangplank where they were being corralled like a herd of cattle into shuttle buses, headed to the enormous land-based downtown casino, the biggest gambling establishment in the state.

"New Orleans is the largest city in Louisiana, right?" Will asked.

"Yep. That's what first-time tourists know it as. For people from around here, in the South, we know it as the place where you have made at least one questionable decision."

Will laughed.

"Don't be laughing now," Ramsey said with a straight face. "You'll see."

"I know, trust me. I've been here once before and it wasn't pretty."

"Oh, okay, then you know what I'm talkin' bout."

Will nodded. "Ramsey, how do I get to Audubon Park from here?"

"You not going to the casino?"

"Nah, not today."

"Oh, okay, that's smart. Audubon Park?" Ramsey thought a brief moment. "Oh, that's easy." He pointed a finger. "See that wide road right there. That's Canal Street. Just walk about five or six blocks up and jump on the streetcar that heads down St. Charles Avenue. It's a straight shot. And if you're hungry, walk a couple of blocks over to Poydras and stop over at Mother's and get yo'self a real good breakfast."

Will reached into his pocket, pulled out a 50-dollar bill and slapped it into Ramsey's roughened black hand. "Thanks for your help and thanks for the Motrin," he said, shaking the pill bottle with a rattle.

"You got it. Now, you behave, Mr. Burke," Ramsey said and walked away.

Will was surprised that Ramsey remembered his full name, but maybe that was his job.

౭ ౭ ౭

HE PURCHASED TWO SNICKERS, A bag of ruffled chips, and a
sixteen-ounce diet soda before disembarking and heading to Canal
Street. He felt a little embarrassed about not stopping to eat in one
of the world's finest culinary cities, but he didn't want to waste
time, intent on getting to the zoo as soon as he could.

A brisk springtime wind channeled down Canal Street,
funneling between the high concrete buildings like a wind tunnel.
Turning onto St. Charles Avenue, Will felt goosebumps under his
thin T-shirt. The air smelled unpleasant as a sour aroma of something like spoiled dairy swirled out of the dark narrow alleyways
leading away from the French Quarter. He wrinkled his nose
as a slight smell of horse manure also insulted his senses. In the
distance, past the branches of 300-year-old live oaks that guarded
St. Charles Avenue like an army of huge green soldiers, Will heard
the distinct clank of the streetcar as it neared.

Except for Bourbon Street, St. Charles Avenue is the most
famous street in New Orleans boasting the oldest continuously
operating street railway system in the entire world. Will paid
his buck and a quarter, climbed up three steps, nodded politely
to the overweight conductor, and boarded the candy-apple-red
streetcar. Being mindful of his cumbersome backpack, he sauntered past an eclectic mixture of individuals: clean-cut businessmen in crisp pinstripe suits, an elderly black woman with
five unruly children too small to be her own, a young man with
a grotesque number of tattoos, his girlfriend who boasted an
overabundance of body piercings, and the obligatory tourist
wearing a necklace of multi-colored plastic Mardi Gras beads
around his unshaven neck, and a T-shirt that read "Follow Me
To Pat O'Briens." Will pushed his way past the crowd to the
last brown vinyl bench seat. He slid across a six-inch gash in the
foam seat cushion to the window.

The streetcar rolled, pitching and swaying, the sound of electricity popping and crackling overhead. Will gazed out the window at the storefronts and trendy cafes lining the road.

"One Shell Square," the conductor yelled as the trolley stopped. Several businessmen got to their feet and exited the streetcar.

Will continued to peer out the window as he awaited new passengers to board and shuffle to their seats. The trolley now pushed away from the stale rankness of the French Quarter and deeper into the richly manicured parts of St. Charles Avenue. Trees of pink azalea blossoms lined the road, accented by wooden barrels planted with an assortment of springtime flowers. He looked up into the clear blue sky, closed his eyes and breathed in another deep scent, the sweet aroma of Confederate jasmine and gardenias filling his senses.

Precipitously, he felt the pain behind his eyes returning, a ringing in his ear, and then that strange and foreboding oblong of light pulsed in rapid succession against his tightly closed eyelids. He grit his teeth and forced his eyes open.

"Ahhhh," he screamed and grabbed his head in pain. As his gaze rose from his lap slowly up to his left, he noticed a young woman seated beside him.

She was lovely, and her clear, pearly eyes locked intently onto his. Will felt an eerie sense of familiarity as he studied her appearance. Soft white skin, thin red smiling lips, a small beauty mark on her right cheekbone. Her short black hair was pushed up into a pink bonnet, and two curls hung down girlishly on each side of her round face.

Will felt awkward and embarrassed for his outburst. "I'm sorry. I didn't see you sitting there," he said.

She continued to stare at him with large welcoming eyes and a pretty smile. She did not respond but simply placed her hand on Will's. He felt a rush of warmth run up his arm, oddly unalarmed by her forward gesture. Before he could utter another word, he heard a man's voice from somewhere.

"Belle, you make me so happy," the deep voice said.

The young woman giggled. "I love you, Julian," she said, staring into Will's eyes.

Will looked behind him but he was pressed against the streetcar's window. No one there. He looked back at the woman. She was closer now and squeezed his hand tighter. He felt her sweet, moist breath on his cheek. Will reached to touch her face but his hand passed through the vision, the emanation warping like tiny flecks of brilliant light around his hand.

He wasn't afraid, but instead was mesmerized with love, a glowing sense of warmth encompassing every molecule of his body.

"What should we do today? It's glorious outside," she said, her lover's gaze never leaving his.

"As you please. As long as I'm with you, Belle, I'm happy," the voice responded.

Will looked behind him one more curious time as the streetcar stopped underneath the shade of a large live oak. When he snapped his head back towards her, Belle was gone.

Will placed his head in his hands and firmly massaged his temples. His body quivered with muddled emotions. "What's going on?" he said aloud, voice shaking. "I'm losing my damn mind."

"Poydras Street, Old Charity Hospital," the driver announced.

Noticing movement from the corner of his eye, Will looked into the face of the skinny pincushioned bohemian as she stood to leave the streetcar with her tattooed boyfriend. She leaned down and regarded him with eyes of dark knowledge.

"It's okay, dude. I've been there. Just be strong. You can get through this," she said sympathetically.

Speechless, he watched as she and her boyfriend exited the trolley along with the elderly black woman and her brood. His face wrinkled in pain as the white flash of light returned. Regaining focus, he again looked out the window. He saw a young woman step down from the streetcar and awkwardly place her feet on the street. It was Belle. She was limping, slowly making her way across the road.

Will grabbed the backpack and sprang out of the streetcar and across the street. He walked behind her for several yards; her gait was labored as she seemed to be struggling to keep her balance. He closed the gap and got next to her. He began to feel as if she were actually leaning against him, the weight of her light body pushing into his for support. As he leaned forward to see her face, he gasped with revulsion. The vibrant glow he had seen just minutes before had been replaced by a pale, frail look of distress, shiny blood flowing in streams from her nose, the beauty-mark hanging like a leech from her sunken, peeling cheek.

Without even realizing it, Will held onto her, supporting her weight, certain she would fall to the ground without his assistance. Her breathing was increasingly shallow and she was drenched in a thick coat of perspiration.

Then he heard the deep voice again, coaxing her along, whispering encouragement into her ear. "We're almost there, Belle, I love you, dear. I just want you to know that I love you," the voice said. Her dry thin lips pursed and tried to reply, but she was too weak.

Will felt a wave of energy leave his body as a large gray cloud passed overhead, shading him from the bright blue sky. Just as fast as it had appeared, Belle disappeared and he was holding nothing more than thin air. As he looked ahead, about a block away he saw an enormous, vacant, and eerily Gothic-style building that covered several city blocks. The partially shattered glass sign out front read, "Charity Hospital."

Founded in 1736, Charity Hospital had served the poor and indigent of New Orleans for almost 300 years. In the early 1900s it was the second largest hospital in the country with nearly 3,000 beds and gained distinction in the decades of urban violence that followed as one of the best trauma facilities in the world for training medical students. After suffering massive damage from Hurricane Katrina in 2005, Charity Hospital never opened its doors again and remained untouched by man but continually scourged by the thick hot and humid elements of time.

Will walked closer to the darkly stained and tarnished hospital. It resembled a crumbling, dying older Empire State Building. With a host of broken windows dotting its 30 floors, its face was spotted with green tears of mildew dripping from beneath the rocky-ledged windowsills. Large cracks up and down its exterior walls burst with dense growths of flora, jutting from the scouring scars like flowering souls of the dead escaping their confines.

Walking just outside the shadows of the building's concrete overhang, near the emergency entrance, he felt the warmth of the sun on the sidewalk. Suddenly, just as before, pain and white light pierced his brain. When he regained his senses, he caught a glimpse of Belle hobbling into the entrance of the emergency room.

Will sprinted to follow. As he entered the door, his heart slapped against the side of his chest wall.

The emergency room was not dirty and stale as he'd assumed but was instead bustling with doctors and nurses dressed in white. There were more than a dozen wooden chairs in the waiting room but not nearly enough for the throngs of sick, emaciated patients lying prone on the tile floor. The sound of curdling coughs and sickly wails filled the thick air.

"I need a doctor!" a full baritone voice called out.

"Julian," Will said aloud and looked to his left. He saw Belle slumped on the floor, gasping for air, a pool of blood gathered beneath her soiled cotton clothes. Before he could lean down to offer her a hand, she disappeared.

His mouth agape, he stood up straight and observed his surroundings. He no longer heard anything other than the buzz of passing cars outside. The previous image of a busy emergency room was replaced by a grimy, abandoned space in a vacant Charity Hospital.

"Belle!" he yelled at the top of his lungs, his voice echoing through empty hallways.

He sat in the musty silence for few minutes, his brain trying to reboot reality, and then, as if something inside tugged him deeper into the hospital, he walked over to a partially open mildewed door and pressed against it. With a slight nudge, it creaked open, exposing a hallway lined with small grimy windows on each side, alternating squares of dark and light illuminating its path. Rotting ceiling tiles hung down, coated with black mold. The floor was covered in a layer of soot and small pools of water or some other fluid speckled the hallway, shimmering in the sunshine passing through dirty broken windows. Will smelled a repugnant twinge of ammonia and mud as this entire hospital seemed to be sinking into the boggy Louisiana marsh.

Frightened but curious, Will stood motionless at the doorway. Closing his eyes, he tried to recall Belle and the distinctive deep voice of Julian. He pictured her healthy face again and felt the intense emotions she pulled from deep within him, from his soul.

"From my memory," he said with bewilderment.

A flash of light struck his closed eyes and he opened them. As he looked down the hallway, the grub and mud of the deteriorating ceiling, walls, and floors was replaced with fresh paint and white shiny sterile tiles. The air now smelled disinfected. He walked forward and rounded the corner, finding himself now standing in a fully functional hospital again, an assortment of white coats, doctors and nurses scurrying from room to room. He could barely hear the doctors as they shouted orders, the sounds of agony from the hospital rooms filtering out their voices.

As he passed the first doorway on his right, he saw several patients crammed into a room no bigger than a large closet, lying side by side on two small beds. The young man's face closest to Will was covered in blood. He didn't seem to be moving or even alive and he looked exactly like the textbook picture of typhoid fever.

Will wiped the sweat from his own forehead and moisture from his eyes; the heat and the somber scene were becoming unbearable. Yet his memory led him to the last room on the left.

As he entered the hospital room, he again saw four patients lying on two beds, a wooden ceiling fan making an uncomfortable rattle, two pitchers of water and several small glasses sitting on a wooden stand between the two beds. Will brushed by several people gathered in the small room consoling their loved ones, making his way to the bed by the window. Belle lay on the edge of the bed, struggling for every breath. Will got down on his knees and looked into her eyes; the formerly beautiful pearls had turned dark and murky. Not blinking, she turned her head ever so slightly and managed to make eye contact as a new bead of blood trickled from her nose.

"Belle, my dearest Belle," Julian cried. "I cannot live without you."

Belle managed to say her last words. "Julian, I will always love you."

Will grimaced with despair and felt a stream of tears run down his face. He raised his hand to wipe the tears but felt none. He looked down at his hand: it was dry. When he looked back up at Belle, her eyes were fixed and her labored breathing had halted. The blood no longer running from her nose.

Julian's scream engulfed his ears. Will covered them from the sound but that did nothing to muffle the noise. He could also feel Julian's devastating sense of loss and he bent over, wincing in pain.

After these intensely painful moments, possibly even more taxing than his parents' funeral, Will opened his eyes and found himself curled in a fetal position. Staring up at the black mold on the ceiling, he blinked forcefully as dripping water pelted his forehead. When he picked himself up off of the floor onto his knees and leaned over, he looked at his wet clothes. He was soaked in water from a surrounding dingy puddle in an abandoned hospital room with broken windows and mildewed walls.

29

UTTERLY EXHAUSTED, WILL MADE HIS way out of Charity
Hospital and meekly rode the streetcar through the Garden District
to Audubon Park. His hair was drenched in perspiration, his camo
pants soiled with soot and his mouth dry from the intensity of the
experience. As he approached Audubon Park Zoo, his gait was
sluggish but quickly steadied at the sight of three sleek black SUVs
parked at the entrance gate.

The front door of the first car opened revealing a stocky,
white, bald-headed man in a black suit and tie, dark sunglasses,
and an earpiece with a clear coiled wire extending from his left
ear. He exited the vehicle and raised his hands outward, palms up,
motioning Will to stop.

"Is Dr. B here?" Will asked. The muscles in his thighs tensed,
ready to run at the first sign of indecision.

Without a word, the man pointed to the zoo entrance. As
he raised his arm, the suit jacket pulled to the side, exposing a
holstered pistol. The man caught Will's eyes staring at the pistol
and he quickly readjusted his jacket to cover it.

As Will entered the zoo, he breathed in the morning dew of freshly watered plants lining the narrow concrete paths. He followed the main path past a Louisiana Swamp exhibit that displayed an old wooden shack and a pirogue, an albino alligator lying lazily on a flat rock in the manmade lily-covered pond.

A few exhibits down, Dr. B was leaning against the metal railing that separated him from the chimpanzee exhibit. Without even acknowledging Will's presence, he began speaking. "Don't you think that Darwin's theory of gradualism is just brilliant?"

Will moved forward, leaned on the rail, and pondered the question, still surprised that Dr. B had not yet attempted eye contact.

Dr. B was referring to Darwin's notion that evolution proceeds in small incremental steps where profound change is the cumulative product of slow but continuous processes. Changes, mutations in DNA, accumulate over thousands or even millions of years and the overwhelming number of these snafus are usually detrimental to the species. Yet, occasionally, a mutation arises that confers an advantage that increases the ability of a particular species to thrive.

Dr. B swept his hand toward the monkey cage as if swinging a magic wand, his voice full of excitement. "Isn't it amazing that only one percent of these monkeys' DNA differs from ours? I mean, how is it that our DNA is nearly 99 percent the same as these beasts?" He shook his head with contempt as the apes swung from branch to branch in the cage. "Such a small difference in DNA accounts for such a massive difference in cognitive ability."

"You mean like the difference between us and the IMS?" Will said.

"Exactly."

"But why do you think that this Inherited Memory mutation occurred? Dr. Greenwood and I think it's just part of evolution. Do you agree? Is it somehow part of gradualism?"

"Yes. Man is still evolving, and there is no need to grow longer claws or fangs. Bigger muscles won't necessarily get you anywhere, not in today's world. Intellect will get you further these days in the mixed-up social soup we live in."

Dr. B turned his gaze towards Will and recoiled with surprise. "Will! You look awful, son. Damn, I hardly recognize you with the dark hair and a beard. You look like a hobo."

"It's been an interesting few days to say the least," Will replied as he stroked his scrappy facial hair.

"First things first," said Dr. B. "How is Victoria?"

"Like I said on the phone, we thought she was with you. I was shocked to hear that she wasn't. We have not developed any intel so far as to her whereabouts or condition. You really have her hidden well, I must say. Where is she?"

Will shook his head. "I'll tell you once we're aboard a plane. I'm not taking any chances with Victoria's life. Where is the plane anyway?"

"It will be here in an hour. Where are we going, Will? I'll need to give the pilots at least 30 minutes heads-up for the flight plan."

Will tensed his eyes and scanned the surroundings, a group of pink flamingos wading in a pool across the path catching his eye.

"It's just me, Will. Well, and those security goons out front. They don't have to know where we're going. I just need to phone the pilot." Dr. B inched closer, staring up at Will's face. "Only you, me, and the pilot will know."

Will's face was strained with tension but he remained silent.

"Will, I'm Victoria's doctor. I care about her more than anybody."

Will bowed his head, believing Dr. B's words. "Okay, I'll tell you but not until we get close to the airport."

Dr. B smiled warmly and nodded in agreement.

"Have you talked to Ross?" Will asked. "I've tried to call several times. I'm starting to get worried." Pulling the cell phone from his pocket, the screen displayed no missed calls.

"He's doing fine," said Dr. B. "I spoke to him yesterday. He arranged for this plane to pick you up and said he would meet us ... wherever it is we are going next."

Will released a deep breath. "Oh, thank god. I was beginning to think the worst. I wonder why he didn't call me back."

The loud cries of howler monkeys echoed from deep in the zoo, filling the morning air as overhead a flock of wild blackbirds noisily cawed in the canopy of limbs.

"Will, everybody is terribly worried about Victoria. You can't hide her away any longer. It's critical that she is totally secure. You cannot protect her as well as the U.S. government. You don't know what you're up against!"

"So tell me. What am I up against? Have they found out who attacked Fort Jefferson?"

Dr. B's lips curled into a tight snarl. "All signs point towards Islamic terrorists. Bastards!"

Will was confused. The men who'd chased him through the casino certainly did not look of Middle Eastern descent.

"That's what I've been told but I'm not privy to all of the classified information, you know." Dr. B placed his hand on Will's shoulder. "My goodness, look at you. What in the world have you been up to? Let's take a walk. We have time."

Dr. B gripped his shoulder tightly and they strolled down the path, deeper into the zoo. "Tell me, I'm dying to know what you found out. Why are you in New Orleans? Is Victoria here?" he said, as if for the first time he realized that Victoria could actually be that close by.

"No, no. I separated from her three days ago. I had something that I needed to do. I needed answers to some questions."

Dr. B looked him in the eyes, his forehead wrinkled. "What questions?"

"Dr. B, when I was at Fort Jefferson, I brought an old family diary with me. It was my great-grandmother's diary. Inside, I found a secret diagram. At the top of the page was the embossed logo of the Blood Memory Society," Will said, his face expressionless.

"The Owl of Minerva? Will, are you sure?"

"It gets better. I traveled to the Dunbars' plantation home in Vicksburg. I found a secret room and what I've learned since has blown my mind."

"Are you telling me that your ancestors had Inherited Memory?"

Hardly able to keep his composure, Will pulled out the documents in his backpack. "It's all right here," he said, then told a condensed version of the story of the Blood Memory Society certificates, the genealogy book, the patents, of Julian and Belle, of Belle's death from typhoid fever, and of his great-grandfather's vaccine.

The look on Dr. B's face as he shuffled through the documents said it all. "I ... I'm dumbfounded, Will. He leaned his back against the lion cage, the lion's mouth now only a foot away but he never noticed. "You are only one generation removed from Inherited Memory. Do you know what this means?" he said so softly that Will could barely hear him over the wild cackles and whoops of the zoo. "Will, I have never known anyone with Inherited Memory to desert or defect, whatever you call it, from the Blood Memory Society or the Inherited Memory Society. As far as I know, your grandfather was the first and possibly the only one."

Hearing this, Will didn't know what to make of it.

Dr. B dragged his words slowly, trying to riddle the importance of it all. "Your great-grandparents must have been devastated. Because ... because a Blood Mother typically only has one child and she wants to ensure that her child has Inherited Memory, so a Blood Mother never conceives outside of IMS. It's not an option. And the men ... the men feel obligated to pass on their memory through Blood Mothers. So they do not copulate outside of the society. If they did have such an indiscretion, that embarrassing memory could be passed on to subsequent generations. That kept them on the straight and narrow." Dr. B folded his arms as he worked out the implications in his head.

"And, Dr. B, there's one more thing. I am directly related to the Stoddard Stock."

Dr. B looked up in surprise, his face now whiter than the albino alligator's.

Will pulled out the genealogy book, flipped to the family tree, tracing the diagram up to the matriarch, Esther Stoddard.

Will knew the news had deeply affected Dr. B. The man shook his head slowly, "Esther Stoddard was the first known person with Inherited Memory. It's possible your grandfather Julian possessed the oldest known memory, probably over 400 years' worth," Dr. B said, his eyes gleaming. "You are one generation removed from possibly the oldest, most powerful memory in the world, the Stoddard memory."

Will reached down and picked up a small loose pebble, and then tossed it into the flamingos' wading pool, splashing the water with a faint plop.

Will cleared his throat and steadied his voice. "Somehow, my grandfather's memories are vividly present in my brain."

"Why do you say that?"

Will ran his hands through his hair. "Ever since I got to Peachtree Plantation in Vicksburg and especially here in New Orleans, I've been seeing these visions. They seem so real. It's like I'm experiencing some type of ultra-intense *déjà vu* or something."

Dr. B took a step closer. "Do you know what *déjà vu* is -- scientifically, medically, what it is?"

Will shook his head. "I guess I don't. What is it?"

"We have all experienced *déjà vu* in our lives. It happens at various times but I have figured out what it is, now that you unknowingly pointed the way with your discovery of ubiquitin.

Do you remember when I told you that all of the male mitochondrial DNA is destroyed by ubiquitin?"

"Yes, when we were in D.C."

"Well, I wasn't telling you the entire truth. We have been conducting a study at Emory on normal patients like you and me." Dr. B shook his head with embarrassment as he corrected himself. "Well, not like you, but people with normal memories like me."

Will felt a faint sense of awkward self-importance.

Dr. B's words drizzled on as though discussing the weather. "In our research, we have been able to detect trace amounts of male mitochondrial DNA in all of our research patients so far. You know. Normal people. We believe every person in the world has some small amount of male mitochondrial DNA in their genes and that *déjà vu* is the expression of Inherited Memory from these tiny strands of DNA. It turns on in certain situations, making the person feel they know someone or have met them before, or that they have been to a certain location before."

Dr. B paused, then asked a question. "Do you know if your father had these visions? What was his name?"

"Samuel. He used to get headaches and told me that he suffered from nightmares as a child and into his twenties but when he moved from Louisiana to Florida, the headaches and bad dreams went away. He thought it was the fresh salt air, a change of scenery or something."

Before Dr. B could respond, an enormous light bulb went on in Will's mind. "That's it. That's why he was so consumed with the Civil War and trying to find out about Julian and the Dunbars. He must have had these images in his head but didn't know what to do with them. He must have felt crazy, like I have for the last couple of days. It's like it's my memory but strangely it's not."

"And I'll tell you something else. The bright blue sky, like today, may be playing a role also. We know blue light helps memory recall. You spent a couple of days in the Blue Bunker at Fort Jefferson, didn't you?"

"Yes. So I don't have a brain tumor after all," Will said, smiling. But he could not stop thinking about his father. "The Lucky Sperm Club!"

"What on earth did you say?"

"Oh ... the Lucky Sperm Club. It's a term that my father used. He used to always tell me that I was a member of the Lucky Sperm Club. But I thought he meant—"

"Do you think he somehow figured it out?"

"Maybe. But he never told me."

"Maybe he intended to." Dr. B grabbed Will's shoulder, his face contorted with intrigue. "This is amazing. You have what I would call partial Inherited Memory, son," he said, certainty in his voice. "I have never worked with someone with partial Inherited Memory before. I need to think about this." He stared up into the dense canopy of limbs for several moments, then scratched his forehead. "Will, this is really exciting. If you were to sire a child with an ubiquitin-free female like Victoria ..." He paused again and broke eye contact.

"What? You think that it's possible that I could restore the Stoddard memory?"

"I think it's highly likely. But I just don't know for sure. We just don't have any data on anyone with partial Inherited Memory. I don't think it has ever happened before."

Will gave him a small knowing smile. "Victoria is not going to believe this."

Then the smile quickly left his face. "Why is someone trying to kill Victoria? She told me that it had to do with the Genesis Project. Do you know about that?"

Dr. B's expression hardened. "It's a bunch of bullshit, is what it is."

"What about it? Ross also mentioned it."

Dr. B knotted his hands, his tone stern. "Oh, your little friend Ross is nothing more than a politician himself."

"Politician?"

"Oh, yeah, the kind of politician that gives bullshit a bad name. It's just a bunch of space junk research. All of the fed's funding is going towards this damn thing. Hell, my last five research projects have been shelved because of it. I mean, what's more important, research that deals with human life, here on earth, or a bunch of damn tin cans floating in space? We're running out of antibiotics faster than you can shake a stick at and they don't give a rat's ass!"

"Tell me what the Genesis Project is."

Dr. B waved his hand in the air. "No, I've said enough."

Exiting the zoo, Dr. B told Will to get into the back seat of the first SUV with him. The bald-headed man with dark sunglasses drove and a man who could be his twin rode shotgun.

"I thought you told me to lie low and out of sight. This is pretty over the top, don't you think?"

"Like you said, Will, we can't take any chances. We have to ensure your and Victoria's safety."

The convoy proceeded out of the Garden District and onto I-10 towards a small private airport on the banks of Lake Ponchartrain. Will stretched back in the vehicle's comfortable cream-colored leather seat and pointed the AC vent above him directly at his face, reveling in the concentrated cool breeze.

"Where should I tell the pilot to take us?" Dr. B asked.

Feeling comfortable, the layers of tension were beginning to peel away along with his drying perspiration. "Marsh Harbour," Will said softly, eyes closed.

"The Bahamas?" Dr. B countered loudly.

Will snapped his eyes opened and pressed his finger to his lips. "Shhh."

Dr. B adjusted the volume of his voice. "Sorry. How in the world did you get all the way over there? I thought for sure that you went into Key West or at the farthest Islamorada."

"It was a long night."

Dr. B pulled out a cell phone and relayed the information to the pilot.

Will closed his eyes again and just as he was dosing off, the crackle of a cell phone awoke him. In his haze, he pulled out the phone in his pocket and checked it. It had not rung. Then he heard the security officer in the front seat answer.

"Hello?"

Will could hear the muted tinny voice of the caller coming through the phone. It did not sound English. The security goon simply answered yes five times in what hinted at broken English, then hung up. Will wrinkled his face. He was not sure if the officer actually had an accent or if his nerves were getting the better of him, only imagining a foreign accent in his mind. The word "yes" was not enough of an utterance to make a precise determination.

Intensely curious, Will leaned forward to make conversation with the man.

"Relax, Will, look we're here," Dr. B said, reaching over and gently pushing Will back, then pointing out the window at a large white sign, "Lakefront Airport."

Securing the backpack to his shoulders, Will exited the SUV and walked with Dr. B across the tarmac to the waiting jet. It wasn't the same G6 that he had ridden on a few days ago but was nevertheless a perfectly crafted piece of modern technology. He hesitated for a few moments and studied the exterior of the plane. He did not kick the wheels like he had with Gregory Albury's Cessna, but the thought of flying continued to cause stitches of edginess on his insides. He stood on the first step before boarding, admiring the glossy whiteness of the plane as it shimmered in the sun but something in his gaze stirred a hair of confusion. Will squinted his eyes and read the registration number on the tail.

Dr. B gave him a gentle nudge in the back. "Don't worry. You're in good hands. Now let's go get Victoria."

Gripping his backpack tightly, he stepped inside the plane. Eight rows of tan leather seats, two on each side of a narrow aisle greeted him. He fell back into the last seat on the right and placed his backpack on the seat next to him, closest to the window. With a firm downward tug, he closed the plastic blind covering the window. Dr. B sat in front of him and five other security officers that were part of the convoy sat in the remaining seats at the front of the plane. Will sighed as his well-cushioned seat wrapped around his exhausted body like a cozy leather glove.

He closed his eyes and began trying to sort out his tangled thoughts about the tail number, the required alphanumeric string that identifies all aircraft, reciting it in his head again. RF-47598. Will was no pilot but he had flown on countless trips with Dr. Lazarus. Since Will was a small boy, certain aeronautical concepts had absorbed like osmosis into his brain. He knew that all aircraft were required to display this information and that each country assigned a designated letter to differentiate the country of registration. Pilots used this registration number as their radio call-sign, and all American tail numbers began with N and Bahamian aircraft began with C.

Will could almost still hear Dr. Lazarus calling Marsh Harbour airport with, "This is N19699 approaching for landing."

His tired body bounced in the seat as the jet began to taxi, the power of the engine revving in his ear. The "RF" in the tail number was confusing him and as he was racking his brain to explain it when the cell phone in his left front pocket vibrated. Will reached in his pocket and snapped the phone out with a quick jerk.

It was a text message from Ross.

"Will, damn, I'm so glad to hear from you buddy. Sorry for not calling you sooner. I have been in the Tortugas trying to piece together everything that has happened. I just got back to D.C. and checked my voicemail and heard your message. That voicemail only goes to my work phone. I'm in an important meeting right now but will call you in 10 minutes. Promise."

Will clenched the phone.

He texted back.

"Man, good to hear from you. I was worried. I'm about to take off in the jet that you arranged for me and Dr. B. We're headed to get Victoria!"

The jet thundered down the runaway and lifted off from the airstrip. Will pressed his bones into the soft seat and closed his eyes as the aircraft gently swayed and rolled up to a cruising altitude of 30,000 feet. Having finally connected with Ross relieved him even more than he had thought and he was not concerned that he would not receive Ross' call in ten minutes but he would call Ross back as soon as the plane landed.

As he dozed into a light sleep, his thoughts returned to Victoria, thrilled to finally be on his way back to her. But just a few short minutes later, his short sweet dream was rudely interrupted by a loud whack, as the lavatory door to his right slammed shut. He opened his eyes and wiped them. As he stared at the labored gait of the man who had just exited the lavatory, a twinge of concern twisted his stomach. He wiped his eyes harder for better focus. As the man turned to sit, he gave a stealthy glance.

Will recognized him. There was nothing remarkable or unusual about his proportional face, just short blond hair and square jaw, and the limp. There was no doubt. This was the man who had chased him through the casino and spat on the ground in frustration.

His pulse quickened and he felt a bead of perspiration roll down from his armpits. He closed his eyes and attempted to envision the man standing on the dock as the *Magnolia Queen* was about to pull away, trying to hear the frustration in his voice again. Will shifted his thoughts to the sound of the voice on the security officer's phone. It was similar, the same dialect. He shifted his thoughts again to the guard's hidden pistol. Will recognized his weapon. He had seen that make of pistol his entire life, it was the same one that was in his father's pistol collection. It was a Russian-made Makarov. He opened his eyes with worry as he deciphered the RF on the tail number.

"Russian Federation," a voice in his head said.

He leaned forward slightly, his eyes barely peeking over the shoulder of Dr. B. A light flickered on Dr. B's lap as he concentrated intently on the screen of his smartphone, moving his finger as he scrolled through what looked like an emailed bank document.

Leaning back, Will tried to calm his brittle nerves. Why was Dr. B involved with these Russians? Hearing a hydraulic hum, he opened the blind and saw the landing gear drop down. His heart raced, his chest pounding harder with each maneuver of the aircraft. As the plane landed and began taxiing, he nervously jerked in his seat as the phone vibrated in his pocket, its signal strength returning.

It was another text from Ross, one that he had sent close to a half-hour ago but one that Will could not receive until now.

"I have not spoken to Dr. B since you and I met with him in D.C. last week. He is on the run. Get off that plane NOW and get rid of that cell phone so they cannot track you."

Will's exhaustion now turned into self-preservation. He desperately struggled to think of what to do next. Victoria's life and his own depended on whatever decisions he made in the next five minutes.

He texted back:

"Run this tail number RF-47598. We just landed. I will shake them and call you back. If I turn off location services I should be fine with the phone, right?"

Ross texted back immediately.

"NO! Every cell phone has an internal GPS. They can track you anywhere."

Will clenched his jaw. He texted back: "Okay. Ross, the killers are Russian!"

He slid the phone into the pouch on the back of the seat in front of him and leaned back.

The jet came to a stop on the tarmac and the cabin door opened.

Dr. B turned around and looked at him. "Okay, let's go. Let's get Victoria."

Will nodded politely, and grabbed his backpack. But before drawing himself fully erect, he shoved his hand deep into the seat pouch, gripped the cell phone firmly, and slid it back into the pocket of his camo pants. Walking across the tarmac, he studied Dr. B's mannerisms. His body seemed to be trembling with nervous energy. Will had thought he looked steady and confident at the zoo but now was perspiring more than he should. His eyes appeared distracted and beady.

The group of seven men easily cleared customs at the familiar Marsh Harbour private terminal without so much of an obligatory "What's your reason for your visit?" They entered the main hallway of the terminal.

Will whirled around to the group. "I need to duck into the bathroom real quick."

The goons' eyes flashed with concern as they looked at each other.

Dr. B stepped forward and pressed a thin smile from his quivering lips. "Of course. We'll wait for you right here."

Will opened the bathroom door and went inside, locking the door behind him by turning the deadbolt. Throughout his life, he had been in this restroom many times. As a child, this was often his first stop after an hour-and-a-half flight from Florida. Thus, he knew about the window high up on the wall above the toilet, leading to the street outside.

Quietly, he lowered the lid on the toilet and stretched his arm fully to unlatch the window. He pushed it open and slung his backpack through, hearing it land with a thud on the street. With a knuckle-blanching grip, he pulled himself up to the cinderblock windowsill and wriggled through. As his red high-tops hit the concrete outside, he was in full stride.

With speed and agility reminiscent of his football playing days, he dodged between several cars as he cut across the two-lane road, dashed through a huddle of tourists standing at an assortment of souvenir stands and headed south. After a fifteen-minute full sprint, his destination appeared just past a large white shell parking lot, the Sand Dollar Marina.

The Sand Dollar was a marina much smaller than the Sea Star and without the resort amenities. Located in the heart of the city congestion of Marsh Harbour, it primarily provided slips to local fisherman and those unlucky travelers with boat trouble. The Sand Dollar wasn't quaint and cute but simply a small and dirty working dock. But when it came to marine mechanic work, it could not be beat. It was known to have the most honest, skilled mechanics on the island. Will had used their services more times than he cared to recall.

As he stood under the shade of a palm tree, he scanned the marina for a target, a candidate, a boat. He knew that there was a good chance that a boat in this marina would have keys on board and would be easily accessible. It was a lazy habit for which the mechanics at the Sand Dollar were notorious.

He strolled down the wooden dock, his eyes shifting nervously back at a large building with a tin roof that sat in the middle of the parking lot, the marina workshop. Studying the small selection of boats, finally he saw a promising one. It was a small center console boat with fresh oily shoe prints on the deck, a good sign that the mechanics had recently worked on this boat.

Will confidently stepped aboard. Pretending as if he were its owner, he unlatched the facing to the upper glove-box and fumbled through an assortment of maps and charts. Nothing. He tilted the white vinyl captain's seat forward, exposing a generous storage compartment. Jackpot. Hoping he had selected a boat in which the problem had been corrected, he put the keys in the ignition. With a twist of the wrist, his ears filled with the sweet sound of four-stroke bliss as the single 115-horsepower engine purred perfectly.

Will now concentrated his attention on an older Bahamian man, a commercial fisherman whose old beat-up twenty-foot skiff was moored loosely on the outside of the last dock. Will watched as the old captain prepared his skiff for a day of fishing. With admiration of the gray-haired man's relentless perseverance, Will saw him make several long walks to and from his truck in the parking lot. With each trip, the captain carried an assortment of fishing gear, rods and reels covered in a layer of chalky salt, a snarled wad of well used tackle and rusty lures, and a large chest full of ice that must have weighed 50 pounds.

As the captain returned to his truck again, Will approached the old skiff, took out the cell phone from his pocket, made sure it was powered on, then placed it under the old captain's seat. Without hesitating, he returned to the purring center console, untied the dock lines, shoved the throttles forward and left the marina without a hitch.

"That should buy me a little time."

His newly commandeered boat blasted through the smooth glassy waters of the Sea of Abaco and into White Sound. Disregarding the "No Wake" signs posted 500 feet from the Sea Star Marina, he glided into the marina faster than was acceptable, a large wake firmly rocking the adjacent boats in their slips.

"Comin' in hot. Slow down, asshole!" a voice shouted from aboard a sailboat across the marina.

When the dock in front of Tiny's marina office came into view, Will grabbed his backpack, threw the dock lines at the young Bahamian dock worker and ran towards the marina office.

"Ta—Ta—Tiny not here, Dr. Dunbar," Eddie stuttered.

"Where is he?" Will asked, out of breath.

"I—I—I don't know. You—you—you dyed your hair."

Will hurried around the back of the office and slammed his foot down on the gas pedal of a beat-up golf cart. At the entrance to the driveway of Tiny's Oasis of the Sea, he stopped, expecting lookout guards to approach him. He looked around and strained his eyes to see into the dense tree line that fronted the yard. He had seen a guard perched in a green deer stand there just days before. No one approached or called out to him.

"Damn!" he yelled, fearing the worst. He traversed the driveway, jumped out of the cart as it was still moving forward and ran into the house.

"Victoria!" he yelled at the top of his lungs. Nothing. He called again. No response. He ran down to the beach, scanning the expanse for any sight of her. "Tiny!" His voice was absorbed by the crashing surf.

Will went back to the villa and snapped the back screen door open with a loud clatter. As he stood in bewilderment running his hands through his hair, a neatly folded piece of paper on the kitchen table came into focus. He opened it.

"Go to the Honey Hole – Tiny."

Will rubbed his eyes, incredulous. He had not thought about the Honey Hole in years. He hadn't been there since he was a boy but still remembered how to get there.

He blasted through the front door and jumped into the old golf cart. With the squeal of rubber, he bulleted down the driveway, took a right and raced to the northern end of the island.

The Honey Hole was a secret place that only he and Tiny knew about and he vividly remembered that there was a bumpy, desolate gravel road that led there. If he remembered correctly, the Leaping Lizard would be due west of the gravel road and Guana Buana just north of it. As he sped down the road, he began to make out a vivid neon-green two-story home. As he got closer, he saw an etched wooden sign on the front door displaying a professionally carved image of a large gecko.

"That's Leaping Lizard," Will exclaimed.

He looked hard to his right. Between two small ferns, he saw the remnants of the old gravel road. The golf cart bounced and lurched for over a mile until he reached the spot where high cliffs met the bright ocean. The salted mist hovered in the air, creating multicolored prisms in the afternoon heat. On the edge of the cliff stood an old coastal oak tree, its brown trunk contorted and twisted, its mangled branches looking like a web of sclerotic veins as they formed a knotted maze.

Will's eyes lit on the trunk of the tree about five feet off of the ground where an oval black opening, a hole, existed. Probably built by a squirrel or raccoon decades ago and at one point inhabited by a swarm of bees, it faced away from the sea and created a dry sanctuary from its surroundings. This secret hole in the tree had been a special place for Will and Tiny. As young boys, they'd called it the Honey Hole.

When Will was young and visited Hopetown, occasionally Tiny would be nowhere to be found, as he would be gone for days at a time, out fishing with his dad to earn money for the family. The boys were close, best friends, as much as friends can be that live 300 miles apart. When Will would arrive, if Tiny could not be found, he would immediately go to the Honey Hole. The boys invented a creative way of communicating even when they could not talk to one another. Tiny would leave local knowledge in the form of notes with instructions on where the best fishing and lobstering had been lately so Will and his dad would have a productive fishing trip. In return, Will would leave a friendly note or candy bar from the States or baseball cards of Tiny's favorite players. Every so often, Will would eagerly place his hand deep into the hole and find treasures of the sea. Sometimes, Tiny left a multicolored or unusual seashell from White Sands Bank or an awesome shark-tooth necklace made from a big mako shark.

Hoping that no new animals had created a den in their secret hiding place, he knocked firmly on the trunk next to the hole and took two steps back. He repeated the thump. With care, he slowly slid his hand inside the dark surprisingly dry abyss. He walked his fingers around the rough, splintery boundary until he finally felt a smooth, hard object.

As he extracted it and held it in front of him, Will's eyes widened further and he took a deep breath. He was holding a black cell phone with a note firmly secured via a red rubber band around it. He stretched the rubber band and removed the note written in Victoria's handwriting.

"Tuesday, 2 pm. Will, I have gone to California, flying into LAX. There is something important I must retrieve. I wanted to go alone, but Tiny insisted on coming with me. Please don't be angry. My cell number is programmed into this phone so call me as soon as you can. Tiny says this phone is digitally scrambled but can be decoded by someone if they really tried so keep communication to a minimum. Do not talk more than 30 seconds at a time. He says to be brief and 'no mushy stuff' -- his words not mine! Come to California and be with me. I miss you so much already. XOXO, Victoria."

Without hesitating, Will pressed the power button on the phone and the LED display lit up. He pressed the Contacts icon to find Victoria's number then pressed dial and stood with bated breath, his heart racing. After four rings the communication went to an un-established voicemail.

He hung up. His next call would be to Ross.

THE SUN WAS SINKING OVER Spanish Cay, sliding backwards into the western horizon as the G6 scorched upward into the sky, leaving spicules of spectacular water crystals in its icy trail. The trip of about 2,000 miles from the Bahamas to California would take only three hours, much faster than Gregory's old Cessna 180.

After trying to call Victoria several times unsuccessfully, Will's next call had been to Ross. After an initial "I'm glad you're okay" conversation, Will arranged for a pickup in the G6 at the next chain of islands only 40 miles to the north in Spanish Cay, wanting at all costs to avoid Marsh Harbour.

He sipped a Coke beside Ross and glanced frequently through the window, his palms sweating. Before leaving Tiny's villa, he had managed to sneak a quick shower and shave, which left him somewhat presentable but did little to relieve his anxiety. Ross seemed relieved to have his friend safe and back in the fold but until this moment had been totally unaware of Will's fear of flying. However, they hadn't flown together since his parents' death.

Will caught Ross' gaze as he stared down at his dirty red high-tops. "What? It's all I have," he barked with laughter. "You should have seen me yesterday. I had on camo pants and had a beard. I looked like a real redneck commando." He tugged on his clean, new beige cargo pants and green crewneck T-shirt that read "Junkanoo Festival 2014."

"I didn't say anything," Ross said, holding his hands up in surrender. "You look like you've been through the wringer, that's all."

"I don't know where to start."

"What were you doing in New Orleans anyway?"

"It's a long story but if these jokers found me in Mississippi, they can find her in California. We have to get to her fast, Ross."

Ross looked confused. He hadn't heard anything about Mississippi. "I don't know what the hell you're talking about but as soon as you find out where she is, I'll have them pick her up. She'll be fine."

"Ross, look, I trust you and I trust Tiny, but that's it. When we get to California, I just want you and me to go to her. No one else."

"Will, don't worry—"

"I'm not telling you where she is unless you promise we will be on our own."

Ross gave a quick scowl, then forced his lips into a smile. "Okay. Just me and you."

Will relaxed and leaned back in his seat.

"Now, when did Victoria fly out of the Bahamas?" Ross asked.

"I'm not sure but I suspect sometime yesterday or possibly last night. Damn, it's been a whirlwind. What day is it anyway?"

"It's Wednesday."

"Oh, yeah, Wednesday. She left me a note and Tiny left me this phone." He pulled out a badly beat-up, flip-style cell phone. A small strip of gray duct tape encircled the bottom third of the phone and held together the battery compartment. He gave it to Ross.

"Tiny? That huge guy that I met that time?"

"Yep. Big ol' Tiny. He's with Victoria right now."

Ross' eyes widened with concern.

"Don't worry. I can't think of anybody I would rather have protecting her right now."

Ross didn't look convinced.

Will handed him a piece of paper. "Here's the note Victoria left me. It's dated yesterday at two p.m."

Ross grabbed the note but first examined the phone like a true detective, unraveling the tape to inspect every inch of the battery compartment and its internal guts. Finding no tracking device, he read the note slowly, then his eyes crept up from the page. Will sensed the tone of the lovers' words were resonating in his head.

Ross tried to look Will in the eyes but Will refused to accept his gaze.

"You did not?" Ross said. He was not smiling.

"No, no. We just went swimming at Fort Jefferson and had some fun on the beach and stuff." Will blushed and continued staring out the window.

"Will, tell me you didn't."

"We just kissed a little, that's all."

Ross shook his head in disgust and began to piece the phone back together. "Damn it, Will."

"What the hell is going on, Ross? Are the Russians involved?"

Ross stopped his busy work with the phone. "Yes. The computer geek on Team X, Timmy Mahoney, saw the face of one of the assassins at JPL. Through CIA files, he was then able to follow the electronic breadcrumbs and piece it all together for us. It seems the killers are from Serbia, hired by the Russians to prevent the Genesis Project from getting off the ground. There were eight of them, but the marshals may have killed a couple of them at Fort Jefferson. We didn't recover any bodies but Rocky saw them drag at least one or two onto the getaway boat."

Will's eyes widened with concern. "Did all of the marshals make it?"

"We lost Double-D, Tex, and Viper." His voice was rigid. "They were asleep in the barracks when it was attacked. Rocky did survive though."

Will was afraid to ask his next question. "What about Dr. Greenwood and the Blue Bunker?"

To his surprise, a smile crossed Ross' face. "The Memory Door was impenetrable. Everything and everybody inside survived."

Will gave a thumbs-up. "Besides Team X, were there any attempts on the lives of other IMS members, you know, the artsy crowd, the Juilliards?"

"Fortunately not. We've secured everyone at different locations around the country. Once the fort was attacked, we changed our plan. It now appears that only Team X was the target the whole time."

Will nodded. "That's good news. We just need to round up Victoria, get her safe, then you guys need to find these Serbian bastards."

Ross agreed. "That's true, but there's more." Leaning forward, he reached down to pick up a leather briefcase. He turned the dials of the gold combination lock and the case clicked open. Will leaned in close. In the briefcase were several large color photographs of two men standing on a gravel road in what appeared to be a vacant lot. Obviously images taken at nighttime from a vantage point high above, the first picture showed a long wooden pier stretching across the entire background. One of the men was tall and thin, dressed in a long brown trench coat, his skin intensely white and glowing from the reflection of an orange sodium vapor street lamp just above him.

"Do you recognize him?" Ross asked. "Was he on your flight with Dr. B?"

Will studied the man's face. The odd-looking, stark-white man was standing in front of a black SUV with his finger pointed directly at the face of the other man in the photograph.

"No . . ." Will's eyes scanned the man's ghostly face again. "Wait, yes. I have seen this guy. I stared him directly in the eyes at the deli in Key West. He's the same dude I saw just before I ran through the casino too."

The other man, wearing a dark shirt and dark trousers, was holding his hands up, as in disagreement, and his back was directly to the camera, face indiscernible. Will reached into the briefcase and picked up a second photograph. In this one, the albino man got into the backseat of the SUV as the other man walked away, his face now clearly visible.

"Dr. B," Will said, pointing at the photograph.

"Yes. That picture was taken 48 hours ago by a DEA security camera at a wharf in Virginia. The man getting into the SUV is the ringleader of the assassins. His name is Igor Milosevic." As Will looked even more closely at both pictures, Ross continued, "Milosevic is wanted for war crimes, like rape and ethnic cleansing, from the Yugoslavian conflict. He's the leader of this Russian-sponsored renegade group. He was instrumental in planning the raid on Fort Jefferson and he masterminded the murders of Team X and the bombing of the NFC."

"But why is Dr. B standing there with him? How is he involved?"

Ross pulled out a bank document. "Timmy was able to trace an account in the name of Joe Emory to the Depository Bank of Zurich."

Will held up the document. "Joe Emory? Wait, I've seen this before. Dr. B was looking at something just like this on his phone on the plane."

"Joe Emory is his alias."

"You kidding me?" Will's eyes glowed with rage as he saw a 50 million dollar payment to the name Joe Emory.

"That's not the worst part," Ross said as he closed the briefcase and locked it shut. "Timmy accessed an email account under the

name Joe Emory on the Emory University server. He uncovered
conversations between Dr. B and Igor. It turns out that Dr. B was
the one to initially contact the Russians offering to expose the
Genesis Project and provide a list of Team X members names for
the 50 million."

Will's response was a shocked stare.

"Yep. The Russians countered his offer with another fifty
million if he allowed them access into the NFC to destroy the
samples, the full payment to be made once all samples were
destroyed and all Team X members were verified dead."

"That son of a bitch!" Will bit his lip, his eyes blazing. "You
know what else? Dr. B called Victoria the morning of the attack.
I was sitting right next to her. He called and acted like he was
worried about her but—"

Ross interrupted, a light glinting in his eyes. "But he was calling
to find out where she was. That asshole wanted to make sure she
was at Fort Jefferson, then he informed Igor and his group." He
cursed loudly. "I can't believe he sold out his country for money."

Will stared expressionlessly at the floor for a few moments. "I
don't think it was just about money. I think he assumed if Team
X was taken out then some of his research projects would finally
get funded."

With a look of disgust, Ross leaned his seat back and stared
past Will at the oval window. Vapor trails created orange and pink
vortices on the trailing edge of the plane's wing.

Finally Ross spoke up. "What were you doing in Mississippi
and Louisiana, and how did the assassins know you were there?"

Will retold the entire story in depth, recounting a detailed
description of the document in the diary, his trip to Mississippi
with the bevy of information about his family that was hidden
away in a secret room, and his frenzied escape from Peachtree
Plantation when tranquilizing darts whizzed over his head. But
he intentionally omitted any reference to his intense episodes

of *déjà vu* or the possibility that he possessed partial Inherited Memory.

"What are you saying, Will?" Ross's words were slow and crisp. "Are you telling me that your grandparents were Blood Memory Society?"

"Yes."

Ross stood up and paced the aisle. "The Dunbar family from a century ago? The doctor who developed the typhoid vaccine? That's your family?"

Will guzzled the last of his soft drink. His wary eyes looked directly into his friend's. "Yes. That's my family."

Ross sat down, his fingers nervously tapping on the rosewood hand rest. "But it can't be. They didn't have a child. They were one of many, many Inherited Memory couples that never bore a baby and—"

Will cut him off. "It's complicated. What I want to know now is why would the Russians be a part of this? Why are they trying to kill our IMS? What is this Genesis Project all about?"

Ross seemed to catch the annoyance in Will's tone and stopped tapping. The air conditioning vent above was blowing hard so he reached up and closed it with a twist.

"The name Genesis Project is a reference to the biblical passage Genesis 1:3. The verse that reads, 'And God said, let there be light.' The entire project is about bringing light to the world, eternal light. An endless supply of light in the form of ... electricity."

"Go on."

"The goal of the Genesis Project is to harness solar energy and convert it into electricity."

Will shrugged. "What's new about that? We've been doing that for years."

"Not like this. I'm talking about collecting solar energy from orbiting satellites in space, converting it into microwaves, and transmitting it in the form of electricity back to Earth, providing an endless stream of energy."

He explained that for the last five years the government had been working on the Genesis Project and that the costs were so enormous that all major NASA programs, including the Space Shuttle Program, were discontinued or put on hold, scuttled in its fiscal wake. Close to fifteen billion annually was being funneled to Team X in an attempt to perfect the capture of solar energy from the sun, in the vacuum of space, and convert it into an infinite and clean supply of energy on Earth.

It was the ultimate green project. No more fossil fuels to smog up the skies, no more greenhouse gas emissions, no more nuclear power plant accidents or hydroelectric dam disasters.

"Why space?" asked Will. "Couldn't you do the same thing on the Earth's surface?"

"In space, there are no clouds, no atmosphere, no nighttime. Immense amounts of solar energy can be collected 24 hours a day, seven days a week, and from what I'm told, there's a billion times more solar output available in space than what we could possibly receive on Earth."

"So what's been the problem with accomplishing it?"

"The ability to beam the captured energy from space to Earth. But that's the only issue. The solar technology is no different than it's ever been. There's no difficulty placing satellites in orbit. That's the easy part. We even know how to store the solar power in batteries. It's ready. That part is perfected. In fact, the government has already built a massive electrical receiver at Cape Canaveral, an enormous battery they call a rectenna. Eventually, once the Genesis Project is up and running, there will be huge battery complexes in all major hubs from Maine to Oregon. Wherever there is a major power grid, there will be a rectenna."

"Is that why Victoria was in Canaveral? To fix a problem with the, uh, the rectenna?"

"Yes. The day before the Genesis Project was to go live, there was a problem. I don't understand it all exactly but what I'm told is that there is a pilot laser that is used to help guide the transmitting laser to Earth. To give it the right direction, like an aiming beam to find the target, I guess. Anyway, there was an issue with the pilot laser and she was flown to Canaveral to fix it, which I'm told she did."

"Transmitting laser. They're using a laser from space to transmit solar energy?"

"Yes. The limiting factor has always been the ability to efficiently transfer the energy to Earth. Back in the 1970s, they tried a lot of times but they never could deliver enough energy from the panels because millions of photons of energy escaped during the process. I think they said that less than one percent of the solar energy actually made it to Earth. Very inefficient, it didn't yield enough electricity to justify the cost. But now, finally, a new technology has been invented—well, invented may be the wrong term. An old technology has finally been perfected—"

"The death ray." Will was in shock, his eyes as big as flying saucers.

"Bingo. The origins of this technology began with Nikola Tesla's brainchild."

"Tesla? Why didn't you—"

"I wanted to tell you, buddy, when you asked me about Tesla, but I couldn't. The material is classified. It was out of my hands, man. I didn't expect us to be here right now, in this situation. But you have a right to know now."

Ross turned and looked directly at Will. "The death ray technology established the basic physics and mathematical computations that were needed. But it took you-know-who to turn it into a reality."

Will grabbed his shoulder. "Victoria and her parents were responsible for perfecting Tesla's death ray?"

"Bingo again. About five years ago, the Van Burens stumbled across Tesla's creation and were amazed at its potential. The government had been trying for decades to perfect Tesla's technology but only for military reasons. The Van Burens demonstrated that it could be used to transfer solar power from space without losing more than one percent of the energy that was harnessed in the solar panels."

"It's 99 percent efficient?"

"Yes. The entire project was coming to a crescendo at Team X Mission Control Center. All the previous tests were promising. The solar arrays were built and positioned in orbit flawlessly. The huge rectenna was constructed and stationed at Canaveral without incident. The only thing left was to fire up the Van Burens laser from space. It was about to happen for the first time but then— well, you know what happened."

"Why would the Russians not embrace this technology?"

Sweat was building on Ross' forehead so he reached up and opened the air vent. "If the Genesis Project succeeds, it'll turn the entire world economy on its ear. There will never be a need for fossil fuels again. And this will particularly hurt Russia because of how they changed their economy after the Cold War."

"I don't know anything about that. What did they do?"

Ross outlined how the Russian economy was essentially gutted after the Cold War.

Around 2000, the Russians reinvented themselves as exporters of natural resources, particularly fossil fuels. By de-emphasizing industrial development and reemphasizing raw materials, they took a different path, one more common to countries in the developing world. Given the unexpected rise in energy prices, this move not only saved the Russian economy but strengthened it to the point where the nation could finally afford to drive its own selective re-industrialization. In an energy-hungry world, Russia's fuel availability was like heroin, it addicted countries once they started using it. This gave Russia leverage in the international system but without the craving for its fossil fuels, Russia was certain to sink back into the stagnant abyss from which it had just emerged, becoming a country with an extreme case of detox."

"Wouldn't countries in the Middle East also want to have the Genesis Project destroyed?"

"I'm sure they would, if they knew about it. That was our initial thought and may have been why we missed the Russian connection originally. Everybody was looking towards the idea that it was terrorists from countries like Iran or Saudi Arabia and such. Fortunately, Timmy put it all together for us."

"Did our president call the Russian president?"

"Yes and as expected, they denied all allegations, saying they never heard of Igor Milosevic or Team X or the NFC."

"But what about the NFC? Why bomb the NFC?"

"Dr. B wanted Team X gone and so did the Russians but for 50 million more, they bribed Dr. B to allow them access to the NFC. I think it's safe to say that he supplied the credentials and documents needed for the assassin to enter the building. At that point, it was a piece of cake to bomb the NFC and effectively destroy America's ability to repopulate its IMS."

"Damn it, man," Will said, the muscles in his jaw tense.

"And we know that Dr. B moved his research out of the NFC to his lab at Emory two months before the bombing."

"Where is that son of a bitch? Did you put a bullet in him yet?"

"He's on the run. He left the Bahamas last night and we tracked him to Arkansas but before we could get to him, his phone went dead and we lost him."

Will stared out of his window, anxious to get on the ground and call Victoria.

❧ ❧ ❧

THE G6 LANDED SMOOTHLY AND began to taxi to the gate. But before Will was able to press dial on his cell phone to call Victoria, Ross' phone rang.

"This is Colonel Chapman," Ross said, putting the phone on speaker.

"Igor is at Victoria's house," Timmy said frantically. "The Serbians are at Victoria's house right now."

Ross' head spun around. "Wait. How do you know that?"

"I used the computer program that I designed, EINSTEIN, to tap Dr. B's phone. Sure as hell, he got a phone call from Igor. Then I used EINSTEIN to lock in on Igor's phone. I'm tracking his location on my GPS right now."

"How did you—?"

"Do not let Victoria go to her house in Malibu," Timmy shouted over the phone.

Will's stomach dropped.

Ross quickly hung up. "Do you know if Victoria was going to her house?"

Will felt sheer terror. "All I know is what you know, what the note said." He hesitated no longer, picking up the beat-up cell phone and pressing dial.

ON THE SECOND RING SHE answered. "Hello. Will?"

"Victoria, where are you?"

"Will, it's so good to hear your voice. I'm laying low in the passenger seat of a rental car across from my house. We just got here."

"You need to get out of there. Whatever you do, do not go inside your house."

"But there's something that I have to get. Very important. It's about the Genesis Project."

"Timmy Mahoney is tracking the killers. He says they're at your house right now. Where's Tiny?"

Will heard Victoria's breath catch. "You talked to Timmy? Is he okay?"

"He's fine. Now where is Tiny?"

"He just got out of the car, doing recon. He insisted on checking out the place before I went inside. He told me to wait here."

"Okay. What kind of car are you in?"

"It's a blue Toyota Camry."

"Stay there. Don't move. We're on our way."

꒰ ꒱ ꒰

WILL'S HEAD THRUST BACKWARD AS Ross stamped on the gas pedal of the government-issued Lincoln Town Car from LAX. They headed west toward the Pacific Coast Highway, running red lights along the way. After a 30 minute wild ride, Victoria's rental car came into view about 300 yards away. Will motioned Ross to pull over.

Ross reached under his seat and handed Will a pistol as Will jumped out of the car and made his way to the Camry, opening the vehicle's rear passenger door and sliding inside.

"Will!" Victoria turned her body toward him, gripped the sides of his head and planted a kiss squarely on his lips.

Will held her tight and looked into her eyes. "God, I missed you."

"Me too," she said. "It's been four days. I was worried sick."

Will scanned the vicinity. "Which one is your house?"

Victoria pointed across the Pacific Coast Highway to an enormous house about a quarter of a mile away.

"Nice digs," Will said. "Tiny come back yet?"

Victoria resumed her posture in the passenger seat, fully reclined and barely able to see over the dash. She wore a dark long-sleeved T-shirt, pink polyester gym shorts that seemed two sizes too small, revealing the outline of her green panties, and a pair of stiff new tennis shoes. "No, not yet." She held up her cell phone, the timer function was running, counting down from 60 minutes. "He said if he wasn't back in an hour, he wanted me to drive away." She looked at the screen of her cell phone. "He's got...eighteen minutes."

"What's so important that you have to go inside your house right now?"

Victoria flashed her eyes at Will. "I broke the law. None of the data regarding the Genesis Project was ever supposed to leave

JPL. But I noticed over the last few months that the security had become very lax, so I saved data and kept it out of there." She bit her fingernail.

"Victoria? You could go to jail for that."

"What was I supposed to do -- just let somebody walk in there and steal everything? This is my life's work. This was my..." She paused and took a deep breath. "This was my parents' life work."

Will leaned up and kissed her cheek.

"Here. Look at this." Victoria held up her phone again.

"What am I looking for?"

"It's the security cameras at my house."

Victoria had not been sitting idly. She had used her smartphone's Internet capabilities to access her home security account. Will watched as she used the very technology she was instrumental in creating. She entered a password and accessed multiple security cameras positioned on her property. With a swipe of her finger, she disarmed her home alarm and unlocked the rear sliding glass door.

She handed the phone to Will. He looked through the car windows again to survey the surroundings. Seeing no one on her property, he shaded the phone from the glaring California sun, held his breath and studied the images. Seeing no evidence that anyone was on the lawn or inside the house, he felt a small, stressful weight roll off his shoulder. His breathing steadied.

"I've been watching for a half hour now," Victoria said. "No one is inside."

Tiny suddenly opened the door and his massive frame barrel-rolled into the driver seat of the small car, lowering the car a full six inches. His head was streaming with perspiration that ran down the collar of his gray cotton hoodie. He was breathing heavily.

"What the...where did you come from, brotha?" Tiny said and reached back to grab Will's shoulder.

"Just flew in. You guys were gone from Hopetown when I got there."

"Look, you know I've always been a sucka for the ladies," Tiny said, flashing his distinctive smile.

Will couldn't be mad at him if he tried. "Where you been? What's it look like?"

Tiny frowned. "I count three men," he said, eyes rigid with determination.

Victoria nervously swallowed.

"You see that do-it-yourself carwash just up the road?" Tiny pointed to a four-bay, green cinderblock self-pay carwash with two vacuum machines positioned on each end of the black asphalt parking lot. "There are two men pretending to vacuum their car."

"How do you know that?" Victoria asked.

Will and Victoria stared hard at the men dressed in dark clothes. Will saw anger build behind her eyes. "Those could be the men who killed my parents," she said as the muscles of her jaw tensed.

"There is also one man on da beach behind your house. He's sitting on a towel with an earpiece in his left ear but he's not listening to da radio, I assure you."

Will did not question Tiny's assessment one iota. He knew that over the past two to three years, Tiny had become very proficient in covert tactics and although he had no formal training, the big Bahamian with an alligator smile had an uncanny sense of street smarts.

"Now, where in da house would I find this information that you need? Is it on a computer or are there papers in a drawer somewhere?" Tiny asked, wiping the sweat from his forehead with the sleeve of his hoodie. His sweatpants matched his hoodie in color and he wore size sixteen running shoes, the soles of which were worn through to his white socks.

"It's not in the house," she said, grinning. "It's in there." She pointed at her dark green Range Rover parked in her driveway.

Tiny looked at the vehicle then back at Victoria, his mouth

agape. "You're telling me dat dis super-important, world-changing information is just sitting in your car?"

"It's tucked away nicely. I had a 12-disc CD player installed in my car. I saved all of the data regarding the Genesis Project on discs and stored them in the CD player. I even wrote the names of bands like Fleetwood Mac and U2 on them."

Tiny laughed hard. "You are certainly a smart one, Miss Victoria."

"My car is locked and I can't unlock it remotely. I need to get the key from inside the house," she said with a twinge of disappointment.

"Tell me where to find the key," Tiny said sternly.

"No, you're not," said Will. "I'm going."

"Guys, you'll never find it. Look. I've already surveyed the grounds and the inside of my house." She pushed the phone up to Tiny so he could view the streaming security images. "You stand guard. I'll go in through the back patio door and get the key. I'll sneak down to my car, unlock it, turn the key halfway without cranking it, and eject the discs. They will never see or hear me."

Will looked at the carwash again, trying to absorb her words and formulate a plan. Fortunately, the men were on the north side, the passenger side, of the Range Rover. He should easily be able to get inside her car unnoticed.

"Okay, but I'm going in with you," Will said and pulled out the pistol from his waist that Ross had given him. "And I'm taking this."

She nodded.

Tiny spoke up. "Now, here's the plan. Let's ease our way back down da block to da public beach parking lot. I'll start to walk down da beach and you guys stay a little ways behind me. Once I have dat guy on da beach distracted, you make your move."

Will called Ross' phone. "Follow us."

ॐ   ॐ   ॐ

TINY PARKED AT THE MALIBU Public Beach lot just across from Pepperdine University and stepped out of the car. In the passenger seat, Victoria removed her dark T-shirt to expose a thin white halter-top. The elastic of her tight shorts was digging into her side, creating an uncomfortable-looking rash, but she managed to squeeze her smartphone between her irritated skin and the elastic.

Ross pulled his car next to them and lowered the passenger window. "What's going on?"

Will spoke up. "There's a thug on the beach and two across the street from her house. Tiny is going to distract the guy on the beach while Victoria and I go inside and get her car keys."

"Car keys?" Ross shrugged it off. "Okay. I'll go back and keep an eye on the two across the street."

Tiny waved his hand. "No. This is real simple. We're gonna go through da back door and come out da back door. Get what we need then come back down da beach right back here. Let's not complicate it any more than dat. You stay here with your car running and we'll be right back."

"But—"

"Tiny is right. Let's keep it simple," Will said.

Ross nodded and threw up his hands.

Will watched as Tiny began the half-mile walk on the beach towards Victoria's house. In front of Tiny, about 300 yards away, he saw the outline of a man sitting on a beach towel. Once Tiny was about 100 yards from the man, he and Victoria left the car and began jogging at a steady rhythmic pace. As they ran, he saw Tiny engage the man in conversation. Tiny raised a finger and motioned out over the ocean as if he was pointing to a whale that had breached just offshore. With the man's back fully to them, he tugged on Victoria's arm, made a swift right turn and ran to the back patio of her house. He drew his gun, quietly slid open the glass door, and placed one foot inside.

He paused, his ears alert. Only the sounds of a humming

air-conditioning unit intermixed with the rolling surf filled his ears. Leaving the door ajar, he stood quietly a few more moments, then motioned Victoria inside.

Victoria pointed toward the kitchen and he watched as she took a few steps in that direction. Will began to follow her then stopped abruptly as a strange rumbling filled his ears. He could not yet figure out where this soft rattle was coming from. With every step, the sound got closer and louder. As he got within fifteen feet of her green suede couch in the living room, he saw a man lying supine. He froze, holding a steady aim of his gun at the man's head as he surveyed his physique.

It was Igor Milosevic. He was pale as a ghost, bald-headed, frightfully thin, and was asleep and snoring. His arms were folded across his thin chest and rose with each breath. His eyes were half shut and a shiny pool of drool had collected on the corner of his dry lips. Within his arms' distance, on the small oak coffee table lay a black pistol and cell phone, a small green light on the phone blinking on and off.

Will's pulse quickened as he stared at the killer on the couch and thought about pulling the trigger. But the man had not budged from his deep sleep. Victoria was already in the kitchen and Will watched as she quietly opened the freezer door and removed her car keys from inside a frozen pizza box.

Will waved his hand to draw her attention. Her eyes grew big as Will pointed to the couch and placed a finger over his lips. He waved for her to come. She squared her shoulders and continued slowly, putting one foot in front of the other as if she were walking on bits of glass.

Gripping the keys tightly, she slowly stepped towards the exit. Now within arm's distance of the sliding glass door, she began to reach for the door handle. Just as her fingers curled around the handle, she was stopped dead in her tracks by the loud piercing alarm on a cell phone.

For a split second, Will thought it was the albino's but then saw Victoria reach toward her waistline. It was the phone she had tucked into her tight shorts, the one she had set the timer on for 60 minutes.

Suddenly, the pale man exploded from the couch with more vigor than his physical appearance suggested possible. Will pulled his gun's trigger but it merely clicked. As Igor reached for his weapon, Will impulsively lunged for Victoria, grabbed her arm, and pulled her through the patio door. A shot rang out from behind her.

"Run, Tiny, run!" he yelled, grabbing the car keys from Victoria's hand.

Hearing his warning, Tiny immediately pulled a pistol from the pocket of his hoodie and ended the beachcomber's life. Will motioned to Tiny, and then led Victoria around the house to the front side. Gun drawn, Tiny followed. Will was kneeling next to the Range Rover with Victoria, attempting to unlock the door as Tiny passed by.

Tiny reached the top of the sloped driveway and began firing towards the two men across the street at the carwash.

Will opened the backdoor for Victoria then entered the vehicle and started the ignition but before he could throw it in reverse, Igor swung open the front door of the house and squeezed off several shots, orange sparkling flints igniting across the hood of the car as the bullets struck metal. Now in reverse, Will floored the gas pedal and the Range Rover began climbing the steep driveway. In the rearview mirror, he saw Tiny engaged in a gun battle, the sound of gunfire ricocheting off the concrete walls of the neighboring homes. In an instant, Will saw Tiny's body shudder backwards, and then lurch forward. He grabbed his abdomen with his free hand.

All the way out of the driveway now, Will put the Range Rover in forward and slung the door open, motioning Tiny to get inside.

As Tiny reached for the car door, another gunshot rocked him backward and he fell into the passenger seat, barely able to close the door.

With fire in his eyes, Will mashed on the gas pedal, plowed through a gauntlet of gunfire that was coming from the two men now standing in the road. As the windshield fractured, Will swerved to avoid the assassins, speeding north up the Pacific Coast Highway.

Looking over at Tiny, Will saw his chest was moving erratically. There was a trickle of blood on his lower lip. A red stain formed through a charred hole in his gray hoodie along his abdomen.

"Tiny, you've been shot," he said.

"Yeah. They got me a little," he managed with tremendous effort.

"I need to warn Ross," Will said but just as he reached into his pocket to grab his phone, his head whiplashed back violently. He looked into the rearview and saw a black SUV no more than three feet from his rear bumper. A smattering of bullets rang out as they pinged the Range Rover. He began twisting the steering wheel in an effort to swerve, to avoid the onslaught.

But the high cliff roads of the Pacific Coast Highway created a narrow passage and Will wasn't able to swerve enough to avoid the bullets. Victoria screamed from the backseat as another burst of shots pulverized the back windshield, sending glass fragments flying into the front seats, covering Victoria as she lay flat.

"Hold it straight," Tiny mumbled as he awkwardly turned his injured body to the left. He held his weight up high, squeezing his torso, and steadied his gun. With one shot, he pierced the left front tire of the black SUV, sending it careening over the steep California cliff.

He slumped down into the seat, examining his bullet wound. Victoria was crying; her hands trembling, she could barely remove the glass shards from her hair.

"We have to get you to a hospital," Will said to his old friend.

"Just go somewhere out of da way, a place where we can lay low for a while. You can tend to me once we get there. I'll be fine. Keep driving, damn it. And call your buddy Ross. Hurry."

Will called Ross and advised him of the situation, including a quick scolding for handing him a pistol that was not loaded, then told him he would call right back once they figured out where they were headed.

After hanging up, there was a long pause in which Will could hear nothing but the hum of the Range Rover and Victoria's sobs. He argued with Tiny for ten more miles about going to the hospital, but with no luck. Finally, he asked Victoria where they could go that was secluded, a place off the beaten path and Will could tend to Tiny's wounds.

Victoria knew the perfect place.

RAIN AND MIST FOLLOWED WILL and the others to Big Sur. The tires of the Range Rover made a low, steady hum along a wet Pacific Coast Highway, pushing high up into the thick fog bank that hovered over the narrow limestone cuts and cliffs on the edge of the Pacific Ocean. The wipers swung in short black arcs.

Big Sur is a sparsely populated region of the central coast of California where the St. Lucia Mountains abruptly rise up from the Pacific. From small rare endangered orchids to towering redwood trees, Big Sur's relative isolation and natural beauty has long attracted artists, writers and transcendental meditationists. It is considered by many to be the ideal place to turn on, tune in, and drop out.

As Will parked the SUV in front of their rented cabin at the Phoenix Inn, which he paid for with cash, he saw a sprinkling of tears roll down Victoria's face. Except for three brief conversations on the phone with Ross, Will had been deathly quiet on the four-hour drive north from Los Angeles. His eyes were misty.

A glint of headlights illuminated the bullet-ridden frame of the Range Rover as Ross pulled his Town Car next to them. Will and

Victoria stepped out of the SUV and hugged tightly, the mists of their breaths melding into one single stream as they kissed and pressed their bodies together, unconcerned at Ross' puzzled stare.

Standing in the damp, cold night air, her hair smelled soothing and her scent was more intoxicating than he even remembered. He finally released his clutch of her.

"I'm sorry, Will. I thought the gun was loaded," Ross said. "Where is Tiny?" Ross asked.

Victoria pointed towards her car. "He's still in the car."

Ross walked over to the passenger door of the Range Rover and opened it. Tiny lay slumped in the leather seat, dried blood on his face, eyes half open, his breathing labored.

Will patted Ross' back and brushed past, securing his arms around Tiny's large waist. "Come on. Help me get him inside."

Using all of their strength, Will and Ross hoisted Tiny out of the car, carried him inside the cabin, and laid him on the couch. Will knelt over him and felt his pulse then assessed his wounds. With a moistened paper towel, he began wiping away the dried blood from his "brotha's" face. He lowered his head, buried it into Tiny's chest, and said a silent prayer as Victoria stood behind him, caressing his shoulders.

"I should have never allowed him to come with me," she said. "Now look what I've done."

Will did not lift his head off of Tiny's chest but simply gripped her hand tightly. As he watched Tiny struggling for life, he felt grief with such intensity that it singed his soul.

"Tiny is doing worse than I thought," said Will. "I don't even think he has feeling in his legs. I'm not arguing about it anymore, Tiny. Ross, we have to get him to a hospital now."

Standing in the small kitchen, Ross jumped as the cell phone in his pocket buzzed before he could answer. He snatched it out and stared at it. "Shit. I can't hardly get any service here."

"Hello?" he said somberly.

Will lifted his head and turned toward Ross. "Who is it?" Will mouthed.

"Timmy, you're breaking up. Let me walk outside," Ross said as he placed the phone on speaker and walked out onto the unusual rear balcony, constructed entirely of glass. His shoes slipped slightly on the wet glass floor with each step.

Will set the bloodied paper towel aside, stood up and followed Ross, stopping in the doorway that led to the balcony. He could hear Timmy's distinctive voice clearly now. Victoria trailed Will, holding onto his waist.

Ross was visibly frustrated. "Timmy? You there?"

"Yes. I keep losing your GPS signal. Where are you? I think you may be in danger."

"We're okay, Timmy. The Serbians are dead. They went over a cliff four hours ago."

"Ross, I'm still concerned. I eavesdropped on a conversation between Igor and Dr. B earlier today."

"What did they say?"

"Igor told Dr. B he was screwed because I found out about his bank account in Switzerland. When I sent that email to you I knew that they most likely had already set up spy software through the NFC's computers. As soon as that software recognized Igor and his buddies' names, they were onto me."

"Try not to worry."

"But Igor told Dr. B that he was going to take care of Victoria first, and then he was going to 'go find that little redheaded pussy.' That's me, Ross!"

"Calm down," Ross said evenly. "Do you have any idea where Dr. B is now?"

"I think he destroyed his cell phone. His last ping came from an interstate in Arkansas." Timmy gasped. "I see where you are now. Your location just pinged on my computer's GPS. I've been tracking you all day but I lost you once you got close to Big Sur."

"What? How are you doing that? I have the same secured line as the president on my cell phone. No one is supposed to be able to track me or eavesdrop on me. I don't understand."

"EINSTEIN can track anybody, even the president. I see your location and I also see Igor's location. He's headed your way, is within a mile of you right now."

Ross tried to peer through the dense California fog but could hardly see more than a few feet. "I can't see anything," he said, aggravated.

"I've got an idea," Timmy suggested. "Igor is using the GPS on your phone to track you. Let's set up a trap, but we have to hurry." Timmy paused. "He's within a half mile."

"That's brilliant, Timmy."

Ross thought for a moment. "I know what to do. I'll put the cell phone on this balcony that I'm standing on, then climb down to the ground. When Igor shows up, he's dead," Ross said as he gripped the holstered pistol under his left armpit.

"I like it. Just stay on the phone with me until he's a hundred yards or so away, then put your phone wherever you want it. I—" Timmy sneezed. His breath caught.

"What is it?"

"I ... I don't know. I think I heard something inside my house." He went silent for a moment but his raspy breathing was audible and he sneezed again.

"Ohhh, my head. This cold is killing me."

"Well, try not to worry. Except for Igor, all of the killers are dead."

"I know, I know. I'm just a little freaked out," Timmy said. "Okay. Everything is good. I just—"

Before he could utter another word, a loud noise distorted the phone's speaker. "Timmy—Timmy? Timmy?" Ross held the phone up in front of his face. The call ended.

ɞ   ɞ   ɞ

WILL HEARD TINY GURGLE ON the couch. He released Victoria's hand and rushed to Tiny's side.

Victoria walked out on the balcony. "What just happened to Timmy?"

Before Ross could look her in the eye, a thunderous barrage of automatic gunfire exploded through the glass floor of the balcony. Ross grabbed Victoria's shoulder as a pulse of blood squirted from beneath his thin cotton shirt. As Victoria reached for him, the combined weight of their bodies fractured the glass beneath them further and both fell through the floor, down the steep cliff.

Will sprang to his feet and ran to the door, stopping short of the decimated balcony. The first image he saw as he peered down was not Victoria or Ross, but the foggy outline of the ghostly albino standing on a narrow terrace of land six feet below. Igor fired a solid burst at Will, missing him. The assassin then turned and ran down the narrow hiking path, like a white leopard chasing prey.

Will stared at Tiny as he lay there. He looked like a man who had been lost at sea for weeks; his body was giving in, sinking down to the depths of its limits. But he was still breathing. That was more than Will could say for sure about Victoria and Ross at this point.

Carefully descending from the broken balcony, Will tried to avoid the sharp points of broken glass. Finally, reaching the small terrace of land from which Igor had fired, he saw the glow of Ross' cell phone as it lay in the grass. Will looked around but Ross and Victoria were nowhere to be seen. They must have fallen farther down the cliff. He picked up the cell phone and sprinted to the trailhead. Carrying no weapon, he edged down the painfully steep cliff, holding firmly to the limestone as he made his way down into an even denser fogbank below. Will's heart was pounding hard. He could hear his pulse in his ears.

Barely able to see the hand in front of his face now, he softly called out. "Victoria? Ross?" He repeated it, hearing only the rustling of wind through the leaves high overhead.

Will came to a turn in the trail. Trying to sidestep several rocks in his way, his sight impaired by the fog, Ross' cell phone lit up.

Will stared at the screen. When he saw the text come through, his faith in the goodness of mankind vanished into the thick foggy air. He caught his breath. Igor was not tracking the GPS on Ross' phone. Ross had been texting the albino.

Ross: "At the Phoenix Inn in Big Sur. Dr. B is dealing with Mahoney tonight. Let's get rid of Victoria now and we'll take care of Dr. B tomorrow then this whole damn thing will be done."

Igor: "On my way."

Ross: "Do NOT hurt Dunbar. He has bought into the entire story that Dr. B is behind this. I'll need a live witness in the days to come."

Igor: "OK."

Igor: "Sorry about the gunshots. Didn't see you. Just saw the girl. Where are you?"

As Will reread the texts in disbelief, he did not see a large root of a massive redwood tree extending into the path. His leg caught the root solidly and sent him tumbling down the side of the cliff for thirty feet until his torso crowbarred around the trunk of a large fir tree, snapping several of his ribs.

As he lay there, writhing in pain, out of the eerie fog appeared the albino's face, gun aimed at Will's head.

"Well, well. Looks like you had a little fall, Dunbar," Igor said in broken English.

Will could not respond, could barely breathe; shattered bones had punctured a lung.

"I understand that you had a revelation of sorts lately—about your family." Igor laughed and pointed the barrel of his Uzi squarely at Will's temple. "Say goodbye to your 400-year-old memory, Doctor."

But before his fingers tensed on the trigger, a sultry voice drew his gaze.

"Leave him alone," Victoria said, arms extended as she approached from out of the fog. "It's me that you want. Shoot me, but leave Will out of this," She looked scraped, scratched, and was limping but otherwise healthy. She stared into Will's eyes as Igor whirled around and took dead aim at her head.

"It would be my pleasure," he said.

33

ROSS APPEARED OUT OF THE shadows, his gun aimed directly at Igor's head. With a bloodied left shoulder, he held the gun only inches away. Igor kept his Uzi on Victoria.

Ross' eyes widened as he noticed the phone in Will's hand. "Goddamnit," Ross yelled with contempt. He looked back at Igor and took two deep breaths. "Why the fuck did you shoot me, Igor?"

"Didn't you get my text? I couldn't see through the fog. All I could make out was the woman standing there so I fired," Igor said, staring into the barrel of Ross' pistol.

Ross spat blood on the ground. "You dumbass."

Will's side was aching and he could barely move as he lay on the dirt trail but he managed a labored voice. "Ross, How could you?" he said as he held the phone up higher.

Ross dropped his aim on Igor and looked back at Will. "Goddammit, this whole thing just gotten screwed up, man. I never meant to hurt you, ever. The Serbians were under strict orders not to harm you. I just needed to get rid of blondie over here." He waved his gun toward Victoria.

"But I thought it was all Dr. B?" Will asked, a speck of blood trickling from his lip.

"That dumbass." Ross waved his gun at Igor. "How was he going to get forged documents to get these Serb thugs into the country? Dr. B. doesn't have access to shit so he approached me, Will, and I ... I sold out. It was a lot of dough, Will ... millions. My family's set for life."

Ross pointed his gun at Will, then dropped his aim. "I can't do it, Igor. You're going to have to take care of him, I got her." He aimed at Victoria.

Seizing his opportunity, Igor whirled around but instead of aiming at Will, he pointed the Uzi at Ross' head and fired, a crackle of bullets exploding Ross' head like a smashed pumpkin. His limp body fell to the moist ground, only a foot from Will.

Igor spun toward Will. "Your friend is a piece of shit, man. Do you know what he is capable of?'"

Will shook his head.

"That son of a bitch is the one that forged the IMS documents and provided the list of your Team X. Hell, he's the one that made the phone call to Fort Jefferson to tell them that we 'checked out.'" Igor laughed loudly. "He even had the idea for the peanuts." Igor lowered the gun. "You know what else? He's the one that gave us blondie's parents' cruise itinerary."

Hearing those words, Victoria bull-rushed Igor from behind, struggling for control of the Uzi. A flash of yellow fire lit up the fog as Igor's finger pressed the sensitive trigger of the gun, sending a flurry of bullets up into the tree limbs above.

Using every bit of energy in his being, Will reached over and grabbed Ross' pistol as it lay next to him. Will swung his long arm and took aim at Igor.

After years of practice with his father at the shooting range in St. Augustine, with the precision of a marksman, Will's bullet pierced the gap between the blue sclera of the albino's eyes. His lifeless body fell to the ground.

34

IT WAS A LATE SEPTEMBER afternoon when the sun finally broke through and began drying the large public dock in the heart of Hopetown. As Will looked up into the wind-blown clouds and blue sky above him, he thought that it was an appropriately delightful day to pay homage to Hopetown's favorite son, Thomas "Tiny" Newcomb.

With the number of distinguished guests who were assembled—General Coleman, the CIA director, and even the Bahamian Prime Minister—it seemed like nothing less than a presidential inauguration than a ceremonial honor. But as Tiny sat in his wheelchair on the small stage on the public dock in the heart of the Abacos and accepted his award for "Bahamian Man of the Year," the crowd in Hopetown erupted with thunderous applause.

The ceremony had finished a half-hour ago but Will still found it hard to leave Tiny's side. He knelt beside his old friend's enormous, well-reinforced wheelchair and tried to sort through his tattered emotions. The outright deceit that he had experienced from Ross' treasonous exploits had left Will deeply scarred.

He would never forgive himself for not recognizing the signs, his ineptitude leading directly to the paralysis of his best friend and brother. The deaths of Team X were horrifying enough, but the guilt and mental anguish that Will had experienced since Tiny was paralyzed from the waist down six months ago, had left him emotionally numb.

Will had resigned his post recently at the Mayo Clinic to accept a position as the new director of the newly constructed NFC in Atlanta. Although he was farther from the Bahamas than he liked, at this point the importance of his new job superseded any extracurricular activities. With the help of the Blue Bunker, Dr. Greenwood, and the invaluable contributions of the Juilliards, Will's 400 year-old memory was filling in nicely. His newfound knowledge was giving him new, interesting ideas, offering fresh approaches to his research, and he was feeling more confident than ever that he would soon solve the ubiquitin enigma, restoring America's IMS.

Yet however turbulent his emotions for Tiny and his professional life had become, his personal life had never been more stable.

As Will knelt by Tiny's wheelchair, he felt a gentle touch on his shoulder. Turning and peering up into the beautiful blue eyes of his wife, Will gave Victoria a genuine smile.

Her face glowed as she leaned down and kissed him.

Just over three months ago, they had married in a small ceremony at the justice of the peace, a quiet and secretive wedding done IMS style. As Will stood and stared at his bride under the bright Bahamian sky, he was filled with love for her and for someone else. He reached his hand out and caressed Victoria's tummy. Her usually tight abdomen was sporting the slightest plumpness today, a sure sign of baby Dunbar growing inside of her.

"Will, I need to show you sumting, brotha," Tiny said, tightly gripping the wheelchair armrests.

Holding hands, Will and Victoria turned toward him. With a

tense grimace on his face and a glistening bald head, Tiny pushed himself up to a standing position. Will's eyes grew big. Then, with stern concentration, Tiny moved his right leg forward one clumsy step, and followed with another step from his left.

Will broke out into roar of delighted laughter. Letting go of Victoria's hand, he hugged Tiny forcefully, supporting his weight. Victoria let out of shriek of joy and the three embraced.

A faint high voice called from behind them. When they turned to look, a redheaded, freckled Timmy Mahoney was strolling towards them, waving energetically.

"Victoria!" he yelled.

She broke loose of the group hug and ran towards Timmy, throwing her arms around him.

"I'm so glad you made it, Timmy."

He smiled widely. "I'm sorry I'm late. Let me see it," he said, staring at her stomach.

Victoria pulled up her sheer white shirt, exposing her precious bulge. Timmy grinned, then turned towards Will. "You're one lucky man, Will Dunbar."

"Thanks, Timmy. Good to finally meet you," Will said. "I've only heard bits and pieces of your run-in with Dr. B. What happened?"

Timmy took a deep breath. "I was on the phone with that loser Ross and Dr. B knocked me in the head with a crowbar."

"Oh my God," Victoria said and put her hands to her mouth.

Timmy continued. "Yeah, and then he jumped on top of me and started strangling me. Seriously."

"How did you stop him? He's way bigger than you," Will asked.

"He forgot something critical," Timmy said with a broad smile.

"Oh, right, I heard about this," Victoria said. "You pulled the ole Mahoney Maneuver on him."

"Yep," Timmy said.

"Mahoney Maneuver?" Will asked.

Victoria grinned. "Timmy's grandfather was a national championship wrestler. He won...how many titles?"

"He defended his flyweight title seven times," Timmy boasted. "He even beat wrestlers twice his size, thanks to his signature move. He called it the Mahoney Maneuver and it's now taught by wrestling coaches all over the world as one of the best moves for getting a pin."

"So you summoned an Inherited Memory from your grandfather?" Will asked with awe. "How does the maneuver work?"

"It involves locking an opponent's leg to his upper body, then simultaneously twisting his ankle and turning him on his back for the pin. It's the synchronicity of the move, not the power, which makes it so successful." Timmy's face was glowing.

He grabbed Will and semi-demonstrated the maneuver. "So I interlocked my lower leg around Dr. B's left foot and, at the same time thrust my knee outward, and then forced his entire femur up to his chest, all the while twisting until he was flipped onto his back, pinned to the floor."

Will and Victoria laughed at Timmy's antics.

Timmy's face turned sad. "Then...then I had no choice. I grabbed the crowbar and cracked him over the head." Timmy shrugged. "He was a bad dude."

Before Will could respond, he felt another tap on his shoulder. He turned to see the charismatic face of General Coleman.

"Will," he said, staring seriously in Will's eyes. "I need you to come with me for a few minutes. And you too, Victoria. Could you both please follow me?"

Will looked at Victoria with uncertainty, then shrugged his shoulders. "Sure," he said catching something in the general's tone.

"What about me?" Timmy asked.

"Okay, come on, Timmy," the general said.

With the three of them in tow, General Coleman steered a shiny golf cart down the narrow blacktop road to the other end of Hopetown, finally stopping at the Sea Star Marina and Resort. Following the much-decorated general down to the dock and out to the last slip on the end, Will spotted an enormous white yacht with dark tinted windows. The name on the back of the yacht was written in bold black script, *The Minerva*, and the bust of an owl was stylishly painted in gold above the name.

"Have you ever seen this boat before?" Will whispered to Victoria as they stood and stared at the shining spotless vessel.

"No. Never."

Standing on the dock next to the boat, General Coleman motioned to two IMS Secret Service agents on the boat and the two men opened a teak door that led to the salon of the boat. As Will watched, an older man slowly limped out of the threshold and stood in the sunshine, propping himself on a cane. Looking to be in his early seventies, with wavy gray hair and about Will's height and stature, his face was covered with deep scars. The IMS agents held his hands and assisted him as he ascended a small set of steps up to the wooden dock.

As the man stood five feet away, his breathing labored, Will's eyes were riveted. He studied the scarred face for only a moment, and then his heart skipped two beats. "Dad?"

A lopsided smile came across the crippled man's face.

Standing in front of Will was his father, Samuel Dunbar.

Blood Memory Society

Book II

Coming summer 2018

Acknowledgements

I WOULD LIKE TO THANK Mark and Marie Fenn for giving me the most supportive home for publishing that I could have imagined. I also thank editor Emily Carmain for her coaching and support. Many thanks go to Erin Brown for her editorial skills, which unraveled a tangled web. Thanks also to Dana Isaacson for your editorial magic.

Special thanks to author Steve Berry, whose splendid instruction enlightened me on the craft of writing.

I owe a special debt of gratitude to Lisa Sandifer, who from day one expressed her unwavering support not only of my story but also my writing.

Thanks to Dr. Jeff Gully and John Handley, for you both had to endure the constant assault of my bouncing ideas for over a year. Both of you provided some wonderful details for the book. I owe a debt of gratitude to Dr. Cayce Rumsey for suspending disbelief and providing a luminous idea.

Thanks to Jimmy and Pam McInnis for believing in me.

A warm thanks goes to Larry and Mitchell Field. You inspire me more than you know.

Thanks to Glen Edelstein for grasping the concept on the cover. Your ability to see things in a different light makes you a true artist.

A particularly special thanks to the following individuals: Curt Englert, Kevin English, Kirk and Tommy Sandifer, Dale and Wolly Wolber. Without our adventures on the ocean, this book would have never been written.

No matter how hard I try to make sure that all facts are accurate and all "i"s are dotted, there is always at least one mistake. I absolve everyone mentioned above. All mistakes are mine.

Exterior view of the bronze door at the
main entrance of the Library of Congress,
Thomas Jefferson Building, Washington, DC.
Created in 1869 by Olin Warner,
it is titled "Memory".

About the Author

A DOCTOR BY DAY AND an author by night, D.A. Field is a collector of memories, whose favorite attire is shorts and flip-flops. Field is just as serious and committed to his family and playtime as he is serious about his work with his patients in his successful periodontal practice. An energetic, adventuring water enthusiast-- just give him his boat, a clear sky, his family, and an open ocean, and you will find yourself in the presence of an ultra-happy man with a great outlook on life.

So how does someone who is a healer find himself lured to writing adventure, action thrillers with a little sci-fi and conspiracy thrown in? Storytelling comes naturally to Field. He has been a musician since age 12. While successfully pursuing his academic goals, he played in several bands and wrote the lyrics for numerous songs along the way.

That talent, coupled with Field's insatiable curiosity about people and science is a winning combo. The spark for the Blood Memory Society series came from a tale about a family member growing up in poverty amid a family of wealthy people. That story has intrigued him since childhood, and his imagination and love of science fueled the rest.

Field lives in Ponte Vedra Beach, Florida, with his wife and their two children.

Visit the Author at www.dafield.com;
look for the second book in the the *Blood Memory Society* series coming summer 2018.

CPSIA information can be obtained
at www.ICGtesting.com
Printed in the USA
LVOW12s0045191117
556874LV00003B/21/P

9 780999 051405